A Killing in Quail County

A Killing in Quail County

JAMESON COLE

St. Martin's Press ≈ New York

Design by Ellen R. Sasahara

Library of Congress Cataloging-in-Publication Data

Cole, Jameson.
    A killing in Quail County / by Jameson Cole. — 1st ed.
    p.   cm.
    ISBN 0-312-13996-9
    1. Teenage boys—Oklahoma—Fiction.   I. Title.
PS3553.O47285K55   1996
813'.54—dc20   95-45734
                                         CIP

10 9 8 7 6 5 4 3 2

To Mary Beth for understanding,
sacrifice, and love

Acknowledgments

To Kay Bergstrom, Chris Jorgensen, Carol Rusley, Karen Thys, Vivian Carter, Gary Calder, Bob Frank, Dale Berndt, Jeff Hansen, Francine Mathews, Joe Simpson, and Marlene Jaquess for their invaluable suggestions and encouragement.

A Killing in Quail County

1

I had a normal childhood except for the murder I was involved in the summer before I turned sixteen. As I look back on it, I guess it all started on a Saturday in mid-July 1957. That Saturday was the last day of my childhood.

I'm Mark Stoddard. Back then, I was just your average-looking skinny fifteen-year-old kid—except for all those damn freckles—and that was the day Ferret, my best pal, and I were going exploring to see if we could find the bootlegger's still south of town.

It was the sort of thing you did as a kid living in Bob White, Oklahoma, back in 1957. I didn't know then that looking for a bootlegger's still would involve me in murder.

I woke up early that morning with bright sunshine spread all over my room. Yesterday's jeans were on the bare hardwood floor next to my worn-out sneakers. I got dressed fast, even put on a fresh T-shirt, and hit the bathroom.

I took care of business, brushed my teeth, and pulled a few grains of sand from my eyes. My mom had told me their color was hazel, but I always thought they were just greenish brown.

The rest of me was pretty normal. Sandy hair with a flattop that never needed combing, five feet eight inches tall and still growing, ears too big for my head, one hundred thirty pounds if I took a deep breath, and already as brown as I was going to get from the hot Oklahoma sun. And too damn many freckles.

I left the bathroom and saw that Jess's door was open. My brother Jess was twenty-four and a county deputy sheriff. He worked a lot at night and last night he'd come home long after I'd gone to bed, but I remembered hearing girlish laughter and giggling, so I knew he had company in his room.

Inside, lying facedown amid rumpled sheets, was a single figure—Jess's company. I hesitated a moment, staring at the bare female back, a hint of breast showing where her right arm had been outflung. Her face was turned away, the short black hair swept back and feathered in a ducktail. I didn't recognize the girl, but the breast was interesting.

Somewhat reluctantly, I went on down the hall to the kitchen, where the smell of freshly perked coffee saturated the air. Jess sat at the table sipping his morning cup, reading the newspaper, and wearing nothing but a pair of Jockey undershorts. Except for being a little on the small side, Jess looked like he was born to be a lawman—five foot nine and one hundred and fifty pounds of solid muscle that had gotten nothing but harder since his high school days of football glory.

"Morning, Jess," I said, walking past him to get the cereal fixings.

"Hey, kid." He didn't look up. Up until last year, Jess used to joke with me, but things were different now. We didn't always get along, and mornings were about the only times we saw each other. We didn't talk a lot. We didn't talk about Mom and Dad's accident at all.

I dumped two Shredded Wheat biscuits into a bowl, splashed milk over them, and layered the cereal with sugar. I sat down opposite him and used my spoon to crush the biscuits into mouth-sized chunks.

Jess must have had a long night. His eyelids drooped, his face looked as stale as moldy bread, and his hair—sandy like mine and short, but not a flattop—needed combing.

I wondered if he'd been chasing girls or . . . someone else. "You haven't found that bootlegger's still yet, have you?"

"Not yet," he answered, shifting a bit, not paying me much attention.

I ate some more cereal, considering how best to continue. "Pretty stupid, if you ask me."

Jess glanced up from his paper, his eyes bloodshot, irritated. "What is?"

"Someone's just asking for trouble—making moonshine in this county."

He put the paper down. "We don't know where the hell it is. Could be somewhere else."

"Could be hidden in the Bottomlands."

Jess shook his head. "Sheriff Adams and I crisscrossed those woods two whole days and didn't find nary a sign."

Jess's eyes were a little bloodshot right now, but they were what he said suckered all the girls to him. Light brown with turquoise flecks and a twinkle that came and went. They glowed like hot-blooded fireflies when he laughed, which wasn't often, not around me anyways.

I swallowed another bite of cereal. "I figure it's in the Bottomlands."

Jess raised one eyebrow. "Don't you go getting any crazy ideas. It's dangerous down there."

I shrugged, pretending indifference. There were some things that Jess didn't need to know—like Ferret and me heading down to the Bottomlands in about half an hour. "Any idea who the bootlegger is?"

Jess's eyes glazed over, getting distant. "Maybe."

"Someone here in Bob White?"

His eyes focused, hostile, as if angry with me for making him remember. "Nah. Someone who used to live here."

"Who?" I persisted, curious.

Jess's voice rose sharply. "You wouldn't know him. He's been gone a while."

"Why won't you tell me? Don't you want to catch him? I could help—"

"Damn it. I am going to catch that son-of-a-bitch. And I don't need anybody's help."

"But, Jess—"

"You stay the hell out of the Bottomlands. It's dangerous for kids."

I felt my neck getting red. Nowadays, Jess only had time to order me around and call me a kid. I figured if I could find the bootlegger, then he'd have to show me some respect. In the meantime, it was best he didn't know a thing about it. I fibbed a little. "I'm going over to Ferret's and we're going hunting for pop bottles to sell."

Jess looked at me doubtfully, then rose. "Just stay out of trouble." Turning, he walked out of the kitchen.

I stared after him, wishing things could be back the way they were when Mom and Dad had been alive. But they couldn't.

Bopeep barked at the back door. It wasn't a real bark, just a whuff. She saved her real barks for emergencies like cats and suspicious noises in the dark. I let her in and she finished my cereal, slurping up the broken wheat strands floating in the sugar milk and licking the bowl across the yellow linoleum floor into a corner. I retrieved it and dumped it upside down in the sink on top of three days' smelly dishes, hoping Jess would break down and wash them, but he always made me do them.

Bopeep followed me outside, down the big concrete blocks which served as steps, and I found her tennis ball. We had a detached garage—Jess's police car was parked outside it—with a fair-sized yard between it and my bedroom where Bopeep and I played catch nearly every day. Bopeep was about four years old and all white except for her black nose and eyes. Mom had named her that and it fit her good.

She was real frisky, almost too frisky, because I could pretend to throw the ball one way and she'd charge off in that direction, then look puzzled when the ball didn't come down.

I'd throw it another way and she'd scramble after it, then bring it back to me as nice as you please. It never bothered her that I'd tricked her.

But I couldn't waste all day playing ball. Ferret should be up by now and we had to get going. I gave Bopeep a big hug and ran fresh water in the bucket by the garage, then left the yard and walked north up Ash Street.

We lived in the southwest part of Bob White. It was a town of about five thousand, a town listless in the hot summer days, a town where not much ever happened, an hour and a half southeast of Oklahoma City. Being that far away, every house had a television antenna on a tower at least fifty feet high so they could pick up the three stations from the City. Some people simply nailed their antennas to the tall cottonwood trees that showered the streets, the yards, and the cars with a snowy blanket of white seedling puff balls every June. Some trees were still going at it.

But that wasn't why our town was named Bob White. And Bob White wasn't the name of the town founder. Bob White was the call that quail made in the fields. And we probably had more quail in our county than in the rest of the state. Our town was also the county seat, and we had some farming and oil field business.

For some reason—I don't know why—I stopped when I got to the corner and looked back at our little house. The white paint was peeling where the hundred-degree sun beat hard on it and the only grass still living was going to seed. It hadn't looked that way last summer. Dad had always kept the paint touched up and paid me a buck to push the lawn mower around once a week. Now the house looked kind of sad, not much like a home anymore.

Standing there in the dusty street, I felt lost. Like it didn't matter who I was. Jess certainly didn't care. I shook off the feeling. I didn't like feeling that way. I couldn't help it sometimes, like now. I decided I had to be tougher.

I walked the two blocks to the Brubakers' house. Most of

the homes in town were ranch-style frame houses mostly painted white. But their house had two stories, with bricks as old and red as Oklahoma clay. They didn't own it. The church did.

A dark blue '54 Ford sedan was parked in front. I prided myself on knowing every car in Bob White. But I didn't recognize this car and as I got closer, I saw it had Louisiana plates. Being in the ministry, Reverend Brubaker had lots of out-of-town visitors drop by unexpectedly, some spending the night, so it wasn't all that unusual.

I could hear the sound of wood being chopped in the backyard, which *was* strange, so I went around to see what was going on. Ferret's dad had his shirt off and sweat was pouring off him, even though it was early morning and only about seventy-five degrees. He was scowling as if he was mad at the logs.

Henry Brubaker was built more like a blacksmith than a minister. His bushy eyebrows were as dark brown as the day he was born. Glistening sweat droplets clung to the hairiest chest in Bob White, but it was mostly gray. And so was the hair that rimmed his head, full and dark gray except for a big bald spot that ran all the way down to his forehead. He liked to tell the little kids that God had kissed him there.

But Reverend Brubaker's most interesting feature was the lightning-shaped scar down the left side of his face. You could see it all the way from the back row of the First Baptist Church. He joked about that too. Said he was struck by a bolt of lightning from God when he was twelve, and that a voice had come out of boiling clouds and told him to be a minister.

He hefted another eighteen-inch-long circular log section from the pile, set it upright on the chopping block, then expertly swung the ax behind him. Upward and down, all in one single smooth motion, the blade sliced down the length of the log, the two halves exploding sideways away from the chopping block and gouging into separate piles.

I wondered why he'd gotten the urge to chop firewood in the middle of July.

Reverend Brubaker flicked the ax loose, then laid it down, and hefted another log into place, as if it weighed no more than a pillow.

"Morning, sir."

He looked up, startled, blinking at me. Then the frown vanished and his face burst into a practiced smile. "Good morning, Mark," he boomed, overwhelmingly.

I grinned, being friendly and showing my respect, but held back a bit. The reverend liked to get right in your face to talk, hovering over you like an angel going to swoop you up and take you to hell 'cause you'd sinned too much. I always felt guilty when he did that.

He pulled a big white handkerchief from his back pocket and wiped his face. "You'll be at church tomorrow."

It wasn't a question. "Yes, sir."

"And your brother?"

"I don't know. He may have to work," I lied, feeling guilty in spite of myself. It was already my second lie of the day.

"You boys still doing all right? Keeping the house right? You know your mom would have expected nothing less."

"Yes, sir." I only answered the first question.

"I don't need to send the missus over to check on it, do I?"

"No, sir." If he did send Ferret's mom over, she'd have a lot of work to do.

"I notice the yard's looking ratty."

Well, he had me there. "I'm going to mow it tomorrow."

"Tomorrow's Sunday."

"I meant Monday, sir." I emphasized the 'sir.' I'd seen a war movie last year where there was a lot of sir-in', and saying it loudly always got the GIs out of trouble. So I had started using it, and darned if it didn't work most of the time.

He looked at me evenly, then nodded. I knew he'd drive by to check, so like it or not, I had me a mowing job to do.

"Is Ferr . . . uh, is Matthew up?" The reverend disapproved of Ferret's name so I had to remember to call him Matthew around his dad.

He frowned, catching my slip, then cocked an eyebrow at me. "You boys aren't going down to the Bottomlands, are you?"

His question caught me off guard, and I must have seemed genuinely surprised. "No, sir. We talked about hunting Coke bottles to sell to Mr. Tucker. Why?"

He shrugged and picked up the ax. "I heard about the bootlegger. Might be a good idea to stay clear of there for a few days." He studied the log standing on the chopping block, as if it represented Satan himself. There was another swish, then a crack, and another log met its doom.

The whole town worried too much about the Bottomlands. But Ferret and I had been there lots, and there wasn't anything to be afraid of. I turned away, and pulling open the screen door, smelled fresh-cooked bacon and homemade biscuits that set my mouth watering. "Hey, Ferret," I called, entering the kitchen.

Ferret wasn't there, his mom wasn't there. Some damn girl was there.

2

I stopped dead, surprised. She had dark black hair, tied into dog ears that dropped onto her shoulders, and bright green eyes. She was about four inches shorter than me, and wore a pink blouse stuffed into blue shorts. I couldn't help noticing she had a perky figure, if you liked that sort of thing. Me? I couldn't have cared less.

"Who are you?" I demanded.

Her mouth split into a wide smile, as wide a smile as I imagined anyone capable of making. But it was a defiant smile. "I'm TJ Gatlin. And I'm spending the rest of the summer with the Brubakers. Who are you?"

Well, I'll be go to hell. So much for the rest of the summer.

Mrs. Brubaker walked in, interrupting my thoughts. "Hello, Mark. Matthew will be down soon." Her smile flashed just for an instant, then faded, and her eyes drifted past me, not really seeing me.

I nodded politely as I could under the circumstances. Josephine Brubaker was still in her house robe. She was as different from the reverend as cats are from hound dogs. In one word, she was graceful. Like a fine dancer.

But today, she was not at all her usual self. Something was bothering her. She didn't glide like a ballerina. Her shoulders slumped and her wide black eyes had red circles round them.

She had long black hair that framed a face that reminded me of Leslie Caron in *Lili*. She even looked French to me, and I knew she was from some place down in Louisiana. . . . Hey, now things got a little clearer.

I peered closely at the girl. Mrs. Brubaker's eyes were black, not green. But except for the eye color, TJ would easily pass for a Brubaker. She would be Ferret's cousin, and the blue Ford would be her parents' car. But why was she suddenly spending the summer with the Brubakers? And why was Ferret's mom sad and his dad angry? Right now the Brubakers were as much a family to me as anybody could be. Something was upsetting them, and I had a feeling it had to do with this girl.

TJ's mouth curled downward, making a face, deliberately mocking me. I looked away, angry with myself for paying her any attention. Girls were nothing but nuisances. I didn't like the idea of her being here, messing up the rest of the summer.

I heard footsteps bouncing down the stairs, squeaking across the hardwood floor, then Ferret entered the kitchen. He nodded.

I nodded back. A lot of the time we didn't have to talk to understand each other. I'd known Ferret my whole life, the two of us having been born in October, a week apart. Matthew and Mark. Somehow, our folks never got around to Luke and John.

He grabbed a biscuit, tore it open, and crammed some bacon in it. He took a bite and then we both started for the door.

"Matthew?" Mrs. Brubaker's voice was firm, like moms' voices get when they tell you something you have to do, and they know you're not going to like it one bit.

We froze and I got this awful feeling.

"You boys invite TJ along with you now. You'll have a good time."

Ferret glanced at me, then dropped his eyes as he saw my face. He turned back to the girl and jerked his head toward the door.

Triumphant, TJ grinned at me and I just couldn't hide my disgust. The three of us ran out the door, my mind already trying to figure out how to dump her. We cleared Ferret's yard, shouting a good-bye to the reverend, and slipped into a smooth walk headed south on Ash Street.

Ash Street wasn't paved. In fact, only Main Street and three others downtown were blacktopped. Here, the street bed had a layer of pulverized red earth a half-inch thick that puffed up little red clouds as our sneakers plopped down.

TJ was nearly shoulder-to-shoulder with me and too damn close. I edged further away. "How old are you, anyhow?"

"I'm fourteen. Why?"

"It figures." I was done talking. High overhead, a gentle breeze streamed through the leaves of the tall cottonwoods, fluttering and hissing overhead.

"Where're we going?" TJ asked.

I glanced at Ferret, hoping he'd answer, but his mouth was full of biscuit. Darn it, she was his cousin, not mine. I guess I'd have to talk to her sooner or later. "Down to the Bottomlands."

"Where's that?"

"It's a ways."

"What's there?"

"Snakes." The word just popped out. And now I had a plan. I'd scare the crap out of her. I felt a grin creeping into the corner of my mouth, so I tucked some cheek between my teeth until the urge passed.

"Snakes? What kind of snakes?"

"Rattlesnakes. Big ones. And cottonmouths, too."

She didn't slow down, matching Ferret and me stride for stride. "We got snakes in Baton Rouge. Rattlers and cottonmouths."

"There's hundreds of 'em in the Bottomlands."

"I been in bayou country. We got alligators. There aren't any alligators in Oklahoma."

"So?" I asked, raising my voice. Uppity girl.

"So why are you going to the Bottomlands?"

"Looking for a bootlegger's still."

"Really? What for?" She lowered her voice. "You going to buy some whiskey?"

"Course not," Ferret answered, wiping his hands on his jeans. He choked down the last of the bacon biscuit and grunted. "That's against the law. And Mark's brother is a deputy sheriff. If we find the still, we'll get a reward. Maybe."

Actually, I hadn't heard anything about a reward. But the whole town was buzzing, wondering who was making it and where it was being made. Except for Hogan's Pool Hall, where 3.2 beer was legal, the county was dry and right proud of it.

"A bootlegger?" TJ said. "Sounds like fun."

"Fun?" I sneered, remembering my plan to scare TJ. "It's plenty dangerous, you know." I lowered the tone of my voice and licked my words out, in my best imitation of Bela Lugosi. "Grown men have gone into the Bottomlands and never been found. If the bootlegger catches you, he'll slit your throat from ear to ear."

TJ considered that for a while. On the other side of her, Ferret grinned and passed his finger across his throat, then made a gagging sound and staggered a few steps. I looked at TJ expectantly.

"I saw a man killed once," she said thoughtfully.

"You did?" Ferret asked. "Golly damn. Who was he?"

"A Cajun. Cajuns kill each other all the time in Baton Rouge. They were drunk and had knives."

"Yeah?" Ferret said. "Slit his throat?"

"No. He just stuck him in the stomach, then lifted the man clean off his feet and held him there till blood gushed out of his mouth."

"Jesus," I said. I looked at TJ with new respect. She did look enough like Ferret to be his sister. Ferret had the same black hair, except his was a little curlier, and his mom wouldn't let him have a decent haircut like my flattop.

Ferret didn't look a thing like the reverend, having gotten

most of his genes from his mom. Ferret and TJ were about the same height. He was about fifteen pounds lighter than me and I could outwrestle him. I could outrun him too, which gave me an idea. We still had about six blocks of town to go before we hit the outskirts. If we could lose TJ, she'd have to go back to the Brubakers' house.

I caught Ferret's eye and winked at him. I stretched and groaned. "Man, I'm stiff. I need to run a little of this stiffness off." I took off running, Ferret right with me, and I knew he knew what I was thinking. We hit top speed in ten paces, but I held back a little so Ferret could keep up. I glanced back. TJ had stopped, staring at us, then she broke into a gentle run, thirty, now forty feet behind. This was going to be easier than I thought.

"Good idea," Ferret said.

"Damn good idea," I answered. I could run a mile if I had to. I looked back again. TJ was maybe a hundred feet behind now and we hadn't run a block yet. We breezed past old Mrs. Jones's house and Tom, her cocker spaniel, raced along inside her fence, yapping at us long afterwards, and I could hear his bark changing as he yapped at TJ.

Two blocks now, and Ferret and I looked back again, hoping she had given up. There she was, only fifty feet back. Damn!

"How'd she catch up?" Ferret asked, breathing hard.

"Shut up and run." I stretched out a little and I could see Ferret struggle with the pace.

Another minute and I glanced back again. TJ had closed to twenty feet. She didn't even seem to be working up a sweat, just gliding down the street, her white socks flashing each time her feet hit, red clouds of dust exploding. Beside me, Ferret's face was redder than the dust. He wasn't in shape, like me. I concentrated on my running.

Then I heard her footsteps. Just behind us. No point in looking back. Maybe we could outlast her. My lungs were raw and complaining with each gasp, but I could stand it.

TJ pulled even, then a little ahead, then backed off and ran along side of me. She wasn't even breathing hard. "In Baton Rouge, I'm on the track team. I run the four-forty and the eight-eighty."

We stopped running right then and there.

3

The Bottomlands was a half-hour south of Bob White, if you had to walk, which was my usual mode of transportation. We took the county road until we could see the long, unbroken stretch of trees. The Bottomlands continued south, getting increasingly dense for a few miles until meeting the south fork of the Clear Boggy River.

The Johnson family owned the land that adjoined the Bottomlands, and they used the fields sometimes as pasture for about twenty head of cattle. Today, there was no herd grazing in the pasture, so we cut right across the field, sidestepping dried patties until we got to the woods. The soil in the Bottomlands wasn't red; it was a rich dark moist loam, and even rocks would grow here. All kinds of trees thrived in the Bottomlands and before we set out in earnest to find the still, Ferret and I would make our usual stop to have our usual smoke.

Here the trees weren't dense and it was easy going, stepping over the occasional fallen log and walking around rotting stumps where trees had broken from disease or from their own weight.

Ten minutes later, we came across a ditch maybe twenty feet wide and nearly as deep, with a trickle of water in it. Here, long grapevines grew up the sides of oak trees. Some of the vines were a half-inch thick, some even thicker. They sent out little runners from the main stalk to attach themselves to the bark.

The vines then climbed up and wound around limbs ten, fifteen, even twenty-five feet off the ground. This cluster of vines extended for a hundred yards or so, as heavy as you might imagine, and vines hung down all over where they had broken away from the tree trunks. As far as we knew, there was no other place in the Bottomlands quite like it, but, of course, Ferret and I hadn't been every place in the Bottomlands.

I sat down on a big old fallen log taking care to see it wasn't covered with ants, and took out my pocket knife. I picked up a four-foot-long broken section of dried vine and cut a healthy-sized cigar and gave it to Ferret. He stuck it between his teeth and pulled out the Zippo that his mom didn't know he had found and lit his cigar, then lit the giant-sized stogie I'd just cut. I sucked hard, taking care not to inhale—if you inhaled, it could kill you—and the end caught fire and flamed up, torchlike.

I didn't cut a cigar for TJ. I figured she wouldn't want one. She watched us puff madly away, sending clouds of white smoke spiraling upward into the cluster of vines and tree branches overhead, then she turned away indifferently. I pulled my cigar out and expertly tapped the ashes onto the ground. "Want a drag?" I offered, enticingly.

"That's disgusting!" she said, crossing her arms.

"Are you . . . chicken?" I didn't have to say anything else.

She held out her hand, defiantly, and I gave her my stogie. Gingerly holding it between two fingertips, she looked at it uncertainly, then raised it slowly to her lips.

Ferret and I watched with increasing interest.

She glanced at us, then pursed her lips and inhaled. The tip flared up again and TJ froze as the acrid smoke assaulted her lungs. Her eyes widened and both Ferret and I started laughing, knowing from our own experience that when grapevine smoke hits your lungs, it paralyzes them.

She got this panicky look on her face, turned white, and threw her mouth open, trying to force out the smoke. "Huh . . . huh . . . ."

Ferret fell off the log, howling. My eyes had tears in them, I was laughing so hard.

"Huh . . . huh . . ." Then her lungs recovered and she coughed out the smoke, or most of it. Her face turned green and she sank to her knees and tried to throw up. But she couldn't, dry retching instead.

About then I realized that maybe Ferret and I were enjoying this too much and I figured any second now, TJ would turn on us and start beating us with her fists or something. But she just sat there on her knees, not retching anymore, kind of weak-like. In spite of myself, I felt sorry for her. "TJ? You all right?"

She nodded, not looking up.

I sank to my knees next to her and said, "Next time, don't inhale. Grapevine smoke will kill you."

She smiled faintly, appreciating my advice, then climbed to her feet. I picked up the cigar and threw it into the ditch. So did Ferret.

"Hey, watch this," I said. I stood up, searching for one of the thicker vines hanging loose from the tree limbs reaching toward the ditch. I selected one, pulled it to me, and tugged hard on it, testing my weight against its strength. Then I backed up and took a run straight for the ditch, at the last second lifting myself up and sailing way out over the ditch.

Ferret and I had done this a lot, playing Tarzan here every summer on a regular basis. I held on and soared halfway across. Then my momentum changed and I swung back to the other side where Ferret and TJ watched. As my feet hit the ground, I ran away from the ditch, building my speed, lifting above the ground again, pausing in midair, then turning back toward the ditch, running again, twice as fast as before. I swung out over the ditch, all the way across to the other side this time, ten feet above the ground. Then I let go and dropped safely down.

As quick as the vine swung back, Ferret grabbed it and repeated my example, dropping beside me moments later. I glanced across the ditch as the vine swung back. TJ's face looked normal now. She was going to live. We all had to inhale once.

"Grab the vine, TJ," I shouted.

"I got it," she said. She backed away, then ran forward, gracefully soaring into the air, her dog-eared hair flying like the Wings of Mercury attached to her head. Then she swung back again to the far side, building up speed as Ferret and I had done, then swinging all the way across.

As she let go up above us, I had a strange feeling. Like I was Tarzan and she was Jane and I was going to catch her in my arms, just like Johnny Weismuller in the movies.

But I didn't catch her. I didn't even touch her. She landed on her feet and grinned, breathless, exhilarated, full of an energy that radiated from her, drawing me toward her. I shook the feeling off, and deliberately turned away, reminding myself that I didn't like her. "Let's go."

A couple of hours later, we had penetrated deep into the woods. We'd seen squirrels and rabbits and sparrows and even one woodpecker. We'd seen deer scat and coyote scat and a pile of black stuff that looked like bear scat, but we weren't sure. That was pretty interesting, but we saw nothing of a bootlegger's still, nothing human, nothing manmade, not even footprints.

This part of the Bottomlands was dense forest and soggy ground. The undergrowth and fallen trees made getting around increasingly difficult. We couldn't see more than twenty or thirty yards ahead, so it would be hard to locate a still unless we just lucked onto it.

After a while, the trees all looked the same. The sun was high overhead and burning hot. I was sweating, but my throat felt like a cocklebur was stuck in it.

"Let's go back," Ferret said. "I'm hungry."

I was glad Ferret said it first. I turned west. "We'll cut over to the county road and it'll be quicker getting back."

After about ten minutes of climbing over logs, the trees thinned and it was easier going. A three-foot gully lay ahead and I could hear water trickling in it. "Might be some craw-dads there."

"Crayfish?" TJ asked, looking interested.

I nodded. When we got there, we spread out, checking for telltale holes and rocks they could hide under.

After a couple of minutes, Ferret said, "Nothing here."

"Guess not. Let's go," I answered, leaping across the little ditch. I landed on the other side and turned immediately to the left, looking again for that bit of color that had flashed in the corner of my eye in the split second of my jump. A bit of yellow. Or gold.

Ferret came over and peered through the trees with me. "You see something?"

"What is it? The bootlegger?" TJ asked, running up beside us and cracking a dead tree branch in the process.

"Shhhh," I said, scolding her carelessness. I didn't see anything there now except trees and more trees. "Come on."

I led the way, hanging close to the ground. If it was the bootlegger, I didn't want him to know we'd seen him. If he moved his business elsewhere, we might never find him again.

"What'd you see?" TJ asked.

"Something yellow. Now keep quiet."

I crept closer, keeping the undergrowth between me and whatever it was I'd seen, avoiding twigs and dead branches as best I could. Behind me, I could hear TJ and Ferret moving, a rustle here and there as they put their feet down. We kept low for another twenty-five yards and I figured that was close enough. Stopping behind a scrub oak bush that gave us maximum concealment, I turned to glare sternly at TJ. "Stay down," I whispered.

Carefully I raised up, my eyes just over the oak bush. Beyond another fifteen yards of trees, a clearing opened. Standing in the middle of that clearing, his face lifted up, looking right into the sun with his arms outstretched toward heaven, was a stark-naked stranger.

4

His hair was bright yellow, and wavy, almost down to his shoulders. He wore it flowed back away from his face, the way Errol Flynn did in the pirate movies. He looked to be about forty, with a rugged face and muscular body. He didn't look much like what I expected a bootlegger to look like.

I half expected him to move or do something, but he just stood there like his bare toes were sending out roots. TJ tugged on my jeans' pocket. I dropped down and turned around. TJ and Ferret leaned forward. "You won't believe this," I whispered.

It was the wrong thing to say, because before I knew what was happening, TJ jumped straight up. Her eyes exploded and she said right out loud, "Holy shit!"

Damn, we were found out. My feet took off by themselves and I could hear TJ and Ferret crashing along behind me. I dodged through the trees and ran for maybe two hundred yards before I thought maybe it was safe to slow down. I stopped and waited for Ferret and TJ to catch up.

"What'd you see?" Ferret asked, breathless.

"You didn't look?"

"Shoot no. I just ran when you did. Was it the bootlegger?" Ferret turned to TJ. "Is he coming after us?"

TJ's face was flushed with excitement and her breath was coming in gasps. She shook her head.

"What did you see, for Christ's sake!"

"I . . . I think I just saw . . . Tar-*zahn.*"

"What? You're kidding!"

"Come on, you two," I said. "We can't stand here jawing. He might be coming after us." Both TJ and Ferret turned to look behind us then started right out, not waiting for me to ask them again.

"Did he see you?" I asked TJ.

"Looked me right in the face."

"Who?" Ferret asked.

"This tall, blond guy."

"Tarzan?"

I shrugged. "Never saw him before."

"He was buck naked," TJ said, grinning.

Ferret's eyes got big. "Golly damn. What was he doing, naked and all?" he asked, suspiciously.

"Talking to God, I guess." I held out my arms and demonstrated how the man had stood.

"That's crazy."

I nodded, and kept moving. The trees were getting thinner and the ground was firm and dry. We were still headed west and the county road wouldn't be much further. "I'm going to tell Jess about him when we—"

An old man swung out from behind a tree, barring our path. I jerked to a halt, not more than three feet from him. TJ and Ferret both bumped into me and froze. It for sure wasn't Tarzan.

This man was a couple inches taller than me, wearing a torn undershirt and dirty coveralls with one strap hanging loose, his gaunt face covered with stubble and stained from chewing tobacco. Scraggly gray hair spewed out from under a John Deere cap and his eyes squinted like they had seen too much sun for too many years.

This man was the third stranger I'd seen today, counting TJ and Tarzan. Mom had always said bad things came in threes. I had a real bad feeling about this man.

"What you little turds doing in these woods?" He spat a stream of foul stuff that splattered my sneakers.

"Nothing," I said. Besides saying "sir" often, I'd learned to say "nothing" to grown-ups when I didn't want to say what I'd really been doing. They usually gave up after a while.

"Don't lie to me, boy," he growled. His right cheek bulged with a wad and his voice crawled out the left side of his mouth. "You been sneaking around, spying."

"No, sir. We were just getting over to the county road." I pointed west, past the man.

He grabbed my wrist and squeezed.

"Hey," I said, and tried to pull away.

His hands were thin, but wiry like the rest of him, and I couldn't break loose.

"Let him go!" TJ's voice cracked like a whip.

The man jerked at the sound of her voice, loosening his grip. I wrenched free and backed away to the side, rubbing my wrist, wary that he might grab for me again. But his attention was focused on TJ, and his glinty eyes traveled up and down her body in a way that made me angry. TJ's cheeks reddened.

"Well, lookee here. Pretty little sass, got her juices all stirred up. Pretty little sass and a pretty little ass." He spat again, at no one in particular, and brown dribble ran down his chin.

"We weren't spying, mister," I said, trying to control my anger. "We weren't bothering anybody and we just need to be on our way."

"What's your name, girl?" He took a step forward and TJ backed up. He laughed, showing ugly brown-stained teeth colored coal black at the roots. He cupped his mouth, holding in the swirl of foul-smelling juice. "C'mere, girl." He wasn't laughing anymore, his voice intense. He lunged for TJ.

But I was ready for his move. I shoved hard against his shoulder. He stumbled, off balance, and nearly fell over a stump. Righting himself, he whirled, his right hand lashing out in a wild roundhouse, with more anger than direction to it. I ducked easily, backing away from his blind rage.

He was out of position now and the path west to the county road was clear. "Get going, guys," I shouted, backing away, keeping my distance from his crazed thrusts.

Ferret and TJ started to run. Then Ferret stopped, calling urgently to me, "Come on, Mark. Now."

I didn't dare take my eyes off him, figuring as soon as he hesitated, I could turn and run.

Then . . . he did hesitate. His eyes opened wide and he looked straight into mine. "Mark?" he asked, in a voice so low I could barely hear him. "Mark Stoddard?"

I looked into his cold, gray eyes, shocked that he knew my name. I'd never seen him before. Of that I was certain.

He rubbed his chin with his left hand and there was something strange about it. He was missing his left thumb. "All growed up now, eh Mark?" His words were growls, ominous, sending a chill down my spine.

I backed away, wanting to run, but held by the man's words, sensing that he knew me, and hated me.

His right hand slipped inside his pocket and he drew out a bone-handled switchblade. Fflickkk.

5

The blade was six or seven inches long, covered with splotchy rust spots, except along the fine-honed edge that caught the sun and flashed against my eyes. He scraped the blade against his throat stubble and laughed, his voice like skittering gravel. "I'll be seeing you . . . Mark . . . Stoddard."

I turned away, surprised, knowing he was letting us go—for now—but wondering if we'd be safe the next time.

TJ and Ferret were twenty yards away, waiting and looking worried. I walked casually toward them, trying not to show how scared I felt inside. Ferret jittered from one foot to the other, while TJ's eyes guardedly watched the old man.

Behind me, I heard an insane cackle that sent shivers up my spine. I kept walking steadily until I reached TJ and Ferret, then we all spontaneously burst into a run.

Minutes later, we found the county road and headed north. The sun was already past its peak and it had to be over ninety degrees in the shade, but we weren't in the shade. Our shadows led us up the merciless county road, which had a layer of bone-dry powder covering a gravel roadbed. Heat rose up from it like a cast-iron skillet over an open flame.

The only car we saw was Mr. Tucker's old pickup rattling south toward us. I recognized it a good half-mile away. Mr. Tucker often delivered groceries to outlying homes, expecting a couple of extra bucks for his trouble. He waved cheerfully as the pickup rumbled over the ruts, but he didn't slow down, and a cloud of dust boiled up and covered us from head to toe before it settled out.

TJ and Ferret wanted to know what the old man had said to me when he quit swinging his fists around. I told them, of course, and then they bombarded me with a ton of questions.

No, I didn't know who that old man was, or why he would know me, or why he would hate me. There was only one thing I did know about that man. "Guess we found our bootlegger," I said.

"Huh?" Ferret said. "That old man?"

"Yep," I said. "As I was backing up, I saw three jugs hidden next to that tree he jumped out from behind. He had them in a gunny sack, but it had slid down and I saw the corks stuck in the tops of those jugs."

TJ and Ferret talked about that for a while, and pretty soon they figured that all we had to do was tell Jess and our problems would be over.

But the still was the key. Without knowing where it was, Jess might not have enough cause to make an arrest. I didn't tell TJ and Ferret that. Let them think their problems were over. In fact, I didn't think they had a problem. I thought it was just my problem. And for sure it wasn't over.

When we got back to Bob White, we were hot, dusty, hungry, and thirsty. Ferret said his mom would make us sandwiches and I was grateful for that. Unless Jess had gone to Mr. Tucker's grocery store, there wasn't much to eat at our place.

TJ said the second thing she was going to do—after eating of course—was to take a bath. I looked at her, and she sure needed one. Her legs were streaked with dust and so was her face. I remembered that I'd just met her a few hours earlier, and that I really didn't know her.

I knew she could outrun me, except when I didn't want to get caught by some weirdo in the woods. I knew she could swing across ditches like a regular guy, and that she wasn't afraid to smoke grapevines, and that she'd seen one man kill another, and that she'd stuck up for me when that crazy old man had grabbed my wrist. Maybe she was all right, for a girl, but Ferret and I didn't need a girl around to mess things up.

The Brubakers' house was now less than a block away. Ferret's mom was out front, down on her knees weeding the flower garden that bordered the drive where visitors parked. She was wearing shorts and a floppy wide-brimmed fishing hat as protection against the sun.

TJ stopped cold. Under the dust, her face was clouding up. Something was bad wrong. "Mom!" she screamed. "Mom!" She took off running, right straight for the Brubakers' house.

Ferret's mom heard her and jumped up, then ran awkwardly forward, her loose sandals slapping the bottoms of her feet. I didn't have any reason to run, but I did and Ferret did too. Mrs. Brubaker's face looked as stricken as TJ's, and I thought TJ would stop and say something. But she didn't.

She ran right by Mrs. Brubaker, jerked the screen door open so hard it banged against the house, and slammed shut behind her. Ferret and I stopped beside Mrs. Brubaker. What in the world was going on?

"Mom!" I heard TJ yell from inside the house. And then it got real quiet.

I looked at Mrs. Brubaker and I could see her eyes were still as red as they had been this morning. And then I realized that where we were standing now, was where the Ford had been parked this morning.

"Where's TJ's parents?" I asked Mrs. Brubaker.

She glanced at me, then looked away. "Just her mother brought her. They drove all the way from Baton Rouge yesterday." She sniffled a bit, then brought out a hankie and wiped her eyes. "I thought she was going to stay at least one day before she went back, but then she said that if she got back today, she could work a full shift tomorrow. We drove all over town looking for you, but when we couldn't find you kids, she said she had to leave anyway." She sniffled again. "So she left."

I looked at the house and thought I could hear TJ crying

inside. TJ's mom had left without saying good-bye. Jesus H. Christ.

"Where's her dad?" I asked, the thought suddenly entering my head that he might be dead.

Mrs. Brubaker's voice got angry, but not at me. "The son-of-a-bitch has left them. They're getting a divorce."

Mrs. Brubaker wasn't your typical minister's wife. She swore when it was necessary and I'd heard her say the same thing once before when she hit her thumb with a hammer. So I wasn't shocked by her language, I just didn't know what to say about divorce. Divorce was one of those things that you knew happened, but it didn't happen in Bob White. All I knew about divorce was that it was supposed to be pretty terrible. Even the sound of the word made me feel bad for TJ.

"I'm real sorry, Mrs. Brubaker."

Her eyes cleared a bit and she looked at me, then smiled faintly. She was a nice lady and I liked her a lot.

"I'll be going now, uh, Ferret," I said, remembering that Mrs. Brubaker didn't mind my calling him by his real name.

"See you later," he said, looking as miserable as I felt.

"You boys hungry?" Mrs. Brubaker asked. She threw her shoulders back and underneath that big old hat, I saw her set her jaw. I guess she'd learn to live with her sister's divorce.

"Could you fry us some bologna, Mom?" Ferret asked.

"Of course I can. Come on in the house," she said.

In the kitchen she put a skillet on the stove, then took off her hat, gave us a quick glance, and sent us to wash up. We dashed upstairs and Ferret used the bathroom first, coming out with about two-thirds of the dust gone from his face.

"Don't tell your mom anything," I warned, remembering that Reverend Brubaker hadn't wanted us to go to the Bottomlands. He nodded and went downstairs. I washed fast, then left the bathroom.

A muffled cry sounded from the spare bedroom down the hall. It was on the north wall behind the closed door. I knew the Brubakers' house like the back of my hand. I'd spent a few nights here last fall until Jess moved back home.

I walked down the hall and opened the door. TJ lay on the bed, her face buried in a pillow, her crying all worn out. I walked over and sat down beside her on top of a frayed quilt with a blue and white pattern that I remembered Mrs. Brubaker had called a Louisiana Star. TJ moved her head just enough so she could see it was me, then she turned her face back into the dust-smudged pillow.

Why did everything have to be so hard? I didn't know what to say, except that I was sorry, and I questioned how that would sound. Last fall, nothing anybody had said to me had made any difference at the time. But I did know how it felt to lose your parents, which was what had happened to TJ, more or less. I reached out and lay my hand on her shoulder, as lightly as I could. I hoped she wouldn't mind.

She didn't seem to notice, just lay still, and I could hear her breathing hard against the pillow. I sat there for a couple of minutes, feeling totally useless, then I decided there was nothing I could do. What was I doing here anyway?

As soon as I took my hand away, TJ rolled over and sat up, throwing both arms around my neck.

6

It caught me by surprise, feeling her body against mine, her holding on like it was a matter of life and death. It was only a few moments later that I realized that my arms had gone around her and that I was hugging her as much as she was hugging me.

Her head was pressed tight against my cheek and in her hair I could smell the dust that Mr. Tucker's pickup had thrown up. I could also smell *her* for the first time—a whiff of perfume underneath all that dust.

It reminded me of the last time a female had held me close. Last fall, when all the church women had thrown their arms around me, saying how brave I was until I was sick of it, wanting just one person in the world to hold me close and to hear my dad grumbling at me to take out the garbage.

But TJ holding me was different. I felt myself being drawn into her again and I didn't want the moment to end. And as soon as I thought that . . .

"Mark?" Mrs. Brubaker was calling from downstairs.

Instantly I let go of TJ and jumped up. "Be right there," I shouted back, starting for the door. Then I stopped and turned.

TJ's green eyes burned into mine, as if she was trying to say something. Exactly what, I didn't know. I just nodded and said, "See you downstairs."

Ferret and I ate our sandwiches together, just the two of us sitting at the kitchen table. Then we played catch for a while until we got bored with that and I decided to go on home. TJ never did come downstairs.

When I got home, it was about three. Jess had left a note for me to do the dishes and pick up the house. After Jess had come back home to live, he'd explained to me that we had to share the work. He brought home the money we needed to live on and it was my job to take care of the house. It made sense, but it sure wasn't fun. I hated housework.

After doing those chores, I took a bath, played "sock" with Bopeep—holding on to one end of an old, knotted sock while she growled and tugged ferociously on the other end—and fell asleep watching the Yankees killing the Orioles on TV. I had this weird dream about a baseball game where all the players were tall, blond, naked men. They had no thumbs, so when they threw the ball, it would fly off at an odd angle. Then I found myself standing on the pitcher's mound, striking out batter after batter, until a girl with black hair and green eyes came to the plate and hit my first pitch, a high fast ball, into the left-field stands.

I woke up when the front door opened. Jess came in wearing his deputy sheriff's uniform, looking sharp with his tan shirt starched and creased down each breast pocket, his silver badge polished like a star at midnight when the moon wasn't shining, and black shoes spit-shined so you could see your face in them. His leather gun belt squeaked when he walked, and I'd seen him explode six tin cans with six shots from fifty feet with his .38 caliber police revolver.

"Hey, kid," he said, looking a little annoyed. "You eaten yet?"

This was his usual way of talking to me—like I was a lot of trouble, like I was interfering with his having fun. "Not yet," I answered.

"Let's go get a bite to eat at the Sonic." The evening news was droning on and Jess walked over and flicked off our four-year-old RCA console TV. Sitting on top of the TV were twenty-one trophies and figurines of baseball players with their bats cocked, and football players stiff-arming imaginary opponents. Jess had played center field for the 1950 American Legion state baseball champs.

But dominating the now-dusty grouping of his past heroics was a two-foot-high trophy for his selection to the East All State squad as second-string halfback. I was eight years old at the time and I vaguely remember going to Oklahoma City with Mom and Dad to see the game, but Jess hadn't gotten to play much and when he did, nothing wonderful had happened.

I stretched and groaned, then gave my usual response to an offer of food. "Sure." Then I added, "Can we take Ferret too?"

"We can ask."

I threw some Purina Dog Chow into Bopeep's bowl, then set it by the back steps. She sniffed at it—as if curious, but not hungry—then stood by indifferent to the food as I gave her fresh water. She had a funny habit of not eating her dog food if I was watching, but I knew it would be gone before the ants got to it. I scratched her ears and ruffled her fur. She was just starting to shed, late as usual, and coarse white hairs covered my jeans legs in seconds.

I ran around front and jumped into the car beside Jess. His cruiser was a two-year-old black-and-white Plymouth Fury with a special police power pack added. Jess touched the pedal and the Fury lunged forward, my back compressing the seat from the sudden acceleration. The hood raised up, as if airborne, and before it had hardly settled back down again, we were at the Brubakers' house.

Jess swerved into the driveway, spewing gravel into the thick Bermuda grass, skidded to a halt, and touched the siren briefly. The circus had come through Bob White last summer and the siren's low, lingering "rrowlll" always reminded me of the way the tigers had protested when Clyde Beatty snapped his whip in their faces.

The screen door burst open. TJ flew out and stopped cold, a worried look on her face.

"What the . . . ?" Jess said, surprised.

I realized that a sheriff's car driving up had set TJ to thinking something bad had happened to her mom. I jumped out of the car real fast so she could see who it was. "It's just me, TJ. And my brother. Is Ferret here?"

Her face relaxed and the tension melted away. She was wearing shorts with a fly front that used to be boys' jeans—but now cut off way above the knees—and a white blouse with a pale blue vest. She ran over to the car. "There's nobody home. They went to the church to get some things ready for the church fair tomorrow."

"Who's this?" Jess said, leaning across the seat to look at TJ.

"Ferret's cousin from Louisiana. TJ, this is Jess."

"Hi," TJ said, smiling and bending over to look at Jess.

Jess grinned. Being friendly to girls came easy to him. "You hungry, girl?"

"I'll have to call the church and—"

"Hop in. I'll call them for you."

I stepped aside and TJ slid across the seat. Soon as I got in and slammed the door, Jess spun the car back into the street and we took off, sending up the usual cloud of dust to blanket the yards bordering Ash Street.

I remembered then that I hadn't told Jess about seeing the bootlegger in the Bottomlands. Jess would be madder'n hell about me being in the woods. I didn't want to tell him now, with TJ in the car. It would have to wait.

Jess picked up the radio mike and keyed it. "Lucy?"

The radio squealed, and Jess reached over and adjusted the squelch knob. "Lucy?" he repeated.

A nasally female voice answered. "Go ahead, Jess."

"Call Reverend Brubaker at the church and tell him that TJ's with me and Mark."

"TJ? TJ who?" You could just hear Lucy's ears perk up.

Jess rolled his eyes. "It's the Brubakers' niece from Louisiana."

"Where from in Louisiana?" Lucy was a busybody and a

pest, acting like she was in charge of all the gossip that ran around Bob White. Most of the time when somebody told you a rumor, it started out, "And Lucy says . . . "

Jess made a face, then pressed the mike key and held it before TJ.

TJ looked at it, took a deep breath, and said, "I'm TJ Gatlin from Baton Rouge, I'm fourteen, and I'm spending the rest of the summer with the Brubakers."

A pause and then, "What's TJ stand for?"

You could see TJ's eyebrows furrow. "None of your business."

Jess burst out laughing and hung up the mike. "You sure told her off. I never heard anybody talk to Lucy Roberts that way," he said. "You got spunk, girl." He threw his head back and laughed some more.

Of course I knew Lucy and I could just see her sputtering her frustration. I started laughing too. "She's probably already making her first phone call."

TJ giggled. "And telling someone how they don't teach manners in Louisiana."

We were still laughing when we pulled into a parking space under the shedlike structure fronting the Sonic. Jess punched the speaker button and ordered burgers, fries, and cherry Cokes.

The gear shift console forced TJ to sit sidesaddle and her right knee touched my left knee and her right shoulder rubbed against my left shoulder. She didn't have dog ears now; her hair was freshly washed and tied back away from her face with a single red ribbon. A feather of a black curl licked her right temple. A few hours earlier I'd held her close.

In Bob White you didn't have a girlfriend until you had a car. After high school started in September, I'd soon turn sixteen and get my driver's license. Maybe then I'd get a girlfriend. I wasn't even sure TJ would make a good one.

About that time, Jess started talking to TJ and she kept asking him questions. He told her about his high school football days, about dropping out of college for lack of money, and about joining the army where he'd been an MP—a military policeman. Inside fifteen minutes of meeting Jess, she knew all about him, his whole life story. But TJ had spent the entire day with me and she hadn't asked me one plain-as-the-mud-on-your-face question. Girlfriend? I needed a girlfriend like I needed a hole in my head.

In a half hour it would be dark. Soon the kids with cars would drag Main, then do a slow circle around the Sonic, then drive back up the mile-long Main Street, honking like they hadn't seen each other in ten years. For now the Sonic wasn't busy and our food came quickly.

A redhead named Joyce brought out the food tray and hooked it to Jess's window, all the while chewing gum like she was afraid it would get away from her. "Hey, Jess," she said, giving him a big smile. She didn't stoop down, she bent over, and the top of her blouse drooped away from her chest.

I tried to keep my eyes on her face but they just naturally drifted in spite of myself. I had to admit it was interesting.

"How's your mom doing, Joyce?" Jess asked. "Lucy tells me that she had surgery in the City last week."

"Oh, she's home now, doing fine. It was just a female thing. I need a buck seventy-seven." She paused her gum chewing to study TJ for a moment, then glanced at me.

Jess pulled out his billfold and paid her. "You tell her I said hello, okay?"

She stood up and put the money away in the change apron around her waist, then bounced back down again. "I'll be off at ten, if you're not doing anything later."

My eyes followed the activity with interest.

Jess shook his head and smiled. "Can't tonight. I'm working until midnight. But I'll call you next week."

She nodded. "I'll be expecting it." She glanced back at me again and winked. "What are you grinning about, Mark?"

Jess and TJ turned to look at me and I'm sure I must have

turned red as a cherry lollipop. "Nothing," I mumbled, sinking back into the seat.

An hour later, we were cruising through the sparse business sections of Bob White, accompanying Jess on his rounds. In the center of town, the old stone courthouse assumed an eerie countenance as the few streetlights splotched dark shadows here and there. Bob White was mostly dead at night, even on Saturdays.

The Palace Theater was all lit up and a John Wayne movie that I wanted to see was playing. We drove to the west side of town, where Main Street turned into the highway, and cruised around Martin's Steakhouse real slow while Jess played his spotlight on the cars in back. Not much crime occurred in Bob White, but occasionally someone would steal hubcaps or siphon gas. We didn't need a police force, and left jurisdiction to the county sheriff's office. Still, it was kind of exciting to watch the spotlight move steadily over and between the cars, the shadows jumping around like dark spooky figures. Nothing happened, but I could always hope.

The southern part of town was the only real bad part of Bob White. Hogan's Pool Hall was a low, flattopped building with a single bare bulb hanging above the doorway and a neon beer sign in a dusty window, flashing on and off. I had been in there with Ferret several times, though we weren't supposed to be allowed inside. There were three pool tables, three snooker tables, and a bar that Hogan himself stood behind.

The Fury's windows were down and the cool night air felt refreshing as we cruised almost silently up to Hogan's. It was pretty quiet except for the frogs and crickets singing from the fish pond that sat about a hundred yards south of the pool hall. The tires crunched softly across the gravel as Jess played the spotlight around the few parked cars and then around the back of the building. We saw nothing.

Jess had just flicked off the spotlight to leave when a crash sounded from inside the building, like glass shattering against the wall. Down at the pond, the singing stopped. Jess backed up the car and called Lucy. "I'm at Hogan's. May be a problem inside."

"Hold on, Jess. Hogan's on the phone." Jess waited patiently. Then, "Hogan says there's two roughnecks drunker than skunks and he's afraid they're going to tear his place up. Wants me to call Sheriff Adams."

"It's all right, Lucy. I can handle it." He got out of the car, then pulled a baton from under the seat and attached it to his belt. "You guys stay here."

We sat perfectly still, watching Jess stride toward the door. He swung it back on its hinges and stepped inside.

I opened the car door immediately. "Come on, TJ," I whispered.

7

TJ followed me out and we ran, quiet-like, to the door. I pushed it open a crack and peered inside.

Jess was leaning on the bar talking to Hogan and I couldn't see anyone else unless I poked my whole head through the door, and I wasn't ready to do that yet. Smoke clung to the low ceiling, swirling in hot little eddies in the dim light. The smell of beer was so strong, I felt a passing urge to puke. I heard a rap and the brittle click of billiard balls caroming against each other.

Behind the bar Mr. Hogan looked worried. He always looked worried. Physically, he was damn near helpless when it came to trouble, and now I wondered why he had ever thought to get into the bar business. If you looked directly into his face, you'd think you were talking to a giant. A ruddy complexion shown from features as wide as they were stretched high. Tufts of red, unruly hair clung to his head like service-station rags. I'd always thought Mr. Hogan had to be twice as smart as most men because his brain seemed twice as large. Then you noticed his arms.

They were as big around as fence posts, and barely longer than my forearms. Mr. Hogan was a dwarf, with a normal-sized body, except his was larger than any man's I knew, including Reverend Brubaker's. But Mr. Hogan's arms and legs were as short as four loaves of bread. Behind the bar, he looked almost like a normal person, but I knew he was standing on a platform made from two planks nailed together and supported on four buckets turned upside down.

Some people made fun of him. That was wrong. He couldn't help waddling on those stubby legs, but his bulging belly made him look remarkably like a duck. Besides, he was a real nice man and had always let Ferret and me hang around for a while before making us leave. We were his future business, I guess.

Jess was moving away from the bar. "Come on in, TJ," I whispered, pushing the door wider.

"No, I . . . I don't want to go in."

I glanced sharply at her. With nothing but dim reflected light, her face was mostly a shadow, but darker than it should have been. Something was troubling her again. "Come on!" I whispered urgently. I didn't want to miss anything.

She hesitated and I knew she wanted to, but something was holding her back. She shook her head.

I didn't say chicken. I just said, "Suit yourself." I squeezed through the narrow opening I'd made and slipped quietly along the left wall until I got to the bar. Mr. Hogan didn't notice me and I glanced back toward the door. It was still ajar.

"You boys looking for some trouble?" Jess stood about six feet from the pool table, his feet spread apart a little wider than you'd normally stand, his thumbs tucked inside his gun belt.

Two men raised up. It was clear from the surprised, dumb-drunk look on their faces that they had not noticed Jess before. One was about Jess's age, his face sunburned the color of hickory chips except for a band of tight white skin just under a widow's peak. He staggered, weaving a bit as he tried to focus on Jess. "We hain't lookin' for trouble," he said loudly, giggling, drunk silly. "Billy Ray? We lookin' for trouble?"

Billy Ray strolled around the edge of the table into the light, a cue stick in one hand, a beer bottle in the other. A few years older than his friend, he wore an oil-stained cowboy hat that probably used to be gray, and he had one eye that looked slightly off to the side, like he'd been hit in the head in the oil fields. He was as big as the Poland China boar hog that had won first place at last year's county fair. If there was anybody that looked like he was looking for trouble, it was Billy Ray.

He sized Jess up and down, then hoisted the bottle to his lips and chug-a-lugged the remaining two-thirds of the frothy beer. He brought the dead soldier down, belched loudly, and suddenly tossed the bottle toward the front wall where it shattered like the one from a few moments earlier.

Bringing the cue stick around in front, he slid it into both hands. "What you going to do about that, Mr. Deputy Sheriff?" His voice was low, menacing, slurring, but not sounding half as drunk as his friend's.

While all this was going on, Jess had not moved. Now he grinned and stretched out his hand in greeting. "Y'all can just call me Jess. Y'all from down . . . Tax-ass way?"

Billy Ray blinked and his face turned red. "You goddamned Okie, I'm gonna break you into little pieces of shit." He raised the cue stick and lunged forward, arcing it at Jess's head.

But Jess wasn't there anymore. The cue stick swooshed as it cut the air. Then Jess raised back up, his right fist flashing forward. Where Billy Ray's nose had been came the sound of crunching cartilage.

"Sum bitch," Billy Ray bellowed, hardly rocking backward. His left hand went instinctively to his nose, while his right lashed out again with the cue stick.

Jess didn't duck this time. His police baton materialized in his hand, and it caught the thrusting cue stick and several of Billy Ray's fingers simultaneously. The cue stick broke into two pieces, one end flying past Jess, dancing across the wooden floor and rolling to my feet. Billy Ray howled again. I figured he was lucky it wasn't his fingers lying at my feet.

Jess thrust the baton forward, end first, and at least six inches went past Billy Ray's longhorn steer belt buckle. He doubled over and Jess clubbed him right on top of his filthy cowboy hat, sending him face-down into the pool-hall litter.

The whole fight was over in less than thirty seconds. I'd heard tales that Jess was tough, but I'd never seen him fight anyone until tonight. My heart was just catching up to the action, pounding furiously, when I remembered that Ferret would want to know all the details. My mind raced through the fight again. Billy Ray hadn't even touched Jess. And Jess had only hit Billy Ray three times, not counting breaking the cue stick.

Now Billy Ray lay motionless except for the trickle of blood coming from his nose. Out cold, or . . . maybe even dead!

Jess's last blow had landed with a sickening thud on the back of Billy Ray's head. My stomach churned at the thought of Jess killing someone, even a drunken Texas roughneck. Then Billy Ray's chest heaved. Relief swelled over me.

Jess strode toward the younger roughneck. Fear crossed the drunken man's face, bleaching it nearly as white as the band up near his hairline. He staggered backward wildly, lost his balance and sprawled across the pool table, scrambling the balls in a furious clicking rhythm. "No!" he cried. "No! Don't hurt me." He threw his hands up before his face.

Then Jess was on him. A quick rake with the baton across the man's hands brought a cry of pain, then Jess thrust his baton against the man's larynx. "You boys been drinking rotgut. Where'd you get it?"

"Oh, goddamn, Sheriff. My hand's broke. I hain't done nothing." The man was practically bawling.

"I can smell it on your breath. Tell me where you got it!" Jess rammed the baton upward into the man's chin.

"Ow, ow. Oh, damn, please . . . we got it here."

"You're lying. Hogan knows better than to sell rotgut."

"No, no. Outside the pool hall."

"Who'd you buy it from?"

"Some old man. I don't know his name."

"You're lying again. Tell me the truth, or I'll ram this stick up your no-good ass."

"I hain't lying. I swear. Some old man. He acted kind of

crazy. Billy Ray and me even laughed about him later. Crazy."

"What'd he look like?"

"I don't know, just an old man." The roughneck's eyes rolled wildly, trying to think back through his clouded memory. "Wait. I remember. He was missin' his left thumb."

Jess raised up, and though I couldn't see more than just the side of his face, I could tell he was shocked. He grabbed the man by the shirt and jerked him to his feet, shaking him like it was urgent. "Where'd he go?"

"I don't know. He drove away in a pickup. Billy Ray and me sat in the car and drank half the jug, then we come in. . . ." The man's eyes rolled and he groaned. "I'm gonna be sick."

Jess let him go and the man fell to the floor and puked out his guts.

Vaguely, I sensed someone's presence beside me and knew that TJ had come in. I didn't look at her. I stood by the bar, stunned, in part by the suddenness of the action and in part by the fact that Jess knew that old man. Jess's face was as grim as on the day Mom and Dad died.

8

In the center of town, Jess turned the packed Fury behind the old stone courthouse, pulling into the lot reserved for county employees. Lucy's red '53 Studebaker Spider was parked in the space marked "Sheriff Adams," which was closest to the back door. Jess parked in the no-parking zone directly in front of the door, leaving the car running.

The Fury's headlights cast warm shadows against the old building. The lowest level of the courthouse was partially underground, and that's where they had stuck the Sheriff's Office and the County Jail. All the windows stood no higher than my chin, and they had frosted panes so you couldn't see inside and half-inch rebar crisscrossing the outside. Three steps led down into a doorwell, dimly lit by a yellow bug light that still attracted a few desperate moths.

I had hoped to watch Jess lock up the two roughnecks, but he glared at me as TJ and I got out of the front seat, and told us to go straight home. He was still mad at me for coming into the pool hall, but I didn't care.

We walked across the parking lot, glancing back to watch Jess pull first one and then the other roughneck from the back seat of the Fury. Their hands were cuffed behind their backs and they leaned forward as they stumbled down the steps into the courthouse.

Cutting across the street, we moved west on Main Street. It

was about nine o'clock, and the cruising crowd had found better things to do than drag Main. The theater wouldn't let out for another half hour, so the street ahead was empty of traffic. Lonely streetlamps stood vigil over the four-block section of Bob White that we called downtown. We walked through mute streets, the only sounds being our rubber sneakers scraping against concrete sidewalks.

Tomorrow I'd tell Jess about the old man in the Bottomlands and find out who he was. But there was another thing I was wondering about. I was wondering why TJ had been bothered about going into Hogan's. She'd seen a man killed—a Cajun, she'd said. So she couldn't be afraid of a little pool-hall fight.

"You see the fight?" I asked.

"What? Sure. 'Course."

"I mean, did you see the whole fight?"

"Wasn't much of a fight." TJ shrugged her shoulders, like it had happened a hundred years ago.

"Heck if it wasn't! That Billy Ray fellow was asking for it and Jess clobbered him."

"The second guy wasn't and Jess broke his hand for no reason."

I stopped cold and grabbed TJ by the shoulder. "What are you saying?"

She pushed my hand away. Under the streetlights, her eyes sparkled, cold and dark. "Your brother's got a mean streak."

"Yeah?" I glared at her. "Well, deputy sheriffs have got to be tough."

"Sure." She rolled her eyes.

"I don't have to listen to this," I said, turning away and walking on, fast. She caught up to me right away, though, just as I turned down Ash Street.

We left the streetlights and sidewalks behind and tromped down the dusty road. I didn't feel like talking anymore. Anybody who said Jess had a mean streak was no friend of mine. Imagine her saying that after Jess had bought her the burger and fries. Pretty darned ungrateful, if you ask me.

I slapped each foot down hard, just to let her know I was mad. Partly, I was mad at myself, for letting her get to me. I thought back at having just met her today and all the emotions she'd made me feel—all in a single day.

At first I hadn't liked her, then I felt sorry for her inhaling the grapevine smoke. But I liked the way she'd take a dare and I liked the way she stood up to the crazy old man. Later she'd cried when her mom had left and I felt sorry for her again. I hadn't liked the way she'd taken up with Jess and I sure didn't like what she'd said about him. Girls!

The night was about as dark as you would ever want a moonless night to be. A dusty haze hung over Bob White, obscuring most of the stars. Ash Street didn't have any streetlights. Even though my eyes had adjusted to the darkness, I could only see fifty or sixty feet ahead.

Somewhere from out of the black night came an ominous sound, almost like a low growl and softly clicking teeth.

"TJ," I whispered, touching her arm to warn her. "There's something up ahead, waiting."

"Huh?" she said, in her normal voice. "Waiting? You trying to scare—"

"Shut up and listen!" I hissed, slowing down. All I could see ahead was blackness, except for huge dark shadows rising against the lighter sky, and I knew those were the cottonwoods. And all I could hear was our sneakers plopping against the dry powder covering the street.

"I don't hear anything," TJ said.

"Walk quiet-like." If something was out there, it could see us in our white shirts, with the glow of the town behind us, long before we could see it. I couldn't see anything except the Thompsons' white picket fence to my right. Still—

TJ froze. "Something is out there. I can feel it."

We held our breaths, listening. Then I heard it again. A ticking sound embedded in a low rhythmic rumble. The sound a sticky engine valve makes.

"It's just a car idling," TJ said, starting to walk again.

"Wait." I held back. "I've got a bad feeling about this."

"Probably high school kids, making out. Let's go." She walked on.

I followed reluctantly. The hair on the back of my neck began to rise, getting pricklier by the second.

Two stabbing beams of light shot through the darkness, blinding me. I threw a hand up, shielding my eyes. The lights were coming from a car or pickup sitting right in the middle of the street, about a hundred feet directly in front of us. The engine revved then slowed, then revved again, and the lights lunged forward, then jerked to a halt.

"He's after us," TJ whispered, her voice croaking like a frog with a sore throat.

The engine revved again, louder this time, and again the lights lunged forward, and again they stopped.

I grabbed TJ's arm and backed up the street, looking for an escape route. Old Man Jenkins's hedge blocked the left side of the street and the picket fence was to the right, the pickets like white spears pointing to the sky. I didn't think we could clear either one. It was forty or fifty yards back to the corner, to First Street. Too far, if we had to run for it.

The engine revved again, higher, straining like hound dogs wanting to be let loose after a squirrel. Suddenly the clutch popped all the way out and the headlights rose in the air, racing forward.

"Run," I yelled, but we were already flying back up the street. Light streaked around us and over our heads and I could feel it plastering my back. Ahead of us unbroken hedge and endless picket fence disappeared into darkness.

The engine roar changed to a high-pitched whine as the driver shifted gears and popped the clutch again. There was no escaping it.

My sneakers slapped the earth rearward. To my right, TJ raced dead even with me, her vest flying half off her shoulders, her blouse glowing like a white-hot blaze.

Behind us, the lights tightened the gap and the engine noise grew deafening.

We had two or three seconds. Then we'd have to go for the hedge, like it or not. I felt my heart pounding inside my chest . . . and the steady roar behind us.

Suddenly, TJ veered right. The hedge wasn't there anymore! I swerved, then lost my footing and crashed into TJ, tumbling onto First Street. A mass of lights and steel hurdled past us flashing up the street toward Main, leaving behind a lingering, dying engine whine and a cloud of dust.

TJ got to her feet first and ran a few steps after the lights. "Bastard!" she screamed.

I got to her just as the lights turned west onto Main Street, away from town. It was hard to tell for sure, what with the dust and all, but it looked like a pickup, an old pickup. One that I'd never seen before.

9

I sensed the morning warmth, then feet walked across my bed. I cracked my eyes open. Bopeep's black muzzle was inches from my nose. Her tongue snaked out and swiped my face with wet drool. I dodged and wiped my face with the sheet, then hugged Bopeep and sat up.

The folding chair was rammed tight under the doorknob. Dad's Winchester Model 12 stood propped in the corner next to the headboard where I could reach it quickly if Bopeep had growled during the night. Luckily she hadn't.

It was Sunday morning and the alarm clock said five minutes past eight. Last night I had pulled the shades down, but left the windows open for the cool air, knowing Bopeep would warn me of a prowler outside. A gentle breeze puffed the shades into the room and bright sunlight stabbed my eyes.

I let Bopeep out of the room and got dressed, putting on the only white shirt I owned and my best pair of jeans.

A few minutes later, leaving the bathroom, I noticed Jess's door was cracked open. Jess lay sleeping, his naked back half covered with a sheet, his face turned toward the far wall, a limp, slender arm dangling across his waist. Some girl was with him, on the far side of the bed. I wasn't particularly interested in who it was this time.

I closed the door softly and went into the kitchen. Bopeep was standing patiently by the back door, so I opened it wide, letting her out to investigate last night's smells. After making a bowl of cereal, I started thinking about last night.

Somehow we'd outrun the pickup to the corner when we shouldn't have been able to. Whoever was in the pickup had held back a little. He'd tried to scare us, not kill us. Or maybe he was having fun at our expense. I didn't think so. And who was the driver? The old man? Why would he be trying to scare us? Nothing made sense.

I was in the middle of my cereal when I heard water running in the bathroom. Moments later, Jess came in, bare-chested and wearing beltless jeans that allowed a lot of groin. His eyes were bleary and he looked like death warmed over. Sunlight from the open door caught him, and he winced, turning his head away, shuffling blindly toward the cabinets.

I took another bite of cereal and grunted when he passed, not expecting an answer and not getting one.

Jess filled the tin coffeepot with cold water, then spilled coffee grounds into the upper tray and set it on our old four-burner stove to perk. Turning, he sat down gingerly in the chair opposite me. "You could be a big help by putting the coffee on when you get up."

I deliberately changed the subject. "We need groceries. We're out of everything."

"I'll go to Tucker's today." The pot made its first gurgle, more like a strangling noise, and Jess looked up at it.

I was afraid he'd realize I hadn't responded to his first comment, so I changed the subject again. "That was a great fight. I can't wait to tell Ferret."

He peered at me with his left eye, the one less bloodshot. Then he grinned slowly. "Bet that Billy Ray will think twice before he tackles another Okie."

"Yeah, bet you broke his nose."

"He'll be all right. Both of 'em are probably still sleeping it off."

"Yeah," I said. My cereal was gone, and I glanced at the back steps. Bopeep wasn't there, so I picked up the bowl and drank the rest of the sugar milk.

"That TJ is downright cute. You sweet on her?"

I glared at him and tried to look insulted. Then I changed the subject again. "You know that old man the roughneck was talking about? The bootlegger?"

Jess frowned. "What about him?" His voice sounded tighter than usual.

"Saw him yesterday."

Jess's eyes widened and then he winced again. "Hell if you did. Where'd you see him?"

"In the Bottomlands. He had three jugs with him."

His eyes flashed with anger. "Damn it. I told you to stay away from there."

I didn't say anything, waiting for Jess to settle down.

"You see his still anywheres?"

"Nope." I shook my head. "Who is he? You know him, don't you?"

Jess hesitated, then got up and went over to the stove. The pot had been gurgling hard for a few minutes, but I could see the color was still light brown as it bubbled into the glass knob of the lid. Jess shook the pot several times, then sat back down, a dark look cutting his face. "His name's Lafe Packard and he's one mean son-of-a-bitch. You stay away from him, you hear?"

Why was Jess so mad? "I think that old man tried to run—"

"God damn it. Listen to me."

"But, Jess—"

"Just stay the hell away from him," Jess exploded, as mad as I'd ever seen him. "And don't let me hear you kids been down in the Bottomlands again." He pointed his finger straight at me, like it was a gun.

I looked at his finger, inches from my face, then back at Jess. He was always telling me what to do. Ordering me around. Never calling me anything except "kid."

Everything just boiled up in me. I spat out the words. "I'll do as I damn well please. You're not Mom and Dad."

Jess looked stunned, then his eyes blazed with cold fire. He lunged across the table, grabbing for my hair.

I ducked down, twisting away, his hand sliding across my flattop, catching nothing. Instantly, I was on my feet, mad and breathing hard, only a couple of feet from the kitchen screen door, and I'd be gone in a split second if he came for me.

He froze half out of his chair, fury written across his face, knowing he couldn't catch me.

"Morning, Mark, Jess." Joyce stood in the kitchen doorway.

Joyce? How long had she been there? Through my anger came the realization that Joyce had spent the night with Jess. "Hey," I answered, feeling some of the tension drain away.

Jess glowered at me, holding his anger inside.

Joyce padded in, barefoot, her red hair uncombed, blinking sleep from her eyes, as cheerful as if she were Bopeep wagging her tail. She was wearing one of Jess's T-shirts that covered all her vital parts, just barely. Joyce seemed awfully casual about some things—a lot different than most girls.

In spite of my anger, I could feel the temperature of my ears rising a bit.

"How about some coffee, Jess?" she asked, picking up the percolator.

"Fine." His voice trembled, then he sat down in his chair and took a deep breath.

I pushed open the screen and paused. "I'm going to Ferret's. And then I'll be going to *church.*" I emphasized "church," hoping to make Jess feel guilty since he never went.

I jumped over both concrete steps, letting the screen door bang behind me. Bopeep was nowhere around. She hates us fighting. I ran some fresh water in her pail and set out.

The First Baptist Church of Bob White, Oklahoma, was located six blocks north of the courthouse, just on the outskirts of town. Sitting on a good-sized rise of ground facing south, the front of it caught the sun's rays most of the year round. Open fields spread out behind it, which at one time had been used for grazing cattle and horses. Now the fields were only a home for mice and quail.

By far the largest church in town, the Baptist Church was half again taller and wider than the Methodist, the Presbyterian, and the Catholic churches in Bob White. Built only two years ago, the sanctuary still smelled new. I remember Reverend Brubaker being away from home all the time, barnstorming the county like a politician, organizing bake sales, squeezing donations out of local merchants, making evangelistic trips to the Baptist churches in the City. He even got Old Lady Hendricks to donate the land. She had no use for it anyway. Her husband Joshua had made his money in oil, then invested it in land which nobody wanted, then passed away.

The church had a real odd look to it, even though it had a large bell tower and a big cross on top. For starters, it wasn't white like churches should be. It was painted a pale butterscotch with a bit of white trim. And it wasn't made of brick or wooden planks; the exterior was some kind of plaster, but not like adobe—it had a sheen to its finish.

If the color wasn't enough to shock you, the style certainly was. Long sleek lines and a stretched, futuristic look. I'd heard an architect from Oklahoma City had designed it. Nothing else in Bob White looked anything like it. The townspeople still shook their heads, saying it was gaudy and that the church members would be forever paying off the debt that Reverend Brubaker had stuck them with.

TJ, Ferret, and I had all gone to Sunday school and listened to the story of Jesus walking on water and saving Peter. It was nearly eleven and TJ and I were in the sanctuary sitting down front in the first pew. Ferret was in the room behind the door on the right with the rest of the choir, and they would be trooping in soon. On my right, Mrs. Brubaker looked prim and proper as a minister's wife ought, wearing a green dress that buttoned all the way to her neck with a white lace doily that spread out toward her shoulders. Ever since Mom and Dad's accident, I'd sat next to her for church service.

TJ sat on my left, wearing a white dress with lace across the front and gloves that snuck up to her elbows. The dress covered her knees and she wore nylons that must have itched because she kept scratching her legs together. A white headband pulled her hair away from her face. All in all, she looked like a regular girl. But she wasn't.

TJ had a strange bundle of emotions inside her that she kept tied double-knotted so they couldn't get out. Twice I'd seen her let loose those strings, and powerful energy had leaped out kicking and screaming.

In the Bottomlands she'd stood up to the old man. Scared as she must have been, she'd found courage in the face of craziness, a face that promised bad thoughts.

Then, when her mom had left without saying good-bye, her grief had poured out like a spring gully-washer.

I decided I wasn't mad at TJ anymore. I couldn't be mad at someone I might have been killed with. Besides, I was mad at Jess. Damn mad. If he wasn't going to listen, then I wasn't going to tell him about last night. I didn't need him, anyway. I could take care of myself.

Yet, someone had tried to scare TJ and me last night. Or had tried to kill us. Jess had said the bootlegger's name was Lafe Packard. Why would a crazy old bootlegger want to kill me?

The organ music was soft and low now—Mrs. Walters played that way a few minutes before the choir came in—and the church deacons were ushering in more arrivals. The door beside the organ opened quietly and Reverend Brubaker entered wearing a royal blue robe. He nodded at Mrs. Walters, then climbed the carpeted steps and sat down in the two-seat pew behind the pulpit. He opened his Bible, looked at it for a moment, then closed his eyes in prayer or thought.

Most of the church windows were colored glass segments

with reds and blues and oranges and greens. Tall and slender, the windows pivoted at the center top and bottom to stand half-way open, letting air flow gently through the church. I could hear a quail whistling somewhere in the fields.

Bob . . . white. Bob . . . bob white?

I listened to its whistle. Its last note ended in a questioning tone, as if waiting for an answer. But no answering whistle came. It whistled again, and I wondered if it was something like a lookout, stationed at an outpost, and signaling to the other quail to gather, that all was well in the field.

Quail were the sneakiest birds alive. They might hear you coming and run away, then circle around behind you. Sneaky. Or they might remain motionless, perfectly camouflaged with their brownish speckled feathers. And you'd never know you passed within a foot of one bird or a whole covey.

You'd never find quail unless you had a hunting dog. And not just any old hunting dog, either. Dad used to have a pointer named Lady. She'd work in front of us, nose to the ground, tail in the air, whirling this way and that, twenty, thirty yards ahead, finally stopping on a dime, her nose inches from a quail. Smelling that quail smell. And that quail frozen also, knowing he'd been found, only his eyeballs twitching.

Lady's whole body would be trembling, but she'd hold until Dad and I came up, shotguns ready, and Dad said "flush em." She'd lunge forward, and then one or maybe a dozen quail would explode upward, the whir of their wings like frantic drum rolls. No matter how many times I'd heard it before, it startled me, and my heart leaped into my throat as I fired.

Lady would stand, unafraid of the shotgun blasts, until Dad signaled to retrieve. Then she'd find the downed birds and bring them back one by one, holding them in her powerful jaws as gently as a momma cat would hold her kittens.

But Lady was Dad's dog and she grieved a lot, missing him. Neither Jess nor I had even thought about hunting since the accident. Jess finally sold Lady last Spring for a hundred dollars. Said we needed the money and couldn't afford a hunting dog. Bopeep . . . well, Bopeep was just a good old dog.

Bob . . . white. Bob . . . bob white?

A secret signal to the other birds? Or lonely? Like me.

Bob . . . white?

Suddenly, I wasn't at the church anymore. I was standing in frozen morning air, icy asphalt pavement beneath my feet. Before me stood the bridge spanning the Clear Boggy River. Wrapped around a steel anchor beam, lay a mass of twisted, blackened, still smoking metal.

Jess was at the station wagon, bending over, prying the door out with a crowbar. He had ordered everyone to stay away, including me. Something he had to do himself, he said. The door snapped open, and Jess got a quick glimpse inside, then staggered back, his face contorted. He turned to look at me and spoke, his mouth ugly, saying things that my mind wouldn't let me hear 'cause I knew they were ugly things.

Then I heard a lonely quail, from somewhere in the fields around us, calling . . . Bob white. Bob . . . Bob white?

But things weren't white anymore. Not white. They were black. Burned black. And dead. And I had wanted to kill every quail on the face of the earth—

I felt a poke in the ribs. Around me, people were rising. The organ music swelled and I couldn't hear the quail anymore. TJ looked down at me like I was a lamebrain. I stood up. The choir had come in and stood poised in their royal blue robes, their hymn books open. Ferret watched me from the front row, a stupid grin on his face.

"Ho-lee . . . ho-lee . . . ho-lee," they sang. I joined in, my mouth dry and creaking, a lump still in my throat.

We didn't have a lot of rituals in the Southern Baptist Church, unless you count standing up and sitting down, and we did a lot of that. We finished the chorus and then Reverend Brubaker stood up and read the scripture. Then we prayed for a minute and sat down. Then the choir sang a song, and then we all stood up and sang a song. We sat down and Reverend Brubaker stood up and talked about tithing and giving the offering. He quoted some Bible verses and made us all feel guilty for not giving enough to the church. He finished by asking the junior deacons to come forward and pass the collection plates.

I met Ferret down front. The other two deacons were Bobby Smith and Mr. Franklin's son, Johnny. The reverend prayed out loud, asking the Lord to bless those who gave all they could today. Mrs. Walters played quiet organ music while we were collecting money. Ferret and I took the left side, each passing a plate down a row of people, then collecting the plate coming toward us, and starting it down the next row. We worked our way to the back of the church and waited for the signal.

Mrs. Walters pounded the keys and the church shook. In massive organ glory, the four of us marched forward and stood before Reverend Brubaker. We bowed our heads while he blessed the offering, then we marched back to our seats and sat down.

Mrs. Brubaker stood up and went down to the steps in front of the pulpit. She climbed a couple of steps and turned to make the announcements. Reminding people of choir practice, worship service on Wednesday, and such, then mentioning a couple of folks who were in the county hospital and where flowers could be sent. Finally, she got to the important business.

"Friends, I just want to remind you of the church fair this afternoon at the park. It starts at three o'clock, and there will be races for the children, baking contests and other events for the women, and trapshooting contests for the men. Mrs. Stack will judge the quilting competition. . . . "

Mrs. Brubaker's voice faded in mid-sentence. She stared at the back of the church. A rustling noise swept the building. Feet shuffled. Elbows bumped the pews as people twisted and turned to look. I half rose and peered over heads and Sunday hats.

Parading down the aisle—barefoot, wearing baggy pants tied with a rope and a flowery shirt with the sleeves cut off and open to the waist—was the blond, long-haired man we had seen naked in the woods. The man TJ had called Tarzan.

10

He walked as a god might walk, boldly, unhurried, oblivious to all the eyes focused on him, his head high and his hair flowing like yellow flames burning away from his face. Over his shoulder was a strap that ran down into a leather bag.

A low buzz swept the sanctuary. I slipped back into the pew and watched. He stopped even with our pew, looking at Mrs. Brubaker.

A startled expression froze on her face and her lips seemed bloodless. Reverend Brubaker rose and approached the podium, his steps uncertain. "Sir? May we help you?"

Tarzan was much taller than he had appeared in the woods, and now when he raised his chin to look at the reverend, I guessed he would tower over everyone in Bob White. "I have come to the House of the Lord," he announced in a clear bass voice, "to hear the word of God." He winked at Mrs. Brubaker.

She blinked and pulled back slightly, catching her breath.

Tarzan turned and stalked past TJ and me to sit at the far end of the pew. The bag at his side was of soft leather, simply made, like Davy Crockett might have carried, except it looked like a ladies' purse. What kind of man carried a purse?

Both TJ and I were watching him, then he looked at us and winked. Both our heads snapped forward and we straightened in our seats, sitting stiffly.

Mrs. Brubaker went back to her announcements, trying to

speak over the whispering in the air. Beyond her, I noticed Mrs. Walters eyeing Tarzan from behind her organ. I remembered she was a widow. Her husband had served with the 45th—the Thunderbird Division—in Korea. Not many single men her age lived in Bob White. I wondered what she'd find attractive about Tarzan. Suddenly she turned red and looked down at the organ. Out of the corner of my eye, I saw Tarzan smiling at her.

A few minutes later, TJ scooted closer and leaned toward me. Her voice was low, tense. "He recognized me. I can feel it."

After church, we all went back to the Brubakers', where TJ changed into the jeans shorts and sneakers she'd had on yesterday and Ferret and I shucked our dress shirts. Mrs. Brubaker fixed a sack lunch of bologna sandwiches and we lit out. The church fair wasn't for nearly three hours and we weren't inclined to let grass grow under our feet. The water tower was our destination.

We trudged north on Ash Street, across Main and then five more blocks before the town petered out. You could see the water tower from miles around, unless the cottonwoods blocked your view.

The water tower was mostly silver and you couldn't see the rust unless you got as close as we were now. The top of it looked like a Chinese coolie hat. And for those people who didn't know where they were, faded white letters proclaimed "BO. .HITE" on one side, with "Seniors–54" scrawled on the other.

Ash Street ended, leaving us a field of sunburned dead buffalo grass and two barbed-wire fences to get through. I spread the barbed wire strands for TJ and Ferret to skinny through, then Ferret held them for me while I climbed through. We started across the field. The water tower was getting bigger with every step.

On the way here, we had been filling Ferret in on last night's action at the pool hall and the pickup that had tried to run us down. "Golly damn," Ferret had said, over and over.

When I was done with my story, he asked, "Did you tell Jess about that old man trying to run you down?"

"Don't know that it was the old man," I said, not wanting to admit I hadn't because Jess and I had fought.

"Had to be," Ferret said, bobbing his head up and down. "Who else could it have been? Tarzan?"

"I 'spect it was the old man, I just don't know for sure."

"You'd recognize his truck, wouldn't you? You know every truck in town."

"Lights were in my eyes, then up my . . . " I glanced at TJ. She was looking up at the tower. Sweat droplets trickled down her face. " . . . up my butt."

Ferret laughed. "Up your butt? Did it light up the place where the sun don't shine?"

"Bright as day."

TJ was still looking up, studying hard on something, pretending she hadn't heard a word we'd said.

"So you couldn't recognize the truck?" Ferret asked.

"Sure I could."

"Huh?"

"I won't forget the clicking sound that sticky valve made."

"Oh? Oh, yeah. Sure."

We climbed through the second barbed-wire fence, taking care not to snag ourselves or our clothes, and craned our necks upward. I felt pretty small, standing under all those steel beams. At ground level, the legs were twenty yards apart and each foot was sunk into a six-foot square block of concrete that probably continued halfway to China. Beside the leg to our right, a steel ladder climbed upward, disappearing into a platform underneath the water tank.

"It's waaaay up there," TJ said.

I wondered if she was scared of heights. "We're only going

up to that first landing," I said, pointing to a small platform about thirty feet up. "You can see just about all of Bob White from there."

I led the way over to the ladder. "Give me that sack, Ferret." He handed me the paper sack containing the bologna sandwiches and I put it between my teeth and started up.

The rungs were an inch thick, rusty and slick with heat. I jammed my right foot tight against the side rail, causing a pinging sound and a tiny vibration to run through the metal ladder into my hands. The sun burned through my T-shirt. Not a breath of air was moving.

I climbed up the ladder, tightly gripping each rung, expecting Ferret and TJ to do the same, and stepped onto the platform. It was a good ten feet square and a great place for lunch. Ferret stepped off the ladder a moment later and TJ was doing fine. I opened the sack and dumped the sandwiches out. Mrs. Brubaker had put six oatmeal cookies in there as well.

"TJ? What the hell?" Ferret called.

I jerked my head around. Above and beyond Ferret, TJ was still climbing the ladder, reaching up for the next rung, grasping it firmly, then steadily repeating the process. "TJ? Don't go any higher. It's dangerous."

"Bring the sandwiches."

Ferret and I looked at each other. I saw shock in his face. I'm not sure what he saw in mine. We both looked up at TJ, framed against the sun twenty feet above us. "TJ!" we screamed.

She ignored us.

"TJ, you come down here right now," I demanded.

She stopped and looked down. I could hardly see her face with the sun behind her. "Mark? You . . . chicken?"

She was mocking me. Saying the same thing I'd said to her about smoking a grapevine stogie. I stomped my foot on the platform and a loud clanging rang out. "Damn you, TJ Gatlin."

She started climbing again. "Heerre, chick-chick-chick-chick. Heerre, chick-chick-chick-chick."

Ferret grabbed my arm. "Don't do it, Mark."

I shook his hand off, then put two sandwiches back in the paper bag and went to the ladder. "Stay here. She's just getting back at me."

I put the bag between my teeth and started after her. My right foot slipped immediately, throwing both legs free. My body slammed against the ladder nearly smashing the sandwiches, but my hold was good. Damn you, TJ Gatlin. Thinking of her had made me careless. Angrily, I scrambled my feet back into place. Locking each hand tight around a rung, I brought my foot up and planted it carefully. I kept going, not looking up, not looking down. Damn you, TJ Gatlin.

My mouth was watering, soaking the edge of the paper bag and making me want to swallow, but I couldn't. Sweat ran into my eyes, stinging, burning. In the distance, I could sense the land shrinking away. Sucking air through my nose starved my lungs and the air got thinner as I climbed higher. I focused on the rung in front of me and the rung just above. Rungs of fire. Burning my hands. But I kept going. Not looking up, not looking down. Damn you, TJ Gatlin.

Then my head poked through the square hole in the platform. The remainder of the rungs were above the platform, all the way up the side of the water tank. Seconds later, I stood on the platform, resting my forehead against the hot, flaking, paint-chipped *T* of what should have been BOB WHITE. Unlocking my aching jaws, I dropped the paper sack onto the steel platform. My fingers felt scalded and didn't work very well. Then I noticed the sound. An eerie whistling from a wind that hadn't been there at ground level.

I rolled against the steel, turning my back to the fiery metal. A four-foot wide platform circled the tank, which was a heck of a lot bigger than it had appeared from ground level. Waist-high, a half-inch metal railing at the platform edge separated me from eternity.

Bob White, Oklahoma lay at my feet. The Baptist Church, the courthouse, Main Street, cottonwoods, Hogan's Pool Hall, and hundreds of miniature houses. Like a Cinemascope movie, the earth stretched before me, a burned-brown carpet with patches of green and white reaching out for miles, far beyond the Bottomlands, far beyond the Clear Boggy River. The sky went on forever, an endless blue so dry and pure I could see a hawk circling the river. I sucked in my breath.

"It's beautiful," TJ said. She was standing beside me, close.

"Yeah," I answered softly.

"Wouldn't it be great if you could spread your arms, leap into space, and soar and fly like the birds?"

"Yeah," I answered, hardly thinking about it. Then I wondered if that was another of her crazy ideas. I sure as hell wasn't going to try flying.

The wind was whipping around the tank, snapping black whispers of hair against her cheeks. She was beautiful. I felt something coming over me.

TJ looked up into my eyes, searching. Her green eyes sparkled and danced, mischievously. "You . . . chicken?"

Chicken? About what? I didn't answer, puzzling about it, finally working it out. I reached for her and put my arms around her. "Chicken? Me? Hell, no."

I kissed her.

I could hear the eerie whistle again and I felt strands of her hair tickling my cheeks, the warmth of her body, the wetness of her mouth. For the first time in my life, I was kissing a girl. Really kissing a girl. And she was kissing back.

A few seconds later, we both relaxed and pulled back. She opened her eyes slowly and they clouded up, not sparkling. I took a deep breath. I needed it. "Wow."

"Yeah," TJ said.

Down below, Ferret looked small, and weird, too, his face tilted up so he couldn't close his mouth. TJ and I lay at the edge of the opening and I was thinking about spitting, just to watch Ferret dodge. Instead, I called, "Come up. It's great."

"Heck no. You guys are idiots. You come down."

"We're going to have lunch," TJ yelled.

"I'm eating down here." Ferret grabbed his sandwich, tore the wax paper off it, and took a bite. "And I've got the cookies here."

"You best eat those cookies," I said. "I reckon we'll be here a spell."

I sat up and opened the paper sack. TJ took a sandwich and sat beside me. I unfolded the wax paper and stuffed it back into the paper sack, the breeze gently rustling it. A fried bologna sandwich automatically set my mouth watering. It had to be the next best thing to homemade ice cream, but I didn't take a bite.

"Aren't you going to eat your sandwich?" TJ asked, her cheek puffed out, full of bread and bologna.

I shook my head, thinking of geometry angles and wind velocities, and winked. I leaned over the platform hole and swished around the saliva that had accumulated in my mouth.

"You're not going to spit on him, are you?"

I grinned, nearly losing my ammo.

"You really are." TJ's eyes lit up and she crawled over to watch. She scoffed. "It's too far. No way you can hit him. No way at all."

Ferret was sitting in the middle of the ten-foot square, looking south toward Bob White. The wind was from the northwest, so I had to spit beyond and to the left of Ferret. "Toohhh!"

I had kept the load fairly compact and it was easy to see as it shot out pretty much along the path I'd planned, then the wind took it and brought it back right at Ferret.

"Jesus!" TJ said. "Ferret! Look out."

Ferret looked up, but at us, not at the small liquid missile homing in on him from the side. "Huh?"

I almost panicked, thinking it was going to land right on

his face, him with his mouth hanging open. At the last moment, he saw it and threw his upper body to his left, but too late. It splat against the seat of his jeans.

Instantly, Ferret leaped to his feet, shaking his sandwich at me. "Golly damn! Dang you, Mark! You messed up my britches."

TJ and I started laughing and I couldn't hear what he was saying. I fell back from the hole in the platform, holding my sides, laughing hard. TJ collapsed on me, giggling hysterically. We had nearly calmed down when she mimicked Ferret, "Dang you, Mark." That set us off again.

We laughed for another minute, then I made a sound like a bomb dropping and a huge explosion. I was as weak as a tuckered-out pup and hardly had the energy to laugh more, but I did anyway, enjoying the way TJ laughed.

"Hey, Ferret," I called, looking down again. He was gone.

I grabbed the railing and looked out. Ferret was in the middle of the field, stomping through the grass. "Ferret?"

He didn't look back.

"Ferret?" I yelled louder. "Don't be mad."

He whirled around and thrust his right arm in the air, his middle finger uplifted. Then he turned and stomped across the field. We watched him climb over the barbed-wire fence, then head on down Ash Street.

"I think he's a little ticked off," TJ said.

"Yeah, well, he would have done the same to me." I grabbed my sandwich and took a huge bite. The moment's fun had passed.

Ferret and I had spitting contests plenty of times in the past, then laughed and hosed each other off. This time he was really mad. Was it because TJ and I had climbed the tower and he hadn't? Was he feeling chicken? Or was it about me being with TJ?

Ferret was my friend. TJ was a girl. There was a big difference between one and the other. I felt uneasy and wished I hadn't spat on Ferret. I wished I hadn't come up here with TJ.

I walked around the platform to the left, feeling more of the wind in my face. The winds almost always blew from the northwest except during tornado season. Far to the northwest I could see shadows in the sky. Black clouds. Thunderstorms were building up. We were going to get some weather later today.

Loud clanging interrupted my thoughts. TJ came around the far side of the tank, hopping on one foot. Playing games on top of the tower? I frowned disapprovingly.

She saw my look and stopped, tilting her head defiantly, then shaking her hair back away from her face, acting like she didn't give a damn. "So where are they having the fair?"

"Will Rogers Park." I pointed toward the far west edge of town. "You see that little stream?"

"Oh, yeah, sure. And the tents."

Ladies were already carrying things into them. A few cars had entered the small lot on the south side of the park. I saw something else, too. Something that sent a chill up my spine.

"You ready to go to the fair?" TJ asked.

"Look." I pointed, pulling her close so she could sight down my finger. "See that old pickup near the stream?"

"Yeah?"

"I bet it's got a sticky valve."

11

Will Rogers Park ran north to south, four blocks long and about two hundred feet wide in places. Meandering southward along the far side of the park was Six Mile Creek, not much more than a ditch. An underground stream broke ground northwest of Bob White along the edge of Highway 48 and flowed past Bob White through the Bottomlands, eventually emptying into the Clear Boggy River, a journey of six miles, more or less.

Here cottonwood, oak, ash, and maple trees thrived, lining both sides of the ditch, thrusting their roots beneath the creek to suck up the precious water that never ceased trickling, no matter how hot the summer got. Six Mile was the best place in the county for crawdad hunting.

Cars spilled out of the parking lot onto both sides of South Mulberry Street. Townsfolk streamed into the park. TJ and I joined them, filtering through the crowd, heading toward the back side of the parking lot.

A minute later I spotted it. A dark green '46 Ford quarter-ton pickup, with a turtle-nosed hood snapped shut over a vertical, scissorslike grille, and bug-eyed headlights perched on round, rust-eaten fenders caked underneath with dried red mud.

"Is that it?" TJ asked.

"Maybe." I glanced around to see who might be watching.

Four little kids were chasing each other on the grass nearby.

TJ and I went up to the truck. Coming from the open passenger window was a sickeningly sweet, familiar smell. The seat cushion was split on the driver's side and stuffing was working its way out.

I moved around the back. Dirty rags and pieces of used lumber cluttered the bed. The driver's door was partially caved in and splattered with brown streaks near the top of the bed and the door window. Tobacco juice—the reason for the foul smell that oozed from the interior.

I pulled the door open—rusting metal hinges squealed in agony—and peered inside. Clutter and filth, but nothing that suggested the owner might be a bootlegger. I started to close the door when I noticed some old rags stuffed behind the seat, like they were hiding something. Reaching in, I moved the rags aside and saw the gun.

TJ looked over my shoulder, and said the obvious. "He's got a shotgun."

"Nothing unusual about owning a shotgun in Bob White, Oklahoma."

"What about hiding it? Concealing a dangerous weapon or something?"

I shrugged. I took the shotgun in my hands and examined it. Most of the bluing had worn off the metal and the stock was dry, with cracks streaking along the grain.

"It's a piece of shit."

I looked at TJ in disgust. She didn't know squat about guns. "It's a Remington 870, twelve-gauge pump with a four-shell magazine, first made about seven years ago. It just hasn't been cared for proper." I checked the magazine. "It's loaded, and the safety's not even on." Instinctively, I clicked it on.

"What're you kids doing with that shotgun?"

I jumped a foot, expecting Packard had caught us.

Standing on the far side of the truckbed was Mr. Tucker, the grocery store owner, frowning, hands on his hips. Skinny as a Popsicle stick, he liked to wear old-timey bow ties fastened tight below his Adam's apple. Relief flooded over me—we were good friends—immediately followed by guilt. "I—"

"Mark Stoddard, you know better than to be messing around with someone else's property."

"Yes, sir." How were we going to get out of this? "We were just curious."

Mr. Tucker walked around the truck. "Curious? Curiosity killed the cat. Is this the young lady staying with the Brubakers?"

TJ nodded. "I'm TJ Gatlin." She held out her hand, then smiled, sweet and innocent like she was still in church.

Mr. Tucker hesitated, then his frown vanished, and he shook her hand.

"Right pleased to meet you," TJ said, doing a little curtsy.

Mr. Tucker's face broke into a grin. "First chance you get, young lady, you come on down to my store and have a soda on me."

"I'm looking forward to it."

Mr. Tucker glanced around, conspiratorially. "Well, no harm done. Better put that back right now." He swiped his knuckles across my flattop, like he did whenever I came into his store.

"Yes, sir." I hurriedly replaced the gun and the rags, then closed the door. "Let's go," I said to TJ.

We ran through the parking lot, dodged around clusters of people, then slowed to a walk. "Raightt pleased to meet you," I said, exaggerating TJ's Louisiana accent.

She stopped and shrugged. "It's just sweet-talking."

I grabbed my jeans legs, pulling them sideways, and dipping down. "Yessir, Mr. Tucker, sir."

She turned the corners of her mouth down, making a face. "I didn't see you coming up with any brilliant ideas."

"Mr. Tucker's my friend. It wasn't a big deal anyway." Still, Mr. Tucker had let things slide awful quickly. He hadn't asked what I was curious about.

"Reckon that's the truck that tried to run us down?"

"I'd have to hear it idling to be sure."

TJ's green eyes clouded. "The bootlegger's here, isn't he?"

I looked around, seeing tents and parents and kids and banner flags and balloons. I didn't see a John Deere cap. "The whole town's here. Might not even be the same truck." But in the pit of my stomach, I had a bad feeling.

Fairs can be lots of fun, even when you don't have any money, which I didn't. Not a dime. Dad had given me an allowance, but Jess said we couldn't afford it.

About once a week, Ferret and I would go hunting for pop bottles. Mr. Tucker paid us two cents for every one we brought in. Sometimes we'd make thirty cents each, which we'd reinvest in Baby Ruths or Dubble Bubble or Popsicles, depending on the weather and how empty our stomachs were. When I turned sixteen, I planned to get a job at Tucker's sacking groceries and sweeping up. Mr. Tucker had promised it to me the day of the funeral.

Anyway, I was flat broke and TJ was too, so we set out to the main tent to find Mrs. Brubaker. Ferret was there and said "Hi," his voice huffy. For the next fifteen minutes, we unstacked tables and chairs, arranging them so people could rest and eat. When we finished, Mrs. Brubaker gave us each a dollar. She was a soft touch. TJ hugged her, but I didn't, even though I felt like it.

Mrs. Brubaker was running the fair for the third straight year as a fund-raising project for the First Baptist Church. The town had taken to it and people came out of the woodwork. Now the other churches had tents as well.

The three of us bought grape Sno-Kones and cruised the stands, avoiding the frequent stampedes of half-pint kids. The paper on the snow cone started leaking, so I ate the ice so fast my teeth hurt. There's nothing better than a grape snow cone on a hot summer day.

Johnny Franklin and Bobby Smith came by, Johnny asking if I was going to enter the trap shoot. I said maybe, and they moved on. Last year I had won the junior shoot, but it cost five bucks to enter and I didn't have even a whole dollar anymore.

Across from the tents, stands were set up with all kinds of games costing a dime or a quarter. Mostly little-kid stuff like fishing in a wash tub with a long pole, a string, and a magnet. You couldn't see what you were fishing for, but eventually you pulled up a wooden fish with a metal ring in its nose. If the fish was blue, you won a pocket knife or a six-inch rubber doll that had blond hair and blue eyes, but no clothes. If the fish was red, you got a package of balloons or a key ring. But if it was white, you only got a pencil. Ferret got a white fish and looked disgusted. We moved on.

The next stand required skill, throwing three baseballs at three stacked milk bottles. It cost a quarter, but had some nice prizes. A man was trying to win a baby panda bear for his little girl. He nicked the last bottle, but it spun around and remained upright. Shaking his head in frustration, he lifted his little girl onto his shoulders, and promised her some cotton candy.

"That's a cute panda," TJ said.

I nodded, doing some quick figuring. The milk bottles were painted silver and had to be half-filled with lead from the way the one had wobbled, then stayed upright. It'd take a solid hit on each of the bottom two to tip them over. But if you knocked them all over, you could take a harmonica.

The harmonica was silver and black, a good six inches long and at least two inches wide with the word "CHRONOMIC" across the top. I really wanted that harmonica. I handed a quarter to the man running the booth.

I hit the bottle on the lower left squarely with the first pitch, knocking it and the top bottle down. TJ and Ferret cheered. My second pitch was a glancing blow that staggered the remaining bottle. My friends groaned. Irritated, I busted loose on the next pitch, and sent the final bottle tumbling.

TJ jumped up and down, hollering as if I had done something special, and I got embarrassed. I usually hit what I was aiming at. Dad had said it was kind of a gift.

TJ's eyes sparkled with a strange intensity, making me feel both good and stupid all over. I grinned back at TJ and when the man asked me which prize I wanted, I pointed to the miniature panda bear.

I gave it to TJ, expecting her to say thank you, but she didn't. She just looked at the bear. His mouth curled upward in a goofy black grin. TJ tucked the bear under her arm and walked away, like she could have cared less about the silly bear.

Girls! Back on the water tower, TJ had dared me to kiss her. Now I do something nice and she ignores me. I should have gotten the harmonica.

Suddenly, I realized Ferret had disappeared. All around, people weaved in and out past each other like one long writhing snake. I scanned rapidly across the crowd, looking for a skinny chest in a white T-shirt, or for a shock of black hair.

My gaze swept right by the cap before my brain registered, sensing danger. Bobbing up and down, forty or fifty yards away. The John Deere cap.

12

Instantly, I swept the area again, not seeing the cap now. Packard had vanished in the crowd. The bad feeling came into my stomach again. Where was Ferret? Where was TJ now?

Seconds later, I glimpsed Ferret hurrying toward the main tent. Beyond him, I caught a flash of yellow hair. A hundred feet away off to the side of the tent entrance, Tarzan stood, talking to Mrs. Brubaker. Tarzan? What was he doing here?

Mrs. Brubaker shifted from side to side, edging backward, wringing her hands, not looking at him. His arms were outstretched, gesturing as he spoke. Ferret's mom looked up and shook her head slowly. Even from here, I could see the muscles tighten in Tarzan's jaw. His arms fell to his sides, then he walked away.

Quickly, I jostled my way through the crowd, and ran after Ferret. Mrs. Brubaker had turned away, holding her hand to her side. I caught up to Ferret just as he got to his mother.

"Mom?" Ferret asked.

She started and whirled, sucking in her breath. Her chin trembled, then steadied when she saw us.

"Mom, are you all right?"

She nodded.

"He bothering you?" I asked, clenching my fists. What had Tarzan said that upset her so?

Tarzan had stopped near one of the other tents, visiting with

Mrs. Walters. The church organist was smiling and flirting like a high school girl. I didn't see what any woman could see in a man who carried a purse.

The soft lines around Mrs. Brubaker's mouth tightened. "He wasn't bothering me. We were just visiting."

Ferret's eyes smoldered. "Want me to get Dad?"

"Don't you dare bother your dad. You boys go on. Have some fun." She forced a smile, then walked back into the tent.

Ferret looked at me, questioning.

I shrugged. "Guess it was nothing."

TJ came running up, clutching the panda, a chill in her eyes, breathing in shallow, quick gasps. "Mark! I . . . "

A knot formed in my stomach. "What?"

She bit her lip. "That old man. He's . . . he's been watching me."

Warily, I scanned the crowd, looking for the John Deere cap. "Packard? What happened?"

"I was walking along the stands, looking at the games and stuff, and there he was. Staring right at me."

"He do anything? Say anything?"

"He just stared at me, grinning. Then he walked away." TJ swallowed hard, then shuddered. "He gives me the creeps."

Ferret spoke up. "Tarzan gives me the creeps."

The contests started a half-hour later. Ferret and TJ entered the sack races. Ferret managed two or three hops before he fell on his face like a lame frog, then repeated the process several times until, finally, someone else was declared the winner.

I held "Andy"—TJ had now decided that was the panda's name—while she raced. TJ easily won the girls' group. She probably would have beaten all the guys as well. Reverend Brubaker officiated the race and presented TJ with a small cross on a thin gold chain. She put it around her neck and got a huge grin on her face. After shaking hands with the reverend, she hugged him.

While waiting for the next event, I taught Andy how to do double back flips with a full twist, then triples. He nearly crashed twice, but I kept him out of the dust both times. He was a pretty good athlete in spite of his fat belly.

Ferret and TJ agreed to team up for the three-legged race and I was going to watch them, until I heard a loudspeaker announcing the trap shoot would start in five minutes. I really wanted to watch the shooting, and it must have showed on my face because Ferret told me to go on and they'd catch up to me later. So Andy and I found ourselves drifting toward the range at the north end of the park. I looked at Andy and shrugged. "They'll just be shooting at clay pigeons." His goofy grin never wavered. He was tough.

By the time I got there, over a hundred people had gathered to watch the contest, and more were coming. The trap range had a three–rail plank fence running around it, and only competitors were allowed inside. The range faced Six Mile Creek and the fence around the big area on the far side had chicken wire nailed to it to keep people and animals from harm's way. Dad had taught me to shoot here and I knew a lot about how the range worked.

I found an open space against the fence, and hooked my arms over the top rail to watch the first group of five men go at it. Some carried boxes of shells. Others wore hunting vests, stuffed with shells of eights or loads of their own choosing. They walked forward, each taking one of the five positions marked by concrete slabs embedded at ground level. The shooter at the first position—nearest me—chambered a shell and looked at the range operator, a man named Red Nelson.

"Anytime you're ready," Red called. He was a small, middle-aged man who owned and operated the range when he wasn't managing the Kerr-McGee service station. He had shooter's eyes, squinty from too much shooting in bright sunlight, and deep creases lined his face like heat cracks splitting parched earth. Red had been good friends with Dad.

The shooter put his front foot on the concrete block and

brought his gun up to a ready position just below his cheek. Twenty-two yards out from the furthermost shooting distance was a small shed about two feet high called the trap house. It was open on the far side to allow the saucer-shaped targets to fly out, launched by machinery inside the shed that automatically loaded the targets and rotated the firing direction, left and right.

The shooter called, "Pull!" and Red pressed the remote firing button. A clay pigeon shot out toward Six Mile Creek. The man swung his shotgun after the rising, spinning target and fired, shattering it.

Firing continued, the men taking a single shot in turn. After each man had taken three shots from his initial station, they all changed stations. They weren't very good. Andy and I snorted whenever someone missed. Finally, after each man had fired fifteen times, only one of them broke as many as thirteen targets.

Lined up outside the fence was the next group of five men, including Jess, with Dad's shotgun. He was wearing boots and blue jeans, his cowboy hat, and a fancy western shirt. Some blonde was hanging on his arm—probably from the City. Jess's group started in.

"Hey, Jess," I called, waving Andy.

He looked around, then found me.

I grinned enthusiastically. "Good luck, break 'em all."

He walked over and scowled. "I like to never found my gun. What the hell was it doing in your bedroom?"

I remembered how I'd thought that Packard might come creeping around the house that night. "I don't know."

He eyed me for several seconds, holding his gaze steady.

I stared back, even-steven, not saying anything.

"You ready, Jess?" Red Nelson called, waving a hand.

Jess turned and stalked to his starting position, joining the line of shotgunners. He was last to shoot, and he hit his first target. I knew he would. Jess was a great shooter.

A few minutes later, Jess had burst all fifteen targets. "A perfect score, ladies and gents," Red announced. "Jess Stoddard wins the men's division." He shook Jess's hand and gave him some cash for his prize. The crowd cheered. I did too. He was my brother.

The other shooters left, but Jess stayed inside the fence, leaning over it, sweet-talking the blonde.

A group of seniors started filing in. They would shoot three yards closer than Jess's age group had. Then the seventeen-and-under junior division would fire from sixteen yards, three yards closer than the seniors.

I felt a bare arm slip lightly around my shoulders. "How ya doing, Mark?" It was Joyce, working hard on her gum. She wore blue shorts and a white blouse with tiny blue forget-me-not flowers on it. It was sleeveless with a good-sized armhole that, I couldn't help noticing, exposed her white bra.

"I'm all right, Joyce," I answered, trying not to move for fear I might jostle something. "You working today?"

"From six until midnight." She looked straight at Jess and the girl, then blew a bubble and popped it.

Jess had his arm around the girl and she was giggling. I wondered how Joyce could watch so calmly. "Must be hard, working that late at night," I said.

"It's no big deal." She put her hand into her jeans pocket and pulled out a one-inch cube wrapped in red, white, and blue wax paper. "Have some bubble gum."

"Thanks." I popped it into my mouth and began to soften it up.

"That's a nice panda bear. You win it?"

The blonde put her hand behind Jess's neck, pulled him toward her, then kissed him right on the lips.

I blinked, remembering Joyce's question. "Yeah. I knocked down three milk bottles." I heard firing in the background. I'd nearly forgotten about the trap shoot, watching Jess and the blonde make out in public.

"You must have a good eye."

"Fair-to-middling."

Jess whispered something in the blonde's ear.

"Jess won the trap shoot."

Her eyes narrowed a bit. "So I see. You going to shoot?"

I looked at the shotgunners on the line, smelling and tasting the burned powder hovering in the air. I felt something inside me stir when she mentioned shooting. I wished she hadn't asked that question. "Nope."

Joyce turned her head toward me. "Is it hard to hit those thingamajigs?"

I grinned. "Clay pigeons, they're called. Yeah, it's pretty hard. You have to swing the gun ahead of the target, and fire at empty space, timing it so your load of shot gets there at the same time as the clay pigeon. If you shoot straight at the target, you'll miss every time."

She nodded. "Who's the girl?"

I looked back at Jess and the blonde hanging on his arm. "Never saw her before. Jess goes to the City a lot. He's always bringing back different girls." I wondered if I'd said too much. "Sorry, I . . ."

"Don't you be sorry for me. Be sorry for that peroxide blonde over there. She's got black roots that you can see from here. All her hair is going to fall out one of these days." She laughed.

I could see the black roots. I laughed too.

Joyce leaned over and whispered. "Can you keep a secret?"

I looked into her eyes. Pale blue, full of good nature and humor. "Sure."

"Promise never to tell a soul?"

I made a pained face. "Cross my heart."

"Someday I'm going to be your big sister."

I pulled all the way back and stood there, open-mouthed, nearly losing my gum.

She laughed, then winked at me and worked her gum furiously. She lay her arms across the fence railing, watching Jess.

I joined her, thinking about Joyce and Jess and the peroxide blonde. "That wasn't fair, making me promise."

" 'Course not. Just thought you'd like to know. See Jess over there? He'll be the last to know. You have to keep your promise now. You can't tell a soul."

I always kept my promises. But the thought of Jess getting married made me feel uneasy. And alone. I shook off the feeling.

Where were TJ and Ferret, anyway? I looked around, not seeing them anywhere. The shooters had finished and another group of seniors was coming in. In the middle, a dingy cap bobbed up and down. It said "John Deere."

Lafe Packard, torn T-shirt and dirty coveralls, came through the gate, carrying the shotgun I had seen in the truck. He veered toward me.

I stepped back as he approached. He laughed and spat a brown ropelike stream in my direction, but way short. He turned away, cackling like the crazy man he was.

"Eeeuuu," Joyce said, turning her nose away. "Who was that awful old man?"

I didn't answer. Jess saw him then. His body tensed, and he brought Dad's shotgun up, holding it before him in both hands, defensively. He started toward the old man, then stopped and looked around, as if realizing where he was. Uncertain, he backed up, his face tense with anger. Or fear. Fear? Jess wasn't afraid of anything . . . or was he?

13

I watched Packard as he took his turns, firing from each station, then moving on. Most good shooters have a routine they repeat each time before they shoot. I noticed Packard would place his left foot in the center of the slab, tap his toes three times, then slide his foot forward almost off the slab.

Not having a left thumb didn't seem to bother him. He had an oily motion, the way he cradled the gun in the palm of his left hand, swinging it smoothly ahead of each clay target, then shattering them, one by one. When the smoke cleared, the old man had broken fourteen of the targets and won the seniors group.

"He's a hell of a shooter," Joyce said. "For an asshole."

"He is," I said, agreeing with both observations. "The only shot he missed was a straightaway shot."

She looked blank. "What about it?"

"Straightaway shots are the toughest shots, because the target is rising and you have to swing the barrel past the target, obscuring it from view when you shoot. Most people shoot right at the target and the load passes underneath. Even the best shotgunners miss those sometimes. You never want to have a straightaway shot."

"He's still an asshole."

I laughed. "A crazy asshole," I said, enjoying the rare opportunity to use swear words in the presence of an adult.

Packard took the prize money from Red, stuffing it in his dirty coveralls. He stayed inside the fence, too, grinning darkly at Jess. Jess glared back, his face an angry mask.

Only four juniors were lined up outside the gate. Johnny Franklin, Bobby Smith, Butch Meredith, and Pauly Adams. Pauly was the sheriff's son. He wore glasses thick as ice cubes.

I just couldn't stand it. I could beat all those guys. "Joyce, can you lend me five bucks?"

"Five bucks? For what? Oh. You want to shoot, don't you?" Her face saddened. "Honey, I'd lend it to you if I had it, but I don't get paid until next Friday."

Damn. The four boys passed through the gate. I slipped through the fence rails and ran over to Jess. "Jess, I need five bucks."

He looked at me, like I was some stranger come up to him on the street. "We haven't got it to spare."

"Jess," I hesitated, not wanting to beg. "Please."

He raised his eyebrows, surprised. "Sorry, kid."

He wasn't sorry. Not sorry at all. I was just a dumb kid.

"I've got five dollars," rumbled a deep voice behind me.

I whirled.

Reverend Brubaker walked through the gate, the scar on his face glistening with sweat. He pulled out his wallet. "One more shooter," he called to Red. "Give him the gun, Jess."

Jess's mouth dropped open. I took the Winchester from him, and shoved Andy into his slack hands. I grabbed the box of shells lying at Jess's feet and dashed toward the shooting line.

The guys had left the nearest station open. I'd have to shoot first and I wasn't ready. I fumbled hurrying the shell into the receiver and almost jammed it. Finally, I got it into the chamber, took a deep breath, and brought the gun up. "Pull."

The pigeon sprang out to the right. I swung the gun after it, fired late, and missed.

While the firing continued down the line, I reloaded the gun and breathed deeply, trying to settle down. The stiff wad of gum seemed to swell in my mouth. I tucked it in the back corner of my cheek. My turn came again, quickly. "Pull." The pigeon shot out to the left this time. Again, I missed.

I was making a fool of myself. Dad had taught me to be a good shooter and here I was, missing everything. Angrily, I reloaded the gun. Then Dad's voice came into my head. 'Listen to the birds.'

Listen? Then I remembered. The machinery in the trap box was old and noisy. If you listened carefully, you could hear the mechanism as it pivoted—"click" when the pigeon was aimed to the far left, "ca-lick" when the pigeon was aimed to the far right. Knowing which way the clay pigeon would shoot out was a tiny edge.

When it was my turn again, I raised my gun and listened to the clicking. "Pull."

I was swinging the barrel ahead of the target almost before it was released. I fired and the target exploded into a thousand pieces. A fast swing shot was the best way to shoot.

We rotated stations and I listened to the clicking from the trap box. Each time I fired, a cloud of fragments showered Six Mile Creek. I vaguely sensed moving through all the stations and finishing out my fifteen shots. I took the last shot, exploded the target, then made sure the gun was clear of shells.

I turned around, hearing Red proclaim me the winner, realizing the crowd was cheering me. I felt embarrassed. I caught sight of Joyce, jumping up and down, setting off secondary bobbing that would have been interesting to think about any other time. I noticed TJ and Ferret weren't here.

The other kids were walking off. Johnny Franklin came over and said, "You should enter the regular division next year." He smiled, so I knew he meant it as a compliment.

I nodded. "I probably will."

Red Nelson gave me a silver dollar and a ten-dollar bill, the prize money for first place. "Good shooting, Mark." He shook my hand. "Gotta reload the feeder." He walked out toward the trap house.

Jess came up, a sheepish grin on his face. He took my hand

and shook it, his hand warm and strong. "Nice going, kid."

I gripped back, thinking this was the best damn handshake of my whole life. "Thanks."

A third hand closed over ours, locking our thumbs together and squeezing, a grip of wiry strength. "You Stoddards think you're real hot shit."

The stench of unwashed clothes and body odor enveloped the old man like an invisible cocoon. I pulled back, but couldn't break loose. Jess's hand flexed, but his was trapped also. I felt cartilage crunching against the bone, and pain shot from my knuckles.

Jess glared at the old man. "Let go, you bastard, or I'll knock your rotten teeth down your stinking throat."

Packard's squinty gray eyes glinted, hard to see under the John Deere cap. "Go ahead. Right in front of everyone. Knock down an old man."

"Y'all about ready for the shoot-off?" Red returned from the trap house.

Jess tore his hand loose and I jerked back as well. "Shoot-off?" I repeated, surprised.

"Folks!" Red shouted to the crowd. "This year, we're going to have a shoot-off. We've got a regular champion, a senior champion, and a junior champion. Let's find out who's the best damn shot in the county. Everybody starts dead even. Rules are five shots apiece. Handicapped of course. Then if anybody's still tied . . . sudden death."

"Won't be much of a contest," somebody in the crowd hollered. "Just give the prize to Jess Stoddard right now."

Cheering broke out. Jess grinned and waved.

"Everybody ready?" Red asked.

"We've only got the one gun between us," Jess said. "We can't be switching guns with each shot."

Red paused only a second. "Then each of you can take all your shots in one turn. All from the center position. In order of age. Packard first, then Jess, then Mark." Red looked at Packard. "That all right with you?"

The old man nodded, his whole upper body bobbing up and down. "It don't matter. Neither one of 'em got a livin', breathin' prayer. Not a livin', breathin' prayer."

Red looked at him, strangely. "Well then, you're up."

Packard took his position in the middle row, center position, spat a stream of brown juice off to the side, and placed his left foot on the concrete slab. Raising his gun, he settled in, getting ready. The crowd hushed, waiting.

I had forgotten about my gum, wedged against my back cheek. It was still fairly hard, so when I blew a bubble, it was small and tight, the skin quickly stretching to its bursting point. Into the quiet, tense atmosphere came a sharp "POP."

Packard flinched. The gun roared, sending a cloud of shot into thin air.

Jess laughed, as did the crowd behind the fence.

The old man whirled, his face full of darkness. "That's cheating, boy," he yelled angrily. "Trying to cheat an old man."

"Keep that safety on until you're ready to fire!" Red shouted sternly.

Packard glowered at Red, then turned away.

A grin cut Jess's face. He leaned over and whispered, "I'm going to beat his butt."

I knew he would, too. Jess was the best shot in the county.

Packard settled in, patted his foot three times, and said, "Pull." Moments later, he had burst all five targets. He got polite applause from the crowd, but nothing like the noisy cheering that Jess got when he walked forward.

As Packard swaggered back from his station, he turned his head casually and shot a spray of tobacco juice onto Jess's station, spattering Jess's boots and jeans. Jess thrust his arm out and grabbed Packard's shoulder, spinning him around. Packard's gun came up leveled at Jess's stomach.

14

"Packard!" Red shouted. "Elevate your gun and clear it. Now!"

Chuckling, Packard slowly raised his gun up the length of Jess's body. He ejected two cartridges and walked back to stand beside me. The stench was more than I could stand. I walked away a few steps.

Jess got ready, his movements angry, jerky. When he started shooting, his timing was off. He ticked the first two birds, which counted as hits though, then shattered the third and fourth. Jess took a little extra time, getting ready for the last shot. As Jess stepped into position, the crowd grew dead quiet. "Pull."

The last target flew out. A straightaway shot! Jess fired. The target spun its way out across Six Mile Creek, settled toward the ground, and shattered on impact. Around me, the crowd groaned.

Jess's shoulders slumped. He cleared his gun, then stooped to pick up his box of shells. He turned and walked away from his station, glanced at me, then dropped his eyes.

My heart sank. "Jess, it—"

He shoved the gun and box of shells into my hands and walked angrily toward the blonde. She had a shit-eating grin on her face which I didn't understand. "It don't matter, Jess," I heard her say. "Come on, let's go back to the City."

Jess took her arm, pushing through the crowd, leaving. Then it sank in. Jess wasn't even going to watch me shoot.

I was all alone. As alone as I'd felt the day mom and dad had died. I let the feeling wash over me and I didn't want to shoot anymore. Jess didn't care. Why should I? I wanted to call out. Jess! Come back! But I didn't. People were watching me. Even as I thought it, I got angry with myself. Dad would care. I wouldn't disappoint him. I'd do my best, win or lose.

I gritted my teeth and looked for TJ and Ferret, but they weren't here, or else they'd be waving. Joyce waved and nodded encouragingly.

Andy the panda was here too. I noticed him sitting against a post on the inside of the fence. Wish me luck, Andy, I thought. He didn't wink or change his expression. I blew a bubble and popped it. I could beat that old man.

Slipping the gun under my arm, I walked forward toward my station, flexing my right hand, the bones still hurting.

Packard waited, his face dark. His voice was a hoarse whisper. "Hurt? Hurt bad, boy? You don't know what pain is . . . boy. But you will. Pain is seeing a living, breathing person gutted, seeing them die. Your brother will die that way. That's pain . . . boy. Real pain." He spat tobacco juice toward my feet.

Expecting it, I jumped sideways and avoided the mess.

"The Day of Doom's a-coming, boy. You won't know when. You won't know where. The day's a-coming." Packard cackled.

The Day of Doom? Gutting Jess? My mind whirled, then settled down. Packard was just trying to rattle my concentration so I'd miss. I walked toward the front station, putting out of my mind what Packard had said. Setting my box of eights down, I noticed there were only six shells left. I took a single shell out and hefted Jess's gun in my hands.

But it wasn't Jess's gun I held in my hands. It was Dad's gun. A Winchester 12 at least twenty years old, well oiled, and cleaned as often as I remembered to do it. Once a month I'd take it out, put three or four drops of gun oil on a clean rag, and run it through the barrel. It was still Dad's gun.

I loaded a shell and got comfortable, my left foot on the concrete slab, feeling that Dad was nearby, helping me out. I listened for the mechanism's rotation. Click . . . ca-lick. "Pull." The target flew out, instantly shattering under the full load of shot I threw at it.

A few seconds later, I had exploded all five targets. We were tied. The crowd cheered. This time I noticed that the cheering was as loud for me as it had been for Jess.

"Sudden death," Red shouted. "Take the first shot, Mark."

I loaded my last shell, trying not to think about how I could get more ammo if it came to that.

Click . . . ca-lick. I listened to the mechanism turning in the trap house. For some reason, I thought about the straightaway shot that Jess had missed. The old man had missed a straightaway, too. You never want to have a straightaway shot.

I settled into position, listening. Click . . . "Pull." The target flew out . . . straightaway! I swung the gun barrel up, passing over the target, obscuring it, and fired. A cloud of fragments appeared before my eyes. I heard more cheering in the background.

I didn't know why I chose to call pull midway between the clicks, giving myself a straight-away shot. Maybe I was trying to prove something to Jess. Or to myself.

I held my gun up, showing Red that it was clear, and walked back away from the line.

The old man was waving to the crowd, strutting, showing off.

He'd tried to fox me, threatening to gut Jess, but it hadn't worked. Packard's station, the middle concrete slab, was just before me. I spat my gum out. It hit the forward part of the slab and stuck. Packard turned and stalked toward me, his lips pulled back from ugly, tobacco-stained teeth into a grin I'd seen in scary picture shows.

As we passed, the old man threw his shoulder against mine. Jarred, I stumbled. Some people hollered "Hey?" but I walked on. I'd sorta expected it, and I wasn't hurt.

Packard took his position, settled in, and raised his gun. I watched his left foot, square in the center of the slab. He tapped the toe of his shoe three times, then slid his foot forward into my gum, where it stuck abruptly even as he called "Pull." The clay pigeon flew out, crossing hard to the right. Packard jerked the barrel after it. The shot went wide, his timing off.

Pandemonium broke out. People opened the gate and stormed in. Joyce slipped through the railings and ran toward me. Other people poured over the fence. Surrounded, I was hoisted into the air, then perched on someone's shoulders. Caught up in the excitement, I held the Winchester over my head and thrust it up and down, like I had won the world's championship. I saw Red Nelson struggling to get through the crowd. Packard had disappeared. Gone to Hell, I wished.

Joyce got through to me and reached up and hugged me around the waist. I bent down from my perch and hugged back, awkwardly. My right hand accidentally jostled her breast and I blushed, but she didn't seem to notice.

We all cheered some more, and finally I noticed TJ coming into the range. She went up to Reverend Brubaker and talked excitedly to him. He said something back to her and she nodded. He immediately hurried out of the range.

Finally, everybody calmed down and I got set back down to earth. Red Nelson gave me two five-dollar bills and a trophy about a foot high with a figurine of a man aiming a shotgun. The little brass plate on the front read, CHAMPION, BOB WHITE, OKLAHOMA, 1957.

After shaking hands all around—my hand hurting worse all the time—the crowd thinned. TJ came up, her green eyes dancing. She threw her arms around me and gave me a big hug. That really embarrassed me and some people laughed.

"Where's Ferret?" I asked, disappointed he wasn't here.

"We fell in the three-legged race. He hurt his ankle and Aunt Josephine took him home."

"Is he hurt bad?"

"She thinks it's just a sprain."

I looked down. TJ's knees and shins were all skinned up. She shrugged.

"See you later," Joyce said, leaving us alone.

"Yeah," I said, and so did TJ.

We started to leave, then TJ said, "Where's Andy?"

Andy? I stopped, looking down. I had the shotgun in my left hand and my trophy in my right. Then I remembered, suddenly worried he'd been taken during the excitement. I looked at the fence post where Jess had left the baby panda. Andy was facedown in the grass. Relieved, I nodded, "There."

TJ ran over, bent down, and picked Andy up. She rose slowly, then turned, tears in her eyes. "Oh, Mark."

I hurried over. The first thing I saw was Andy's goofy grin. Then I saw his stomach. He'd been gutted.

15

It was early evening. The wind had come up, at first in gentle refreshing puffs, pushing aside the day's heat, then stronger, stiffening. The northwest sky grew dark. At ground level, thunderheads boiled, reaching up about as high as clouds could go. From low in the west, the sun's rays sneaked underneath the ominous clouds, making their bellies seem on fire.

As TJ and I left the park, people frantically tore down the tents. In Oklahoma, a strong wind could shred a tent in minutes and take the roof off two or three houses just for good measure. We have lots of hail and tornadoes, too, when cold wind comes blustering down from Canada and collides with hot air sweeping up from Texas. Tornado alley, that's Oklahoma.

We walked east toward home, the wind whipping up dust devils. TJ hugged Andy close to her chest so his insides wouldn't fall out, carrying my trophy in her left hand. I shifted the shotgun to my right hand and slung my left arm around her shoulders. It seemed the natural thing to do.

TJ raised Andy up a bit, studying his stomach. Her jaw was set, her voice angry. "I'm going to ask Aunt Josephine if she can sew him up."

"It should sew up okay," I said, looking again at the sharp, clean cut. I felt bad about Andy's getting gutted. TJ had cared about the panda all along. She must have been too embarrassed to say thank-you.

"Who would do this? Some kid?" TJ asked.

"Packard did it with his knife."

"That bastard. He tries to run us down, then he cuts Andy. You've got to tell Jess."

"We don't have proof he's done anything. I don't know that telling Jess would do any good. Jess hates him anyway."

"He's crazy," TJ said, shaking her head. "Somebody's going to get hurt."

Packard had threatened to gut Jess. He'd cut Andy. Was this his way of saying his threat was real?

We stopped at my house to check on Bopeep. Storm or no storm, she needed grub like anyone else. We went in the house and I put the shotgun in the hall closet where we always kept it. I thought about clearing a place for my trophy on the TV, but that could wait. I left it on the floor of the closet and went into the kitchen.

Bopeep was waiting at the back door. Her tail helicoptered when she saw TJ. I let her in and she jumped all over TJ, licking and shaking and talking. TJ did her best to pat Bopeep and love her, but I could tell her heart wasn't in it. The wind whistled in the back door, so I dashed through the house, slamming windows shut.

I retrieved Bopeep's bowl from beside the back porch and scooped up a generous helping of chow from the sack near the stove. TJ and I carried it and her water pail outside and into the garage, setting both next to her bed, an old green army blanket stuffed into a large flat cardboard box.

Thunder rumbled in the distance. Bopeep immediately put her tail between her legs and slunk into bed. She'd be okay there. Dad had cut a doggy door in the back of the garage so Bopeep could get in and out. She hated storms and would cower in her bed until it was over.

TJ and I stepped outside into a stiffer, darker wind. Clouds were approaching rapidly. We'd have to hurry. All around us, cottonwoods screamed, their leaves hanging on for dear life. The leading edge of clouds slipped further southward, obscuring the sun. Lights flashed on all over the neighborhood. People scrambled to close and latch outside shutters. Our house didn't have shutters. Once we'd had three windows broken by hail as big as walnuts.

We had two blocks to go—north, almost directly into the storm. TJ and I started running for the Brubakers' house, the wind slapping at our faces, stinging our cheeks.

We were still a half-block away when the first big drops pelted down—one at a time at first, each exploding on landing—creating tiny craters in the dusty street. A block away, a solid wall of rain approached, drumming insanely on the rooftops of houses, roaring closer and closer. We ran faster, trying to reach the Brubakers' house before—

It hit. Huge raindrops beat on us, freezing cold like icicles had melted on their way down from the heavens.

Ten seconds later, we landed on the Brubakers' front porch, drenched. A brilliant flash of light exploded, nearly blinding me, the crack of thunder deafening. The ground shock lifted the Brubakers' wood porch up two inches and their front door rattled. We flew into the house almost before our feet settled back down on the porch.

In the kitchen, Mrs. Brubaker took charge, tossing us several towels, helping us soak up the water that poured off us. Goose bumps tightened my frozen skin underneath my soaked T-shirt. Shivering, I wrapped a towel around my shoulders. TJ's hair hung in dripping black strings. Even Andy was soaked.

TJ showed him to Mrs. Brubaker and almost started crying again. Ferret's mom's eyes got sad but she said she'd fix him up right after supper. She shooed TJ upstairs to her room to change, then followed her up to find some of Ferret's clothes that I could squeeze into. I doubted there were any big enough.

Ferret lay on the living room sofa, his right ankle propped up on a pillow and wrapped in a towel wet with melting ice cubes. His bony toes protruded like stubby Tinkertoy pieces. Ferret said he couldn't feel anything 'cause his foot was frozen, but I was welcome to look at the bruise, if I wanted. I unwrapped enough of the towel to see pale blue swollen tissue around the ankle.

The wind burst against the house, thrashing it with sheets of rain, trying to breech the walls. The house shuddered with each onslaught, as if fearing imminent destruction. Having lived in Oklahoma all my life, I was plenty used to bad storms.

I was telling Ferret about the shooting match when Mrs. Brubaker found me dripping on her living room carpet instead of in the kitchen where she'd left me. Scolding me for my transgression, she hustled me into the bathroom, thrusting some clothes into my arms.

Ferret's briefs were snug but stretchy in the right places. I slipped on a pair of blue-striped pajamas that fit fine. They had to be too big for Ferret. The only problem was the bottoms had only one snap in front and a drawstring. I worried that they might gap a little, so I left the top out and reminded myself to keep my arms down.

An hour and a half later, the rain settled down to a pesky drizzle. Mrs. Brubaker invited me to spend the night, which was double fine with me. Supper was fried chicken with mashed potatoes and cream gravy. We dug in, everyone having seconds.

Across from TJ and me, Ferret perched sidesaddle, his right leg on another chair, wrapped in a cold wet towel. He placed his knife and fork across the top of his plate. Mrs. Brubaker was a stickler for manners. "Dad?"

"Yes, Matthew?" The reverend had already finished the gizzard and the liver, and now was picking bits of meat from the neck bone with his fingers. Ferret's dad liked all the chicken parts that I didn't.

"I was thinking about that long-haired blond fellow who came to church today."

Forks and knives had been scraping against Mrs. Brubaker's Melmac dishes. Now you could hear the rain sprinkling outside. I had a spoonful of biscuit and gravy halfway to my mouth, and it hung there while I gaped at Ferret, wondering what he was about to say.

Reverend Brubaker carefully replaced the neck bone on his plate and wiped his fingers on his napkin, his eyes hard, angry. "The arrogance of that man. Comes into my church, interrupts the service, marches right down the aisle, and stands there, like he was the most important man on earth. Then says he wants to hear the word of God. I didn't believe him, not for a minute."

"He's strange, isn't he, Dad? I mean strange like a . . . three-dollar bill."

Mrs. Brubaker gasped. "Matthew Brubaker!"

"For gosh sakes, Mom. He carries a purse. That's fruity."

"It doesn't mean he's . . . strange that way."

TJ spoke up. "He's just different-looking than people around here. He's tall and he's handsome, like a movie star."

"Yeah, like Milton Berle wearing a wig," Ferret said.

I laughed. "Put a dress on him. Sweetest thing I ever saw."

"He looks all man to me," TJ said, grinning.

She was remembering seeing him naked in the Bottom-lands. I warned her with my eyes. Some things parents didn't need to know.

"Any man carries a purse has got to be queer. Right, Dad?"

"It's against the laws of God and nature. It's an abomination."

"Henry. He isn't that way."

"Now, Josephine. The fact of the matter is that he is strange. The townsfolk ought to keep one eye on him and one on their kids. Don't be naive." His tone was final. The reverend always had the final say.

A scarlet flush appeared on Mrs. Brubaker's cheeks.

Sometimes I felt sorry for her, for the way the reverend talked to her, like he'd talk to me or Ferret.

She pushed her chair back, picked up her plate, and carried it to the sink. Then she turned, a folded white dish towel in her hands, squeezing it, turning it, twisting it. "Matthew. I don't want you talking about him anymore. Making fun of him. It's not Christian."

The room was silent again. Mrs. Brubaker's hands worked the dish towel. If it had been alive, it'd be dead by now.

"I don't think he's Christian."

We all looked at the reverend.

"I think he's Jewish."

The rain stopped around eight-thirty. Mrs. Brubaker asked me to call Jess to tell him I'd be spending the night. There was no answer, which wasn't surprising. Reverend Brubaker drove his car down to my house to leave Jess a note on the kitchen table so he wouldn't worry. Mrs. Brubaker took a spool of black thread from her sewing basket and repaired Andy's black stomach. The stitches didn't show too much. TJ decided he looked good as new. I thought Andy looked as good as anybody who'd been gutted, and better than most.

TJ's mom called a little after that and we all went into the living room allowing TJ her privacy to talk on the kitchen phone. After about ten minutes, she came out clutching Andy under one arm and a numb look on her face. I guess we all felt uneasy about her folks getting a divorce, because no one said anything.

Finally, TJ herself broke the silence. "Mom said it was a long hard trip back to Baton Rouge."

"Oh, dear," Mrs. Brubaker said, looking up from the sofa. "Is she all right?"

"Yeah. Except she's real tired. And then she had to put in a twelve-hour day today."

Reverend Brubaker frowned. "I wish she didn't have to work on Sundays."

The room fell silent again. TJ looked around. We all sat there like bullfrogs with sore throats. "I'll be going to bed now." TJ took Andy upstairs.

"Me, too," Ferret said. I helped him navigate the stairs and hobble into his room. I was pretty bushed, so I said good-night and went into the bedroom next to Ferret's room. Besides Ferret's room and the one TJ was using, there were two more bedrooms upstairs for guests. I fell asleep inside of five minutes.

Much later, I opened my eyes to eeriness and silence. Holding my breath, I listened. Something had awakened me.

Moonlight filtered through motionless window curtains. I scanned the room, seeing shadowy shapes of a desk and lamp, a chest of drawers, and closet depths. Then a tiny squeak sounded near the bedroom door, as a floorboard might sound rubbing against another.

Someone moved toward the bed, a creeping, stealthy, tiptoe walk. Lafe Packard? Nah. It couldn't be. Another step revealed the pink color of a short nightgown.

"Mark?" came a soft whisper.

"TJ? What the . . . "

16

She climbed onto the bed, her hand quickly finding my face. Her fingers touched my lips, slipping down to caress my cheek. Leaning forward, she brushed her lips against mine. After a moment, she pulled back and sat on her heels. Her black hair hung forward, loose and undone for the first time since I'd met her, framing her pale face. Her eyes were barely visible in the dim reflected moonlight.

I breathed shallowly, a lingering sensation on my lips, imagining her fingertips still touching my cheek. I wanted those feelings to last a long time.

TJ sighed, then climbed over me and settled into the bed beside me, pulling the sheet up to her chin. I couldn't have been more surprised if I'd been Father Flanagan.

Her body was only inches from me. I couldn't help thinking romantic thoughts and those thoughts brought every part of my body alive, like bursts of pulsing energy. And under all that energy, I felt something else. Almost like I was in awe. But that couldn't be.

I lay still, feeling like a thousand-year-old mummy with petrified limbs that might crumble if I dared move them. I wondered if she'd say "You chicken?" again. And I wondered what I'd say and do, if she did. Was she waiting for me to roll over and put my arms around her?

TJ sighed again, a long slow sigh, breaking the stillness of the room. "What was your dad like?"

"Dad?" I repeated, surprised. An image formed in my mind of Dad—a handsome, ruddy face that he said used to have more freckles than mine until the sun melted them all together. He wore a hunting cap pushed way back on his head, a tan vest with a few shells filling loops sewn into the coarse waterproof fabric. "Dad . . . was fun to be with. He liked to hunt."

"Did he drink?"

I rolled over and looked at TJ. Nothing was showing below her chin. She gazed back at me, her face shadowy and innocent. This close, I could see her eyes, but not well enough to figure out what she was thinking. I wondered why she wanted to talk about my dad. "No," I answered.

"Not even beer?"

I pulled my pillow down from the headboard and tucked it underneath my arm pit. "He didn't think it was right to drink. He supported the drys."

TJ uncovered her arms and crossed them over her stomach. The pink night thing she wore had frilly white edges around the neck and shoulder straps. "My dad drinks."

"Yeah?"

"He gets drunk all the time."

"Why does he drink?"

She shrugged her shoulders. "I don't know. I guess he likes it."

"He gets real drunk?"

"Really drunk. I've seen my dad so stinking drunk, he couldn't walk or stand up unless he had something to hold onto. It's . . . it's not funny."

"Can't you . . . " I paused, remembering her mom and dad were divorcing. "Couldn't you get him to stop?"

"I tried . . . I . . . " TJ was having trouble. Her eyes were blinking fast.

"You okay?"

She squeezed her eyes shut and turned her head away. "No."

Maybe I should have shut up, but I felt like she needed to talk it out. So I spoke slow and easy. "Your dad? Did he get . . . mean drunk?"

I could hear a hollow pinging as rainwater formed slowly into drops and ebbed cautiously over the lip of a down spout to plunge earthward, striking the flat turn at the bottom.

TJ was biting her lip, trying—I guess—to keep from saying what needed to get out. Then she started talking fast and breathing like she was running. "He came home late one night, drunk. Just last week. I heard him in the kitchen. I got up and tried to talk to him. He looked at me, strange. Like he didn't know me. He . . . he had me down on the floor. His weight was crushing me. His hands . . . he was tearing my clothes . . . then . . . then Mom came in. She started screaming. Beating on him. He knocked her down and started for her and then I was screaming and pulling on him, trying to keep him from hitting Mom."

She paused, but still breathing short and fast. Her eyes were wide open, looking up at the ceiling, but not seeing it. She was remembering that night. I waited for her to go on, to get it all out, to finish it.

TJ's voice came again, slowly, a low whisper. "Then he just stopped and . . . and . . . looked at us and started crying. He said he was sorry and that he was leaving . . . and wouldn't be coming back. He staggered out the door and took off."

I was silent for a long time thinking of what her dad had done. I didn't know what to say after hearing a story like that. I just knew I had to say something. TJ had put a lot of trust in me and I knew she needed me to understand.

Finally, I thought of something to say. It wasn't much, but I felt maybe it was true. "I don't think he's a bad man, TJ. I guess the whiskey has got him. And deep down he knows it. Maybe . . . maybe he decided the best thing he could do was to take himself away from you and your mom."

Nothing more needed saying. I leaned over and kissed her lips, as softly as she'd kissed mine earlier. Then I pushed my pillow back up and lay down, listening to my own breathing, trying not to think about what her Dad had nearly done.

After a while, TJ rolled over and draped her arm across my chest, and snuggled her face against my shoulder. My right arm was free. I reached up and took her soft hand in mine. I felt strong, like I could protect her. The last thing I remembered was thinking about the Brubakers and hoping they wouldn't come in and find us sleeping together.

"**M**ark!" The voice was sharp, angry.

I bolted to a sitting position, blinking sleep from my eyes. Bright morning sunshine splashed across the room.

Braced against the door frame, a pajama-clad Ferret balanced on his left leg, a scowl on his face, his black hair unruly.

My voice caught in my throat, and I glanced toward TJ. Only rumpled bed sheets remained.

"She just left," Ferret said, his dark eyes flashing.

"Ferret, did—"

"No, Mom and Dad don't know." Ferret placed his weight gingerly on his right toes and hobbled into the room, closing the door behind him. "At least, not yet."

My mind whirled, still groggy with sleep. "She was—"

Ferret limped toward the bed, clenching his fists. "What the hell do you think you're doing?"

"Ferret, wait. Nothing happened . . . " My mind wasn't working.

Ferret launched himself into me.

17

Knocked backward, pinned beneath his thin body and tangled in the sheets, I struggled to free my hands. Our faces inches from each other, I saw something strange in his black eyes. Not hate, not anger, it was a look that said I'd betrayed him.

Ferret pushed himself upright and threw a hard right at my face. Twisting my head to the right, I dodged most of the blow, receiving a glancing, stinging punch to my left ear. My own fury erupted, and I wrapped my arms around Ferret, rolling over on top of him. His arms flailed against my back. I pinned him under my chest, then grasped first his left hand, then his right, pressing them into the bed beside his head.

"Ferret, stop it," I shouted, hovering over his face.

Ferret strained against my grip. "Golly damn. Golly, damn, damn, damn!"

"Damn nothing. Nothing happened." Suddenly, I heard the strength of my voice and worried that we might have been heard downstairs. "We didn't do anything," I hissed.

The resistance ended. Ferret lay still, his arms pinned beside his head, his breath coming in gasps. Gradually his eyes unclouded and focused on me. "She slept in here all night. What were you doing?"

"Truce?"

Ferret jerked his right hand down, and it slid on the sheets, but I held fast. I pulled his arm back up next to his head. "Truce?"

Ferret glared at me, then nodded.

I let his hands go. You didn't break a truce unless you gave the other guy fair warning.

He shoved against my chest, pushing me off him, and sat up. "So?"

"She just wanted to talk."

"About what?"

TJ's father was drunk out of his mind, having his way. I couldn't tell Ferret that. "Nothing really. Just stuff."

"What stuff?"

"It's none of your business."

"It is my business. This is my house and she's my cousin."

"She's your cousin, not your girlfriend. So why do you care?"

Ferret got a sullen, pouting look on his face. "It ain't right. That's all."

I eyed him pointedly. "Well, nothing wrong happened, and you'd better not be telling anybody that it did."

"I suppose nothing happened up on the water tower."

"I spat on you. I'm sorry."

Ferret looked at me curiously, then climbed out of bed, wincing as he placed his right foot down, and hobbled out.

I went downstairs, still in Ferret's pajamas.

Mrs. Brubaker had a big box of Wheaties on the kitchen table with a picture of Mickey Mantle on the front, and she was dressed up like she was going somewhere. TJ was there wearing a white dress with tiny blue dots all over it.

"We're going shopping in Oklahoma City," Mrs. Brubaker said.

As soon as Mrs. Brubaker turned her head, TJ made a face and rolled her eyes, as if bored by the whole thing.

Ferret limped gingerly into the kitchen, a sour look on his face.

"Matthew, you going to be all right today?"

"Sure," Ferret grumbled, answering his mom.

"What about you, Mark?" she said, turning to me. "You'll spend some time with Ferret so he won't be lonesome?"

I nodded, unable to see Ferret behind Mrs. Brubaker. "I've got some stuff to do at home, but I'll be around later."

As soon as TJ and Mrs. Brubaker left, Ferret hobbled back upstairs, leaving me alone. I found my clothes, dry now, got dressed, and started for home.

The street dust had been washed away, exposing bone-hard Oklahoma clay. The sun was already burning away yesterday's rainstorm, drying up the puddles. I could feel the steam rising from under my feet. The air was fresh and I could smell the grass growing and hear the cottonwoods breathing.

Bopeep was lying on the front porch, guarding her property. She rose, wagged her tail, and stretched herself—first her front legs, then her hind legs. She stretched herself more than any other dog I knew. I scratched her ears, feeling guilty again for having neglected her. She licked my face, forgiving me for my sins. I hugged her, coating myself with two-inch-long white dog hairs. "C'mon, girl."

I ran around the side of the house with her chasing me and found her tennis ball. We spent the next ten minutes playing catch, dodge ball, and tag. She loved it. Finally, out of breath, I sat down on the back steps and leaned against the screen door. Bopeep watched me briefly, then figured out the game was over. She climbed up the steps beside me and lay down panting, her head resting across my leg and her eyelids drooping within seconds.

I closed my eyes, thinking again of Ferret. We'd been best pals as long as I could remember. Now I felt guilty just for liking TJ.

I sighed, wondering what I was going to do today. Ferret was mad at me and lame, besides. TJ was on her way to the City. Jess was . . . well, it didn't matter. He didn't want me around. I felt lonely again.

The back door opened. Air sucked at my back as it swooshed

into the kitchen. Bopeep shot off the steps and disappeared around the corner.

"Hey, Mark."

I pushed off the steps and turned around. Joyce opened the screen door, smiling as big as she had yesterday when I won the shooting contest. She was dressed in yesterday's clothes, blue shorts and a white blouse.

She must have noticed my eyes taking in her clothes. "Jess came by the house last night about nine. Remember what I told you, and don't tell nobody."

"Is Jess here?" I asked, unable to think of anything else to say.

"He's just getting up. Come on in. I got fresh homemade biscuits coming out the oven. You hungry?"

Fresh homemade biscuits? My mouth watered. Hot bread liberally buttered and topped with strawberry jam. I grinned. "I could manage a couple."

I sat down at the table. Joyce pulled out a glass pan filled with biscuits, steaming and golden brown. "Butter those quick," she said, setting them on top of an old blue pot holder, discolored with burn spots. She got butter and jam from the icebox and sat down to help.

Jess came in, already dressed, his gun holstered at his side and handcuffs jangling from the belt. He glanced at me and frowned. "Thought you were at the Brubakers'," he said, pouring himself a cup of coffee.

"I was." I split the last biscuit, buttered it, and set in on my plate. I needed to tell Jess about Packard's threat to gut him and about Andy the Panda.

Jess sat down, grabbed a biscuit, and spread jam in between the two buttery halves. "You been spending a lot of time there lately."

"I suppose." I spooned a generous helping of jam into my biscuit and took a bite.

His voice got sterner. "Don't you be imposing on them, you hear?"

"I'm not imposing on anyone. Ferret's my best friend."

Jess glanced at Joyce. I could tell he was holding back on account of her being here. "Friends are just friends. They're not your family."

Reverend Brubaker had paid my entry fee yesterday. I figured that had a lot to do with this conversation. "I expect I won't be seeing them much today."

Jess took a swallow of coffee. "Joyce said you outshot Packard."

"He missed by a foot," I said, and then grinned at my unintentional joke.

Jess's eyes narrowed. "What's so funny? You watch out for him. He doesn't forget. Stupid kid."

I felt the grin die on my face. Jess talked like he wished I'd lost. Then called me a stupid kid.

"Where'd you put the gun?"

"Closet yonder," I said, keeping my voice flat. "Shells are all used up."

"I'll bring home a couple of boxes today." He rose to leave, then paused, swallowing down the last of his coffee. "I'll drop you by your house now, Joyce."

Joyce got up, stacked all the plates and set them in the sink. "I noticed you boys are plumb out of food."

"Damn it. I forgot to go to the store yesterday." Jess pulled out his wallet and took out a ten-dollar bill. "Mark, you go to Tucker's today and pick up some stuff. Nothing expensive, you hear me?"

"Ten dollars won't go far," I said.

"You got money. Use some of it."

Joyce spoke up. "Jess, it's his prize money."

"That ten-dollar bill was my prize money too. I don't see that it makes much difference where it comes from."

I glowered at Jess. He was a real tightwad.

"Say," Joyce said. "Why don't I fix you two a real home-cooked meal tonight?"

Any offer of food was an offer accepted. "Sure."

"I don't know if we should do that," Jess said, looking a little trapped.

Joyce smiled at me. "Be at my place about six. Okay?"

I nodded. Jess and Joyce left. I hadn't told Jess about Packard's threat.

18

Later that morning, about ten, I went downtown to get the groceries. For a Monday morning, Bob White looked pretty busy, half filled with cars parked in the business section and people going in and out of stores.

Tucker's Food Store was in the middle of town, facing north, looking right at the courthouse. The four diagonal spaces in front were taken, and two cars were parked in the vacant lot next door. Unlike the other stores, Tucker's sat a little way back from the street and had a long wooden porch fronting it that was covered and caught a lot of shade.

Old Sam, part hound, part everything else, sprawled half off the edge of the porch, his tongue lolling out the side of his mouth, dripping enough water to fill a slop bucket. He was Mr. Tucker's dog. I stopped to pet him and he raised his head appreciatively. Old Sam was about my age, of a motley liver color with real short hair, feet half as big as my hands, and tired eyes. He appeared to smile as I rubbed his shoulders, rearranging his loose skin. God made a mistake with dogs, giving them too short a life.

Mr. Tucker kept a half-dozen chairs out front so people could sit down and rest. At least that's what he said. But I heard someone else say that he did it so people would sit out there thinking about all the good things inside they could be eating. Then they'd just have to come inside and buy something.

I didn't think it mattered much either way. Mostly, old men sat in them, wearing hats they'd owned for more than twenty years and resting gnarled canes between their legs. Their yellowed eyes watched all the goings-on, and shrunken jaws spoke of people who had died before I was born. Sometimes they whittled. Sometimes they coughed. Mostly, they just sat.

Today, Mr. Tubbs, Mr. Roscoe, and Mr. Davis were sitting with their chairs pulled close together so they could hear each other. The townsfolk called these three "the graybeards," which was strange since what was left of their hair was well past the gray stage, more like dirty snow. Only Mr. Davis had a beard— one that might have looked like Robert E. Lee's at one time. I had to pass by the trio to go in the front door. Although not expecting an answer, I nodded anyway and said, "Morning, sirs."

A hand snaked out and bony fingers seized my arm. "Boy?" It was Mr. Davis. He squinted so much all I could see underneath his hat was a gleam behind each narrow slit.

"It's me, Mr. Davis. Mark Stoddard."

He still had hold of my arm, his grip like a feeble claw. The rest of his arm shook with a palsy and his head twitched rhythmically from side to side, about a quarter of an inch, two or three times a second. "I know who you are, boy. Think I can't see, do you? I can see fine. Don't you be disrespectful."

"I didn't mean to be, sir. Excuse me."

He continued like he hadn't even heard me. "Understand we got a strange one in town. Real strange. You see him yesterday? At the church?"

"I saw him."

To my right, Mr. Tubbs cleared his throat. A cigarette dangled from his lips and smoke drooled from his mouth as he spoke, his voice not more than a wheeze. "We hear he's a tall feller. Hair as long and blond as a girl's. Carries a purse."

I nodded, wanting to get on with my business. I glanced around. Mr. Roscoe looked dead, his mouth hanging open, his eyes vacant.

"You ever see him before?" Mr. Davis asked.

"I never did."

"They say he likes kids. Boys especially."

"I wouldn't know about that."

"You best stay away from him." He squeezed my arm and found a nerve.

I pulled loose from Mr. Davis's grip and backed toward the door to Tucker's store.

His beard jutted forward and his voice scratched as he spoke. "He comes around here, we'll take care of him."

Childlike, Mr. Tubbs raised his cane like he was holding a rifle, pointed it at me, and pulled an imaginary trigger. "Blooey," he said.

Mr. Roscoe came unfrozen, and I knew he'd been listening to the whole conversation. "Maybe we'll cut his balls off."

"He ain't got any." Mr. Davis laughed, his white beard bobbing up and down.

Roscoe and Tubbs both started laughing too, except Mr. Tubbs started coughing and hacked something up on the porch.

I turned away, pulled open the screen door, and went inside. Mrs. Tucker was at the cash register, ringing up groceries for Mrs. Franklin. A few other customers were shopping. It was almost as hot inside as out. The store had a high ceiling and four large fans hung down from it, revolving ponderously, beating the air downward, making it harder for the flies to maneuver.

Mr. Tucker came trudging up the cookies-and-cereal aisle toward the front of the store, wearing a long white apron and carrying two cases of Coca-Cola in wooden trays, the floor squeaking in protest. Above his usual bow tie was a lean face ravaged with pock marks. His brown hair was slicked back with Brylcreem, every hair plastered into place.

"Morning, Mr. Tucker," I said, greeting my future boss with a friendly smile.

"Morning, Mark," he answered cheerfully. He plopped the

soda cases down on the floor next to the rusty red cooler near the doorway, then stood up and rubbed his knuckles across the top of my head.

I ducked away, grinning.

"Saw you at the fair yesterday. Mighty fine shooting. Mighty fine indeed!" His eyes twinkled like he really meant it.

"Thank you, sir. I got a little lucky." Hoping to get a little luckier, I decided to hang around a while. Sometimes he gave Ferret and me a cold one free.

He slid the top of the cooler back and began shuffling the remaining bottles closer to the front. "Guess you won't be bringing me any stray pop bottles, what with all that money you won yesterday."

"Well, I might, if there's any that need picking up."

He nodded toward the cases on the floor. "Reckon we've got any from Tucumcari?"

Mr. Tucker thought it was neat to find a Coke bottle that had been made in some faraway place. He would take it in his hands, turning it this way and that, and make up some crazy story of how it found its way to Bob White, Oklahoma.

I squatted down and picked up two Coke bottles, examining the raised letters on their flat bottoms. "Durant and . . . Lawton," I said, handing the two bottles to Mr. Tucker.

These were just ordinary, but still he glanced at the bottoms before he put them in the cooler. He had a collection of over fifty Cokes in his front window that had been made all over the United States. He really wanted to find one from Tucumcari, New Mexico. Said he'd lived there as a boy.

I went through the cases on the floor, hoping to find the magical "Tucumcari" Coke, but without success. Four bottles remained in the second case when I realized he hadn't taken the two I was holding up. I looked up. He was staring out the store front window, a puzzled look on his face.

I stood up. Across the street, Sheriff Adams's patrol car turned into the no-parking zone in front of the courthouse, lights flashing. Something important was going on.

Pulling up to the right of the sheriff's car was Jess's Fury, his lights flashing too. A man in the rear seat bent forward as if his wrists were handcuffed behind his back.

I had to go. Mr. Tucker was mesmerized. "Mr. Tucker? Sir? Mr. Tucker?" I asked, raising my voice.

"Huh?" He glanced down. I shoved the Cokes into his hands and pushed open the screen door.

Sheriff Adams hit his siren. A howl rolled out, loud enough to wake up everybody in Bob White. He let it wail for half a minute, then killed it and climbed out of the car. People poured from the courthouse and from every store on Main Street. Jess got out and hung over the Fury's door. I dashed across the street, intending to ask him what was going on, but he frowned and told me to shut up.

Sheriff Adams watched the crowd gathering, nodding at his friends and acquaintances. He knew everybody in town, and everybody called him "Brahma" from his rodeo days. He was tall and lanky, with bowlegs that came from locking themselves around bulls and wild broncos when he was in his prime. He still made good money raising rodeo stock on his ranch north of town. He had an honest-to-goodness salt-and-pepper handlebar mustache that made his worst frown look like a smile. Although stove up from a dozen broken bones, he was six feet tall and tough as nails.

Sheriff Adams lifted his cowboy hat and mopped his brow with a wrinkled red bandanna that he pulled from his back pocket. Ducking back into the patrol car, he flipped some switch on the police radio and exited with the microphone, stretching the cord to its full length.

"Howdy, folks." The radio was set to bullhorn mode, and the sound of Sheriff Adams's voice crackled through town. "We got us a little problem here. Jess? Bring that fellow out here. Bring him out where everybody can see him."

Jess reached into the back seat of the Fury and hauled out the handcuffed prisoner. He was a small man, not much bigger than Ferret and not much older than Jess. His T-shirt looked freshly torn and he had a bruise starting over his left eye. He looked angry. Jess walked him to the rear of the sheriff's car, where everybody could see him good.

Sheriff Adams keyed the microphone again. "Folks, we got us a rumrunner here. Caught him speeding down the highway. Had ten cases of Old Crow in his car. Bringing illegal whiskey into our county. Where you from, son?"

The rumrunner didn't answer, smirking defiantly at the crowd.

"Son? You done got resisting arrest to go along with possession and intent to sell illegal whiskey. I don't want to have to ask you twice."

Jess jerked the handcuffs upward toward the man's shoulder blades. The man staggered, lost his balance, and fell to his knees. Jess grabbed him before he fell on his face and hauled him to his feet.

Sullen, suspiciously, the man answered, "I'm . . . I'm from Oklahoma City."

"That's better, son. Now, being from Oklahoma, you are aware that Oklahoma is a dry state and that it's against the law to bring liquor across the state line."

"I got me a federal license."

Sheriff Adams reached into his breast pocket and pulled out a yellow piece of paper. He unfolded it and held it up so everyone could see it. "Why so you do, son. I got it right here. It's got an official U.S. government stamp on it. Says you have the legal right to buy whiskey wholesale and then to distribute it and resell it in the United States. But we're not talking about federal law that allows . . . sinful drinking. We're talking about Oklahoma law, made by good . . . honest . . . God-fearing people. This here piece of paper ain't worth spit."

Sheriff Adams took a match from his pants pocket, popped his thumbnail across the head, and set the flame to the paper. He turned it in his hand as it burned, then dropped it on the street, where it died out.

"Aw, Sheriff," the rumrunner pleaded. "Ain't no call to

done that. I'm just a good old boy trying to make a living by giving people what they want. How about . . . just letting me pay my fine so I can be on my way." He smiled real nice when he said "pay my fine."

Sheriff Adams exploded. He dropped the microphone and walked toward the rumrunner, shouting. "This isn't Choctaw County. You're not in Creek County or Latimer or Pushmataha. Son, you're in Bob White, Oklahoma, and we don't have itchy palms that need greasing. You're in the heart of the Bible Belt and this is dry country."

The rumrunner turned pale as the sheriff approached. He cowered a bit as if expecting Sheriff Adams to hit him. Then his mouth started spewing words. "Reckon there's got to be some way we can work this out."

Sheriff Adams stopped two feet from the man and leaned over him, menacingly. "Son, here's how we're going to work things out. Someday you're going to get out of our jail and leave town and never come back."

The rumrunner's voice trembled. "If you could just give me my merchandise back, I'd be happy to pay the fine and be out of your hair forever. Gone and forgotten."

"Hell! You aren't ever going to forget being here. Jess! Get a case of Old Crow out of my car."

Jess shoved the prisoner toward Sheriff Adams, opened the car's back door, pulled out a case of whiskey, and set it down a few feet from the car.

Sheriff Adams stepped forward, ripped open the cardboard box, and pulled out a bottle. He held it over his head and the sun caught the color inside, a dazzling burst of reds and golds like the pot at the end of the rainbow. "Friends, this is what we been fighting against for fifty years, ever since we become a state. We got prohibition written into our constitution and still people are bringing this stuff across our borders. Now we got another damn bootlegger back in the county."

He turned to the rumrunner. "You got ten cases of this to

sell. Twenty-four bottles to a case. Two hundred and forty bottles. What's that worth to you, son?"

The rumrunner had a worried look on his face. He shrugged his shoulders.

"I'd say that's worth about a thousand dollars to you. That right, son?"

The rumrunner looked the sheriff in the eye and this time agreed, nodding his head.

Sheriff Adams hefted the bottle twice, then turned and fired it against the curb, shattering it into a million pieces. Old Crow and glass silvers splashed everywhere.

"Aw shit. That's good money you're—"

"Hear that, folks? It's all about money." He pulled another bottle from the case and threw it against the gutter. The golden contents exploded on impact. I could smell the booze from where I stood by the Fury.

Sheriff Adams looked at the crowd. "Any of y'all want to help me smash this whiskey? Come on up here and smash a bottle."

People's heads swung back and forth, looking at each other, surprised by the sheriff's invitation, hanging back.

"I reckon I can help out the law." Mr. Tucker grinned and stepped out of the crowd. He strode proudly up to the sheriff and pulled a bottle from the case. He hefted it twice, then hurled it against the curb, the bottle exploding in a shower of red and gold. He turned to the crowd and grinned, "Oklahoma was born sober. We don't want whiskey in our state."

"Attaboy, Roy," someone called. Some folks cheered and others clapped their hands.

Sheriff Adams waved the crowd forward. "Come on, folks. Roy Tucker ain't afraid to fight the devil. We got us a thousand dollars' worth of booze to bust. Jess? Get those other cases out of my car."

The townsfolk moved forward—men and women included—at first taking turns picking out a single bottle, tossing it into the gutter, and cheering when it broke. Then the action picked up, and the bottle throwing got faster and faster. People were tearing at the boxes, grabbing two and three bottles at once, jerking them away if someone else's hands closed on "their" bottle. The air was electric. Shouts and laughter and cheering swept the crowd. Shards of glass and golden Old Crow splashed everywhere. It didn't take long to bust up a thousand dollars' worth of liquor. The gutter was full of broken glass and pools of booze.

I felt stunned. It was strange seeing grown-ups acting like kindergartners. I didn't feel a bit sorry for the rumrunner, but I felt sorry for the people of Bob White. It reminded me of what I imagined a lynch mob would be like.

Sheriff Adams got back on his radio–bullhorn, grinning behind his handlebar mustache. "I want to thank y'all for helping me teach this rumrunner not to bring illegal whiskey into our county. I don't expect he'll be coming back anytime soon with a load of whiskey. Y'all can go on about your business."

But not many people left right away. Faces were flushed and juices were flowing. This was an event, and they had to talk about it. Jess put the rumrunner back in the Fury and slowly backed out, except people stopped him and patted him on the shoulder and shook his hand, like they were doing to the sheriff as well. Finally, Jess started around the courthouse toward the jail, driving real slow, "rrowllling" his siren.

I looked for Mr. Tucker, but didn't see him. I wondered if the crowd would have joined in if he hadn't smashed that bottle. Maybe. I decided I'd better get the groceries.

I turned away, then stopped, catching a glimpse of Old Sam through the crowd. Mr. Tucker's dog had gotten off the porch and, like everyone else, had come over to see what all the excitement was about. Something was wrong with Sam. He staggered, then fell down.

"Lookit that dumb dog," someone said. "Drinking that Old Crow."

Sam? Drinking the whiskey that flowed down the gutter? I

ran forward, dodging the people between me and Sam, then stopped. Sam struggled awkwardly to his feet, then staggered sideways, walking like he had only three good legs, but not figuring out which three to use. He fell again, letting out a mournful howl. People had come up behind me, and were laughing themselves silly.

"Goddamn dog'll kill hisself, drinking that lightning. Har, har. Git up, have another snort, pooch."

Sam's legs pawed the air, seeking traction and not finding it. He lifted his head, struggling to rise. The effort weakened him. He dropped his head, his nose striking the concrete.

I could see blood glistening on his muzzle. He must have swallowed some glass slivers along with the booze. "Mr. Tucker?" I yelled toward the store, as loud as I could. Not waiting for an answer, I ran to Sam and got down beside him, cradling his head in my lap, wrapping my arms around him.

"Help 'em up, boy. Make him walk around. Like a chicken with its head cut off."

"It's Mr. Tucker's dog," I said. "He's bleeding. Somebody get Mr. Tucker."

"Shitfire. He's drunk some glass. I didn't see him drinking, not until it was too late."

I looked down at Sam. His eyes were glazed and his mouth hung open. Blood oozed from his tongue onto my jeans.

"Damn dog is done for, boy. That glass'll shred his insides as it goes through him."

Gently, I touched Sam's head, trying to comfort him. He sighed, then heaved, trying to throw up. His eyes closed and his mouth opened wide, every fiber of his body straining as his stomach rebelled.

"Easy, boy," I said. "Easy."

A handful of bloody soup dripped forth. Sam's body gave a quiver that ran from head to toe, then all his breath drained out.

"Lookie there. His heart must of give out."

I felt tears running quietly down my cheeks.

"Sam?" Mr. Tucker was at my side, scooping his arms underneath the animal. "Sam?" he whispered.

Mr. Tucker looked sick. I helped him gather the old dog into his arms, then stood helplessly as he carried the dog across the street and into his store.

"Hell, it was just an old dog. He would've died of old age inside a year anyway."

I set my eyes hard. I didn't want to look at whoever was talking. I didn't want to have bad thoughts against them. Clenching my fists, I turned away and started for home. I needed to be with Bopeep.

God made a mistake with dogs, giving them too short a life.

19

Back home, I just about wore out Bopeep playing with her, soothing my soul. Old Sam had just been thirsty. It could have happened to any dog. Even Bopeep. I was glad that she was a stay-at-home dog. She never left the yard except for the times I invited her to go hiking, usually with Ferret.

The thought of something happening to Bopeep—losing her—scared me. My folks had died. Old Sam had died. I didn't want anyone else dying. I remembered Packard's threat. Where was he? Sneaking around somewhere? Making more moonshine?

About one o'clock, I went back to Tucker's and bought nine dollars and eighty-seven cents' worth of groceries from Mrs. Tucker. She had a long face, so I didn't ask her about Mr. Tucker or about Sam. Jess's ten-dollar bill went a lot further than I had thought it would, but then hamburger meat and franks didn't cost much. At home I fried a couple of hot dogs, wrapping each one in a slice of mayonnaised white bread. Bopeep finished off the crusts and she got the last bite of each frank, too. She deserved it just for being a dog.

While I was putting away the groceries, I remembered that I had told Reverend Brubaker that I would mow the lawn today. Relaxing was my preference over work anytime. But I liked keeping my word. Dad had said that you couldn't respect yourself if you didn't keep your word.

I went out to the garage, pulled out the dusty mower from behind a clutter of tools, and started shoving it around the yard. Our push mower hadn't been sharpened since last summer, which made the job a lot harder. The mower was stubborn, its wheels complaining and sliding across the grass, the blades refusing to turn consistently. The weeds were stubborn too, and sometimes I'd reach down and yank them out after failing to cut through their tough skins.

In Oklahoma, the days after a storm were always blistering, with the sun baking down, steam rising up. I shucked my T-shirt and got an old cap from the house. After slurping cool water from the outside faucet, I resumed cutting the seedy grass and the weeds that thrived in our yard.

I was about halfway through when the reverend drove up in his station wagon, a 1956 Chevy Impala. I propped the mower handle up vertically and rested my arms across it, watching the reverend get out of his car. He walked forward, his shirt sleeves rolled up to his elbows, a vee of sweat soaking through his shirt front. The large bald area above his forehead gleamed under the hot sun.

He surveyed the mangy yard and shook his head. "Yesterday's rain was sorely needed."

"I'd have to agree with that, sir."

"A little more watering on your yard wouldn't hurt."

I nodded, and reached into my pocket, feeling the crumpled prize money I had won at the fair. "I forgot to pay you back yesterday. Thanks for loaning me the five."

The reverend shook his head. "Why don't you just keep that five, Mark? I know you boys can use the money."

I thrust a five-dollar bill forward. "Thank you, sir, but we're fine. Win or lose, I was going to pay you back."

He took the money and stuck it into his pocket, almost absently. I could tell he was thinking hard about something. I wondered if it was about what happened in town this morning. "You hear about the rumrunner today?" I asked.

He looked at me blankly, then his eyes focused. He nodded. "I heard. Wish I could have been there."

"I wish it never happened."

"Whiskey is a bad thing, Mark. A bad thing."

"Yeah. I just didn't like all that bottle smashing."

"People were carrying out God's will."

Puzzled, I looked at the reverend. "Smashing all those bottles was God's will?"

"God was angry. Very angry."

Reverend Brubaker was the smartest man I knew. Seems like he had a good answer for everything. Yet his answer bothered me. "What about Sam?"

"Sam?"

"Mr. Tucker's dog died."

"God works in mysterious ways."

I looked at the reverend closely, afraid that maybe I was asking too many questions, questions that he might take exception to. But the reverend seemed distracted today. "Why did Sam have to die? Was that God's will?"

"The Lord God was very angry."

"God was angry at Sam? Mr. Tucker's dog?"

"God was angry with his children. The people of Bob White."

I knew this all made perfect sense to the reverend, so I tried hard to understand. "The people? They were just there. The rumrunner was passing through on his way to Oklahoma City. Why would God be angry with the people of Bob White?"

"There's an evil presence in town."

Evil? Packard? He seemed evil to me. "Sir?"

"Evil begets evil. One evil man comes to town, and evil spreads."

"I don't understand. Someone in town is evil and God is angry so he has a dog die?"

The reverend didn't seem to hear me. His eyes darted up Ash Street and then down again. Edgy, he turned his upper body this way and that. "You haven't seen Mrs. Brubaker, have you?"

"No, sir. They back from the City already?"

"They got back about one-thirty."

"Oh. Well, no. I haven't seen them. Something wrong?"

"No, nothing. Just need to talk to her." He shrugged his shoulders for no apparent reason and started back to the Chevy. "Be a good Christian now, you hear?"

He drove away, raising a billow of fresh dust from the totally dry street, which showed no sign of last night's violent storm. I watched him drive past his house, slowly, then go on toward Main, headed downtown.

I felt the sun beating down, burning my shoulders. Sighing, I looked at the weeds in front of me, then lowered the mower handle, and shoved hard. This time the wheels didn't skid across the grass. The blades flailed furiously, decapitating seed heads that failed to bend backwards in time to escape the dull blades.

The reverend's words bothered me. How could God be angry with a dog?

I reached down and tore out some weeds I'd missed earlier.

"God is angry?" I said aloud. I was angry. Angry with Jess, with Ferret, with Reverend Brubaker, with Lafe Packard, with God. Angry with God for taking things away that had no business dying. Like Sam. Like my parents.

I mowed hard.

Ten minutes later, sweat was pouring off my body. Every so often a salty drop would slither through an eyebrow and burn into my eyeball. I had one more row to finish, not counting the stray slips and singles that had escaped fate, when I felt something small and stinging strike my back.

"Ow." I whirled around, one hand instinctively reaching for my injury.

20

"Gotcha," TJ said, grinning. She stood about ten feet away, holding a slingshot in her hand. I recognized it as belonging to Ferret.

"TJ! Damn it to hell. What are you doing, shooting people with that thing?"

"Awwww. These teensy-weensy stones wouldn't hurt a fly." She held out a handful of pea-sized pebbles. "You're not hurt, are you?" she asked, talking like she'd talk to a little kid.

"Hell no," I grumbled, pulling my hand from behind my back. Under the skin, a good-sized lump was growing. "You guys weren't gone long," I observed.

TJ shrugged her shoulders and said, matter-of-factly, "Aunt Josephine bought me two dresses, then we had lunch, and came home. No big deal."

TJ was looking at my bare chest. Suddenly self-conscious, I was sorry I didn't have bigger muscles, and there was hardly enough hair there to be respectable. She grinned, and I hoped my fly hadn't slipped down. I didn't dare look.

"Ferret's got a neat slingshot," she said, relieving me of my anxiety.

"I've got one just like it."

"You make it?"

"A couple of summers ago, me and Ferret carved 'em from a hickory tree felled by lightning."

"Yeah? Is that why the wood's so dark? The lightning?"

"Naw. We soaked the yokes in linseed oil. It hardens the wood."

"It looks expensive."

"It's as good as any professional slingshot," I allowed.

"Where's yours?"

"In my room. It needs new rubber."

TJ nodded, and glanced briefly at the yard. "You finished?"

"Done," I said, not wanting to turn my back on her again, not while she still had ammo. Bopeep came bounding around the corner of the house, alerted by the sound of voices.

TJ bent down and hugged her while Bopeep wriggled all over. "Let's go swimming. Ferret says there's a couple of places nearby."

"How's his ankle?"

"Big as a pumpkin. Getting better, though."

I eyed TJ. Red shorts. Blue blouse with strawberries sprinkled on it. Hair pulled back behind her head and banded into a pony tail. "Where's your suit?"

"Got it on underneath. You going or am I going alone?"

I felt a drop of sweat trickle out of my right eyebrow and spiral down my nose. "I'm going."

I put on last year's swimming shorts underneath my jeans— they were getting a little tight in the waist. The three of us set out due east—I'd decided Bopeep needed an outing—cutting across to the railroad tracks which bordered the town. When we ran out of street, we mounted the embankment and used the ties for a road.

"Train come through here often?" TJ asked.

"There's one in the afternoon. It'll be coming up soon on its way to the City."

"Ever stop in Bob White?"

"Sure. Sometimes." Usually it kept going, clacking lazily through the crossing on the far side of town.

"I like trains," TJ said.

I enjoyed hearing her say that. I liked trains, too.

We followed the tracks southeast, having a couple of miles to go to get to the Clear Boggy River, at the east edge of the Bottomlands. Bopeep ranged ahead of us, stopping to sniff or squat at every interesting spot. I pretended not to notice, hoping she wouldn't do number two in front of TJ.

TJ gave up on the pea-pebbles, and advanced to railroad chat, which fit the pouch better. She wasn't particularly good at bean-flipping, but you wouldn't know it to hear her talk. She shot more for distance than accuracy, holding the yoke awkwardly, pulling the pouch back well away from her face. When she released it, she yanked the yoke downward, giving it some extra kick but nearly always shooting across her line of sight.

Finally I couldn't stand watching her mess up any longer. "You'd do better holding the pouch next to your cheek."

She eyed me, her right eyebrow lifted questioningly. "Yeah? Like you're an expert or something?"

I sure knew a lot more about bean-flipping than any girl. "Quit aiming at the target. Just point your left hand, like you're pointing your finger. Then let go of the pouch. And don't pull it back so far."

"If you're so good, smarty-pants, show me. Hit that telephone pole over there." She held out Ferret's slingshot.

I ran my fingers over the smooth wood, then flexed the rubber straps, testing their strength and pull. Tiny rot spots dotted the length of them, growing bigger as I stretched the straps out. Like mine, they needed to be replaced. One was bound to break sooner or later.

I bent down and selected the roundest piece of chat I could find. The pole was maybe forty yards ahead. "That's easy."

TJ turned toward the pole, set her hands on her hips, and thrust her chest out.

My thoughts shot back to last night. Her sleeping in my arms, and my letting that opportunity pass without even accidentally doing something—like feeling her bare breasts underneath her nightie. I sorta knew what breasts felt like, but not from any significant experience. A few accidents here and there, but mostly imagining. Feeling breasts had to be just about the most pleasurable thing a fellow could do.

"You going to take all day?" TJ pivoted her hips toward me, pointing her left breast at my chest.

I felt my ears turning red so I raised the yoke and fired. The stone whistled by the pole, missing it by at least a yard. Damn.

"That's easy," TJ said, mocking me.

Angrily, I handed the slingshot back to her. "Try it yourself. You might get lucky this time."

TJ picked up another stone, held the yoke out, and drew the pouch back to her cheek, not unlike the way an expert shotgunner would handle his piece, releasing the pouch smoothly.

The stone whizzed through the air, whacking sharply against the creosote wood, ricocheting to one side. Bopeep popped her head up from some weeds well to the right of the pole, looking curiously for the source of the sound, then back at us, probably wondering what kind of foolishness we were about.

TJ cocked her head and lowered her voice an octave, drawling out the words. "Just lucky, I reckon."

I knew it wasn't luck. She'd been leading me on. "Where'd you learn to shoot?"

Her eyes lit up remembering. "My Dad—" She paused, and her eyes darkened, turning wistful. "It was a long time ago."

"Yeah. I guess so." I figured it was time to change the subject. "I'm surprised that Ferret loaned you his shooter."

"He didn't. I borrowed it." TJ grinned.

I allowed a grin back, and we walked on down the tracks. I put my arm around her shoulders. She smiled, appreciating it. I bet she'd stuck her chest out on purpose. Being this close to her, I could see partway down her front, where her chest started to swell before being hidden by her blouse.

The tracks mounted a little rise. Clearing it, we had a panoramic view of nearly all of the Bottomlands spread out to the southwest and the Clear Boggy River meandering southeast on its way to join the Red—the river that saved us Okies from being Texicans.

The valley before us was old and shallow, most of it criss-crossed with plowed farmlands of alfalfa, corn, green beans, and turnips. A haze filtered the view, giving the green fields a beautiful bluish tint. As far as I could see, only three farmhouses dotted the landscape. I liked coming down here. I felt like part of nature.

"Train's coming," TJ said.

In the distant southeast, a tiny train twisted like a woolly caterpillar, trailing maybe twenty cars or so behind it, weaving its short length down the far side of the valley. "On its way to the City," I said, matter-of-factly.

The three of us moved down the track a couple hundred yards, Bopeep cutting back and forth across the tracks, making sure every opportunity got explored, checking on us every minute to make sure we didn't get lost.

The tracks crossing the river were positioned on two-foot-wide pilings sunk through the water, deep into bedrock. The Clear Boggy wound out of the edge of the Bottomlands and made a sharp turn just before it passed under the tracks. It was a perfect swimming hole, having been widened and deepened to slow the river's pace to a crawl.

The "trestle" was where Ferret and I usually went swimming. The banks of the Clear Boggy were lined with small trees and bushes which provided peaceful and secluded surroundings. I looked around, enjoying the view, then realized that Bopeep had vanished.

"Bopeep!" I called. We waited. TJ put her two little fingers in the corners of her mouth and whistled the most godawful shrill screech I'd ever heard. I glanced at her enviously. I'd never been able to do that.

Still no Bopeep. "Oh, she'll be along any minute. She's been here lots of times. Knows this ground like the back of her paw. Come on, let's go swimming."

"This is great," TJ said. Handing me the slingshot, she ran

out onto the trestle and stood looking down at the water. The river was maybe thirty yards wide and the trestle twice as long, about fifteen feet above water level, a great platform for flips and cannonballs.

TJ stretched out her arms and turned slowly around, like a goddess in charge of the whole world. "Eeee-yow-oh!" she yelled, to no one in particular. "Eeee-yow-oh!"

I knew how she felt. I'd done the same thing many times. But now, beneath my sneakers, I felt vibration flowing into the tie on which I stood. A couple hundred yards south, the track curved behind the trees that guarded the river so I couldn't see how close the train was.

But I could hear the chugging strain of the engine approaching. "TJ! Come on back. Train's getting closer."

"Fraidy-cat?" she said, spreading her arms into wings and hopping across the open ties, fluttering like a butterfly, moving further out along the trestle.

"TJ! Don't be stupid."

"You chicken?" She bent down, untied her laces, and then kicked her sneakers off, sending them flying toward the bank. Pausing, she looked at me, expecting me to come running out.

But I was on to her tricks now, and I didn't feel like being taunted into doing something every time TJ wanted her way. I stood my ground, hands on my hips. "I ain't chicken, and I ain't crazy either. You best be getting off the tracks now. The train'll be coming around the curve any second."

"How deep's the water?"

In spite of myself, I did some figuring. She was about twenty feet from the bank. "Where you are, it's maybe a dozen feet." The train noise grew louder. Like it was right behind the trees. "Get off the track—"

An old, big-nosed locomotive roared around the curve, pulling a chain of noisy, gyrating cars behind it, going fifty miles an hour at least. It'd be on the trestle in seconds.

For a moment I froze, immobilized by the terrible scene.

TJ stood smack dab in the middle of the rails, facing the approaching train.

It wasn't slowing down. There wasn't time for it to stop even if an engineer was looking out the window, which he wasn't.

"TJ!" I yelled into the approaching roar. I ran forward, stumbled, then awkwardly regained my balance. I couldn't get to TJ in time.

21

Ahead, I saw TJ jerking her blouse off, then stepping out of her shorts. She wasn't wearing her suit underneath, just a bra and panties.

The train roared onto the trestle, sending a shock wave through the ties that stopped me cold.

TJ slipped her bra and panties off, then tossed the whole bundle of clothes behind her, where they landed on the edge of the bank. Casually, she stepped across the rail and posed on the edge of the visibly shaking tie.

Relentlessly, the train rushed toward us.

Another split second, then TJ leaped feet first and spread-eagled off the trestle, just as ungraceful as a turtle might, stripped of its protective shell.

A laugh caught in my throat and I became aware of the gigantic mass of metal hurtling toward me. My frozen muscles burst into life, and I leaped off the trestle onto the river bank. The train roared by, and I felt its hot breath on the back of my neck.

I hit the grassy incline and rolled halfway down toward the water, my ears full of the rattle and clatter and roar of the train. Deafened, I struggled to my knees, feeling the ground trembling underneath.

Ripples spread from the spot where TJ had landed in the water, but she was nowhere to be seen. I waited a couple of seconds. No TJ. The time stretched into five seconds, then ten seconds. No TJ.

The caboose jerked across the trestle, and the sound of the train faded quickly. The ripples in the Clear Boggy died away.

I jumped to my feet, shouting, once again able to hear my own voice. "TJ!"

She might have been hurt after all. I thought of how I'd nearly laughed when she'd jumped, and felt instant guilt. I had to save her. Hurriedly, I jerked off my tennis shoes, then shucked my T-shirt. A splash of water burst from the river.

"Come on in," TJ called. She was treading water about halfway across the river. Her hair glistened like black silk, clinging to the back of her neck. Her green eyes sparkled and I was never so glad to see anyone in my life.

"Damn you, TJ. You could have gotten killed. Hellfire, shit, damn. You could have gotten me killed."

TJ stretched out and took a few strokes toward me. She paused, treading water again. "I thought you wanted to go swimming."

I glared at her, feeling my anger fading away, yet near speechless. "Damn you."

TJ laughed, and it was a wonderful laugh—full of life. Full of being fourteen, being a girl, and dodging trains. She swung an arm out of the water, splashing a handful toward me that fell way short.

I remembered she was nude, but I couldn't see anything below her neck. I glanced sideways at her clothes strewn on the grass. Everything was there. She was really nude. It wasn't my imagination.

"You lied to me," I said. "About your swimming suit."

"So? So what?"

"So . . . you lied, that's what," I said, deliberately making my jaws hard, yet glancing lamely down at my feet.

"So we don't really need suits, do we?"

I looked up. TJ wasn't grinning now. Her eyes were a real deep green and her voice sounded husky.

"Guess not." I stood there thinking about taking all my clothes off, thinking about TJ nude in the water, wishing that the Clear Boggy was a little clearer. Suddenly, I wasn't sure I could undress in front of a girl. "Turn your back."

TJ laughed again, a sparkle of laughter bright as a crystal bell. "Hell no."

I could see the swirls of water and catch glimpses of her arms moving. I thought of her breasts just under the water and knew that I'd be touching them in a few seconds. I could almost feel them now.

I unbuttoned my jeans and stepped out of them. TJ was watching, interest on her face. My swim trunks were boxer type with a lining underneath and they provided a lot of concealment. I knew if I took them off, I'd be embarrassed for the rest of my life. I decided to take them off after I got in the water. I stepped forward into the edge of the water, feeling its warmth flow around my toes.

"You chicken?" TJ said. "Here chick, chick, chick. Here chickee."

I jumped back out of the water, and scowled angrily. "I ain't chicken." I put my thumbs inside the waistband and took a deep breath. A sharp noise, like a dry twig snapping, startled me.

The sound came from upstream. About fifty feet away, a large bush grew along the bank and hung out over the river. Through its leaves and branches, I could see a dirty John Deere cap bobbing up and down. Lafe Packard stepped out from behind the bush, carrying an old gunny sack, walking down the river bank toward us. "Here chick, chick, chick. Here chickee."

Packard!

My blood ran cold.

He took a few more steps, an evil smirk across his face. He was getting too close.

"Hold it right there, Packard," I shouted.

He stopped, and the smirk turned into a toothy, yellow grin. He spat a stream of tobacco juice into the water. "I's right about you, girl. I's right all along. Pretty little ass. Nice tits, too. Come down here to fuck her, eh, boy?"

Clenching my fists, I glanced at TJ. Her face was red. She slipped closer to shore, water still up to her neck, her arms criss-crossing her chest. She wasn't treading water anymore. Her feet were touching bottom.

I turned back to Packard. He was trying to make me mad. Like back at the trap range. Well, I was mad. "Just get the hell out of here."

"I ain't gittin' nowhere. This is my place. The Bottomlands. The river." He cackled wildly and danced kind of a little jig. "I live here. I sleep here. I eat here. I shit here."

"Get out of the river, TJ." I glanced quickly at her, not wanting to take my eyes off Packard.

She shook her head violently. "Not with that old man there."

He grinned at TJ. "Come on out, missy. Lemme see between your legs again."

I felt my mind explode with anger. "Shut your dirty mouth," I screamed. I started forward. I could whip his butt. I'd out-shot him at the trap range. He wasn't that much bigger than me and I wasn't going to be afraid of him. "I'm going to knock the shit out of you."

Packard held out his right hand. Fflickkk. The switchblade glinted in the sunlight.

I stopped, trembling with rage, yet knowing I wouldn't have a chance. With Packard, it wouldn't be a fair fight.

"You cheated me at the shoot, boy. You cheated me. You ain't no better than that scum brother of yours."

"I beat you before, Packard. And I'll beat you again."

"Remember what I told you, boy. Said I'd gut your brother. Right before your eyes. Maybe I'll gut you, too." He reached up with the switchblade and scratched his scraggly neck with it. Then he shook his head. "I ain't gonna kill you yet, Mark Stoddard. Not yet. It ain't the Day of Doom yet. I want you to suffer some. Like my boy did. Suffer. The Day of Doom will come soon enough. Then you'll see Jess die. Then you'll die."

"TJ, get the hell out of the water."

"You like snakes, boy?" Packard raised the gunny sack up a little.

I looked at the sack. Something inside moved against the cloth, a slow curling kind of movement. I felt my blood turn cold and a shiver ran up my spine. Snakes! I hated snakes.

"I like snakes. Like to eat snakes. Some folks say they taste like chickens." He laughed. "You ever eat snake, boy?"

I didn't answer.

"Answer me, boy!" Packard roared. "You ever eat snake?"

"Never did," I shouted back.

"Truth is, snakes don't taste like chickens. Snakes taste like snakes. You ever been bitten by a snake, boy?"

Suspicious, I looked at the sack. "You're crazy."

"I been bit. Lost count of how many times. Water moccasins, rattlesnakes, all kinds of snakes."

"Too bad they didn't kill you."

"I'm immune to snake venom. I don't even get sick. Never been sick a day in my life."

Packard brought the knife to the top of the sack and cut the twine wound around the top. He folded up the switchblade and put it into the pocket of his coveralls. Slowly, he squatted down and peered into the sack.

Suddenly, his hand darted inside, and jerked a live wriggling snake out. He held the snake behind its head, its length coiling spasmodically, trying to wrap itself around something. A cotton-mouthed water moccasin.

My eyes riveted on its pale mouth and fangs. "Thought you were going to gut me?" I said, desperately playing for time. I had to figure some way out of this thing.

"I am, boy. This is just for fun." Packard whirled the snake around his head. "It ain't for you."

He launched it right at TJ.

The snake twisted in the air, writhing, angry. TJ screamed.

22

The moccasin splashed into the water about five feet in front of her, flipped itself upright, and started swimming erratically in circles. TJ lunged backwards, frantically splashing water toward the snake. "Mark!"

TJ swam backwards, further into the river. The water moccasin turned downstream, and darted away.

"You crazy bastard," I shouted, turning back to the old man. He held another snake in his hand, whirling it around his head. He released it, and I saw it would land upstream from TJ, and likely swim right for her.

I had to do something. I couldn't go in the water. I'd be just as helpless as TJ. Desperately, I looked around the bank. The slingshot lay halfway up the slope where I'd dropped it when I'd jumped off the tracks. I turned and ran toward it. Behind me, I heard the splash as the snake hit the water. I grabbed the slingshot and raced up the slope to the tracks.

"Mark!" I heard frantic splashing. TJ was fighting the snake. I scooped up a handful of chat from the embankment and ran out onto the trestle. TJ was backpedaling, splashing water toward the moccasin coming straight for her. The old man was dancing along the edge of the bank, waving another snake in the air.

The snake was almost on TJ now. I had time for one shot. I loaded the slingshot and fired at the moccasin attacking TJ.

It whistled forward, zinging through the air. A geyser of water erupted beside the snake's head. I'd missed.

Quickly, I placed another piece of chat into the slingshot and pulled it back. Below me, the moccasin rolled and twisted, its belly flashing as it writhed in agony. I hadn't missed after all. I saw a flash of white skin as TJ dodged around the snake, then glanced up at me, her eyes filled with fear.

Another moccasin splashed upstream from TJ, righted itself, and began swimming for her. I pulled the slingshot back. Ssnappp. The broken rubber strap backlashed, popping the bridge of my nose. Tears flooded my eyes and I couldn't see. TJ screamed again.

I threw the slingshot aside and rubbed my eyes, trying to clear them. Blurry images appeared. Frantic, TJ splashed water at the snake. I took one stone between the fingers of my right hand, and transferred the remaining ones, two of them, into my left hand. I fired at the snake. My aim was off—a geyser erupted to the right front of the snake. Confused, the snake changed course, circled, then swam toward TJ again. I fired again, sending a shower directly in front of it. The snake veered past TJ, darting downstream.

On the bank, Packard stood, holding another writhing snake by its head. "How many more rocks you got, boy? I got more snakes than you got rocks. Maybe I'll just drop this next one right on top of her."

"You go to hell, Packard."

The old man whirled the snake around his head, grinning, taunting me.

Behind him Bopeep came trotting up, wondering who this stranger was, ready to be friendly. She stopped abruptly, a few feet from Packard, glared suspiciously at the gunny sack, and growled.

Packard turned at the sound. "Well, another one of them fucking Stoddards. Here, pooch. Wanna play with a cotton-mouth?" He jabbed the snake at Bopeep, its white mouth open and fangs exposed.

Bopeep jumped back and started barking furiously. She darted halfway around Packard, faking a charge.

Packard jabbed the snake toward Bopeep again, sending her into a spasm of excited lunges and dodges.

"Bopeep!" I yelled.

She paused, glancing at me.

Packard thrust the snake at Bopeep, nearly catching her before she leaped away, racing to the top of the bank. Packard laughed and turned to me. "Hot damn. I'm gonna kill your dog," he cackled.

His words sent a chill through me. An image came into my head. An image of Bopeep lying in my arms, all the breath draining out of her, dying like Old Sam had done. Rage poured through me, and I fired my last stone straight for Packard's head.

Not expecting it, he blinked, then ducked, late, the stone smacking against his left ear. He howled in pain.

It was my chance to get more ammo. I raced down the trestle, toward the embankment and the chat lining the rails.

Packard's back was to Bopeep, and from the slope above him, she charged, a blur of white fur leaping straight for his head. Her jaws grazed his cheek and her shoulder banged against his head, sending Packard sprawling down the slope, the gunny sack flopping loosely on the ground above him.

And opening.

And snakes sliding out. Little ones, big ones, fat ones. Writhing, angry, mean.

I froze, watching the hoard of snakes tumbling down the slope toward him.

Packard rolled to his knees and reared back, his eyes wide open. "Goddamn, son-of-a-bitch."

He must have forgotten about the snake he held in his right hand, because he dropped it, and it struck his right forearm, and clung to his arm. He looked at it in horror. "Shitfire."

The wriggling mass approached. Packard jumped to his feet and danced sideways, away from the other snakes.

Bopeep dodged also. She had a healthy respect for snakes.

Packard jerked at the snake on his arm, trying to pull it loose and not having much luck with his thumbless left hand. "God-damn," he cried, as it pumped its venom into his arm.

Finally he wrenched it loose and cast it aside. Bopeep growled and bit his calf.

From the embankment, I grabbed a handful of chat and let loose volley after volley, firing them as hard as I could, the stones hitting Packard's chest, his arms, his head.

Cursing, he took off running back up the river.

Bopeep raced after him, snapping at his legs.

"Bopeep! Come back!" I yelled. She chased Packard into the Bottomlands, barking angrily, and disappeared from sight.

The snakes were slithering toward the water.

In the river, I saw TJ swimming toward the bank, trying to get out now that Packard was gone. She couldn't see the snakes coming right for her. "TJ! Stop!"

She looked up at me, and kept coming.

"Stop! The snakes are all loose. Swim upstream."

She stopped, looking toward the bank. A fat six-footer slipped into the water. "Holy shit," she said, turning upstream, splashing vigorously through the slow-moving water. She was getting around them.

I grabbed two more handfuls of chat, then began tossing the stones at the snakes, hurrying them along into the river.

When they were gone, I went down the bank next to the trestle and gathered up TJ's clothes. I wondered how I was going to get them to her so she could get dressed. I turned to call to her.

She stood before me, naked, not covering herself, her face pale, trembling.

I looked at her for a moment, holding her clothes awkwardly in one hand, realizing that TJ had nearly been killed. Then, instinctively, I held my arms out for her.

She folded herself into me, leaning her head weakly against my neck.

I hugged her, tight and hard, pulling her wet body into mine, feeling her hair damp against my cheek, her wet breasts against my bare chest. I felt a need deep inside my body, a feeling I didn't quite understand. But it wasn't any kind of romancy feeling—not a feeling of wanting her body or anything like that. I needed to hold her tight, so I did. And, as I held her, I knew I wanted her arms around me.

We stood there for a couple of minutes, then I pulled back. She raised her head up and I could see that her eyes were misty. "You okay?" I asked.

She nodded, and smiled. "Okay."

I bent down and kissed her lips.

She kissed back.

I felt a kind of strength flowing through my body. A wonderful feeling, bigger than life itself. And I marveled that there could be such power in me. The feeling bound me to TJ . . . as if we were one person . . . and lasted.

Moments later, I heard a bouncing, huffing noise and pulled back.

Bopeep came charging up, tail wagging and tongue hanging out. She sat down before us, looked up, and whuffed as if to say, "Well, I took care of that old bastard."

Both TJ and I laughed.

Noticing TJ's nakedness, I thrust her clothes into her arms, then turned my back so she could have some privacy. I didn't know if it was really necessary. I'd already seen everything, but still, it seemed the respectful thing to do.

I stepped into my jeans and pulled them over my swim trunks. Bopeep wandered over as I was buckling my belt. The excitement was over and she'd calmed down now. I'd worried about her chasing Packard. But she could take care of herself. She spied my sneakers and went over to sniff them. Immediately, she lay down on top of them, her back arching against the grubby things.

I pulled my T-shirt on, watching Bopeep rubbing her muzzle and then rolling her whole body across the shoes.

"What's she doing?" TJ asked from behind me.

"Covering her scent."

"You mean like dogs rolling in stinking dead fish? That's gross."

Suddenly embarrassed, I said, "Bopeep, quit that."

Bopeep stood up, looked at me curiously, then shook her fur back into place.

"Why don't you get new shoes? Those are worn out."

"They're good enough." I shrugged it off, but she was right. If they weren't coming apart, I wouldn't have room for my toes. I'd asked Jess for new shoes, but he'd said I could get by until school started.

About the time I finished working my feet into my sneakers, TJ walked into my view, all dressed and none the worse for wear. "I hope that snake killed Packard," she said sincerely.

I looked straight into her eyes. They were angry and steeled, like the way I felt. "He wouldn't be messing with those snakes unless he really was immune. He won't die."

Wagging her tail hopefully, Bopeep came over to us. I leaned down and scratched behind her ears. She stretched her neck out, lowering her head, then half-closed her eyes.

"Maybe he'll leave us alone now," TJ said.

"Heck if he will. Besides, he said he's going to gut Jess."

TJ paled a bit. "You think he'll really try?"

"He's sick in the head. Crazy. He gutted a toy panda bear, and threw snakes at you. He'll try all right."

"We could get him arrested for throwing snakes at me."

"He'd be out before you'd know it. And he'd tell everybody you were skinny-dipping."

TJ made a face. "I don't care."

"I care."

TJ looked at me, her eyes softening a bit, kinda dopey looking. "You care?"

"Well, yeah. And there's no need for the Reverend and Mrs. Brubaker to have to listen to people talking about—"

"Oh, good grief." TJ rolled her eyes.

I took that to mean she agreed. Standing up, I said, "Let's go back now."

We started walking back up the river bank slope, toward the railroad tracks. Bopeep trotted ahead, scouting the territory, looking for scents she might have missed earlier.

I took TJ's hand in mine, and we walked down the tracks together.

"Mark? Packard said 'the Day of Doom.' What did he mean?"

"He said it once before, during the trap shoot. He wants to kill Jess on a certain day."

"What day? When?"

"I don't know."

"We've got to do something."

I already knew that. An idea had been forming in my head. "If I can find his still, Jess and the sheriff can arrest him. Then he'd be tried and convicted and sent to McAlister."

"McAlister?"

"The state pen's there."

"How're you going to find the still? Looking in the Bottomlands—if that's where it is? That's like looking for a needle in a haystack."

I considered that for a moment. It was a problem. The Bottomlands was too big and too dense for just one searcher—and that was my intention. I was worried about TJ, and Ferret, too, for that matter. It was my fight, not theirs. I didn't want them getting hurt. But how could I find Packard's still?

"You know how moonshine's made?" TJ asked.

I shook my head. "Not really. Do you?"

She shrugged her shoulders.

An idea came to me. "Mr. Hogan knows about making moonshine."

23

Afternoon sunlight roasted the earth and Hogan's Pool Hall looked a whole lot different in the light of day. Boards were tacked here and there around the squatty building to keep out the frequent, piercing Oklahoma storms. Torn, rotting tar paper curled lazily across the roof top, and red Oklahoma dirt served as paint for the walls. A fifty-foot-wide gravel carpet circled the dunghill of Bob White.

A single frog croacked a lonely bellow from the fish pond south of the building. Bopeep's ears perked up, her attention focused. The frog croaked again. Bopeep cocked her head curiously and set off in a trot, wagging her tail in a friendly fashion.

"It looks closed," TJ said.

There wasn't a car in sight. "Sometimes he doesn't open if there's no business."

We got to the front door, and TJ pushed against it, hard. "It's locked."

"Try knocking."

TJ pounded her fists against the door. The whole wall rattled violently, dust shaking loose and drifting downward. We waited, hearing nothing.

"Let's try the back," I said, leading the way.

We walked around the side of the building, avoiding the weeds that lined the building's foundation, and the debris trapped in its clutches. Out back stood a single car—Mr. Hogan's huge silver Cadillac. He'd had it modified with a special seat and built-up pedals to accommodate his unique frame. Empty beer cans spilled underneath the car. It had skidded to an awkward stop, its left wheel splintering a wooden crate, its bumper smashing two fifty-gallon oil drums that overflowed with uncollected, smelly trash.

On its side beside the back door lay an empty moonshine jug, the spitting image of those I'd seen poking out of Lafe Packard's gunny sack in the Bottomlands on Saturday.

TJ saw it too. "Moonshine."

I nodded.

"Packard couldn't be . . . " TJ looked anxiously at the half-open door, a shadow deepening in her eyes.

TJ was a curious girl, sometimes scared, sometimes bold— mostly around me, though not always. I couldn't figure her out, probably because she was a girl and guys weren't supposed to understand girls. I shook my head. "His pickup isn't here. He couldn't have gotten across the Bottomlands, then up here this quick." I pushed the door open, lodging it against the gravel.

Hogan's small storeroom was filled with heavy cardboard boxes, some stacked orderly, others empty and discarded haphazardly. A narrow path wound through the clutter toward the main room. A shaft of light from the late-afternoon sun penetrated the windowless storeroom. I led the way, TJ following, her hand touching my shoulder.

The interior door swung open into the dark pool room. The bar where Hogan served legal 3.2 beer was to our right and we stood beside it, looking out toward the pool tables, except it was too dark to see them. I smelled spilled beer and old cigarette smoke oozing from the woodwork, and listened.

I could hear breathing. Mine. TJ's. And someone else's.

"Mark?" TJ whispered.

"Shhhh. Someone's in the room."

TJ sucked in her breath, and shrank behind me.

I peered into the darkness, alert for any sign of movement, waiting as my eyes adjusted to the poor light, watching dark shapes turn into pool tables as if by magic. One dark shape on the floor beside a pool table remained a dark shape—about the size of a very large man, except it had short, stout arms and legs.

I glanced at TJ, then saw the light switch on the wall behind her. I flicked it up, and across the room, several lights blinked on, casting a dim, eerie glow over each pool table.

Hogan lay face down, his red-tufted head angled toward us, his arms outstretched beside his head, unmoving.

I ran over and knelt down beside him. "Mr. Hogan, Mr. Hogan." It was hard to see his face.

"Is he dead?" TJ asked, standing beside me, her voice a hoarse whisper.

I shook his shoulder gently and heard an answering snort in return. "No. Help me turn him over."

We rolled him onto his back. With his layers of fat, he was at least two hundred pounds. His eyes were closed and saliva had dribbled from the corner of his mouth, smearing across the side of his flushed face. A strong odor rose up from him. Moonshine.

"He's dead drunk," TJ said.

"Ummm . . . not drunk enough," Mr. Hogan said thickly, slurring his words. His right eye opened as far as a skinny slit, but he made no effort to move. "Can shtill feel the pain."

TJ looked at me questioningly. " 'The pain?' " she mouthed.

I shrugged my shoulders. "Mr. Hogan? Are you hurt?"

He raised a stubby arm and wheezed weakly. "Help me up, kid. Need to sit in a chair."

With TJ helping, we managed to get Mr. Hogan up on his feet. We waddled him toward the nearest table, his knees buckling.

He was more than a foot shorter than TJ, stout as the stump of a hundred-year old oak tree, except for his bulging belly. We sat him into a chair, his butt occupying only the front edge of the seat, sitting as little kids would sit.

He propped an elbow over the table and supported his head in his massive fist, his eyes half-open. "Jug's under the bar. Get it, kid."

He looked pretty drunk to me. I figured he'd pass out again if he had more to drink. "Mr. Hogan, I don't think you need to drink any more—"

He slapped his palm against the table, his face dark and angry. "What'd you know about what I need?" Then his expression softened, his will breaking. "Get it for me, Mark," he whispered. "Please?"

In his eyes, I saw a lot of sadness. Sadness and pain. Mr. Hogan must have been through a lot during his life, being a dwarf. I remembered laughing at dwarfs and midgets clowning in the circus. How would I feel if I were a dwarf?

"All right," I said. I went over to the bar, behind the makeshift platform of planks that Hogan stood on while he worked, and found the corked jug sitting on the floor. I grabbed it—surprised by its heavy weight—and a glass from underneath the counter, then returned to the table.

"Thanksh," Hogan mumbled, taking the jug, ignoring the glass. He twisted the cork out, and thrust his index finger through the jug handle, then raised the jug, supporting it on the back of his forearm. His Adam's apple bobbed slowly and a stream of moonshine trickled down his chin.

"I didn't know you drank."

Hogan lowered the jug, wiped his face with the back of his hand, and sighed, satisfied. "Whensh the pain's bad."

"The pain? What pain are you talking about, Mr. Hogan?"

Hogan's lips twisted in a loose, rubbery grimace. "Back and joints. Worse than arthur-itis. A hunnerd times worse. All—" He belched. "People like me got it. Born with it. Pain every fucking day of my life. Gets worse. Then we die."

He smiled, an unsteady, unsettling smile of resignation.

"Somedays ain't worth livin'. Might as well's be dead." He raised the jug to his lips again and took a big swig.

Mr. Hogan was a real nice man and I liked him, but I didn't like hearing talk like that. I didn't want to hear about real people dying. Especially people I liked.

TJ leaned forward. "Uncle Henry says it's wrong to drink."

Mr. Hogan turned and squinted at TJ. "Who'sh Uncle Henry?"

"Reverend Brubaker."

Recognition twitched across his ruddy broad face. "You 'is niece?"

"Yeah."

"You in here Saturday night?"

"Yeah."

He belched again, and the smell rolled across the table. "Reverend Brubaker don't know shit." Mr. Hogan grinned silly.

"He's a Baptist minister," TJ said, hostility edging her voice.

"So what? Know who invented bourbon? Fucking Baptist preacher. Invented Kentucky bourbon. Baptists are fucking hypocrites."

"You could take medicine to kill the pain," I said, changing the subject, trying to avoid an argument.

"Medicine?" Mr. Hogan laughed bitterly. "Doc tells me to take aspirin. I can take a whole bottle. Don't kill the pain in my back. Nothing does." He raised the jug again.

I waited until he'd finished his pull. "So you drink whiskey and beer?"

"Beer? Hell no. Beer's too weak. Go down to Texas once a month. Bring back the good stuff. Sheriff Adams knows. He don't care, long as I don't sell it."

"That jug's corn liquor. You didn't get it from Texas."

His half-hidden eyes were swollen and cloudy. "S'not corn liquor. S'sugar whiskey."

"Sugar whiskey?"

He tilted the jug, filling the glass half-full with a pale liquid. "Pure as a newborn baby's piss."

"What's the difference?"

"Corn tastes better . . . but sugar cooks faster and has more kick. Try it."

"Huh? No. I don't—"

He pushed the glass toward me. "It'll put hair on your chest."

I hesitated, remembering I didn't have a lot of hair on my chest. I'd never had a drink and now wasn't the time to start.

"Don't try it, Mark." TJ insisted, a stern look on her face, her voice ringing.

I glared at TJ. "Heck if you've got anything to say about it. I'll drink it if I want to."

TJ frowned, her cheeks flushing.

I took the glass and swirled the liquor into a miniature whirlpool. TJ shouldn't be ordering me around. But I really didn't want to drink the stuff. What I wanted was information. "Moonshine must be hard to make."

Mr. Hogan shook his head, and the loose skin on his face and cheeks jiggled. "Hell, it's easy. All you need for the still is a boiler and some copper tubing."

"And the sugar whiskey?"

"Lotsasugar . . . fresh water . . . little yeast."

"Yeah?" Fresh water? Where in the Bottomlands was there fresh water? An idea came to me.

He nodded. "Sometimes they'll use . . . berries for flavoring. Sometimes . . . snake venom."

I froze. Was he joshing me? "Snake venom?"

24

He grinned in a way that said he was telling the truth, as he knew it. "Some say it gives a special kick. But too much venom and your muscles get petrified, permanent-like."

I held the glass a little further away, then looked at TJ, wishing she'd tell me one more time not to drink it.

She didn't say anything, just sat there, holding her breath and staring wide-eyed at the glass I held in my hand.

Mr. Hogan burped. "Of course, if you're afraid, you don't have to drink it."

"I'm not afraid." For the first time I noticed some dark specks in the bottom of the glass. I held it up before his bleary eyes. "What's that stuff there?"

"Nothing. You're scared, aren't you?"

"Hell if I am." I raised the glass and tilted it slowly, until I felt the liquid lightly tickle my lips. I parted them slightly and felt a warm smoothness penetrate and pool between my teeth. A tingling began on my tongue. Something was happening. This wasn't going to be a pleasant experience.

Over the top edge of the glass, my eyes slid to TJ again. "I told you so" was already written on her face. No matter how bad it was, I'd never let her know. I let it trickle over the back of my mouth and swallowed.

A fireball flashed in my throat, racing downward. Involuntarily, my stomach clamped shut against the coming onslaught and my esophagus rippled upward, carrying the liquid lava back upstairs. Then, everything stopped working. The burning liquid plunged into my stomach.

I wanted to jump up and down, and cough and gag. But I couldn't. I couldn't even breathe. The fire burned white-hot, shutting down my insides. The room revolved in slow motion.

I lowered the glass, and noticed TJ looking at me expectantly. I forced a stupid grin, wondering if I'd ever be able to take another breath. Mr. Hogan was saying something, except I couldn't hear what it was. He stopped talking, his blubbery lips fluttering in a strange, silent laugh.

Suddenly, my muscles returned to life and I sucked air into my lungs trying to cool the raging fire in my chest. "It's good," I croaked, fighting a sudden urge to throw up.

"S'a hunnerd and fifty proof." Mr. Hogan pulled the glass from my hand. "Let that be the last drink you ever take. You don't need it, like me."

I nodded and stood up, slowly, my muscles stiff and wooden. I worried about the snake venom. "We better be going. You be all right, Mr. Hogan?"

"Yeah. Won't be opening today. Don't get many customers no more. Don't know why I bought this business, nohow."

TJ scraped her chair as she stood. "Are you buying that moonshine from an old man named Packard?"

Mr. Hogan's head shot up, an anxious look in his eyes. "Better forget you ever heard that name. You might be too nosy for your own good."

TJ put her hands on her hips. "You are, aren't you?"

"Shut up, TJ," I said, grabbing her arm and pulling her toward the open storeroom door.

She stumbled a couple of steps, then regained her balance and jerked her arm away. "Let me go!"

I didn't turn around, urgently needing fresh air. "Suit yourself."

I stumbled through the storeroom clutter and burst outside into the dazzling late-afternoon sun. My insides were rolling that moonshine around, trying to cool it off. I leaned against the building, wanting to gag and throw up.

TJ came out, one eye closed against the sun, squinting out the other. She put her hand on my shoulder, genuine concern on her face. "You all right?"

"Heck, yes," I said, straightening up. In my head, something stabbed me with a miniature sword. "Where's Bopeep?"

She turned and looked at the fish pond. "I see her." She put her little fingers in the corners of her mouth.

"No. Don't whistle—"

The shrill shriek silenced all the natural sounds of man and nature except for the sword in my head that swished and slashed this way and that.

"Here she comes," TJ said.

"Great."

"Where to now?" she asked.

My stomach had settled, but my head was killing me. "I better talk to Jess."

We headed toward the courthouse. Along the way, we got to the street that ran past my house and I sent Bopeep home. She trotted reluctantly down the street, checking ever so often to see if I'd changed my mind.

When we got to Main Street, I was feeling better. My headache was gone and my muscles were slippery as a runny nose. I wasn't going to die from the snake venom and I felt like dancing. But TJ and I had work to do.

The old men who'd been sitting in front of Tucker's store had wandered home, and Mr. Tucker was sweeping his wooden porch with a broom. He didn't look up.

I decided not to call out to him, figuring he was probably feeling bad about Sam. I was feeling great.

It was about five o'clock. Most of the county offices had closed and people gone home by now. I wasn't sure if Jess would still be here, or just Lucy—she always worked the evening shift from four until midnight.

We walked up the wide and broad front courthouse steps

and through the open double-wide doors. High overhead, a huge fan drooped ten-foot blades that turned like a tired mule. The courthouse wasn't air-conditioned, but its stone construction and marble floors sucked a coolness from the earth's depths.

Downstairs, we walked through a musty confined hallway, past the rest rooms and the reinforced metal door that led to the jail cells. "COUNTY SHERIFF" was stenciled on the upper glass part of the next door.

Inside, sitting at a desk cluttered with magazines, two phones, and an old Motorola base-station radio was a plump blonde lady about thirty-five years old. Lucy was wearing a white dress with big blue and pink flowers on it, and talking on the phone. Her desk held stacks of the latest movie magazines, and she knew the Hollywood gossip as well as the goings-on in Bob White.

I didn't see Jess. We walked in. Lucy glanced up, then spoke into the phone, "Gotta go, call you back."

"Hi, Lucy," I said, closing the door behind me.

"Hi, Mark." Lucy smiled sweetly. She wore the reddest lipstick and had the blackest eyebrows in Bob White. High cheekbones rose near her blue eyes, giving them a permanent crinkly, smiling look. She eyed TJ. "You the Brubakers' niece?"

"That's me."

"Fourteen and spending the rest of the summer here?"

"That's me."

"Hmmm." Lucy's curiosity framed her face. "How come you're up here and not back in Louisiana?"

TJ shrugged.

"You don't talk much, do you?" Lucy said, disappointment filling her voice.

"Not me."

The sheriff's door was open but I couldn't see inside from my angle. "Is Jess here?"

Lucy shook her head. "He left already. Said he had plans."

I hesitated, trying to think what to do next. I could warn

Jess later, but I couldn't help wondering what Packard had against Jess. Jess might not even tell me. He'd probably get mad again and order me to stay away from Packard. Talking to Jess was likely to be a waste of time. But talking to Lucy might help. The gossip queen of Bob White, Oklahoma.

"Lucy, you know who Lafe Packard is?"

"Packard? Yeah. He's scum. Why?"

"Yesterday, at the range, well . . . he hates Jess."

"I expect he hates most folks."

"Why does he hate Jess?"

She picked up a magazine and began thumbing through it. "I don't know nothing."

"What don't you know?"

She turned a page. "I don't know nothing about Jess and Packard."

"Lucy, I know you know something."

"Not me."

"If you do know something, you've got to tell us."

She glanced at TJ and smirked. "I'm minding my own business. Y'all better be running along."

I leaned across her desk, pleading. "But Lucy . . . " I burped unexpectedly, before I even knew it was coming.

She turned toward me, getting a good whiff of my accident. Recoiling, her eyes widened. "Why, Mark Stoddard! Have you been drinking?" she whispered.

"Damn it, Lucy! I think Packard wants to kill Jess!"

Lucy's mouth fell open.

"What's going on out here?" Sheriff Adams walked out of his office, a sweat-stained cowboy hat atop a lanky form wearing a blue workshirt, faded jeans, and scuffed boots. Except for the badge over his left breast, you wouldn't know he was anything but a common ranch hand.

I calmed down, not wanting the sheriff to find out about TJ skinny-dipping. "I was wondering about Lafe Packard."

"Packard?" Behind his handlebar mustache, Sheriff Adams spat the word out. "Heard you hog-tied his ass at the trap shoot. What're you wanting to know about him for?"

"I think he's the bootlegger."

"Shit. Of course he's the bootlegger."

"You can't arrest him, can you?"

"Not yet, but as soon as we find his still, we'll put him away for a long time."

"There at the range, sir, he seemed real mad about something."

"He's an ex-con, meaner than a bad-tempered bull. Better stay away from him."

"I think he wants to kill Jess."

"That's crazy. Nobody wants to kill Jess."

"He said something about his boy."

Sheriff Adams's eyes narrowed. "His boy? What'd Packard say?"

"Something about his boy suffering. Like it was Jess's fault."

"Jess never done nothing what didn't need doing. You got your riggin' twisted. Packard ain't going to kill nobody."

"Sir, I need to know—"

He jammed a crooked finger at me. "Mark, your brother can take care of himself. Settle down."

"Yes, sir."

He glanced to my right. "Who's your pretty little friend?"

"This is TJ. She's from Baton Rouge."

TJ didn't say anything.

He nodded. "Oh, yeah. Staying with Reverend Brubaker. You ever ride a horse?"

"I never did."

"No? You look like you'd sit a horse good in a barrel race." He winked at her.

TJ grinned. "Thanks."

The sheriff reached up, lifted his hat, exposing a dry-weathered forehead creased with deep lines, then smoothed his thinning salt-and-pepper hair. "Been a long day and I got horses and cows to look after. You git on home and quit your worrying."

Back outside, we paused on the front steps. Inside my stomach, frustration and worry boiled. "Damn it. The sheriff didn't pay any attention to us."

"You'd look right pretty sitting a horse," TJ said, mocking the sheriff.

"They expect us to act like adults, while they're still treating us like kids."

"Think Lucy will blab that you were drinking?"

"It'll be all over town inside of an hour. Jess will shit a brick when he finds out."

"Now what?" TJ asked.

I sighed. "I don't know."

"Well, think about it. I'm going to the bathroom." TJ turned and went back into the courthouse. I heard her sneakers squeaking on the marble stairs leading down to the lower level.

I sat down on the front steps and looked at Tucker's store. People were doing their last-minute shopping for supper. I remembered Jess and I were supposed to be at Joyce's at six.

Lucy knew something. Why wouldn't she tell? Then I remembered what she'd said. The "not me" and "minding my own business." She'd been mimicking things TJ had said.

TJ hadn't told Lucy why she was spending the summer here and Lucy was getting even. TJ could have easily made up a good story for Lucy's benefit. Now we'd never find out from Lucy.

Minutes passed. I glanced over my shoulder, then stood up impatiently. What was keeping TJ? Girls and bathrooms! Then TJ's sneakers squealed coming up the basement stairs.

She ran up to me, her chest jiggling excitedly. "I found out why Packard hates Jess," she whispered. "Lucy told me."

25

I stood there, openmouthed.

"Packard and his son were involved in a car theft ring a few years ago. Jess arrested them and they were sent to McAlister State Penitentiary. The son was killed last year in a prison fight. Got himself beaten to death. Packard got released and now—"

"He blames Jess for his son's death." It all made sense.

"Mark, the Day of Doom is—"

"The day his son died." I looked hard at TJ. "When last year was Packard's son killed?"

She shook her head. "Lucy didn't know. She said it was about a year ago. Said she wasn't sure she could find out."

"A year ago? The Day of Doom could be tomorrow."

TJ and I started home, talking about Packard and Jess. Now we knew why Packard wanted to kill Jess. He had to be put away, that was all there was to it. And that meant I had to find his still. I had to find it before the Day of Doom, before the anniversary of his son's death, whenever that was.

Finally, I got around to wondering how TJ had gotten Lucy to talk. "I thought Lucy was mad at you for not telling her why you were spending the summer here."

"Yeah. I offered to tell her why. As a trade."

"You told her about your folks? Everything?"

TJ shook her head. "Just that my parents were getting a divorce and I was staying here until it was settled. She promised not to tell anyone. She won't, will she?"

"Lucy's never kept a promise in her life. She'll call up her close friends, then tell them on the condition that they promise not to tell anyone. Then they'll call up their friends, making them promise not to tell anyone. The whole town will know before bedtime."

TJ was silent for a while. "It's okay. I guess I knew, deep down inside, that she'd tell. I don't care."

She was lying. She did care. She'd made a real sacrifice for me. I took her hand and squeezed it.

TJ looked up and smiled, then squeezed my hand back.

The Brubakers' house was down the street. Near the street, Mrs. Brubaker held a garden hose, spraying her marigolds and petunias. She had on her wide-brimmed floppy hat and wore loose, faded blue jeans and a white blouse.

I was suddenly conscious of holding TJ's hand and having Mrs. Brubaker see us, so I let go.

Except TJ didn't let go. "Hi, Aunt Josephine," she called, waving her free hand.

Mrs. Brubaker turned and paused, looking at us curiously, unaware the hose was sprinkling the street. "Hi."

"Evening, Mrs. Brubaker," I said, feeling trapped, waving my left hand awkwardly.

She smiled in a way that embarrassed me, then turned back to her spraying again, showering the flower beds vigorously.

TJ and I walked around to the driveway, avoiding the spraying, then to the front door.

"You can eat with us, if you like," TJ said, her eyes dancing proudly. She still held my hand, now by the fingers.

"I can't. Joyce is expecting me and Jess for dinner tonight."

"Oh," TJ said, not trying to hide the disappointment in her face. "Well, then I guess I'll see you tomorrow. We're going to get an early start, right?"

I knew what she was thinking but I asked anyway. "Early start?"

She glanced at Mrs. Brubaker and lowered her voice to a whisper. "Yeah, looking for Packard's still. Maybe Ferret's ankle will be—"

"You're not going."

TJ's face froze, a look of incredulity turning it into a mask.

"And neither is Ferret. I'm going alone."

TJ leaned forward, whispering insistently, "I am too going. You need me."

"I don't need anybody. It's too dangerous for girls."

TJ's face quivered. Her face turned red and she struggled to control herself. But she couldn't hold it back and she cussed me right out loud. "Damn you, Mark Stoddard!"

She jerked her hand away, and stormed into the house, slamming the screen door behind her.

I'd done the right thing but that didn't make it any easier, knowing I'd hurt TJ, especially after she'd made that trade with Lucy.

I turned to leave. Mrs. Brubaker was watching me. She must have seen and heard nearly everything. I flushed, embarrassed that she'd seen TJ and me holding hands, and then having a fight. I jumped off the porch and started down the driveway toward home.

"Mark?" She had a worried look across her brow.

Apprehensive, I stopped. "Yes, ma'am?"

"Come here a second, please."

I worked my hands, reluctant to talk about girl stuff with Mrs. Brubaker. But I made myself walk toward her. I stopped a few paces from her, not wanting to get so close she could smell my breath.

"Mark, you and TJ have been spending lots of time together."

I didn't want to lie to Mrs. Brubaker, but I figured it was best to leave things a little unclear. "Some."

"All afternoon?"

"I guess so."

She was silent for a while, as if thinking hard about what to say next. "Why is she mad at you?"

"I told her I'd be busy tomorrow. Doing other things."

Mrs. Brubaker looked relieved. "I see. What did you do today?"

"Nothing much. She came over after the reverend left and then we just goofed off."

"Henry was at your house today?" Mrs. Brubaker's voice sounded shaky.

"Yeah, he came by while I was mowing the yard. Asked about you. Then he left and TJ showed up."

"Oh."

I glanced at the sun, thinking I had to leave to get to Joyce's on time. I thought about the reverend, and how Mrs. Brubaker seemed scared of him.

Mrs. Brubaker walked toward me, directing the spray downward, splattering the flower bed soil.

I backed up to let her go by, then stepped across the hose. "Your flowers are right pretty, Mrs. Brubaker," I offered, trying to change the subject.

She didn't take notice of my comment. "You know TJ's upset about her folks getting a divorce?"

I nodded. "That'd be hard on anybody."

"Well, right now she's real . . . vulnerable."

"Vulnerable?" I looked at her, wondering what she meant.

"She feels guilty about her folks. Somehow responsible."

"Why would she feel guilty? It's not her fault."

"People just do, when things like this happen. She needs time to sort out her feelings. You understand what I'm telling you?" She twisted the nozzle, turning the water off.

I didn't answer. I must have looked pretty confused because I was.

"Right now she's liable to do some . . . extreme things."

An image of TJ—standing on the trestle, taking her clothes off, and the train bearing down on her—flashed through my mind. That was as extreme as you could get. "Yes, ma'am."

"Things she might regret later."

I remembered hugging and kissing TJ, her bare flesh dripping wet, and noticing her nakedness.

"That's what I meant about her being vulnerable." Mrs. Brubaker looked deep into my eyes.

I nodded sagely. "Yes, ma'am."

"She needs understanding and caring."

"Yes, ma'am."

"You're growing up, Mark. Getting older. More mature. And it's important you be responsible. Can I trust you to do the right thing?"

I wondered how I could be responsible for TJ. She did as she damn well pleased. I remembered that she wouldn't get off the trestle when I'd told her to and that she'd jerked her hand away from me at Hogan's. "Yes, ma'am."

Mrs. Brubaker looked away, far down Ash Street, as if she could see all the way to the Bottomlands. "A woman needs a responsible man."

I looked also, but there was nothing in particular to see, just houses and cottonwood trees. A moment of silence passed. The conversation seemed over. I started to edge away.

"Things aren't always black or white," she said, her voice as distant as her face looked.

I wasn't sure she was even talking to me, but I answered her anyway. "Yes, ma'am," I said, smiling uncertainly.

Mrs. Brubaker glanced sharply at me, then turned and walked toward the house, dragging the hose with her.

I started down the street. What she'd said—about things not always being black or white—stayed with me. I wondered why she'd said that. I knew what the words meant, but I had no idea if she was referring to me, or TJ, or somebody else.

26

At home, the kitchen clock said six-twenty. Jess must have already gone to Joyce's. Hurriedly, I dished up some chow and ran fresh water for Bopeep, scratched her ears and told her I was sorry I couldn't play right now, then set off at a run for Joyce's house, six blocks away.

As I ran, I thought about tomorrow, and about finding Packard's still. I'd tell the sheriff—no, I'd tell Jess so he'd get the credit. Jess would arrest Packard and send him back to the pen. Then Jess would shake my hand, put his arm around my shoulders, and things would be perfect again.

No, it could never be perfect again.

Things were changing. Again. Joyce had said she was going to marry Jess. If they got married, she'd move in with us.

Maybe they wouldn't want me to live with them.

But they couldn't kick me out, at least not until after I got out of high school.

Jess treated me like I was a little kid. Jess would say I was in the way. Maybe Joyce would start treating me like I was a little kid, too. Maybe she was just acting nice to me to get on my good side.

She'd better not treat me like she was my mom!

I decided I didn't want them getting married. It would be their family, and I'd be an outsider. Yesterday, I'd thought going to dinner at Joyce's was a great idea. Now I wasn't so sure.

I arrived at the Weavers' house, hot, sweaty, out of breath, dying of thirst, and half angry.

Joyce Weaver lived with her mom in a house smaller than ours. White clapboard siding, a roof like a book open face down. No garage and no porch—just two small concrete steps before a screen door. Jess's black and white police Fury was parked in front, the right front wheel straddling the depression that separated the street from the Weavers' yard. Parked on the grass next to the side of the house was Mrs. Weaver's rattle-trap '51 Ford. It leaned toward the driver's side as if one of the springs had cracked.

In the west, the sun had already set and twilight hung over us like time standing still. The living-room lights were on and a few early-evening June bugs had attached themselves to the screen door like large brown buttons. A TV set blared and, beyond the screen, gray images of a cowboy show flickered. Scattered around the living room were a small sofa, some easy chairs, and two table lamps.

I didn't see Jess or Joyce. I knocked on the door frame.

A moment later, Joyce came into the living room followed by Jess. My attention focused on Joyce. She wore tight yellow shorts and a white blouse with blue and yellow daisies, and she'd tied the shirt-tails together in front so that it looked like bunny ears drooping over her bare midriff. She had a nice stomach.

But what really caught my eye was the way she jiggled when she walked. My eyes fastened on her nipples, thrusting against the cloth. Lately, it seemed that I was getting a lot of experience on breasts. I decided Joyce couldn't be wearing anything underneath her blouse.

"Hi, Mark," she said, smiling and pushing the screen door part-way open, waiting for me to move back so she could open it all the way. "Mind the bugs."

Bugs? I imagined Joyce's nipples, as big and as brown as June bugs, and all my anger went away. I couldn't be mad at anyone with such a nice smile and such interesting breasts. I jumped down off the step and grinned shyly. "Hi," I answered.

She opened the door just enough so I could squeeze past her into the living room.

I enjoyed that. The smell of her perfume reminded me of the taste of honeysuckle flowers, plucked with the tips sucked and chewed. "Sorry I'm late."

"That's all right, honey," she said. "I was just getting ready to put supper on the table."

Wearing boots, jeans, and a T-shirt, Jess had his feet planted wide apart, hands on his hips, scowling. He looked me up and down. "You're a mess."

Joyce waved toward the back room she'd come out of earlier. "You can wash up at the kitchen sink."

I was still breathing hard so I didn't say anything to Jess, just followed Joyce into the kitchen.

"Be right back," Jess said. I heard him walking down the hall to the bathroom, leaving Joyce and me alone.

She put a towel beside the sink and turned on the faucet for me. "About an hour ago, I heard a silly rumor."

I soaped my hands and washed them under the kitchen sink faucet. "Yeah?"

"Oh, just something about drinking and the younger brother of a certain deputy sheriff."

I wondered if Jess had heard. He was bound to hear eventually. "That's a pretty silly rumor, all right."

"When I was at Tucker's today, I noticed he'd got in some rum-flavored jawbreakers."

I hesitated a moment, thinking about what she'd said.

She winked at me.

Then it sunk in. I grinned. "Yeah. They're real good. Mighty strong flavoring, though. The taste hangs with you a long time."

She grinned, then went over to the stove, picked up a large

spoon and stirred a pan of white cream gravy. Sizzling in a skillet were three large chicken-fried steaks, and ummm-good, batter-fried okra chunks were keeping warm in another pan. A cloud of stream rose up from corn ears tossing in boiling water.

"Wow," I said, my mouth watering.

"And I picked up a nice bone at Tucker's today for Bopeep." She carried the corn to the kitchen table and put an ear on each plate.

I glanced around, getting familiar with my surroundings. Everything was spotless and either put away or situated in just the right places. A bright blue, brand-new-looking cloth covered the kitchen table, and it was set with three plates, each with knives and spoons and forks and paper napkins arranged etiquette-like. Daisies spilled merrily out of a skinny glass vase and she'd set out two tall blue candles.

Noticing there were only three plates, I asked, "Where's your mom?"

"Tonight's her league bowling night. She and her buddies are eating at the bowling alley."

Jess reentered the kitchen, scraped a chair from under the table, and sat down. "Let's eat."

Joyce's dinner was great and I drank a gallon of lemonade. Jess's sour attitude vanished and he was laughing and joking the way I remembered when he was in high school. Joyce's chest swelled up even more when Jess told her he couldn't remember having such good food.

After supper, I plopped down on the living room sofa to watch TV. "Cheyenne" with Clint Walker was on. A few minutes later, Jess came in. He studied me for a while, then flicked the TV off and pulled a straight chair up and sat down. "I hear you been talking to Sheriff Adams."

"I was looking for you."

"You was asking about Packard. I told you to stay away from him." Anger radiated from Jess's face, his voice sharp. "You got no call to be thinking about him."

"He . . . plans to kill you, Jess."

Jess blinked. "Where'd you hear a fool thing like that?"

I'd heard it today, from Packard himself, but I didn't want to have to explain about TJ being nude, and about the fight with Packard. Jess would really get mad then, and probably tell Reverend Brubaker. "At the trap shoot, he said he'd gut you."

Jess scoffed, waving his hand loosely. "He was trying to scare you."

He wasn't taking this seriously enough. "I know about his boy."

Jess froze, his eyes boring into me.

"I know about the beating. I know about McAlister."

Jess's eyes narrowed. "What exactly do you know?"

"I know his boy died from getting beat up in prison, and Packard is bent on revenge."

Jess's lips seemed white and bloodless. "I arrested him and his boy, and the judge sent them to prison. That was the end of it."

I got a strange feeling. Like there was something more I didn't know. Something Jess knew and wasn't saying. "How come Packard's boy got killed? What happened in prison?"

"Stole something from another con, so I heard."

"Then how can Packard blame you?"

"He's crazy. How would I know? You haven't seen him, have you?"

The lie slipped off my tongue easy as spit. "No. I haven't seen him. But I could help you find him. I—"

Jess laughed, his voice loud, derisive. "Kid, you couldn't find a puddle under an unpapered dog. So stay the hell away from him."

"I'm not a kid! And quit telling me what to do."

"As long as you're at home, I'm telling you what to do."

"Maybe I'll be leaving as soon as I can."

"You'll be leaving home when it's time. And don't you be bothering Sheriff Adams with fool talk." He paused, then let his next words trickle out. "People will be thinking I'm scared of Packard."

The way he said that . . . stopped me. As if something deep inside him snuck out, before he even realized it. I wondered if Jess *was* afraid of Packard.

Joyce came in, drying her hands on a towel, looking first at Jess, then me, then back to Jess, a worried expression on her face. She smiled uneasily, then put a cheery note in her voice. "Hey, what's going on in here, guys?"

"Stupid kid," Jess growled. He sounded embarrassed.

"Oh, Jess," Joyce said. "He's fifteen, and he's growing up. The whole town thinks he's a hero for outshooting Packard." She leaned down and hugged me.

Her breasts pressed against the back of my neck and the smell of honeysuckle enveloped me. Joyce was always doing something to make me aware of her breasts. I wondered if she was using me. I felt like a little kid.

"Poor thing," Joyce said. "He's lost his mom and dad. We all need to be nicer—"

I exploded, bursting upright, jerking her arms away from me, whirling. "Shut up! Leave me alone."

Joyce looked shocked and hurt.

I felt a hand grab my shoulder. I twisted around, defensive, fists clenched.

27

Jess's eyes glinted with anger, as mad as I'd ever seen him, his fingers tightening on my shoulder, hurting me. "What the hell's got into you? You apologize to Joyce, you hear me?"

The whole world closed in on me. I was suffocating. I had to get away . . . away from Jess . . . away from Joyce . . . away from people telling me what to do.

I threw my left arm up, breaking Jess's grip, then fired my right fist into his stomach, as hard as I could, catching him unexpectedly.

Jess's air burst from his lungs and he doubled over, gasping.

I turned away, feeling the room spinning. Vaguely, I sensed Joyce moving toward Jess, crying out his name. I pushed past her, then stumbled out the front door into the darkness. The steps fell away from my feet, and I sprawled onto the baked-hard earth. Coarse, dried grass scratched my cheek, and I heard the screen door bang closed behind me. My fingernails clawed the ground, and I staggered upright. I ran down the darkening street, not crying, holding my emotions inside.

I walked aimlessly, thinking and not thinking, not figuring anything out. Just feeling alone. Truly alone.

Hours later, I found myself approaching our house. Jess's Fury wasn't outside, so I knew he wasn't home. When I got close enough, Bopeep emerged from the shadows of our porch, recognizing me, wagging her tail. Ignoring her, I walked into the house, into my bedroom, and closed the door. I fell into bed, tossing and turning for an hour before dozing off.

A dream came. Of craggy mountains and a mirrored lake and the smell of fresh pines filling the cool air. A blanket was spread on the ground and covered with all kinds of food that Mom was taking from a huge picnic basket. Dad had just come up from the lake, a stringer of lake trout in one hand, his rod in the other. We were all laughing about something. Laughing 'cause we were happy. It was the most wonderful dream I ever had.

I got up early the next morning, knowing it might be a long day. Jess's door was closed, so I knew he was sleeping, but I didn't know if Joyce was with him. Or some other girl, I hoped.

I was mad at Jess and he had to be mad at me, but it didn't change what had to be done. Packard had to be put away. Or else he might kill Jess.

I filled my canteen with water, slapped together a peanut butter and jelly sandwich for lunch, then stuffed everything into an old Army knapsack that Dad had given me. I decided not to take Bopeep. She wouldn't stay close and I'd be forever worried about her getting into trouble. After feeding her, I set out toward Six Mile Creek.

Lafe Packard lived somewhere in the Bottomlands, and I knew of only two sources of fresh water that filtered through those woods. The Clear Boggy River was one, except the water really wasn't all that clean, and it'd probably already been searched by Jess or the sheriff. The other source was Six Mile Creek. Fed by an underground stream, the water at least started out pure, and stayed pretty clear as it trickled southward through the Bottomlands, eventually emptying into the Clear Boggy. By Packard's standards, it was probably clean enough for making moonshine.

Ferret and I had been down Six Mile many a time, hunting

for crawdads and such. But once we'd got into the Bottomlands, we'd veered off on some wild goose chase, so I'd never actually followed the creek all the way to the Clear Boggy.

Of course, it was possible that Packard's moonshine still wasn't in the Bottomlands, but somewhere near Six Mile Creek, so I figured I'd best explore all of Six Mile that was south of Bob White. The creek was maybe ten feet across and only three to four feet deep, meandering mostly due south on its short journey, and creeping under fences and through culverts that farmers had laid down and built roads over.

I moved alongside it at a good pace, slowing down to inspect clusters of trees that might offer Packard enough concealment for a still and enough dead wood to feed the fire under the boiler. Between Bob White and the Bottomlands, only three places offered a possible hiding place for a still and none of them showed any signs of burned wood, or footprints, or recent human goings-on.

Thirty minutes after I'd started, I trudged across a field of fenced stubble owned by the Johnsons. A quarter-mile to the left was the county road that Ferret, TJ, and I had come up after running into Packard on Saturday. Further east was the jungle of grapevines where we'd smoked cigars and swung across the ditch. Straight ahead lay the dense swampy forest known as the Bottomlands.

It looked altogether different from when I'd seen it before. A mysterious aura, dark and ominous, oozed from its depths. Standing in the open stubble field, I felt exposed, as if the forest itself were watching me.

I walked along the creek until I got within thirty yards of the woods, then turned sharply left and ran to a loose section of the wire fencing in the Johnson's property. I slipped through the strands easily and ducked into the woods, feeling an immediate increase in humidity. I paused, listening and glancing around. Patches of sunlight streamed down through holes in the leafy canopy, washing out all the forest colors, imparting a camouflaging effect to everything. The sounds of birds singing and other forest noises filtered through the trees, and told me that everything was okay.

I moved quietly through the trees until I got back to Six Mile. The trees didn't seem any denser next to the creek than anywhere else, making me wonder how the forest kept its growth, how every tree somehow found enough water to sustain its life, and why the land was so marshy.

I followed the creek southward, looking for footprints or freshly broken branches and logs. Along the way I checked out every clearing and cluster of trees near the creek that offered a hiding place. It was slow going.

By mid-morning, I decided to eat my sandwich, and straddled a fallen tree, shucking my knapsack. The peanut butter sandwich was hot and sticky, but the first bite recharged my energy. I devoured the whole thing, chugging half my water to wash it down. Licking jelly trails that had run between my fingers, I listened to the water splashing and trickling on its journey toward the Clear Boggy. Hearing the stream and . . . nothing else. No birds singing. No insects chirping.

The hair on the back of my neck rose.

I slipped off the log and crouched down, listening hard. After a moment, I heard a sound, a voice coming from off to the left away from the creek. Indistinguishable. No more than a few words somehow filtering through the trees.

I replaced my canteen, slung my knapsack on, and started toward the sound, moving from tree to tree, careful where I placed each foot. Ahead, the woods thinned, opening into a clearing. Another sound came, again indistinguishable, long and drawn out. Like someone was hurt and moaning.

Keeping low, I crept forward to the edge of the clearing, concealing myself behind a thick bush. The clearing was perhaps forty yards wide and mostly circular. Directly across, on the far side of the clearing, was a tent about the size of a small shed. Opened toward the right, a large rectangular flap extended horizontally, supported by two poles, covering the entrance to the tent.

Near the tent, a doughnut of stones encircled a pile of ashes. The grounds were neat and orderly, a sharp contrast from what I'd come to expect from Packard. I didn't see any sign of a still. One thing for sure, this wasn't Packard's camp.

The side of the tent moved as if someone inside had jostled against it. I heard voices, and realized there was more than one person inside.

From my vantage point, I couldn't see inside the tent. I backed further into the woods, merging with the shadows, then circled around the clearing until the opening became visible. Inside, I could see the legs of two people intertwined. They were . . .

I felt my face turning red. It was a man and a woman, naked, making love.

28

They were mostly hidden in the back of the tent—I couldn't see their faces—but I was sure that muscular body belonged to Tarzan.

The woman's body was unfamiliar, but of course I wasn't familiar with any female's body, except TJ's.

Half hidden beneath Tarzan's body, the woman's arms encircled his waist, pulling him to her. Her legs rose rhythmically against his thighs, and he strained against her body. I'd seen dogs and cattle doing it before, piggyback style, but this was different, and fascinating. All the guys had talked about sex, but seeing it firsthand gave me a totally different understanding of what it was all about.

Inside the tent, the activity heated up, and Tarzan's butt began rising and falling, as if he was pummeling someone with his hips. I held my breath, staring at the furious action. Sex sure made people do some pretty ridiculous things with their bodies.

If Ferret had been with me, we would have looked at each other, then busted out laughing.

Mrs. Brubaker had said TJ was vulnerable. Had she wanted to make love to me down at the trestle? I'd heard guys talking big, and I'd talked big too. But now, thinking about TJ, it made sense that if you made love to someone, then you ought to be in love with them.

Inside the tent, the two people froze. Then the man pulled back, his head moving down the woman's body, kissing her breasts, then her stomach. His golden hair hung over his face. It definitely was Tarzan.

That talk—back in town—had been wrong. Ferret was wrong, Reverend Brubaker was wrong, the congregation was wrong, the old men in front of Tucker's—all of them were wrong about Tarzan—or whatever his name was. He wasn't queer. Of course, folks didn't know that Tarzan had a woman traveling with him. All they knew was he carried a purse and was different from everyone else.

All of a sudden, I felt real embarrassed watching Tarzan and his woman. Seemed like a personal, private matter. Nobody's business, especially not mine.

I turned and crept stealthily through the trees for thirty yards before straightening up. Relaxing, I set out toward Six Mile Creek again, and stepped right onto a dry branch hidden beneath some leaves. In the silence, the crack echoed as loud as a gunshot. I froze, turning to see if Tarzan had heard, but I couldn't see the tent. Carefully, I hurried away, not waiting to see if Tarzan was coming.

A half-hour later, sweat was pouring off me. The woods were sultry, with no breeze able to penetrate to ground level. I drank the last of my canteen water. If I had to, I'd refill it from Six Mile Creek. The Bottomlands became increasingly marshy, sucking at my tennis shoes, and the creek's banks were dense with undergrowth, at times forcing me to veer away and then cut back to it after I'd gotten around the obstacles.

I hadn't seen any human signs since I'd left Tarzan and his woman. I wasn't sure how much further Six Mile would go before it dumped into the Clear Boggy. At this slow pace, I'd be at least another hour following the creek. If I didn't find the still, then I planned to work my way down the Clear Boggy, looking for footprints or other signs of Packard.

Another dense thicket blocked the sides of the creek, obscuring the view downstream. Sighing at the prospect of another long side trip, I turned east again, following the edge of the thicket in a wide circle.

These hundred-yard jaunts out and back again were taking too much time. All the time I'd been searching, I'd kept my eyes peeled. Packard was sneaky, and even though he'd said he was going to gut Jess, and then me, I wasn't so sure he hadn't changed his mind after yesterday. Maybe he was sick from the snake bite, and holed up somewhere.

I got around the thicket, turning west again. I walked at least a hundred and fifty yards when I realized I was on the far side of the thicket, circling to the north. Six Mile Creek had disappeared.

The thicket was still on my right. Had I gotten turned around? I checked a couple of trees and found some sage-green moss growing on the north side, confirming I'd gone west and was now circling back toward the north. Where was Six Mile Creek?

I looked closer at the thicket. Its bushes were eight to ten feet high and densely packed with small, dark-green leaves with sharp, stickery edges, and tiny red berries that looked poisonous. A growing suspicion told me there was something hidden behind it.

There didn't appear to be a way into it unless I hacked through it, and I didn't even have a knife on me. Six Mile was somewhere behind that thicket. And maybe nothing else was, but I'd check it out and know one way or the other.

I circled back the way I'd come, looking for an opening. Soon, I found a pile of dead brush I hadn't paid attention to before, all of it lying with its limbs reaching upward. It had been stacked.

I pulled the nearest branch away. The base had a diagonal slice across it. Carefully, I removed another branch and found a similar cut. Packard's still had to be hidden in the thicket. I tried to suppress my excitement. I had to be quiet, in case Packard was inside right now.

I pulled the last branch away, and saw a small passage tunneling through the thicket. On the ground, leading into the thicket, was a heel print. I hunkered down and crept forward, taking care not to snag my knapsack. I moved slowly, quietly.

A few feet further led me to an opening on the interior side of the thicket. Cautiously, I peered out. Inside the thicket were more trees, but not as dense. And beyond the trees, there appeared to be a wide clearing.

I moved forward, gliding from tree to tree, staying behind cover. The clearing opened before me, a wide expanse of grass surrounding a small pond. I could see Six Mile Creek trickling into it on the far side. I realized that if Six Mile emptied into the Clear Boggy, then it flowed out of the pond, going underground again for some distance. But here was the water supply that Packard needed for making moonshine.

On the other side of the clearing, through some trees, a torn, patchwork tent sagged halfway to the ground. My eyes quickly scanned the shabby dwelling. It looked like something Packard would live in. Something shiny caught my eye. Further back in the woods was a small boiler with copper tubing that coiled upward, then turned down into a jug. I'd found the still.

In front of the tent, something moved. Lafe Packard squatted under his John Deere cap, rocking on his heels, looking straight at me.

29

Shit! I ducked. A moment ago, he hadn't been there. Or I hadn't seen him.

"No use 'n hiding, Mark Stoddard," he called. "Knowed you was coming long time back."

He knew I was coming? Slowly, I raised up and peered at Packard, not saying anything, hoping he hadn't really seen me.

Packard stood up, his eyes riveted on me. He grinned and expelled a dribbling mouthful of tobacco juice. His hand emerged from the pocket of his coveralls. Fflickkk! He tossed the switchblade upward in a single revolution, then caught it by its bone handle. "Been waiting for you. Seeing if you was smart enough to find this place."

I was glad he was on the far side of the clearing. That would give me plenty of time to get away from him, if he tried anything. "How'd you know I was coming?"

"Heard you barging through the woods a half-hour ago."

Heard me coming? How could he? No matter. "I know where your still is now, Packard. The sheriff and Jess will be arresting you, and sending you back to McAlister."

Packard spat again, not bothering to wipe off the brown stains running down his cheek. Even from this distance, his eyes looked sick. Sick and crazy. "Know what I been doing while you been crashing through the woods? I been using a whet rock on this here knife. Sharp enough to slice tin. Can't let you be getting back to town. I got to kill you now, you little Stoddard shit."

"Yeah? Well, how you going to catch me? I can outrun you any—"

"Be waiting for you. I know these woods. There's trails here that only I know about. I know where you'll be going, and I'll git there before you."

"I'll see you in Hell, Packard."

Menacingly, he sliced the air with his knife. "You'll be there all right, waiting for your brother. I'm coming for you now, Stoddard. Gonna gut you."

I backed away, watching Packard carefully.

He leaped forward, then crouched and cut two wide swaths in front of him, like he was slashing me into three parts.

Whirling, I ran back to the thicket, straight for the passageway leading out.

An eerie cackling pierced the air. "Remember, Stoddard. I'll be waiting for you."

Half-diving into the tunnel, I duck-walked through, emerged on the other side, and ran. I dodged through the trees, around undergrowth that clutched at my jeans, and over logs that heaved trying to trip me, making enough noise to set chickens to flying. I ran—if you could call it that—tripping and stumbling, dead straight east toward the county road.

The footing was bad, slow going. The effort soon had my breaths coming in short gasps. If I could make the road, I could outrun him. Packard would expect . . . Jesus! I was going right straight where he figured I'd go.

I stepped on a log that rolled under my weight, and fell over it, thrusting my hands outward against the soft, damp earth, breaking my fall. Sudden fear that Packard was on me brought my heart up into my throat, thumping, choking, but I forced myself to freeze, holding my breath, listening.

All the birds were quiet, probably scared by my thrashing around. My heart was pounding so, I could feel it in my fingertips. Then I realized it wasn't my heartbeat I was feeling. I was feeling footsteps pounding on the earth.

Packard was coming.

My mind screamed. Run! No, hide! I slithered off to the side and rolled under a leafy bush, hoping I wouldn't find an unfriendly snake waiting there. Now I could hear his footsteps, and the occasional swish as his body swiped against a branch of undergrowth. He was almost on me.

"Yeeee-hawww!" Packard screamed.

The sound electrified my nerve endings and I almost burst from my hiding place. Packard charged by, not ten feet north of me. Gradually, the sound of his footsteps faded away.

I crawled from under the bush and sat up. If I'd kept on going, stumbling through the undergrowth, he would have got me for sure. He must have been following a trail, the way he'd been running a heck of a lot faster than I'd been able to run.

I looked around, getting my bearings. I was in some sort of small clearing. Around me, the undergrowth parted, forming a narrow trail, running north and south.

What if I followed this trail north instead of east? I could go north for thirty minutes then cut east to the road, or find Six Mile Creek again and follow it back to town.

What if I went south? Packard wouldn't expect me to go south. But going south would just put me further away. I'd have to turn north sooner or later. That settled it.

Rising, I crept softly up the trail. A branch snagged my knapsack, then tore free, zinging loudly. I grabbed it, silencing it. The knapsack was a problem I could do without. I shucked it, slipping it under a bush, out of sight.

I moved up the trail as cautiously as I ever did in my whole life. Every so often, I'd pause and listen, then move on. A half-hour later, I was pretty sure I'd lost Packard. A few more minutes and I'd cut over to the road. In case he was watching and waiting somewhere in his pickup, I'd stay in the edge of the woods, until maybe somebody I could get a lift with came along.

Ten feet ahead, something caught my eye, lying in the trail.

Something man-made. My olive-green knapsack!

I ducked down low, knowing that Packard had to be watching. I listened, hearing nothing except a few birds blithely singing away somewhere to my left. Unconsciously, I shrank back down the trail, as if my own knapsack were something deadly. Turning, I—

"Yeeee-hawww!" Packard blocked the trail, not three feet from me. Fflickkk! His switchblade flashed. His gray eyes clouded, lusting for death. "Here chick, chick, chick. Here chickee."

I watched, frozen with fear.

He held out his left hand, an ugly white scar where his thumb had been, his four bony fingers curling toward him like an obscene invitation from the Grim Reaper. Then he lunged.

I whirled to run, but his left forearm snaked around my neck and the knife blade pressed against my right cheek, its sharp edge grabbing and scraping the flesh.

"Gotcha now—"

I slammed an elbow into his scrawny ribs, and ducked down, twisting. Packard's blade sliced across my right ear, but I was free. I backed slowly up the trail, wary of turning my back on him again, my arms raised defensively, ready for his next attack, blood trickling down my cheek.

"Fucking bastard," Packard growled. He lunged again, slashing his knife at me.

I jumped backwards, escaping the downward, ripping thrust, and fired my right hand at his head.

He ducked, avoiding most of my blow, but my fist caught the John Deere hat, spinning it into the underbrush.

Packard staggered backward, then regained his balance, keeping his knife pointed right for my stomach. Ugly gray hair spewed wildly in a hundred directions and his eyes were narrow slits of hatred glinting like the blade in his hand. He was more cautious now, guarding against my counterattack. "You can't never beat me, boy. Soon you'll be holding your guts in your hands, trying to push 'em back in."

"Rot in Hell, Packard!"

He faked a lunge at me.

I jumped backwards.

Laughing, he jabbed the knife at my groin.

I leaped backward again, this time catching my heel on something—my knapsack—tripping, falling. I hit the ground, flat on my back, my head thudding hard against a rock.

Stunned, I watched Packard slinking toward me, then kneeling. My arms were lead weights and my head felt like I'd been jolted with a thousand volts of electricity. Blackness closed in. I fought for consciousness. Gritting my teeth, I forced my right hand up and made a fist.

Packard slapped my hand away and jabbed the heel of his left hand against my throat, closing off my windpipe, forcing my head back. I couldn't breathe, and all my strength was gone. I felt my T-shirt being pulled from my jeans, tearing, then felt the knife zigzag lightly across my belly. He was toying with me.

Packard's grizzly face loomed inches from mine, tobacco juice oozing from between his teeth. "Now, Stoddard. Now. For what your brother did to my boy."

Packard's hand pressed harder against my throat, choking me. The knife appeared in front of my eyes, catching a flash of sunlight, then rose high over my stomach.

I watched the blade, helpless to avoid the final thrust.

Packard's hand froze in the air, fingers appearing around his wrist. Packard turned to look behind him. "What the—"

An arm came into view, muscular, tanned . . . then broad, bronze shoulders . . . and . . . golden hair.

I passed out.

30

A tiny lawnmower whirred in my head. Gently, peacefully, I floated, away from dark nothingness to a damp coolness across my forehead. But the tiny whirring continued.

Reaching up to my face, I touched a wet cloth and pulled it from my eyes. The light was subdued, yellowish. Disoriented, I glanced around. Everything was different from when Packard had me. I was lying on soft blankets, not damp ground, and there wasn't a rock under my head. I was lying on top of a bedroll inside Tarzan's tent. I smelled something strangely familiar. The smell of wildflowers.

The back of my head hurt. I touched it gingerly, feeling a lump as big as a silver dollar. The skin wasn't broken so I guessed it'd be all right in a day or two. I wondered if my ear was still all there. My hand went to it, cautiously feeling the diagonal slash across the back part of the cartilage. It was tender, but not deep, and it had crusted over. The blood that had run down my neck had been cleaned away. And my stomach felt fine. Packard hadn't gotten me.

I rolled over and looked out the tent. A few feet away, Tarzan sat, cross-legged, holding a wooden contraption in his left hand and slowly turning a crank with his right, a tiny whirring droning steadily. The world seemed entirely peaceful now. Where was Packard? What had Tarzan done to him?

I studied the man before me. Bare to the waist, chest muscles like armor plating, a manner as relaxed as a sleepy kitten snuggling up to a warm stove. In the sunlight, his hair streamed away from his face, then trailed across his shoulders like a lion's mane. He was clean-shaven and the strength in his jaw mirrored that in his biceps. His baggy pants were tied with a rope around his waist and his stomach rippled like the belly of a crawdad. This was the man who had saved my life.

Tarzan looked up, his eyes soft blue, friendly, like a morning sky in springtime. He stopped turning the crank and smiled. "Welcome."

I crawled out of the tent, realizing my T-shirt had been removed. I looked around for it, and saw it spread out on a bush, washed clean of my blood and drying in the sun.

"Your name's Mark, isn't it?"

"Mark Stoddard," I said, wondering how he knew my name. He held out his hand.

I shook it solemnly, my hand small in his. "Thanks for saving my life."

Tarzan shrugged. "I prevented one man from performing a crime against nature."

Uneasily, I glanced around the campground, checking the edges of the woods. "Where's Packard now?"

"You don't need to worry about him."

I felt a strange peace coming over me. I felt safe being with Tarzan. I hadn't felt that way in a long time.

"What are you doing?" I asked.

Tarzan grinned, then flipped a lever on his contraption— something I had never seen before but now realized was a kind of portable drill press. Removing a marble-sized shiny blue stone, he peered closely at the small hole he'd drilled in it. He handed it to me. "I make jewelry."

I turned the stone in my fingers, recognizing it as a blue agate, noting it was slightly oval, polished to perfection, and a brilliant, clear blue, the color of a blue lagoon in the South Seas, or so I imagined. "Wow," I said, expressing my admiration the best way I knew how. I handed it back to him. "What kind of jewelry do you make?"

He placed the agate in a leather pouch beside him, then rose and ducked into his tent. Bringing out another leather pouch, he pulled the drawstrings open, then poured the contents out into his hand. It was a woman's necklace, made of shiny carved seashells and brilliant agates and other polished stones I didn't recognize.

My fingers went toward it involuntarily, touching it lightly, feeling its smoothness, noting the symmetrical perfection that Tarzan had crafted into it. "It's . . . it's beautiful."

"The gray gemstone are smoky quartz, the green are moss agates, and the whites are moonstone. Some of them came from Six Mile Creek."

"From Six Mile Creek? Really?" I thought of all the pebbles I'd tossed carelessly around there.

"The shells are sand dollars, from the Gulf. They're very fragile."

"What's that large brown stone?" I said, pointing to an oblong, two-inch-long pendant hanging at the bottom.

"That's amber. I got that in Burma last year. If you look closely, you can see a mosquito inside."

I pulled the pendant close and peered into its murky, swirling depths. The insect materialized, ugly with stiltlike legs and a needle-nose snout nearly as long. "That's an awfully big mosquito. How does a mosquito get inside a stone?"

"It's prehistoric. Amber is fossilized resin from trees."

"Oh," I said, truly impressed.

Tarzan placed the necklace in my hand. "I want you to have it."

I looked at it in amazement. "Me? Why?"

"A gift."

"A gift? But . . . I can't accept it. It's too valuable."

"You can give it to your mother."

The words shocked me. I looked down. "She's . . . she's dead." My voice sounded strange, saying that. I passed the necklace back to him, its colors sparkling in the sun.

Tarzan replaced it in the pouch, drawing the strings carefully. "What if . . . if I made you a bracelet?"

I kinda liked the idea, but then I thought about what Ferret and the guys would say, seeing me wearing a bracelet of shells and stones. "It's nice, but I don't wear bracelets."

"You could give it to your friend."

I blinked, realizing he was referring to TJ. Tarzan had seen us together in church. "TJ's mad at me."

"All the more reason for a gift."

I thought about that. She'd really liked Andy the Panda. Maybe if I gave her a bracelet, she'd forgive me for not taking her to the Bottomlands. "Okay."

"I'll meet you at Tucker's store tomorrow. Mid-morning?"

I nodded. Then I remembered the whole town was jawing about Tarzan. I got an uneasy feeling about Tarzan's coming to town. "What are you doing here, anyway?"

"Passing through."

"From where?"

"Various places . . . Vancouver, Los Angeles."

"Where're you heading?"

"South, eventually. I follow the sun. You are very curious, my friend."

"You just wander around?"

"I travel. I experience the beauty of nature."

I'd never heard anyone around Bob White talk the way he did, not even Reverend Brubaker when he was sermonizing. Remembering Tarzan's visit to the Baptist Church, a thought occurred to me. "Are you a minister?"

Tarzan laughed. "No, but I am a man of God."

I considered that for a moment. He must mean he was a Christian. "You sure got the whole town talking."

"I mind my own business. I harm no one. No living thing."

"They think you're strange."

"I am different, but not strange. In what way do they think I'm strange?"

I hesitated, not wanting to offend him.

"It's all right. Please continue."

I dropped my head a bit, wishing I hadn't brought the subject up. "They . . . think you like boys, but I know . . . I figure they're wrong."

Unoffended, Tarzan shook his head. "They are mistaken. I don't need any kind of human love. I'm in love with nature. I love the beauty and simplicity of nature."

How could he say he didn't need human love? He'd made love that very morning. Maybe he didn't like boys, but he sure liked women. And that was human love.

I looked around. I didn't see any woman things, things you'd expect if Tarzan had a woman living with him. I remembered Mrs. Walters fawning over him at the fair. Could she have come out here and—?

"There's no one else here, Mark."

I jerked my head toward him, surprised. Did he know that I'd seen him making love earlier? "I . . . I was just . . . "

"The man who attacked you isn't here."

Relief flooded over me. I stammered, "Yeah, Packard's his name. Lafe Packard." Suddenly a vision of Packard entered my head. Packard leering over me, his knife upraised. Then Tarzan's hand. "I wish I hadn't passed out. I'd have liked to have seen him get what was coming to him. Did you . . . " I started to say, "kill him."

"I let him go about his business."

Incredulously, I looked at Tarzan. "You let that crazy bastard go?"

"Some people have said I'm crazy."

"He oughta be locked up. He's a bootlegger."

"Jesus turned water into wine."

This man was too nice. Nothing riled him. Discouraged, I said, "I found his still."

"Yes, I know."

I was getting impatient with Tarzan. "Bootlegging's against the law."

"Yes, but I believe it's wrong to cage a man, just as it's wrong to cage an animal."

He was dismissing my concerns, just the way the sheriff had, the way Jess had. "Packard wants to kill my brother."

Tarzan's eyes met mine. "No man should harm another, Mark. I'll keep an eye on Mr. Packard. If it becomes necessary, I shall again dissuade him."

How could Tarzan keep an eye on Packard, and be there when he was needed? It was up to me to do something about Packard. I rose to my feet. "I've got to be going. I've got to tell the sheriff about Packard's still."

"I understand." Tarzan rocked forward, uncrossed his legs, and stood up. Even in his bare feet, he was a good head taller than me. He stepped over to the bush, removed my T-shirt, and held it out. "It's nearly dry."

I slipped it on, noticing the tear on the bottom left side. I tucked the shirttail into my jeans so the rip wouldn't show.

I hesitated, realizing Tarzan had risked his life in saving mine. "Packard won't forget what you did. He might come back."

Tarzan shrugged. "Thanks for the warning."

I wasn't surprised by his indifference. "Thanks again for saving my life."

He smiled. "I'll see you tomorrow."

I turned away, walking east toward the county road when another question popped into my head. I stopped and looked back.

Tarzan had sat back down and was turning the crank on his wooden drill press.

"Hey?" I called.

He looked up, questioningly.

"What's your name?"

Slowly, a broad grin spread across his face.

I waited, half expecting to hear him say "Tarzan."

Instead, he said, "Jonathan Goldwyn."

31

Minutes later, I emerged from the woods next to a dead cottonwood split wide open by lightning. The county road had been cut right through the Bottomlands and long branches hung over the road like giant fingers laced together. But a few hundred yards north the Bottomlands ended.

I thought about Tarzan. Jonathan Goldwyn was just about the most unexpected name I could imagine. I remember Reverend Brubaker saying he thought Tarzan was Jewish. Was Goldwyn a Jewish name? I didn't know. There weren't any Jewish folks in Bob White. The only Goldwyn I'd ever heard of was the movie studio guy. M-G-M. Somehow, I couldn't think of Tarzan as Mr. Goldwyn. The name Tarzan was stuck permanently in my head.

I walked up the dusty road, wondering where Packard was, maybe lying in wait somewhere up ahead. Waiting with his knife.

Maybe his pickup would burst from the woods and run me down. I walked faster. I'd best be getting to Jess as quick as possible. As soon as I did, Lafe Packard would not be bothering people any more. He'd be going to jail.

A sudden rumbling coming up the washboard road startled me. Whirling, I expected to see Packard's rusty, turtle-nosed pickup. Silhouetted against a trailing cloud of dust, Mr. Tucker's delivery truck straddled the road, trudging toward me.

Relieved, I walked toward the approaching pickup, waving my hands. Slowing, Mr. Tucker peered through the windshield at me. In this heat, I wondered how he could wear a collared shirt, buttoned stiffly around his neck, his black and white polka-dot bow tie choking him. I stepped aside as the pickup eased to a halt, and grinned, glad as hell to see him.

Mr. Tucker pulled alongside and stopped, looking puzzled. The trailing dust cloud overtook us, and a layer of powder grit draped itself over me, filling nooks and crannies all over my body and clothes. After it settled out, I licked my lips and spat out the reddish-brown mixture.

Mr. Tucker frowned, uncertain, his eyes darting up the road, then back at me. He cleared his throat. "What brings you down in this neck of the woods?"

I didn't want to answer that directly. I wanted people to think it was Jess that had found Packard's still, not me. I said the first thing I could think of. "Hunting for crawdads, sir." Actually, I had kicked over a rock or two as I'd gone down Six Mile.

"Alone?"

I looked at him, thinking immediately about Packard, and then Tarzan. But he couldn't mean them. "Ferret twisted his ankle."

He nodded slowly. "Oh. Yeah, I did hear that." He frowned again. "Well, you take care now."

I needed to get to town fast. "Sir? Uh . . . sure could use a ride back to town?"

Mr. Tucker seemed nervous and distracted. "Oh. All right."

I ran around the back of the pickup—noticing a tarp thrown over something in the truck bed—and climbed up beside him. "Thanks, Mr. Tucker."

He pulled the crooked floor-shift lever into first gear and revved the engine, easing the pickup forward. He let the clutch out too suddenly, and we jerked a couple of times before smoothing out. We jerked just as badly shifting to second and third before reaching his cruising speed—about forty miles an hour. From high up in the tall cab, the truck seemed to poke along, rocking from side to side.

I looked out the window as we approached the cottonwood skyline of Bob White. Tall television towers appeared, followed by small white frame houses and sagging clotheslines. I was glad to get back to civilization.

Mr. Tucker slowed, shifting into second gear. The pickup whined, as impatient as I was with the snaillike pace. "Where can I drop you?" he asked.

"At your store is fine. I want to say hello to Jess."

"Thanks for helping Sam yesterday."

All I'd done was hold Sam in my arms, and it was too late then. "Wish I could have done more. I liked Sam."

Mr. Tucker looked sad. "Had him for sixteen years."

He'd lost his dog only yesterday. That explained his nervousness, why he wasn't his usual self. "Where'd you bury Sam?" I asked, wondering if that was an okay question.

"I didn't. I thought about burying him back of the store, but you know how some people talk. The missus said I should have the vet take care of him, so I called Doc Bailey."

Doc Bailey lived out west, just off the highway, with some acreage for his home and his business as well as kennels and a pet cemetery. "Seems like the next best thing. Then you can go out and visit him every so often."

Up ahead I could see the courthouse on the left and Mr. Tucker's grocery store on the right. Mr. Tucker hadn't answered me. "You could even take some flowers to put on the grave."

"I had him cremated."

The words stunned me. I'd forgotten about Doc Bailey's incinerator. "You had Sam burned up?"

Mr. Tucker's face colored a bit. "Doc Bailey wanted fifty dollars for the plot. It was ten for the cremation." He shrugged, his voice defensive. "He was only a dog."

Sam had been burned. Dogs ought to be buried in cemeteries, just like people. I was glad my folks were buried. I couldn't imagine having them burned because it was cheaper.

I looked at Mr. Tucker, seeing him in an entirely different light. He'd loved Sam, but he'd had him burned up.

Movement out the back window caught my eye. The tarp flapped in the breeze, then slipped sideways a bit, exposing two large boxes that said PURINA in large letters on the sides. The boxes rode heavy in the truck bed like they were full of something.

Mr. Tucker glanced over his shoulder, as if he'd forgotten about the boxes in the back. "Just errands."

"Oh," I said. I hadn't asked him a question. Curious, I turned in my seat to look closer at the boxes—

"That's a nasty cut on your ear."

I jerked my head around, thinking fast. "Scratched it on a thorn."

Just then Mr. Tucker turned in behind his store, braked to a stop, and killed the engine. "Come into the store. The missus will put some iodine on it."

I climbed out of the pickup and slammed the door. I didn't want to wait. I had to tell Jess about finding Packard's still. "Nah. I'll take care of it later. Thanks for the ride." I ran around the building toward the courthouse.

At the sheriff's office, Jess was sitting at Lucy's desk—she wouldn't be in for another hour and a half. His back was turned, setting his coffee cup down. The sheriff's personal office was dark and gloomy. Jess was alone.

I was as excited as I'd be if I'd found a hundred-dollar bill. Slamming the door behind me, I hurried toward him. "Hey, Jess!"

He turned, his deputy's badge flashing in the light, his mouth open, staring at me like I was crazy.

I'd saved Jess's life. I wasn't some lamebrain kid. "I found Packard's still!"

Jess's jaw muscle tightened. Behind him, the Motorola radio hummed. A metallic voice, belonging to Sheriff Adams, crackled from the speaker. "Jess? Is that your brother?"

Jess grimaced, then turned back to the desk, pressing a button on the table mike. "Yes, sir. It's Mark."

"Mark? Git over here and tell me what you know," the sheriff's voice commanded. "Where'd you find it?"

I hadn't planned on the sheriff finding out. Leastways, not until after Jess had all the credit. Reluctantly, I stepped next to the desk. "In the Bottomlands."

"Where in the Bottomlands?"

"Hidden in a big thicket. It's west of the county road, halfway to the Clear Boggy. I'd have to show you exactly."

"Packard see you?"

"Well . . . I reckon so."

"Shit!" Jess said. "Then he's lit out by now."

The radio was silent for a moment. Then it crackled, "Yeah. Well, damn it, Jess, we'd better git down there anyways. Bring an ax and the camera so we can collect some evidence. I'll meet you on the county road in ten minutes."

Jess pushed the mike away, opened the lower left-hand drawer, and pulled out his gun belt. Standing, he strapped it around his waist, then brushed past me and walked over to the closet. He dragged a double-edged ax from the back corner and leaned it up against the wall. "Grab this. Mind you don't cut a foot off."

I hurried over, and hoisted the ax by its neck.

From an upper shelf, Jess pulled down a satchel, then carried it over to Lucy's desk. He removed a large camera and inspected it. Satisfied, he nodded. "Let's go."

I followed Jess out the back door of the courthouse and climbed in the Fury.

Jess accelerated down Main Street toward the county road. Wind whipped through the open windows, buffeting my face. Jess always drove fast, expecting everything to get out of his way. The cottonwoods lining the street obliged and shrank away from the Fury's approach, their leaves shivering as we passed. "What happened to your ear?" he asked.

"Cut it on a thorn."

At Ash Street, Jess braked hard, the Fury sliding into the turn. Straightening the car up, Jess accelerated south. We passed the dead cottonwood marking Tarzan's camp and drove a few miles further. "This'll be about right," I said.

The sheriff showed up within minutes, and I led the way into the Bottomlands. It took me a half hour to relocate the thicket. There was no sign of Packard, just the moonshine still.

Sheriff Adams stood next to the four-foot-high still with the ax. Jess took several pictures and I knew they'd be in next Sunday's paper. Then the sheriff handed me the ax and stepped back. "You found it, Mark. You can bust it up, if you want."

The inert tin metal boiler stood on four stubby legs, its bottom blackened from the silent fire pit beneath. Overhead, an eerie breeze whistled through the sparse canopy of treetops, dipping a warm invisible finger down to swirl the ashes. Then they settled, rustling, crinkling, the tiny black chips reminding me of the fate that had consumed Mom and Dad. I thought of Packard, wanting to kill Jess.

I lunged forward and swung the ax. The edge bit deeply into the round shiny midsection, toppling the still to the ground, its contents sloshing violently, the sweet smell of fermenting yeast and sugar surging from its mortal gash. Anger flowed into my veins—anger at Packard and the world that had taken my folks away. Again and again and again, the ax fell.

Finally I stopped, sweat pouring off me, a ripped and crumpled mass of metal before me. I caught my breath, then felt a tingling sensation behind my ears. Turning, my eyes focused on the far side of the clearing, searching through the odd shapes the bushes made. In the sunlight, moisture glistened like beaded sweat on leafy arms and bodies. Further back, closer to the thicket wall, dark shadows crouched like wolves waiting to spring. I saw nothing that nature hadn't made.

But I could feel Packard watching me.

Suddenly, a hand was on my shoulder, jerking me around. Jess's voice was tight and hard. "I told you not to come down here."

"I found Packard's still, didn't I?"

"So you found his still. How will we prove it's his still? I suppose it has Packard's name written all over it."

"I saw him. I'm a witness."

"You see him making moonshine? Bottling it?"

"Yeah. I mean . . . no, not really."

"So you think all you have to do is testify in court that he's the bootlegger?"

What was Jess saying? "Why not?"

"No Oklahoma judge would send a man to prison for bootlegging on the testimony of a minor. You didn't think about that, did you?"

I hadn't given it a single thought. A bad feeling came over me, now understanding what Jess was getting at.

"Packard can't be convicted. You better listen when—"

"Jess!" Sheriff Adams frowned. "Lay off the kid. He meant well."

Jess turned red, and glared at me.

The woods seemed dead quiet. Yet I could sense Packard laughing at me, and planning on getting even, somehow.

32

About five o'clock, Jess dropped me at the house, saying he was going into the City. Before he left, he lectured me about how everything was all my fault. He also allowed as how I owed Joyce a favor, since she'd talked him out of chasing me down last night and beating the crap out of me. I didn't say good-bye when he left.

Feeling miserable, I sat down on the front steps. Bopeep trotted around the side of the house and lay down beside me. At least she was happy to see me.

I couldn't forget about Packard. And I knew Packard wouldn't forget about Jess and me. He hated us both now, and he wanted to kill us.

He was out there somewhere, laying low. Sooner or later, he'd be coming for us. But when? When was the anniversary of his son's death? I couldn't just sit around and wait for Packard to make his move. Something had to be done. But what? Nothing came to mind. By finding his still, I had thrown away the only chance I really had to stop Packard before he killed Jess. Damn it. Damn it to Hell.

After feeding Bopeep, I opened a can of Vienna sausages. They tasted pretty slimy even wrapped inside white bread. In the living room I turned the television on. The news was on all three channels. I turned it off, my eye catching Jess's trophies standing on its dusty top. Remembering my gun trophy, I went to the closet.

Two new boxes of shotgun shells had been shoved against it, knocking the trophy on its side. Concerned, I picked it up, but it wasn't broken. I looked at the inscription again. CHAMPION, BOB WHITE, OKLAHOMA, 1957. Dad would have been proud of my trophy, but Jess had pushed it aside. I set it in the far corner, out of the way.

Dad's shotgun stood where I'd put it Sunday afternoon, uncleaned. I felt guilty about that. Dad would have expected me to clean it. I took it to the kitchen table with the cleaning kit and set to work oiling the gun and running a cloth through the barrel. When I finished, I peered down the long end of the barrel, sticking my thumb into the magazine chamber. Light reflected off my thumbnail, illuminating the barrel's insides. Clean as a whistle.

The Winchester 12 was a fine gun. Suddenly, a thought popped into my head. A crazy thought. A wild thought. There was another way I could stop Packard.

I could take Dad's gun down to the Bottomlands, find Packard, and shoot him.

I slid my left foot forward into a shooting stance, raised the gun to my cheek, and imagined Packard in my sights. Blooey!

Blooey? Old Mr. Tubbs had said the same thing when he raised his cane, pretending to shoot Tarzan. I felt guilty for thinking I might kill someone. Saturday night, at Hogan's Pool Hall, I'd worried that Jess might have killed the roughneck. How would I feel if I killed someone?

Bopeep jerked her head off the floor, turned her nose to the back door, and whuffed. Someone was coming around the house, shuffling carefully. Instantly uneasy, I stood up, holding the gun ready, even though it was unloaded—looking through the screen door. The shuffling sound got closer. Shuffling like Packard. My senses jangled, like I had sat in an electric chair. Packard was coming to kill me! I gripped the gun tight, wishing I had a shell in the chamber.

Bopeep stood up, wagging her tail, then Ferret's skinny body appeared on the steps. He pulled the door open and slipped in, shuffling with his limp. "Hey, Mark."

My mind was still frozen with fear. "Hey, Ferret."

He looked at me, curiously, then at the gun.

I managed a grin, and mumbled, "Ankle okay now?"

"S'fine. Long as I don't try running. You got my slingshot? TJ said you had it."

"Yeah. I'll get it." I carried Dad's shotgun into the living room. Ferret's slingshot lay on the sofa where I'd tossed it yesterday.

He stretched the broken rubber straps, inspecting it closely. "Needs new rubber."

"Mine does too." I walked over to the closet and set Dad's shotgun against the back wall. I wondered what I'd have done, if it had been Packard and there had been a shell in the chamber. Would I have fired?

"She's pissed at you."

Turning, I eyed Ferret closely. "TJ?"

He grinned. "Yeah."

I shrugged. "So she's pissed. So what?"

Ferret shrugged. "So let's go over to Red's and get some rubber for our slingshots."

"All right." Red always had torn inner tubes lying around the Kerr-McGee station that we could cut up and use for slingshots and rubber guns. Mom had outlawed rubber guns after I'd shot down a wasp's nest and she'd been stung.

"Okay if we take your BB gun along?"

"Sure." I went into my bedroom and retrieved it. It was a Daisy pump rifle that I'd gotten when I was ten. Ferret and I had done lots of target shooting with it over the years. Mrs. Brubaker wouldn't let Ferret have a BB gun. The reverend was against guns, though he'd learned you didn't preach about it, not in Bob White, Oklahoma, where darn near every able-bodied man went hunting.

I handed it to Ferret. I really wasn't interested in shooting it, not today. Not after thinking that Packard was coming for me.

He shook it and the BBs chinked against the insides. "Plenty of ammo."

We headed out, the three of us. Bopeep was always glad to go on an outing, even a short one. The Kerr-McGee station was at the far west end of Main Street. Heading straight west toward Six Mile Creek would give Ferret more chances to shoot along the way. Shooting BBs in town was against the law.

"So what'd you do today?" Ferret asked.

"Found Packard's still."

"You did? No shit?" Ferret's eyes lit up, but behind them was envy and hurt that I hadn't taken him along. Of course, I couldn't with his ankle and all.

Ferret was so interested in everything that we walked all the way along Six Mile Creek to Main Street and he forgot to shoot a single time. I left out the part about Packard catching me and all the stuff about Tarzan. And I hadn't told him about TJ skinny-dipping, or about Packard throwing the snakes, or about the "Day of Doom." I worried about what he might tell his folks. Probably I'd tell him most of it later.

When we arrived, Mr. Nelson was busy filling a customer's car with gas. "Hi, Red," I said. Everybody called him Red.

He turned away from the tank, his hand still on the nozzle, his clothes streaked with oily grime. His forehead was smudged where he'd swiped an oily hand, and the bill of his cap was turned up in a friendly fashion. "Hi, guys. How you all doing?"

"We're fine," I said. "We were wondering if you had any rubber for our slingshots."

"I reckon there's plenty. Take what you need." He nodded toward the back wall, then glanced at the clicking pump counter.

"Thanks."

We went into the garage, did a balancing tightrope walk along the rails of the car lift, and found a pile of torn inner tubes. I selected a foot-long piece, stuffed it in my back jeans pocket, and we left.

We moseyed down Six Mile, in no particular hurry. The sky had another hour or so of daylight, and there was nothing else to do. Ferret plinked at a few tin cans and sunflower faces that offered big targets. BBs were big enough and slow enough so you could see them in midair. Ferret had never been much of a shot, the barrel waving all over the place as he pulled the trigger.

After missing a large violet flower growing out of a stickery weed—three times, from ten feet—Ferret sighed and said, "I'll be glad when TJ leaves."

I looked at him questioningly.

"She's a nuisance."

I thought about how I'd dumped TJ last night, and hadn't taken her along today. I was glad I hadn't. She might have gotten hurt. "I guess she's all right."

Ferret turned toward me, his eyebrows raised, defiant. "Oh, yeah? Well, I don't like her."

I didn't understand how this argument was getting started, but I felt like I had to stick up for TJ. "I like her okay."

Ferret froze, looking hard into my eyes. He shifted his gaze and turned away. "You like her better than me, don't you?"

"Hell no, Ferret. It's different with her. You and I are pals."

"Sure it's different. You're trying to make out with her."

My hackles rose. "If I was trying to make out with her, it'd be none of your business."

"Oh, yeah?"

"Damn it, Ferret. I like her in a different way, that's all. Besides, she'll be gone at the end of the summer. And we'll be pals forever."

"Pals forever," he echoed sarcastically, still angry.

"I mean it, Ferret. Word of honor."

"Word of honor?"

Neither of us had ever broken our word of honor. "Yeah."

"Well, all right then." He still sounded doubtful.

I remembered I was going to give TJ a bracelet. How would Ferret take that?

"Hey, look." He pointed at a sparrow sitting on the limb of a bush across Six Mile Creek. Raising the rifle, he fired. The BB missed by a mile. The sparrow didn't even realize it'd been shot at, instead cocking its head this way and that, and twittering.

I frowned at Ferret. "Hey, you know better than that. Shooting at a bird that's sitting. It's not fair."

"Why not?"

We'd had this argument plenty of times before. It had never kept Ferret from shooting at sitting birds. He'd never hit one, ever. "It's just not fair," I repeated, rolling my eyes.

"Well, I don't see how you hit them when they're flying, even with a shotgun."

"You swing the barrel past the bird, and shoot while you're swinging it. Shooting has got to be instinctive."

"Instincts don't work for me."

Over the years, Dad had tried to teach him to shoot at the range, but Ferret was too uncoordinated. "Well, some day you'll get the hang of it."

Across the creek, the sparrow chirped, twitched its tail dropping a load of do-do, then took off, crossing in front of us.

Ferret raised the rifle, swinging it past the sparrow, and fired. The brass BB, clearly visible, streaked toward the little bird, and struck it squarely in its head. The sparrow folded its wings and crumpled to the ground, tumbling on impact.

Ferret turned to me excitedly. "I did it!"

I couldn't believe my eyes. A million-to-one shot. I walked over and squatted down next to the sparrow, then picked it up, gently. The white feathers of its chest were soft, almost like fur. The brown-and-gray speckled head lolled across my index finger, its eyes shut, a small trace of blood. A sick feeling came over me. "It's dead."

"It is?" Ferret asked, surprised.

"Yeah." I'd killed many a quail for food and sport. This was different. In all the times I'd been hunting, I'd never, ever shot at an innocent little sparrow.

Yet earlier, I'd thought about killing Packard. Somehow, my thinking about killing Packard now seemed like it was Ferret's fault. It didn't make any sense, but it didn't matter. Angrily, I turned toward him, intending to yell at him, to curse him.

But Ferret's face was somber, full of remorse. His eyes glistened. "I'm sorry."

My anger melted. It seemed as if my heart broke. "It's all right, Matthew. I know you didn't mean it. It was an accident."

Bopeep came over to investigate and sniffed the dead bird in my hands. I lay the lifeless body down on the bank of Six Mile Creek and rested my hand on Bopeep's head.

Killing someone was something I couldn't do. There couldn't be a worse feeling in the whole world. I could never take Dad's gun and hunt down Packard. There was nothing I could do to stop him. Packard could do anything he damn well pleased.

33

The next morning—Wednesday—I stood by Jess's open door. He'd come home late, and alone. Watching his bare chest rise and fall, I was glad he was alive, glad nothing had happened to him. What was I going to do about Packard? Maybe Tarzan could help.

I got dressed and went over to the Brubakers'. Mrs. Brubaker was out back hanging towels on the clothesline, a sack of clothespins tied around her waist.

"Morning, Mrs. Brubaker," I said, hiding my worries.

She looked at me and grinned. "We're having buttermilk biscuits, cream gravy, and country sausage for breakfast. Interested?"

"You bet." I started inside and hesitated. "Is TJ up?"

"She's making breakfast."

"Oh? TJ's making breakfast?"

Mrs. Brubaker gave me a stern look that said "be nice."

TJ was cooking? I wasn't sure I wanted to eat food that TJ fixed. Then my stomach growled. "Lordy," I sighed, under my breath. "I sure hope she's a good cook."

I went into the kitchen, letting the screen door slam. Alone, TJ stood by the stove, wearing one of Mrs. Brubaker's aprons around her waist, stirring gravy with a large wooden spoon. She turned, then frowned, seeing me.

"Hey, TJ." I smiled, pretending everything was fine.

She turned her back to me. "I'm not talking to you," she said, shaking her head, her ponytail swishing like a frisky week-old filly.

I walked over and stood beside her. Besides the gravy bubbling like milky lava, golden brown sausage sizzled slowly in a pan and a pot of coffee gurgled, its percolating about done. And the oven oozed heat, along with the hearty aroma of rising biscuits that had to be ready to pop into your mouth. In spite of everything, my mouth watered at all the activity on the stove.

I felt awkward, wanting to make up to her, but not knowing how to start. "Cream gravy sure looks good. I love fresh homemade biscuits, smothered in hot cream gravy."

She rolled her eyes and got a sarcastic look on her face. "Good grief. It's just plain old gravy."

I didn't want her mad at me. I wanted her to understand. "TJ? About yesterday—"

"There's nothing to talk about," she snapped. "You just go on about your business, important fellow that you are."

"I couldn't take you to the Bottomlands yesterday. It was dangerous—"

"Didn't sound dangerous to me. Ferret said that you just went down there, found the still, told the sheriff, and became a big hero again."

"It wasn't that easy, and for sure I'm not a hero."

"I don't need to know anything about it. I told you to go on about your business, so go on. Scat."

Scat? She sure had a nerve, talking to me that way when I was trying to be nice and apologize. "I'm not going anywhere. Mrs. Brubaker invited me for breakfast, and I'm going to have me some biscuits and gravy."

She glared at me. "You're staying for breakfast? Well, in that case, I'll make it real special." She scooped a spoonful and pretended to taste it. "Needs more salt." She grabbed the shaker and shook it vigorously over the skillet.

"TJ! What—"

"Needs more, you say? All right. We aims to please at the Brubaker Breakfast Café." She shook more salt into the skillet, stirring briskly.

She was going to ruin the gravy. I had to stop her. "How'd you like to meet Tarzan?"

She paused, eyeing me suspiciously, the salt shaker suspended over the gravy. "Maybe I would. Maybe I wouldn't."

A couple of floorboards squeaked. Reverend Brubaker entered, dressed in black trousers and a white shirt, his sleeves already rolled up, a blood-red tie knotted around his neck. "Good morning, TJ. Mark."

"Sir," I said, nodding respectfully.

"It's a fine morning, Uncle Henry," TJ said, speaking louder than I had. She busied herself stirring the gravy, the shaker concealed against her body.

The reverend walked over to the stove and inhaled deeply. "Smells wonderful."

"Thank you. I hope it's half as good as Aunt Josephine's."

The reverend took the percolator from the stove and poured himself a cup. He blew ripples across the steaming surface, then slurped it noisily.

He turned toward me, leaning so close I was afraid scalding coffee might spill on me. "Mighty fine thing you did yesterday, mighty fine. Doing the Lord's work, busting up that still."

"Yes, sir."

Behind him, TJ stuck out her tongue at me.

"I'm starving. Where's Matthew?"

I went into the other room. "Matthew?" I yelled up the stairs, remembering I'd called him "Matthew" after he'd shot the sparrow.

Upstairs, the bathroom door slammed against the wall, then Ferret appeared, walking almost normally down the steps. "Hey."

"Hey back at you," I answered. "Don't eat the gravy."

"Why not?" Ferret said, cocking his head like Bopeep did whenever I talked to her like she was a real person.

"TJ's salted the heck out of it."

He frowned. "Why'd she do that?"

I shrugged and walked into the kitchen. Everyone was seated at the table, waiting for us. Ferret and I sat down across from TJ. Then the reverend intoned grace, thanking Him especially for the food TJ had prepared.

I peeked at the gravy bowl, certain it was going to be unfit to eat. TJ seemed totally unconcerned.

The reverend finished the prayer and said, "Pass the biscuits, please."

TJ handed him the platter, smiling sweetly. He took two biscuits, and passed the platter to me. I took one and paused. Reverend Brubaker shredded his biscuits, then buried them under a mound of gravy. I passed the platter of biscuits to Ferret, then took the gravy bowl from the reverend and looked doubtfully at it. I offered the bowl to Ferret. "Guess I'll just have a biscuit and sausage for now."

Ferret eyed the bowl like it was poison, then held it toward his mom. "Me too."

Mrs. Brubaker's voice whipped across the table. "Matthew Brubaker! TJ has fixed a nice breakfast and you'll take a good helping of everything. You too, Mark."

Ferret looked at me questioningly.

Reverend Brubaker cleared his throat, attracting my attention. He leaned forward, hovering over the kitchen table, his hairline and baldness reminding me of the seams around a baseball. "Boys," he said, a warning clearly in his voice.

The skin around Ferret's eyes paled. "Yes, sir."

"Yes, sir," I echoed.

I took enough gravy to be respectable and so did Ferret. After everybody had been served, Reverend Brubaker scooped a huge portion of gravy-saturated biscuit into his mouth.

Ferret, TJ, and I watched. I held my breath.

A moment later, his vigorous chewing came to an abrupt halt, his mouth absolutely still, a surprised look on his face. If it had been anyone else, I would have laughed out loud, but this was Reverend Brubaker. The look on his face made his lightning-shaped scar stand out more than usual. He swallowed hard and declared, "It's delicious, TJ. Best biscuits and gravy . . . " He cleared his throat. " . . . I ever ate."

We ate the salty gravy mostly in glum silence, taking a bite then washing it down with a swig of orange juice.

The reverend finished his breakfast quickly, then poured himself another cup of coffee. "What have you three got planned today?"

Ferret answered. "Nothing much. We're going to fix our slingshots, then do some target practice near Six Mile Creek."

TJ looked accusingly at me. "I thought we were going to meet Tarzan."

Dumbfounded, I looked at her. Wouldn't she ever learn when to keep her mouth shut?

"Tarzan?" Ferret asked, suspicion clouding his voice. "We're going to meet Tarzan today?"

He was probably wondering why I hadn't told him. Frankly, I hadn't wanted to get into that and then have to tell him I was giving a bracelet to TJ.

Reverend Brubaker cleared his throat. "I think it would be best if you kept away from that man. All of you," he said pointedly, sweeping his gaze from face to face.

I didn't want to argue with the reverend, but Tarzan wasn't bad. "I've met him. He makes jewelry."

The reverend glanced at me, but then his eyes darted away, ignoring me. His voice boomed across the table. "You kids stay away from him. People like that come into town, first thing they do is make friends with the kids."

"Henry?" Mrs. Brubaker shifted uncomfortably, making her chair creak. "I don't think we should be so hard on the man. Things aren't always what they might seem. We know he's a churchgoer."

Reverend Brubaker leaned forward and lowered his voice.

"Going to church is all part of his plan. That man . . . does unnatural things. Defiling himself before God. And God will punish him."

Unnatural? I'd seen him in the Bottomlands, lying with a woman. Seemed pretty natural to me.

"But, Henry—"

"Josephine!" The reverend sat straight up in his chair, rising at least six inches taller. "I've said my mind!"

A red flush rose into Mrs. Brubaker's cheeks. She looked down, clasping her hands together. Sitting at the foot of the table, hunkered over her plate, she was a small bookend to the reverend's oversized one.

Mrs. Brubaker was only trying to be nice and forgiving, the way the Bible said. I felt somehow responsible for the way Mrs. Brubaker was getting treated.

I wanted to say something, but a rock-firm righteousness cloaked Reverend Brubaker's body. There was no use arguing with him. He wouldn't listen to me.

Then, to my right, came Mrs. Brubaker's small voice, hurt, yet defiant. "Henry . . . it's not right . . . to accuse people wrongly . . . that's not the Christian way."

Reverend Brubaker's posture crumbled, his mouth open. A moment stole by, with utter silence. Then his voice came in a whisper, trembling, but one I could have heard if I'd been in the back pew of the First Baptist Church. "How dare you speak to me this way? To accuse me of an un-Christian thing? In God's eye, that man is an abomination. That's the Bible talking."

Mrs. Brubaker sat, unflinchingly. "You are wrong, Henry Brubaker. And there, I've said my mind."

She met his glare evenly, then rose and stalked from the room, her head high and her shoulders back.

The reverend stared at Mrs. Brubaker's empty chair, an ugly, incredulous look on his face.

34

The Brubakers had tried hard to be like parents to me. Seeing them fight made me feel sad and lonely. Yet I was glad Mrs. Brubaker had stood up to the reverend. Reverend Brubaker *was* wrong, and he couldn't stop me from meeting Tarzan.

We fixed our slingshots, then went over to Six Mile Creek for target practice. Ferret came out last, and I for damn sure didn't let TJ win. When mid-morning came, we left our slingshots at Ferret's house and went downtown, Ferret not even hesitating about going along.

Bob White was already bustling with activity, the parking spaces along the street filled with cars, people traipsing in and out of stores, shopping, visiting. As Bob White was the county seat, there were always a fair number of goings-on at the courthouse, what with legal transactions and taxes and such. Jess's Fury was parked in its usual spot in back of the courthouse.

I didn't know where things were headed between Jess and me. The way he saw it, all I'd done was cause trouble for him. Sheriff Adams and Jess blamed me for not catching Packard at the still. They were looking for Packard—just for questioning, the sheriff had said. What if Packard found Jess instead?

We walked down the sidewalk toward Tucker's, getting more than our share of glances and howdys. Some people congratulated me for finding the bootlegger's still.

Three chairs in front of the store were pushed back against the storefront, out of the hot sunshine. Mr. Davis's head slumped on his chest, half buried in his long beard, his face hidden by his hat. A pile of whittlings lay at Mr. Tubbs's feet, and Mr. Pemberton had the third chair, gesturing and jawing away at the empty space before him, probably retelling one of his tired World War I stories, but nobody was listening.

I walked around the shavings, getting a wary look from Mr. Tubbs as he sliced off another thin strip of whitish wood. Mr. Pemberton didn't miss a beat flapping his gums. I heard Mr. Davis snoring as I passed, and smelled something that told me he'd just farted in his sleep.

"Eeeyuuuu," TJ said, wrinkling her nose.

"C'mon, TJ," I whispered. "He doesn't even know he did anything."

"He wouldn't care neither," Ferret said, grinning.

I pulled open the screen door to go inside. Behind us, a sound came from Mr. Davis, a high-toned single note changing in pitch as it squealed out, like in the movies when an airplane spirals down from the sky. We jumped inside, avoiding the onslaught from Mr. Davis's bottom, laughing, letting the screen door slam behind us.

Inside, the floors looked freshly scrubbed, and the air was heavy with the smell of disinfectant, a welcome relief from the smell just outside the door. A couple of carts clanked in the aisles and Mrs. Tucker was checking out a customer with a heavy load of groceries. I didn't see Mr. Tucker or Tarzan.

I treated TJ and Ferret to soda pops, then walked over to Mrs. Tucker and put three nickels on the checkout counter. If you took them with you, you were supposed to pay a two-cent deposit on the bottles. "Okay if we bring the bottles back later?"

She smiled. "Why sure, Mark."

Avoiding the old men outside, we walked across the street to the courthouse grounds and sat in the shade of a big cottonwood. We settled down, our backs to the tree trunk, taking big swigs followed by bigger sighs of relief as our thirsts were quenched.

I savored the coolness flowing down my insides and glanced at the bottom of the glass bottle. "Bartlesville, Okla." I wondered if Mr. Tucker would ever find a Tucumcari bottle.

Ferret hiccuped, attracting my attention. He took a deep breath and held it in, grinning like he was going to conquer the hiccups just that simply. I waited, anticipating his next hiccup. Still grinning, he glanced at TJ, then the air in his lungs burst out into a large belch, interrupted by a hiccup.

The three of us laughed.

I swallowed some air and belched twice as loud as Ferret.

We laughed some more. Ferret's hiccups vanished as quickly as they'd started, then we rested in silence, waiting for the next subject of interest to occur.

TJ sat up, leaning forward, tense.

Ferret and I sat up, looking across the street, expecting to see Tarzan, but seeing nobody of consequence. TJ seemed to be concentrating on something. "What is it?" I asked.

A tiny little "burp" burst from her mouth.

I fell over laughing.

TJ collapsed onto me, giggling, then Ferret piled on and all three of us rolled around on the grass, belching.

Finally, we separated, weak from laughter, and lay on our backs in the cool grass, relaxing. Above us, cottonwood leaves fluttered as a breeze curled through the branches. Lying there next to my friends gave me a sense of comfort and peace that pushed my troubles way back in my mind.

Next to me, TJ sighed. "I can climb that tree."

The tree was at least seventy-five feet tall, and the slick, shiny-bark limbs nearest the ground were nearly a foot around, making it difficult to get a good hands-hold. It wasn't something I'd go out of my way to do. But I knew enough about TJ now to know that if she decided to climb that tree, then by damn she'd climb that tree.

"I can climb all the way to the top," she said, drawing out her words.

"Ummmhmmm," I said, knowing she'd be at it, given the slightest provocation.

"It's risky to climb cottonwoods," Ferret said, lying on the other side of TJ.

"Oh, yeah?" TJ said, an edge of stubbornness in her voice.

"Yeah. You never know if a limb's rotted out. May look fine, but when you put your weight on it . . . ccrackkk!"

"You mean like that big one, just above us? It looks pretty solid to me."

"Yeah, but, golly damn, it could break any minute and kill us all."

TJ waited for a moment before speaking. "Then we'd be dead."

"Uh-huh," Ferret agreed cheerfully.

"And the whole town would be sorry."

"Yeah." Ferret didn't sound so cheerful now.

"Wonder what it's really like to be dead?"

"My dad says Heaven's wonderful."

"What do you think?"

Ferret thought for a moment. "I don't know that being dead is so wonderful."

"Maybe being dead is like being a cloud in the sky."

"I don't know, and I don't want to find out."

Silence fell over us again. Then TJ asked, "Mark?"

I'd been listening to them talk, not wanting to get involved. Death was too real to me. "Yeah?"

Her voice was soft. "How'd you feel when your folks died?"

TJ had a way of talking about stuff nobody had any business talking about. "Numb at first. Then just shitty."

"Did you feel sorry they was dead?"

I'd felt like something was crushing the air from my lungs. Lonely. Feelings of despair. Those feelings were coming back.

"Did you feel—"

"For God's sake, TJ. Will you just shut up?"

We lay quiet for a while. Then TJ rolled over and stood up. "I'm going to climb this tree." Leaping up, she wrapped her arms around the lowest limb, then hooked her left leg over the branch and into the tree fork, leveraging herself upward.

I got this image of TJ lying dead at my feet. It scared me. "TJ! Don't!"

I jumped up and put my arms around her waist, getting mostly bare skin because her blouse was riding up. I hugged her tight, my face against the back of her neck, her hair streaming against my face, getting tickles running up and down my nose.

TJ freed up her left elbow and jabbed at me, jarring my biceps muscle. "Let me go!" TJ yelled.

"You let go," I yelled back, jerking hard.

She struggled, clinging determinedly to the tree, but losing ground. Her legs came undone, swinging down suddenly, loosing her grip, her whole body crashing into mine. The two of us tumbled to the ground, her on top of me. Twisting, she beat at my chest. "Damn you . . . "

She froze, looking beyond my head. "Oh," she said, her eyes traveling upward. "Oh."

35

TJ scrambled off me and stood up, backing up a step or two. I rolled over and rocked backwards to my feet.

Tarzan stood there, his leather pouch slung over his shoulder, barefooted, a sleeveless, buttonless, loose-fitting shirt showing his rippled stomach. "Hello, Mark."

"Hi." I stood there awkwardly, not knowing exactly what to say. Ferret climbed to his feet and stood beside me, not saying anything either.

"I've seen your friends before, but you can introduce me."

"Oh, sure. Ah . . . " I almost said Tarzan but caught myself in time. "Mr. Goldwyn, this is TJ and Ferret."

"Hello, TJ." He smiled and nodded. TJ nodded back, her eyes wide.

Tarzan turned and held out his hand. "Hello . . . Ferret?"

Ferret hesitated, then held out his hand. "It's really Matthew."

"Your friends call you Ferret."

Ferret nodded slowly.

"Then I shall call you Ferret."

Ferret's dark eyes were full of suspicion. "I hear you like to travel. Ever been to Hollywood?"

"Yes. Lots of times."

"Met any movie stars?"

Tarzan laughed. "Some."

"Who?" Ferret challenged.

"They're just people, Ferret. Ordinary people like all of us." Tarzan turned to me. "I've got something for you." Reaching into his pouch, he took out a leather thong to which was attached a dozen or so small stones and shells, and placed it in my hand.

"Thanks." I recognized agates, moonstones, and the shells I'd seen at his camp, but there were other gems that I didn't know.

"That's hourglass selenite," Tarzan said, pointing to a thin, tubular crystal about the size of a stick of gum. "And the petal-like crystals are called desert roses. Both are native to Oklahoma."

"Where do you find these? I've never seen anything like them."

"Mostly I trade with the Indians. Recognize this stone?"

"It's turquoise, isn't it?"

"It's beautiful," TJ said, stepping closer. She touched it, tentatively. "It looks fragile."

I placed it in her hand, not quite ready to tell her I was giving it to her. "Thanks, Mr. Goldwyn."

He winked. "You can call me Tarzan if you wish."

"What? How . . . "

He shook his head. "Never mind. I've got to pick up a few items at the general store. See you later."

We watched him crossing the street, his long barefoot strides strong and graceful. TJ was still admiring the bracelet. I motioned to Ferret and we slipped away a bit.

Lowering my voice, I asked, "What am I going to do with that bracelet?"

"Huh? What'd ya mean?"

"That bracelet. I can't wear it. It's too pretty."

"Oh. Oh, yeah." Ferret grinned. "Here comes Mark with his bracelet."

"Guys don't wear bracelets. I ought to give it back."

Ferret shook his head. "You can't do that. Wouldn't be nice."

"Well, heck with it then." I waited, not wanting to solve my own problem. Deliberately, I turned toward TJ, hoping Ferret would get brilliant.

He did. "Why not give it to TJ?"

Inside I grinned, happy that he'd suggested exactly what I was hoping for, but outside I kept my poker face on. "TJ?"

"Yeah. She already likes it."

I shrugged. "Why not?" I turned and walked over to TJ. She looked up as I approached, then held out the bracelet.

I shook my head. "You keep it."

She got this stunned look on her face. "You're kidding."

"Nope. Just promise me you'll take care of it."

TJ's eyes deepened, as if holding something in that was filling her up. "I will. Always."

I backed away, shaking my head and breaking the spell. Embarrassed, I didn't look Ferret in the eyes. "Come on. Let's go take back our bottles."

Back inside Tucker's, we put our bottles into some slots in a wooden case half-filled with empties, then walked down the aisles looking for Tarzan. We found him in the women's cosmetics section, holding a five-pound sack of flour in one hand and studying something in his other hand.

Ferret nudged me in the ribs. His eyes narrowed suspiciously, and he mouthed the words "golly damn."

I knew what Ferret was thinking, but I knew Tarzan wouldn't be here without a good reason. "What're you buying?"

Tarzan looked up. "Emery boards. I scrape off the grit—it's garnet powder—and use it for drilling holes in the harder stones." Tarzan's eyes shifted past me.

I felt someone coming up behind me, and turned. Mr. Tucker stood there, a white apron covering most of his front. "Hi, Mr. Tucker," I said, always anxious to be on good terms with my future boss.

He looked at me and nodded, then his eyes focused on Tarzan, a hard look on his face. "What are you doing in my store?"

Tarzan's smile remained friendly. "I need a few things. I have money."

Mr. Tucker shook his head. "I don't want your money. Get out." He jerked his thumb toward the door.

Tarzan made no effort to move. "I need the flour for bread. I use the emery boards in my work."

"We don't want your kind around here. And you'd better stay away from our kids if you know what's good for you."

Unflinchingly, Tarzan stared at him, a look of amusement on his face. "All right," he said softly, not moving.

Mr. Tucker's eyes darted away from Tarzan's, settling briefly on me, a guilty, nervous glance. Then he glanced back at Tarzan, not quite meeting his eyes. "See that you're out of here in five minutes or I'm calling the sheriff." He paused, eyeing the rack holding the other emery boards, then pushed past us, going toward the front of the store.

Tarzan sighed and replaced the emery boards. He started walking toward the front of the aisle, carrying the sack of flour. We fell in beside him.

"Mr. Tucker shouldn't have done that," I said, wanting to apologize for what had happened, but knowing I had nothing I could apologize for.

"It's happened before. Don't worry about it."

"It isn't right."

"No, but it's his way of saying I'm not welcome in Bob White. He thinks I'm a threat to his way of life." He paused, holding the flour sack in his hands, checking the aisle to his left.

TJ spoke up. "I'll take the flour back for you." She slipped in front of him and held out her hands.

"Thank you, TJ." Tarzan handed her the sack, covered with the fine white flour dust, and smiled, noticing the bracelet tied to her wrist.

TJ flushed, and hurried down the aisle with the flour.

"I think she likes the bracelet," Tarzan said. His smile faded.

Ferret and I walked outside with Tarzan, getting ugly looks from the old men on the porch. Mr. Tubbs raised his cane, blocking the sidewalk and pointing it at Tarzan. He didn't say a word, but I remembered how he'd said 'blooey' a couple of days earlier. Big talk for an old man.

Ignoring them, we walked between the cars and out into the street, heading west. TJ came running up, a concerned look on her face. "How are you going to eat?" she asked Tarzan.

He ran a hand through his golden hair, then lifted his chin and inhaled deeply. "There's plenty of food in the forest, if you know where to look. Berries, bark, roots, mushrooms."

"Mark!" The shout came from behind us, and I recognized Jess's voice.

We turned toward the courthouse. Jess was hurrying down the courthouse steps, his hands on his hips keeping his gun holster and police baton from flapping. Mr. Tucker emerged from his store, half-running down the street toward us, a dark look cutting his face. Something was wrong.

"Arrest him, Jess," Mr. Tucker yelled. "He's a thief."

Ferret and I looked at each other, then at Tarzan, all of us puzzled. People on the sidewalks stopped and stared.

"Damn it, Mark," Jess said, nearing us. "You've got yourself into more trouble."

"Me? I didn't steal anything."

"Shut up! Roy, what did you say was stolen?"

Mr. Tucker's cheeks were red and his fists were clenched. "Some emery boards." He pointed at Tarzan. "That man stole them!"

Emery boards? Tarzan had put them back. I'd seen him. But Mr. Tucker's anger seemed genuine, coming from deep inside him. I glanced around. Over thirty people had moved into the street surrounding us. Their faces were suspicious, hostile.

Jess stepped forward, demanding. "Give me those boards."

Tarzan held his hands out slowly, then looked Jess in the eye, a steady gaze. "I do not steal."

"Search him, Jess. You know he's got them in that leather purse."

"Empty your purse on the ground," Jess ordered.

"Do you have a search warrant?"

"Don't get smart with me." Jess grabbed the strap and yanked the purse from Tarzan's shoulder. He watched Tarzan's reaction, as if expecting him to start fighting.

Tarzan stood quietly, passively, meeting Jess's gaze calmly.

Jess turned the purse upside down. The contents clattered to the blacktop street—several gemstones, a few rings, and other trinkets, as well as a large wallet. "See any emery boards there, Roy?"

Mr. Tucker bent down and ran his fingers over Tarzan's things. "No . . . no . . . they're not here." He picked up the wallet and opened it, pulling a wad of money out and looking inside. "There's no emery boards here, but he's sure got a lot of money." He stood up and gave the wallet and money to Jess.

Jess flipped through the wallet, then frowned. "Where'd you get all this money?"

"I make jewelry. I sell it. You can see that for yourself," he said, indicating the gemstones scattered on the pavement.

Mr. Tucker pointed at Tarzan again. "The emery boards. He hid them in his clothes. Search him, Jess. You'll see."

Jess replaced the money and tossed the wallet to the ground. "Turn around," he ordered.

Slowly, Tarzan pivoted in a circle, his hands away from his body. The way he did it made me think he'd had to do this before.

"What are you waiting for?" Mr. Tucker asked. "Search him."

"Hold your horses, Roy." Jess raised the palm of his hand toward Mr. Tucker. "He's got no pockets in his clothes. You want him to disrobe here on Main Street?"

Mr. Tucker looked confused for a moment, then his eager-ness returned. "Arrest him. You can search him in the jail."

"Settle down, Roy. You got any proof this man stole half-a-buck's worth of emery boards?"

"He was looking at them in the store. And now one box is missing. I checked. He took it."

"No, he didn't." I spoke up, surprised at the sound of my voice. "He put it back and we left."

Jess glared at me. "Shut up, Mark. Roy? You go on back to your store."

"But Jess? Damn it! You sticking up for him?"

"You ought to know better than that, Roy. Now you go on back to your store and count those boards again. We got no proof of shoplifting."

Mr. Tucker's chin trembled and his voice shook. He stepped forward and thrust his index finger inches from Tarzan's face. "If you ever come in my store again, I'll have you arrested for trespassing."

He turned on his heel and stalked away, pushing his way through the crowd.

Jess watched him leave, then turned to Tarzan, and smiled, real friendly-like, reminding me of how he'd talked to the roughnecks in Hogan's. He spoke, low and slow, so the crowd around us wouldn't be able to hear what he was saying. "Listen, you fag. People don't want you in our town. You want to avoid more trouble, you'll get out right away."

"I have no desire to leave."

"I didn't ask you. I'm telling you."

"I am sorry. But I cannot leave right—"

Jess's right hand shot up, backhanding Tarzan across the face.

Tarzan reeled backwards, his face turned sideways from us, staggering, trying to hold his balance. Several people in the crowd laughed, and I heard an old man's voice call out, "At-taboy, Jess."

Jess stepped forward, raising his voice. "Don't you be smarting off to me. I told you to get out of town and I mean to see that you do, one way or another."

Withdrawing the police baton in a lightning fast move, he rammed it into Tarzan's stomach. Tarzan doubled over, gasping for breath, then fell to his knees.

"Jess!" I yelled. "Stop it!"

Jess raised the baton.

I lunged forward and grabbed Jess's arm, holding on with all my might. "Stop it. He didn't do anything."

Jess hauled me around in front of him, then shoved hard, sending me sprawling onto the asphalt. I fell, skinning my elbows.

Jess raise the baton again.

"Jess!" Mrs. Brubaker burst forward, coming from somewhere in the crowd.

At her voice, Jess hesitated.

Mrs. Brubaker strode forward, stepping between Jess and Tarzan. "Jess Stoddard! You put that club down."

Jess lowered his baton and glowered defensively. "You've got no business here. You're interfering with the law."

Mrs. Brubaker raised herself up as high as she could, her back straight as a board. "Since when does the law beat up innocent men?" She stepped right up to Jess, as if daring him to touch her.

Jess backed up a step, then looked embarrassed. He glanced at the crowd, then his eyes returned to Tarzan sitting back on his heels, one hand braced against the asphalt to support his weight. "You're lucky this time. I'm warning you one last time. You get out of town or else."

He turned and walked back toward the courthouse, the crowd parting ahead of him as if he were a king.

Mrs. Brubaker's eyes swept the crowd. "Haven't you all seen enough for now?"

The solid circle of people dissolved, and the stillness in Bob White broke into an uneasy rustle as people resumed their normal goings-on.

Mrs. Brubaker turned to Tarzan, all her anger gone. "I'll give you a lift back to your camp." She held out her hand.

He shook his head, then climbed to his feet, a stiff smile on his face. "That's not necessary."

Mrs. Brubaker put her hands on her hips, the firmness in her voice returning. "Nonsense. There's too much trouble in Bob White now. I'll see you get safely out of town."

Tarzan's eyes narrowed and he shrugged. "All right."

"And maybe you had better think about leaving. Things are unsettled. The whole town is uneasy."

Tarzan's voice was so quiet I could barely hear him. "I will think about it."

"Come with me. My car's over here."

TJ, Ferret, and I helped gather up Tarzan's things off the street, then he and Mrs. Brubaker climbed into her car. She backed out, then made a U-turn heading west.

I watched the car turn south on Ash Street, and remembered the night Jess had beat up those two roughnecks at Hogan's Pool Hall. TJ had said then that Jess had a mean streak. I had to admit she was right.

But still, I didn't understand Jess's anger, and I didn't understand the hate I sensed from Mr. Tucker and other people in the crowd. They thought Tarzan was queer, and maybe I should have tried to set things straight. But if I did tell them what I'd seen, I might make things worse for some lady in town. People would talk, and Mrs. Walters had already seen enough grief.

"It's all my fault," TJ said quietly.

36

I turned, surprised. "What?"

She had a sick look on her face. "The fight. Everything."

"What are you talking about?"

TJ flushed, and looked down at her feet. "I wanted to thank Tarzan for the bracelet and he needed the emery boards, but I didn't have any money. I took them anyway. I was going to pay for them later. I didn't realize . . . " TJ pulled the emery boards from her pocket, then bit her lip, trying not to cry.

"Golly damn. That was dumb," Ferret said.

"I know. I'm sorry. What am I going to do?"

TJ had done the wrong thing. But she'd meant well. She felt bad enough already. "You best put them back. Just don't let anyone see you do it."

"Shouldn't she tell Mr. Tucker?" Ferret asked.

I shook my head. "It'd only make matters worse."

"Dad always says telling the truth is—"

"She couldn't say anything that would change Mr. Tucker's mind about Tarzan."

"But then he'd know Tarzan wasn't a thief."

"This thing isn't about stealing."

Ferret and TJ looked at me and nodded slowly, understanding what I now understood.

TJ turned and ran toward Tucker's store, slipping quietly

inside. Moments later she emerged and came running up to us. "Maybe he'll think he miscounted."

"Anybody see you?" I asked.

TJ's confidence had returned. "Course not. I'm going to the Bottomlands," she announced.

Ferret and I exchanged glances, surprised.

"I've got to apologize to Tarzan."

I knew there'd be no stopping her, but I couldn't let her go there alone, where Packard might get her. "I'll go with you."

"Me, too," Ferret said.

An idea popped into my head. "We ought to do more than just apologize."

TJ looked at me. "What do you mean?"

"Mom's got . . . I mean . . . there's some emery boards in the medicine cabinet at home that are going to waste."

"Hey," Ferret said. "We can get some flour at my house and take it to him."

"Why not take along some of TJ's biscuits as well?"

Ferret grinned. "Good idea. But not the gravy."

We all laughed, especially TJ.

"I expect that's been thrown out already," she said.

We started toward the Brubakers' house. A little later, I hung back with TJ so I could speak to her alone. "I'm sorry I made you so mad that you salted the heck out of the gravy."

"You are? You're really sorry?" TJ slipped her hand into mine, and we walked along together.

Ferret turned. He saw us holding hands and grinned. I knew then that the three of us would forever more be a team, but that Ferret would understand when TJ and I did things without him.

"Yeah, I'm sorry," I answered, remembering TJ had asked me a question.

TJ turned her green eyes upward, catching my gaze. "I didn't do it to get even with you."

"You didn't?"

"Heck, no. You think I want to be doing any more cooking this summer?"

When we got to the Brubakers', neither of Ferret's parents were home. Ferret suggested we make fried bologna sandwiches and take them over to the park to eat. TJ volunteered to cook the bologna, which surprised the heck out of me. After getting the flour and biscuits, we picked up the emery boards at my house.

A half hour after eating lunch at Will Rogers Park, we were tramping down the county road nearing the Bottomlands. A lone quail whistled in the stubble field to my right. Bob . . . white. Bob . . . bob white.

It reminded me of the quail that had whistled when my folks had died. I shook my head. I had to stop thinking about things like that. It was just a plain old ordinary quail whistling, and it didn't have a special meaning.

We left the stubble field behind, following the county road directly into the Bottomlands. On either side of us, a wall of dense woods formed a tunnel nearly encasing the road. Tarzan's camp wasn't far, maybe a quarter-mile farther south, and then a few hundred yards west of the road.

Ferret spoke up. "I don't know that we ought to be coming down here."

I glanced at the dark, spooky woods and thought of Packard hiding in them, lying in wait for me. But I didn't think that was what Ferret had meant. "How's that?"

"Well, you know." Ferret shrugged. "Tarzan being queer and all."

"He isn't queer," I said defensively.

"Yeah? Well, how do you know that?"

I guessed I'd have to tell them the truth. I sighed. "Because I saw him with a woman."

"So you saw him with a woman. So what? I saw him talking to Mom today."

Ferret hadn't caught on, but I saw TJ's eyes widen. "I mean,

I saw him and a woman . . . doing it in the woods yesterday."

Ferret stopped, grabbing my shoulder, spinning me around. "You saw . . . Jesus, Mark. Golly damn. And you didn't tell me!"

"I'm telling you now."

Ferret's dark eyes flashed and he set his jaw. "You should have told me yesterday. Who was he with?"

I shrugged and resumed walking down the dusty road. "I couldn't see her face."

Ferret caught up with me and spoke, his voice softer now. "Are you just saying that?"

"Honest Injun." That's what we always said when we were telling the God's honest truth.

Ferret threw his shoulders back and got this dreamy look on his face. "They really were . . . doing it?"

"Yep."

He grinned, looking off into space. "Both of them naked?"

"Of course."

"And you could tell for sure it was a woman?"

If TJ hadn't been with us, I'd have said "Tits and ass," but I didn't out of respect for her. "I'm not blind. She was full growed, that's for sure."

Ferret's dreamy state changed to one of curiosity. "Someone from Bob White?"

"I can't rightly say. Don't know that's any of our business."

"There's not a whole lot of single women in Bob White he could be interested in."

"Maybe she's not from Bob White," TJ said. "Maybe she's like those girls that Jess brings down from the City."

I considered that possibility, then said, "Maybe so. I don't know."

The dead cottonwood tree was off to our right. I saw car tracks leaving the road where Mrs. Brubaker had stopped and let Tarzan out. The tracks veered back around in a semicircle where she'd turned around and gone back into town. I led the way off the road and stopped beside the dead tree. Lightning had split it right down the middle, leaving a black streak on both sides of the split halves. One half leaned north and the other half south.

"How far is the camp?" Ferret asked.

I pointed into the murky forest. "Just off yonder through the trees."

"What if he's got that woman with him again?"

"Not likely. There's no cars around."

"Could be one hidden in the woods. The ground's not marshy here." He stomped his foot hard on the solid ground.

"I suppose there could be."

He lowered his voice. "What if we just sneak up on 'em?"

"Ferret Brubaker!" TJ said, exasperated.

"It'd be fun, wouldn't it? You ever see people doing it?"

"No, and I don't want to. That's private."

"Yeah. Well, I bet we can sneak up on 'em anyway."

TJ glared at Ferret. "I think we ought to warn him we're coming." She put her little fingers in her mouth and whistled, a piercing shrill.

I cringed, hearing ringing in my ears even after she'd finished. "Damn it, TJ. Do you have to whistle so loud—"

Bammm! The explosion coming from the woods in front of us stunned us. I had a sudden fear. Then I realized the shotgun blast wasn't near us. It had to have come from Tarzan's camp. The Bottomlands was completely silent. Not a single bird chirped or sang.

Bammm! Another blast!

37

"It's Packard!" I yelled. "He's after Tarzan." I dashed forward, jumping over logs, dodging around trees and bushes. TJ and Ferret crashed after me. "Yell! Let 'em know we're coming. We've got to scare Packard off."

"Eeyyaahhh," TJ screamed.

"Aahhhuhaahhhuhaahhh." Ferret's yelling reminded me of the movie Tarzan's jungle cry.

"Yahhhh!" I yelled.

We smashed through the woods, making enough noise to scare an elephant, yelling, tramping on leaves, snapping dead branches. A few minutes later, I burst into the clearing and saw Tarzan's camp. Stopping, breathing hard, I held my hands out, warning TJ and Ferret to stop. "Quiet now," I whispered. "Watch out for anything."

The camp was silent, neat and orderly, as it had been yesterday. A lonely wisp of smoke spiraled upwards from Tarzan's burned-out fire pit.

"Where's Tarzan?" TJ asked, crouching beside me.

My eyes scanned the clearing and swept deeper into the trees on the other side of the camp, seeing nothing except forest. "Not here."

"Who fired the shots?" she asked, her voice a low whisper.

Ferret stood up, speaking in a bold tone of voice, startling me. "Whoever it was, we scared him away."

"Maybe the shooting didn't come from here," TJ said.

"It had to have come from here," I answered, convinced I was right. I'd heard plenty of shotguns fired in the fields before.

"Then who fired at what?" TJ asked.

"I don't know. Keep your eyes peeled."

We approached the tent cautiously. I kept my eyes on the bushes beyond, searching for any sign of Packard, seeing nothing special.

"I'll look in the tent," TJ said, starting forward.

I grabbed her arm, pulling her behind me. "Heck if you will."

I circled around to the tent entrance. The flaps hung open, the tent seemed empty. Crouching low, I peered inside. The strangely familiar smell of wildflowers wafted from the interior. I pulled back. "Nothing here."

"I'll check the other side," TJ said stubbornly.

"TJ, stay back."

"Heck if I will." She marched around the tent and froze, her eyes fixed on the bush where my T-shirt had dried yesterday. "Mark!" she screamed.

I ran around the tent. Half-concealed by the bush, Tarzan lay still, flat on his back, his chest and stomach a bloody mass. His eyes were open, glassy. They flickered. He was alive.

"Tarzan!" Kneeling, I cradled his head in my arms.

Tarzan looked up, his eyes full of pain. His lips moved, trying to say something.

"Hang on. We'll get help. Ferret!"

Ferret knelt beside me. "Oh, Jesus, golly damn," he moaned.

Tarzan glanced at Ferret, and the corners of his mouth turned upward.

Was he smiling? Somebody had just shot the hell out of him. "What happened? Who did this?"

He took a breath, his throat gurgling, bright red flecks of blood appearing on his lips. "It's . . . no use."

He was dying. I looked at his ravaged chest. His shirt half

shot off, pieces of fabric embedded in his flesh, he couldn't have much time left. "Who shot you?"

I felt a shudder pass through his body, reminding me of when Mr. Tucker's dog Sam had died. "It doesn't . . . matter," he said, straining against the pain.

How could it not matter? I was to blame. Packard had shot Tarzan for helping me. "Did Packard do this? That bastard!"

Tarzan looked up at us and forced another faint smile. "Thank you . . . for being friends. . . . " The light in his blue eyes faded and his head turned slightly away from me. I felt the heaviness of his head then. Gently I laid Tarzan's head down and stood up, tears in my eyes.

"Holy shit!" TJ yelled, pointing toward the woods.

I whirled, expecting to see Packard coming out, his shotgun pointed at my belly. But no one was there. Deep in the woods, a good fifty yards away, I saw a quick movement, then nothing, then another blurred movement, further away, moving toward the county road.

"It's Packard. He's getting away. Stay here." I charged after him, jumping and dodging through the forest, feeling bushes and limbs tearing at my arms and legs. I tried to keep my eyes on the movements ahead, but managing only a glimpse now and then. Then, nothing.

The forest lay suspended in time before me. I slowed and stopped, suddenly worried that he might be lurking ahead, waiting for me to catch up so he could shoot me.

I started again, low and slow, not knowing if Packard was running or waiting to ambush me.

A motor roared to life. Near the road. Damn it. He'd been running while I'd been creeping. I raced through the woods again, caution be damned. Ahead, I could hear gears shifting, engine sounds moving away. I had to see Packard's truck. That would be evidence enough to convict him.

A couple of minutes later, I emerged from the woods and dashed onto the county road, still hazy with lingering dust. Far to the north, a cloud of dust rose, obscuring what had to be Packard's truck.

I stumbled down the road. I'd tried to warn Jess and Sheriff Adams about that bastard Packard. Now it was too late. Suddenly, I remembered what Reverend Brubaker had said. His prediction had come true. Evil begets evil.

Up ahead, a quail whistled. Bob . . . white. Bob . . . bob white.

"Damn you," I screamed. "Damn you to Hell!" I stopped, sick in my heart, and listened to that stupid quail continue its plaintive call.

TJ and Ferret came running up.

"You should have stayed with Tarzan," I said softly.

TJ shook her head. "I'm not staying there."

"Me neither," Ferret said.

I shrugged, tired, all my emotions spent. "I guess it doesn't matter."

"Did you see Packard?" TJ asked.

I took a deep breath, forcing myself to respond. "Vanished in a cloud of dust," I said, jerking my head toward Bob White.

TJ's eyes widened. "Holy shit! He's coming back."

I whirled. Somebody was coming. Dust boiled upward, indicating a high rate of speed. Would Packard be coming back?

A few seconds later, I could tell it wasn't a pickup. It was a car. Jess's police car. We waved furiously. A minute later, Jess slid to a halt, gravel spewing off both sides of the road. We backed up, avoiding the dust drifting east.

"What's going on?" Jess asked, getting out of his car, shoving his hat on his head, adjusting it as he came around in front of the Fury.

"Lafe Packard's killed Tarzan," I shouted, my voice filled with anger.

"Packard killed the queer?" His eyes shifted from mine to TJ's and Ferret's, then back again. "What? How?"

"He shot Tarzan and then took off into town. You must have passed him."

Jess frowned and glanced back up the road. "I didn't pass anybody."

He had to have passed someone. Surely he believed me. "You saw the dust, didn't you?"

Jess nodded. "Yeah. Somebody had been up the road." He looked toward the forest, right at the dead, split-wide cottonwood tree. "Where'd it happen?"

"Back at his camp."

Jess cocked his head and looked at me suspiciously. "Are you certain he's dead?"

I nodded. TJ and Ferret nodded also.

"You see Packard do it?"

"Not exactly. We heard two shotgun blasts."

"You heard the killing?"

"Yeah."

"Did you actually see Packard?"

"Well no, but—"

"See his truck?"

"I guess not."

"You guess not. Well, shit."

I didn't say anything.

Jess turned and went back to the car and pulled out the radio mike. "Sheriff? This is Jess. You there, Brahma?"

The radio crackled, "I'm here, Jess. What's up?"

"You best get on down to the Bottomlands. That queer's been murdered by persons unknown."

38

Sheriff Adams arrived in five minutes and took charge, ordering us to take him and Jess back to the camp. It was just as we'd left it, a wisp of smoke still curling from the fire pit. The sheriff inspected the body and allowed as how Tarzan was dead all right. The sheriff had us tell what happened, then had us tell him again, and then a third time, so we wouldn't leave anything out, he'd said. Finally, we all went back to the county road and Sheriff Adams started calling people.

We got told to stay put in Jess's Fury. It was hot, so we opened up all the car doors and solemnly watched the goings-on without saying much. During the next couple of hours, the county road practically filled up with official vehicles with their lights flashing and motors running with no one in them. Besides Jess's Fury and Sheriff Adam's car, there was the Bob White Fire Department truck, the fire chief's car, the ambulance from the Dwayne Mulhair Funeral Home, Mr. Mulhair's county coroner's car, and two Oklahoma State Highway Patrol cars that just happened to be in the neighborhood. In addition, Mr. Stack, the mayor of Bob White, showed up with a reporter from the *Daily Gazette,* and about thirty people from town had come down to see what all the commotion was about. The firemen cordoned off the area to keep the towns-folk from entering the woods. We could hear them making rank jokes, then laughing and enjoying their rowdiness.

Finally Jess returned and said he was taking us to the station to get our statements down on paper. On the way back, he asked if we were okay, and we all nodded and mumbled "yeah." TJ didn't look all right, especially for someone who'd seen one Cajun kill another one. Her face was pale as ash, her eyes more white than green.

Ferret was . . . well, just pretty much the same old Ferret, except he was quiet, maybe out of respect for the dead. The reverend had been involved with death a lot, so Ferret was probably used to it. I didn't think he ever liked Tarzan. Maybe in his head, he couldn't overcome the image of Tarzan as an abomination, as the Reverend Brubaker had claimed.

I'd seen too much trouble in my life, with more to come. Lafe Packard's threat was real. He would have gutted me yesterday except for Tarzan, and now he'd taken his revenge on the man who had saved my life.

And the damn thing about it was he might get off scot-free. If I hadn't told TJ and Ferret to yell, Packard wouldn't have been warned off and we would have caught him in the act.

I felt my face burning, but not from the heat. I was burning from inside out.

Lafe Packard was a man who needed to be killed.

The thought exploded into my head. As soon as I thought it, the hot spell vanished and a chill went up my spine. What was happening to me? This was the second time I'd thought of killing someone. I scrunched down in the car seat, feeling the outside air buffeting my face, suddenly wondering who I was.

At the Sheriff's Office, Lucy was on duty. She always dressed like she was going out—but Lucy never dated. The big purple flowers on her white dress made her seem larger than she was. Her puffy blond hair looked glued on, and her eyebrows seemed like they were painted on with black Crayola.

Lucy was on duty all right, jabbering away on the phone, letting someone know what she knew about the murder, speculating, talking big, hinting that she knew more than she really did.

She knew everyone in town on a first-name basis. I wondered whether she had some kind of pecking order established for who to call first, who second, and so on. She barely nodded when we came in, but she'd be all ears as soon as we started giving our statements to Jess.

Jess sat us down in chairs surrounding his desk and put a fresh sheet of paper into his typewriter. Lucy immediately hung up and pretended to be reading her movie magazines. It took more than half an hour for Jess to type out all his questions and our answers. Through it all, I sat numbly, not saying more than I had to. I hadn't told anyone that Packard had nearly killed me yesterday or that Tarzan had saved my life, so none of that went into the report. I guessed it wasn't important now anyway.

Jess pulled the statement from the typewriter and slid it across his desk for me to sign. I signed it, not bothering to read what he'd typed.

Behind me, I heard the office door open. A startled expression flashed across Jess's face. Across the room, Lucy gasped.

Standing in the doorway, a shit-eating grin cutting his face, was Lafe Packard!

Warily, I rose to my feet. "You son-of-a . . . " The words caught in my throat.

"Hee, hee, hee," Packard cackled. A bulge protruded from his left cheek and tobacco juice dribbled down his scraggly chin. "Lookee here. Jess Stoddard wet-nursing three piss-ant kids."

Jess's lips tightened into a thin, bloodless line, and his voice hissed out of his mouth like a snake ready to strike. "You come to give yourself up?"

Packard shuffled across the room, the fraying cuffs of his filthy overalls swishing against the floor, his John Deere cap cocked at a jaunty angle. "Give myself up? What for? I heared you was looking for me so here I am. You want to talk? Then talk."

I backed further away as he approached, a foul odor preceding him, a smell like dead mice in the walls of a house.

His thumbless left hand shot out and grabbed the chair I'd been sitting in. TJ and Ferret bolted from their chairs, shrinking back beside me. Packard sat down and propped his feet up on Jess's desk.

Jess glared at Packard's mud-encrusted boots, his eyes as hard as I'd ever seen them. "You expect to be doing any walking, Packard, you best be getting your filth off my desk."

Their eyes locked and seconds of time ticked by, reminding me of two arm wrestlers straining their guts out, but evenly matched, their arms frozen, immobile, with not the slightest quiver between them. Holding his eyes on Jess, Packard dropped his feet to the floor. "Why shore, Mr. Deputy Sheriff, I'm happy to oblige. That's why I'm here. To help you." He smiled, revealing his sickening tobacco-stained teeth.

"All right," Jess said quietly, his eyes never leaving Packard's. "Where were you this afternoon?"

"When this afternoon?" Packard smirked.

"Between one and three."

"Between one and three?" Packard looked up at the ceiling, pretending to be racking his brain. "Oh, you mean while that queer was getting hisself killed?"

He was practically admitting it!

"Yeah," Jess answered.

"Between one and three. Now, lemme see. Well, hell. You know . . . " He acted surprised. " . . . I was over at Hogan's having me a couple of beers."

I gasped. "You were at Hogan's?"

"Shut up, Mark. That right, Packard?"

"That's right, Mr. Deputy. You can ask him yourself."

"I will. Lucy?" He turned, for the first time taking his eyes off Packard.

Lucy was looking right at Packard, as if mesmerized. She didn't answer.

"Lucy!"

Her eyes fluttered, and she looked at Jess, her mouth sputtering, "What . . . oh, sorry, Jess." Her cheeks reddened.

"Call Hogan. Tell him to get his butt over here right now." Lucy picked up the phone immediately, whispering into it. Jess turned back to Packard, his eyes as intense as a hawk's.

Packard leaned back in his chair, letting his eyes half-close. Then his smile faded and his voice turned into a low, gloating growl. "Got any more questions, Jess Stoddard?"

"You live down in the Bottomlands, don't you?"

"I been known to spend the night there, sometimes. My official address is Gen-ner-el De-live-ry, Bob White, Oklahoma."

"You ever see a tall, blond guy in the forest?"

"Naked as a jaybird, most of the time."

Jess blinked, then nodded as if he understood. "Ever talk to him?"

"Fuck, no."

Across the room, Lucy's eyes were as big as saucers.

"Ever fight with him?"

Packard's eyes closed and he didn't answer.

"You answer my questions or I'll throw your ass in jail."

The old man chuckled, opening his eyes to tiny slits. "Only one I ever heared fought with him is a Mr. Deputy Sheriff."

Jess flushed, and I could see the anger building in him, trying to take over. "You better watch yourself, Packard."

The old man held up his hands, and I couldn't help staring at the scar on his left hand, where the thumb had been. Packard grinned. "Just trying to help you out."

"Where'd you get the boiler for your still?" Jess asked quickly. "You buy it in the City?"

"Boiler? Still? Now where would I get the money to buy a boiler?" Packard's voice changed, getting hard and bitter. "I just got out of prison."

"We know the still was yours. We know you been selling moonshine. We got witnesses."

"You ain't got shit. You ain't got witnesses. I don't know nothing about no still." He turned toward me, his eyes piercing like knives. "Your baby brother knows more about stills than me. He knows how to smash 'em up real good."

I remembered the feeling I'd gotten just after I'd busted up the still. Of Packard hiding in the bushes, watching me.

No one said anything for a moment, the silence hanging in the air like stale cigarette smoke.

Then Jess spoke. "You're lying, you old bastard. And I'm going to prove it. You're a god-damned liar."

Packard sat up slowly, his eyes smoldering like he was ready to kill again. "And what are you, Jess Stoddard? You're a—"

"I'm here, Jess." Mr. Hogan waddled into the office on his stubby legs, his face red as his patchy hair, his breath coming in quick gulps.

Packard swiveled in his chair and Mr. Hogan froze. For a brief instant, their eyes locked, then the dwarf averted his eyes in a trembling, jerking motion. Awkwardly, he looked around the room, blinking when he saw Lucy, blinking again when he saw me. Finally, he looked at Jess and swayed from side to side. "What . . . uh . . . what did you want to see me about?"

"When did you last see this man?"

Mr. Hogan glanced at Packard, then licked his lips. "Uh . . . earlier this afternoon."

"When?" Jess snapped, rising suddenly from his chair.

Mr. Hogan's eyes jerked upward at Jess, and his face paled. "It was between one and three. He had a couple of beers."

"Who else saw him there?"

"Uh . . . no one. My place was closed."

"Closed? Then what was Packard doing there?"

Mr. Hogan clasped his hands together, squeezing first one then the other. Nervously, he glanced at Packard again. "I mean, it wasn't closed. There was just no one else there." He focused on Jess again, a pleading look in his eyes. "You know my business has been bad, lately."

Jess sighed. "All right, Hogan. You can go now." Jess sat down, as if he were really tired.

A relieved expression on his face, Mr. Hogan glanced at Packard again, then started backing toward the door.

"Ask him about the jugs beside his back door." TJ's voice rang into the stillness.

Jess turned to stare at TJ, surprised and puzzled by her outburst. "Jugs?" He looked at the dwarf. "What jugs?"

Mr. Hogan twisted his hands and it must have been painful, because he winced. "Jugs? Oh . . . uh . . . Just some stuff I picked up in Texas. For medicinal purposes. You know about that, don't you, Jess?"

Jess nodded. "Yeah, I know about that." He glared at TJ and she dropped her gaze. "You go on home now, Hogan."

Mr. Hogan backed slowly out of the room, rocking from side to side in his distinctive gait. He pulled the door closed behind him, like a little kid would do to keep the bad things from getting him.

Packard swiveled around to face Jess and shifted his chaw from his left cheek to his right. "So the little fucker's been drinking sugar whiskey. I don't know nothing about that."

Jess leaned forward, his eyes burning into Packard. "Sugar whiskey? How'd you know it was sugar whiskey?"

Packard's mouth gaped open, exposing a swirl of ugly brown liquid, but no sound came out.

Jess pointed his finger at Packard. "I know Hogan's lying for you, and I'm going to keep after him until he admits it."

A dark shade descended over Packard's face and he didn't say anything.

"You killed Tarzan," I said, "and you're going to jail."

Packard turned toward me, his eyes suddenly blazing with hate. "What's that on your ear, boy? Cut yourself? On a thorn? You oughta be more careful?" He laughed, and stood up. "Got any more questions, Jess Stoddard?"

Jess looked strangely at me, then shook his head. "Get out."

Packard cackled, then stomped each foot a couple of times on the floor, dancing in this way to the office door, bobbing his head up and down in time with his feet. He opened the door, stepped halfway out, then stopped. "Good-night, folks." His face broke out into a grin, evil and wild. "Sleep well."

39

Packard spat a stream of brown tobacco juice across the floor toward Lucy. Then he closed the door.

"Lord-a-mercy!" Lucy said, clutching her hand over her ample bosom. "That's the nastiest man in the world."

I couldn't stand it. That bastard was not going to get away with it. Not if I could help it. I ran across the room and yanked open the door.

"Mark! Stop!" Jess said.

I ignored him. Packard's legs were vanishing up the back stairs and out the door. I ran after him, intent on catching him in the parking lot. As I burst through the back door, a hand grabbed my right wrist, jerking me to a halt, pulling me toward a foul-smelling face.

"Nothing's changed, Mark Stoddard," Packard whispered, spitting tobacco juice droplets into my face. "Remember, I'm going to gut your brother and I'm going to gut you."

I tried to wrench loose, but he had me tight. "You killed the nicest, gentlest, most peace-loving man in the state. You bastard."

Packard laughed, genuinely amused. He raised my hand up, then popped his fingers wide, freeing my wrist. "How do you know your own house ain't dirty, boy?"

I stood there, slack-jawed, my mouth wide open.

Packard laughed again, then turned and shuffled to his pickup.

TJ and Ferret came running out the back door, nearly colliding with me. Packard climbed into the seat and backed out of his parking space. He swung his truck around in front of us and stopped, his eyes on TJ, glinting as they traveled up and down her body.

Angrily, I clenched my fists, wishing I had a rock or a sling shot in my hands.

Packard took his sweet time looking TJ over, so I stepped in front of her obscuring his view. Packard grinned at me. "The Day of Doom's a-coming!"

He revved his engine and popped the clutch. The pickup leaped away, catlike, and exited the lot. We watched until he disappeared, heading west on Main Street.

"The Day of Doom?" Ferret asked.

"The anniversary of the day his son died," I answered, knowing I'd have to explain to Ferret later. The way Packard had said the Day of Doom was coming meant that it wasn't today.

"Did you hear his engine?" TJ asked.

"His engine?" My mind left Ferret and drifted backward in time, recalling what I hadn't paid any attention to a moment ago. "Yeah. It's got a sticky valve that clicks when it idles."

"Yeah. The pickup that tried to run you down." Ferret said.

"Did you hear a clicking this afternoon, I mean, after Tarzan was shot?" TJ asked.

I thought back, hearing the engine starting up, then shifting gears, roaring away. I shook my head. "I can't remember."

The back door swung open and Jess came out. His eyes swept the parking lot, then settled on me. "Packard's crazy. It might be best if you spent the next few nights at the Brubakers'. That all right with you?"

I was surprised that Jess asked me. "Sure. If it's all right with the Brubakers."

Jess looked worried. "I'll give them a call and see if it's okay." He went back inside the courthouse.

When the three of us got to the Brubakers', Mrs. Brubaker hugged us each in turn, asking if we were all right. She told us we had to be strong, though her own chin trembled as she said it. The reverend wasn't home. Mrs. Brubaker said he had an appointment in the City and he'd be getting in late.

She offered to fix our favorite food for supper and we all voted for fried bologna sandwiches and ice cream. After eating I remembered I had to feed Bopeep. The sun was setting when I ran home. We played fetch until it got dark, then I fed her and ran back to the Brubakers'.

None of us felt much like talking, so when Mrs. Brubaker suggested we get a good night's sleep, we went upstairs. Packard had said "Sleep well." He meant to come for me while I was sleeping and least expecting it.

I climbed into bed, thinking about TJ. It wouldn't be right of me to visit her room uninvited, but I hoped she'd slip down the hall. She didn't. I fell asleep, all alone.

Sometime in the night, I woke up. Packard's last words kept bothering me.

"How do you know your own house ain't dirty?"

What did Packard mean?

Packard had to be the killer. He was the only man in Bob White mean enough to kill someone. But what if Packard hadn't done the killing? Who else would want to kill Tarzan? Who else hated Tarzan? Mr. Tucker? That was ridiculous.

"How do you know your own house ain't dirty?" Was Packard saying Jess had killed Tarzan? That was stupid. Why would Jess kill Tarzan? Because he thought Tarzan was queer? My mind went back to when Jess knocked out that roughneck, Billy Ray. At first I'd thought that Jess had killed him.

Jess couldn't be a murderer. He couldn't be. Packard had to be the killer.

"How do you know your own house ain't dirty?" "How do you . . . "

The words kept coming at me, making me toss and turn so I couldn't sleep. I decided to get dressed and go home. I'd check on Bopeep and maybe I could get some sleep in my own bed.

I slipped my clothes on, then sneaked downstairs as quietly as I could. The Brubakers' bedroom door was shut but a light showed through the crack. Voices were talking. Angry voices. I didn't want to hear them arguing again. I hurried into the kitchen and out the back door.

When I got home, I saw Jess's Fury out front. Bopeep appeared from the vicinity of the garage wagging her tail, having recognized me in the dark. I grabbed her and hugged her, and I'm sure it embarrassed her because she struggled to get loose. I let her come inside with me—she liked sleeping on my bed.

Inside I turned on the living-room lamp, and looked down the hallway, noticing that Jess's door was shut. Joyce was probably with him.

"How do you know your own house ain't dirty?"

Tarzan had been killed with a shotgun. I looked at the closet door. Dad's shotgun would be there where I'd left it. It had to be there. I turned away, then glanced back at the door. Was it really there?

I opened the hall closet. Dad's shotgun leaned against the wall, a familiar, comfortable sight. I sighed in relief.

The two boxes of shells that Jess had bought sat on the floor exactly where they'd been last night. They looked odd in the middle of the closet floor. Mom would have moved them off to the side, out of the way.

Bending down, I picked up the boxes to move them, and felt a shell shift inside the one in my right hand. I shook the box. It rattled. A bad feeling came into my chest. I pulled the top flap open. Two shells were missing. Exactly two.

The shotgun leaned against the back wall, now strange and different. I'd cleaned it last night and put it away. Reaching for it, I hesitated. Had it been fired? No, it couldn't have. Yet, two shells were missing.

I picked it up and carried it into the kitchen and sat down. I slid the bolt back, made sure the gun was clear, then stuck my thumbnail into the chamber and looked down the barrel. Light reflected from my thumbnail. But the inside walls of the barrel were dirty with powder residue. And the smell wafting from the barrel wasn't gun oil. It was burned powder.

40

Dad's shotgun had been the murder weapon. I shook my head. It couldn't be true. A numb feeling came over me.

I sat there over an hour trying to sort things through. Questions kept nagging me. Questions I didn't have answers to. Could Jess have killed Tarzan? No, he couldn't have.

But had Packard seen Jess shoot Tarzan? Had Packard seen Jess with the gun? How would Packard even know about the gun? Would he know I'd check the gun?

I kept coming back to Packard's accusation. Nobody in the world would believe him. Everybody in Bob White thought Packard did it. And everybody could damn well keep thinking that.

The shotgun was the only evidence against Jess. I got the cleaning kit, and ran an oily rag through the barrel. After I put the shotgun back in the closet, a terrible feeling of guilt washed over me. The only thing I was sure of was that I had to find out the truth.

"Mark? Wake up." I felt someone shaking me and rolled over, seeing a shock of red hair and a gum-chewing jaw. Joyce sat on the edge of my bed, an expression of concern touching her face. "You all right, honey? I was worried about you."

Groggily, I blinked and sat up, clutching the sheet around

my waist. "What time is it?" I asked, groaning, feeling like I had just gotten to sleep.

Joyce smiled, soft and easy. "It's nearly ten o'clock. We didn't even know you were in here until we heard Bopeep scratching to get out."

Bopeep? I remembered that I'd let her spend the night with me. Then I remembered last night and discovering that the shotgun had been fired. "Is . . . Jess here?"

Joyce raised an eyebrow, questioning my serious voice. "He left a while ago. Busy day for him, I expect."

"I need to talk to him. Know where he's going?"

Joyce's expression got more worried. "No, I don't. But Mark, there's something we need to talk about."

I'd learned to be wary whenever an adult started a conversation by saying they'd like to talk to me about something. "Yeah?"

She fixed her eyes steady on mine. "I want us to be friends."

Was that all? I relaxed. "I reckon we're friends all right."

She maneuvered the gum into the side of her mouth and smiled. "Well, you know the other day at my house? I'm sorry about upsetting you."

I remembered she'd said I was a poor little kid or something like that. But now I felt bad about having made a scene, especially right after she'd cooked up such a great meal. Looking down at my hands, I said, "I don't know that it was your fault, exactly."

"And I'd like to see you and Jess get along."

I didn't answer, turning my face away. I thought about the way Jess had been treating me, and about the shotgun being fired. Jess could be a murderer, and I'd destroyed the evidence. Maybe I was as guilty as Jess.

Joyce broke into my thoughts. "Mark? He loves you."

Love? Since Jess had come back home, I couldn't remember one thing he'd done that I could consider being done for love or friendship. "I doubt that."

Joyce moved closer to me, and put her hand on my shoulder. "He does love you. He wants you to grow up right."

I rolled my eyeballs. "I'm growing up just fine without him, thank you."

Joyce laughed. I guess my eyeballs must have looked pretty funny. "You are growing up just fine." She leaned backward, studying me. "If Jess and I do get married—and I'm betting we do—you'll have a place with us. Until you're ready to be on your own, of course."

If they get married? I tried seeing in her head, wondering how she'd like living with a murderer. I shook my head, clearing it of thoughts I didn't want to think. "Excuse me, but I'd like to get dressed. I've got things to be doing."

She stood up and backed away. Bopeep wandered into the room and whuffed. Joyce reached down and picked her up, then scratched her ears. Contrary to the nervous way Bopeep acted when I held her, she enjoyed it, licking Joyce's chin. "That's a good girl," Joyce said, putting Bopeep back down. She glanced at me and grinned. "You going over to see TJ?"

"Probably so," I answered. Seeing TJ and Ferret was something I had to do. I wasn't sure what I could tell them—maybe nothing about Dad's shotgun being the murder weapon—but I had too much worry on my mind to be alone.

"You're kinda sweet on TJ, aren't you?"

I felt embarrassment coming on. I acted bored. "She's okay for a girl."

Joyce laughed, then leaned down and hugged me, her hair sweeping across my face. Bopeep barked, the way she always did when she wanted to be part of the action. She jumped on the bed, grabbed some sheet between her teeth, and shook it ferociously. Joyce pretended to bite me on the neck, then growled. That set Bopeep off on a tear, dashing around the room from bed to floor and back again, barking so loud it hurt my ears.

Joyce let me go, standing up, laughing at Bopeep's antics. Bopeep made a final leap onto the bed to stand stiff-legged facing me. She barked once more to let me know she was still in charge, then jumped off and trotted down the hall. Joyce followed her, closing the door, giving me some privacy.

I sat still for a moment, remembering the flow of Joyce's hair across my face, tickling my nose, smelling the scent of honeysuckle. It reminded me of something. Something I'd smelled recently.

My mind went back to Tarzan's tent, and the smell I'd noticed when I woke up. A smell of wildflowers. But it wasn't wildflowers exactly, it was perfume. Was it the smell of honeysuckle? I couldn't remember exactly. Could Joyce have been the woman in the tent with Tarzan? If she was, then Jess might have . . . I shook my head, feeling sick.

Ten minutes later, I opened the Brubakers' back door, and walked into their kitchen. Reverend Brubaker sat at the kitchen table, an empty coffee cup near his right hand. He was reading his Bible, scowling, and making notes in a journal. I figured he was concentrating hard on his next sermon, because he didn't look up. I walked over to the table and leaned against a chair, scraping it a couple of inches.

The reverend's head shot up, his eyes focusing on me. He licked his lips, but said nothing. Not his usual greeting, not his normal "Good morning, Mark."

I guess I'd intruded into his thoughts. Feeling uncomfortable in the situation, I said, "Morning, sir. TJ and Ferret around?"

The reverend barely nodded. "They're upstairs. I think they're in Matthew's room." He turned back to his Bible.

I started toward the hall, then paused. His being here at this hour was pretty strange. "Is everything all right?"

The reverend's eyes were distant, far away. He spoke so low I had a hard time hearing him. "Josephine's not feeling well."

"It's not serious is it?"

He shook his head, then put his pen down. "She's under the weather. She'll be fine in a few days."

I was relieved to hear that. I'd hated to see them fighting yesterday, even though I expect most married folks did a little fighting now and then.

People said the reverend had a way of making them feel better about their problems. And I had plenty of problems right now. It seemed a good time to ask his help. I walked back to the table. "Sir? You've said to come talk to you if ever I was troubled? Well, I guess I'm troubled about Tarzan being murdered."

He studied me for a moment, not moving, as if he never expected me to come to him. Then he seemed to understand, because his eyes softened, and he took my hand in his. "It's God's will when any man has to die. We must accept God's will. The man you call Tarzan died for his sins."

"His sins?" I asked. The reverend had called Tarzan an abomination.

"Whatever his sins were, the man is dead now and the living must carry on. Best I can do is give him a decent burial."

That surprised me. "You're conducting the funeral service?"

"A graveside service." He closed his Bible and stood up. "I'm working on the service now. Perhaps before he died, he asked to be forgiven for his sins. To be allowed to enter the Kingdom of Heaven."

The reverend's words sorta made sense if you worried about his soul getting into Heaven, but they didn't help at all in understanding why he'd been murdered. "As far as I know, he didn't. But I'm sure Tarzan would appreciate your help."

He bowed his head. "I'm only doing God's work. I am the right hand of God." Rising, he took his coffee cup to the sink, then came back and collected his Bible and journal.

When people died, you had to do the right thing. The right thing was going to Tarzan's service. I hadn't known him long, but he was a good man and had tried to make friends. "When's the burial?"

"Sunday afternoon. Two o'clock."

"Isn't that rather quick?"

"Sheriff asked me if I could do it then. The autopsy was done last night and Brahma thought it would be better for all concerned if we got this whole matter taken care of and forgotten as soon as possible."

"Forgotten?"

"Sheriff said none of the other ministers wanted anything to do with the service. The man's Jewish—actually, we don't know for sure—but I'll give him a good Christian burial."

Reverend Brubaker nodded toward me, then strode briskly out the back, letting the screen door slam. It bounced back from the frame, then settled closed.

The house seemed quiet, with a certain finality after the door slammed. Like the way folks in town wanted to get Tarzan buried as soon as possible. Dead and buried.

A strange feeling came over me. I felt drawn toward the back screen door. I walked over and pushed it open. The reverend's station wagon was just disappearing around the corner of the house. I let the door swing back and bang shut again. Something about the door was bugging me.

I pushed the door wide open again, then caught it before it could bang again. I hesitated, noting it was unlocked, as usual, remembering that I'd come over and just walked right into their house, as easy as pie. Nobody in Bob White ever locked their doors, not even at night. You didn't have to, not in Bob White, Oklahoma. Anybody could walk into anyone else's house . . .

Packard could have slipped into our house, taken Dad's gun, killed Tarzan, then replaced it, with no one the wiser. Later he could accuse Jess of the murder. Jess would go to jail and Packard would have his revenge. Packard had changed his plan. Instead of killing Jess, he'd have Jess sent to jail like Packard's son had been. Maybe that was Packard's warped idea of revenge.

Somehow I had to stop Packard again. But I couldn't tell anyone about Dad's gun. Not yet, anyway.

Going upstairs to Ferret's room, I found TJ sitting crossways in an arm chair by the window, looking out. Ferret was sprawling on his bed, propped on his elbows, reading a comic book. "Hey, guys."

TJ looked at me strangely and said nothing. Ferret rolled over, looking relieved I was here, and said, "Hi."

"Let's go," I said, motioning toward the stairs.

TJ turned back to the window. "I don't feel like going anywhere."

I put my hands on my hips. "We got work to do."

Ferret sat up, curious. "Work?"

I nodded. "We've got to get the goods on Packard."

"He's got an alibi," TJ said, still looking out the window.

I walked over to the window and stood in front of it, forcing her to look up at me. "Bullshit. He killed Tarzan and deserves to go to jail. Or Hell."

Irritated, TJ squirmed around in the chair, avoiding my eyes. "We can't prove that. Mr. Hogan—"

I was glad she was finally showing some life. "Maybe we'll get Packard for bootlegging instead."

Ferret got up and came over to us, speaking to TJ. "You gonna sit around all day feeling sorry for yourself?"

"I'm not feeling sorry for myself," she said, wrapping her arms across her chest.

"Yeah, you're thinking it was your fault Tarzan got killed and you're wishing you had thanked him proper for the bracelet." Ferret reached out and shook her left wrist, jangling the stones and shells together.

Frowning, she jerked her hand away. "Shut up, Ferret."

Ferret wasn't using the right approach. I caught his eye and winked, then started for the door. "Come on, Ferret. TJ would just get in the way, anyhow."

Behind me, I heard TJ's sneakers clump against the floor. "All right, I'll go. You guys would be lost without me along."

41

I let my feet bump across the stair edges, sledding my way down the stairs. Short of jumping, it was the fastest way of getting downstairs. Going out the back door, I cut into the alley, heading north, my pals right beside me.

"So where are we going?" Ferret asked, walking fast to keep up.

"To get some answers. Red Nelson's first."

"Why?" TJ asked, not figuring anything out.

"Red knows guns better than anyone around."

No customers were at the Kerr-McGee station. Red was sitting in the office, oil-stained brown shoes crossed on the front of his desk, balancing himself on his chair's hind legs. He wore grimy overalls and a service cap with the emblem torn off. A copy of *Shotgunner's World* in his lap, he saw us coming and waved it enthusiastically at us.

The three of us trooped into the oily-smelling office and I greeted him. "Hi, Red."

He hadn't shaved, and the lines across his leathery face had collected plenty of station dirt. He nodded agreeably. "How you kids doing?"

"Fine," I answered.

His crinkly eyes shifted, studying each of us in turn. "Yesterday must have been pretty hard on you all."

"We're okay . . . except . . . "

He cocked an eyebrow, suspicious. "Except what?"

"We wanted to ask you a few questions about the shooting, if it's all right."

Red's hands were embedded with the black from grease and oil. He rubbed the back of his right hand against his chin, puzzling. "You were there. You oughta know more about it than anyone."

Ferret butted in. "We don't know more'n anyone else. We didn't see Tarzan get shot and he didn't take the trouble to tell us who did it."

"Took the killer's identity to the grave, did he? Why do you suppose he did that?"

Shrugging my shoulders, I said, "I don't have a clue. You sound like you don't think the killer will ever be found."

"Wouldn't surprised me none."

"Someone in town is a murderer." TJ said. "What about justice?"

Red took his service cap off and scratched his head, then readjusted the cap to a comfortable position. He acted uneasy about the fact that someone he knew might be a killer. "A man's . . . uh . . . choices in life are his own business. Ain't none of mine. I never even met the man, though I seen him at the fair."

Red hadn't answered TJ's question—on purpose I figured. No matter. I'd come here to ask some questions about the shooting. If anyone would know the answers, Red would be the man. "You heard he was gut-shot?"

His interest picked up. "Shot twice, at close range. Died pretty quick, I expect?"

"A few minutes," I agreed.

Red dropped his chair to the dusty floor, standing up. He stepped into the doorway and leaned against the frame, his back to us. "Tore him up inside pretty bad. I've known men who got shot on the range and men who got shot a-hunting. Twenty years ago I accidentally killed my own dog through damn fool carelessness." He shook his head. "Never saw a man gut-shot with a twelve-gauge before."

I had. "It was pretty bloody . . . but hey, you said . . . twelve-gauge?"

He turned around, facing us, and leaned his other shoulder against the frame. "Sheriff Adams brought some of the pellets by the house late yesterday. Asked my opinion. I figure it was a twelve-gauge. Could be wrong though."

"How's that?"

"Same size shot could be loaded in sixteen and twenty-gauge guns. But most shotguns are twelve-gauge, and Brahma thinks the first shot came from about ten feet. For a twelve-gauge, that'd make the pattern about six inches."

"The pattern? But how . . . "

"Brahma said the autopsy showed pellets in him from the lower rib to his testicles." His eyes darted to TJ, as if he'd just remembered she was with us. "Oh, sorry, excuse me, miss. Anyway, that'd be a twelve-gauge. Don't know of anyone in the county who's got a sawed-off sixteen- or twenty-gauge."

"The first shot was from ten feet? What about the second?" TJ asked.

"Brahma said it was fired point-blank. Tore a hole clear through him."

"Jesus Christ!" TJ said, her voice trembling. Her face was white, but I could tell from the way her jaw was set that she was damn mad about the way Tarzan had been killed.

A man had held a shotgun pointed at Tarzan's belly, and Tarzan probably stood calmly, facing death like he hadn't a care in the world. Bammm! Then the man had come up to him, and put a second shot right into his belly. Bammm!

I couldn't imagine why Tarzan had taken the killer's identity to the grave. Why hadn't he told us? What if Jess really did shoot Tarzan? Would Tarzan keep silent so I wouldn't know my own brother was a murderer?

"The man who killed him had to be heartless," Ferret said, clenching his fists.

I decided to ask the question that had been worrying me since last night. "Any way to tell which gun fired the shot?"

"No way in hell. It ain't like pistols or rifles where you can match the rifling patterns on the slugs. Shotguns ain't got rifling. If you want to shoot someone and get away with it, a shotgun's just about the perfect weapon."

Ferret had a tough look about his face. "You think Packard done it?"

Leaning against the door frame, Red gave a one-shouldered shrug. "Could be. He's got a twelve-gauge. Lives in the Bottomlands. Could be practically anybody in Bob White excepting old ladies and ministers. But I hear he's got an iron-clad alibi."

"Some people don't believe his alibi," TJ said, a dark, determined shadow across her face.

Red hesitated, then his eyes narrowed and focused on me. "You kids watch yourselves. Snooping around like you are."

"We'll be careful. Let's go, guys," I said, motioning with my head.

Red turned aside, letting us pass. "Say, Mark. Some kids been trashing the range. You ain't heard tell who'd that be, have you?"

I shook my head. "I've been out of touch lately."

Red nodded, then turned his attention to a car that was just driving up.

When we had cleared the service station, TJ said, "So what does all that mean?"

I shook my head. Nobody could prove that Dad's gun had done the killing, and I hadn't needed to clean the gun last night. "Maybe something will make sense later. Let's go see Mr. Hogan."

"Yeah," TJ said. "He lied yesterday. Let's see if we can get him to fess up."

It was a good twenty-minute walk. When we arrived, the squatty building was shut up tight. Mr. Hogan's Cadillac wasn't around back, either.

"Now what?" TJ asked, frustration creeping across her face. "His house is only a few blocks away."

Mr. Hogan lived in the nicest part of Bob White, in a red brick house that looked as normal as the rest of the neighborhood. Shrubbery out front, lawn well kept, a house you'd never expect to belong to a dwarf. He'd inherited it from his parents. The roof line came down over the front porch, which had been fully screened in. Folks around here liked screened porches. They could sit and visit, catch the evening breezes, and not get pestered by mosquitoes and June bugs.

Through the screen I could see the front door had been left open. Banging was coming from somewhere inside. I knocked on the screen door. The racket inside suddenly ceased, followed by dead silence. After a moment, I knocked again.

"Who . . . who's there?" Mr. Hogan called.

"It's me, Mr. Hogan. Mark Stoddard," I yelled back.

Another pause. "Go away. I got no reason to talk to you."

I wasn't giving up that easy. Motioning for TJ and Ferret to follow me, I opened the screen door, and led the way across the porch and into the house, discovering a living room filled with normal-sized furniture. Toward the back was a dining area and kitchen. A hall led off to the left. "Mr. Hogan?"

The short, stout man waddled rapidly from a back bedroom and hesitated, still in the hallway. His large, red-tufted head peered cautiously at the three of us, his eyes blinking. "Go away. Get out of my house."

"I'm not leaving," I said firmly. "Not until you talk to us."

Nervously, he licked his lips, shifting his eyes from face to face. "I don't have time to talk. I'm going on a trip."

"Huh?"

He jerked his head in a quick nod. "Going on a long vacation. Maybe never coming back."

The hell he was! "You're scared of Packard, aren't you? You're running."

"My business is . . . bad. Gonna sell out. Live somewhere else."

Angrily, Ferret spoke up. "You lied yesterday, protecting Packard. Now you're gonna take off and forget about it?"

"I . . . I didn't lie. He was in the bar—from three o'clock on."

"Yesterday," TJ's voice cracked like a whip, "you said from one to three. Which is it?"

He looked confused. "I don't know. Whenever." He glared at TJ. "I don't have to answer questions from you."

"At least tell us about the moonshine. If you'd testify that Packard was selling you the whiskey, he could be put away for a long time."

"No!"

I raised my voice, practically yelling. "You lied, because Packard threatened you. I saw the way he looked at you yesterday. How can you protect that slime?"

His eyes darted toward the front door as if afraid someone outside would be listening. "Shut up. Go away. I'm leaving." He turned and waddled down the hall into a room.

I followed him, TJ and Ferret right behind. Mr. Hogan's bed was a cluttered jumble of pillows and rumpled sheets on which lay an open, packed, very large suitcase. For as long as I could remember, I'd known Mr. Hogan. "How can you leave? You were born here. You've lived here all your life. Your folks are buried here."

He turned and stared at me, wide-eyed, as if realizing the enormity of his decision to leave. Panic seized him. He grabbed a towel lying on the bed and buried his face in it. "Get out, leave me alone," he screamed.

"Coward!" TJ yelled fiercely.

Mr. Hogan jerked the towel from his face, his hands clenched, his eyes wild with fear. "Packard will kill me."

"Mr. Hogan. This is your home. Stay and tell the truth."

He collapsed on his bed, shaking his head, sobbing. "I'm sorry. I'm so sorry. I just can't."

I felt sorry for him. Anger was in my heart on account of his protecting Packard. But he was frightened, and there was no changing his mind. I held out my hand. "Good-bye."

He didn't look up.

The three of us left Mr. Hogan's house, and headed west. We hadn't gotten more than a block away when his screen door slammed open. Mr. Hogan lumbered from his house like an overweight duck, carrying a suitcase nearly as big as he was. He stuffed it in the back seat of his Cadillac, then climbed in. The car roared by, raising a cloud of dust, heading toward the highway. As he passed, he glanced away. The car went as far as Six Mile Creek, then turned north, avoiding Main Street.

I watched the car disappear, then wondered what the hell to do next. "If he'd just been honest about the whiskey."

"Sugar whiskey," Ferret corrected.

I shrugged. "Yeah, sugar whiskey."

"Sugar whiskey?" Ferret said again. "Sugar whiskey! Golly damn!"

42

Ferret's dark eyes were shining, like he'd discovered buried treasure. "Where did Packard get all that sugar?"

"You're not thinking of Mr. Tucker, are you?"

"I sure am."

It was too obvious. "Sheriff Adams would have asked Mr. Tucker."

"So what if Mr. Tucker said he didn't know anything about it?"

"The sheriff would have let it go, trusting him."

"Packard might have gotten the sugar from Texas," TJ offered.

I frowned, feeling my memory kick into gear. Something was bugging me.

She continued. "Or from any town within fifty miles. He could haul a ton of it in his pickup."

Then I remembered. I got excited. "Except . . . "

"Excepting what?" Ferret asked, knowing I was on to something.

"Except when Mr. Tucker gave me a ride back to town, after I'd found Packard's still, he said he'd been delivering groceries to Mrs. Johnson."

TJ knitted her eyebrows together. "Yeah? So?"

"Then why were there two grocery boxes in his truck on the way *back* to town?"

TJ and Ferret looked at each other, getting the picture.

"Because maybe they weren't groceries, after all. Maybe they were filled with sugar . . . and he couldn't find Packard to deliver them, because Packard was chasing me."

"It all hangs together," Ferret said, proud of himself.

TJ snapped her fingers. "If we can sneak into his storeroom—"

"Yeah," I said, interrupting. "We can find those boxes."

We set out for Tucker's General Store. Arriving downtown, we came up behind it. Mr. Tucker kept things looking pretty orderly behind the store, with lids sealing all the trash cans tight and boxes stacked in neat piles for people to pick up and use if they had a need. The area was deserted except for Mr. Tucker's pickup, parked a few feet away from the door to the storeroom. Whatever had been in the pickup bed had been removed.

"Reckon the back door's locked?" TJ asked.

I knew it wasn't. I'd been in and out of it lots of times helping Mr. Tucker unload stuff. "No need to lock anything in Bob White, except maybe at night, in case of strangers."

"Then let's go," she said, starting forward.

Ferret grabbed her arm. "We can't just barge in. Mr. Tucker or his wife could be in the back."

Angrily, TJ jerked her arm free.

"Hold it," I said, trying to avoid a last-second squabble between the two. "I'm the only one knows what the boxes look like, so I'm the only one needs to go in. Ferret, you and TJ go round and see where they are, then send TJ to tell me it's okay to sneak in. Then both of you go in and hang around. If you see Mr. or Mrs. Tucker starting toward the back, then, Ferret, you keep 'em occupied until TJ can come around and warn me."

"Okay by me," Ferret said, starting around the side of the building toward the front. TJ glanced at him, then me, then chased after him. They disappeared around the corner. A couple minutes later, TJ came dashing back. "They're both working in the store, waiting on customers."

"Okay, go on back and help keep watch."

"I'm going with you." She grinned, like my plan had fit perfectly with hers.

Irritated, I pointed toward the front of the store. "We need you in the store to help Ferret. Go on, damn it." Even as I spoke, I knew it was the wrong thing to say to her.

TJ walked over to the back door, swung it wide, and walked in.

I jumped forward and caught the door just before it banged shut, then followed TJ inside. The room was as big as most people's houses, well lighted, and more or less filled with boxes of all kinds of grocery stuff that didn't require refrigeration.

"What do the boxes look like?" she whispered.

"They've got 'PURINA' on the outside, and they're really big." I held my hands wide, sizing a two-by-three-foot box.

Five minutes later, we found the boxes, not far from the back door. Their tops were cut on three sides, making lids. I raised one up. Neatly stacked to the top were five-pound bags of sugar and a few packets of yeast.

"Holy shit!" TJ said. "You were right. Look at all that sugar."

"What's going on in here?" Mr. Tucker stood in the open doorway, his hand still on the doorknob. Behind him, I could see Ferret, looking half sick. He shrugged, indicating there was nothing he could have done. Mr. Tucker looked at me, a puzzled expression on his face. "I'd like an explanation, Mark."

Feeling a little sad about the whole affair, I stood aside so Mr. Tucker could see the boxes of sugar that we'd discovered. "I know you've been selling this to Packard."

His face turned white. He licked his lips nervously, then looked at TJ. "Sweetheart, wait outside while I talk to Mark about this little misunderstanding."

TJ glanced at me, apprehension on her face, then turned and walked through the door toward Ferret.

Mr. Tucker shut the door firmly, then walked over to the

boxes of sugar and flipped the lid closed. "It doesn't mean anything, Mark. Anything at all."

"You've been supplying Packard with sugar. You can prove he was bootlegging. You could testify—we could testify and send him to jail."

His shoulders sagged. "I can't do that. If people knew . . . I'd been helping Packard, I'd be destroyed. I . . . I might go to jail."

I thought about having known Mr. Tucker for years, as good a grownup friend as I'd ever had. "Why'd you do it?"

He took a long time answering, then said simply, "Just for business, Mark."

"We've been friends a long time, Mr. Tucker," I said, feeling like my friendship had been betrayed.

Mr. Tucker smiled, speaking earnestly. "A long time, Mark. I was friends with your Mom and Dad. I promised you a job here at the store. Remember all those free pops. Remember helping me look for the Tucumcari bottle?"

"I remember."

"Then why make a big deal of it? It's over now anyway. You busted up the still. Nobody got hurt."

I shook my head. "Packard killed a man."

Mr. Tucker snorted. "Is that what this is about? It's not about bootlegging? It's because a queer got killed!"

"He's got to go to jail one way or another."

Mr. Tucker looked grim. "Damned if I'm going to lift a finger for a queer."

"You hated him, didn't you?"

He glowered, not trying to hide his feelings. "I hate all people like him. You bet I do. You don't understand. I know about these things."

"You don't know anything about him."

Mr. Tucker threw his shoulders back, lifting his head high, kinda reminding me of the way Reverend Brubaker acted sometimes. "He got what he deserved."

He was glad that Tarzan was dead. There was a lot about

Mr. Tucker that I didn't understand, that I'd never under-stand. That tore it for me. "And you'll get what you deserve. It's got nothing to do with Tucumcari Coke bottles."

He looked worried. "Come to work for me. I'll pay you dou-ble."

"I don't want your money."

"Now what?" he asked, nervously clenching his fists.

"Either you tell about Packard's bootlegging or I'm seeing Sheriff Adams."

Mr. Tucker licked his lips. "I'll call you a liar. Everybody knows you've had run-ins with Packard. You're out to get him. Who's going to believe you?"

"TJ saw the sugar. Ferret saw the sugar. They'll believe us." I started to leave.

Mr. Tucker stepped in front of me, a real hard look around his eyes. "Don't do this, Mark. You'll be sorry."

"Get out of my way," I said, staring coldly at him.

He stood rock-solid for a moment, then his eyes wavered and he took a half-step aside. I pushed past him and opened the door, joining TJ and Ferret. They didn't speak and fol-lowed me out the front door, past the old men sitting in their usual spots on the porch.

On the way to the sheriff's office, I told TJ and Ferret what had transpired. When we arrived, Jess wasn't there, and I was surprised to see Lucy on duty, since it wasn't yet four o'clock. She was on the phone, talking as usual, but seeing us come in, she hung up quickly.

"Hi, Lucy."

"Hi, y'all," she answered, as curious as if she'd had six eyes and matching ears as well as antenna and feelers. "What's going on?"

She'd find out soon enough. "Sheriff Adams in?"

"He's on the phone." She leaned backwards, glancing into the office. "Oops, now he's off. You can—"

I barged into the office. Sheriff Adams was writing some-thing down on a note pad. "Sir?"

He looked up and frowned, the corners of his mouth turning down in exact opposition to the tips of his mustache. "Well, if that don't beat all. I just this minute got a call from Roy Tucker." He looked behind me, seeing TJ and Ferret hanging back. He motioned at them. "You two better come on in."

I didn't wait for the sheriff to get started. He'd already heard from Mr. Tucker, and I wanted him to hear the truth straight away. "We've got proof that Packard's the bootlegger. Mr. Tucker's been selling sugar to Lafe Packard to make moonshine with."

The sheriff froze. "What?"

TJ spoke up. "He's been hauling it down to the Bottomlands in his pickup."

Sheriff Adams glanced sharply at her. "What the hell . . ."

She nodded. "We just saw it in his storeroom."

"I rode back to town with him a couple days ago, in his pickup, and saw it then," I added quickly.

"He admitted this to you?" the sheriff asked incredulously.

"Yeah. Said now that the still was busted, it didn't matter. Asked me not to tell. Then tried to bribe me. Then he said if I told, he'd say we were lying."

The sheriff nodded, as if considering all I'd told him. "That's what he said, all right; and that you'd been stealing."

"If we'd been stealing, would we be here now?" I looked him square in the eye.

Sheriff Adams stood up and reached for his hat. "I think I'll have a talk with Roy."

"Now you can arrest Packard."

Sheriff Adams paused at the doorway and said, "Even if Tucker was selling him sugar, I can't arrest Packard unless Tucker testifies against him. This whole thing about Packard is a mess. Mark, I don't know what the hell you think you're doing, but I'll be talking to Jess about it later."

43

I had a sneaking suspicion that Mr. Tucker wouldn't be admitting anything. Nothing I did seemed to be working out without getting worse. I wasn't any closer to getting Packard thrown in jail.

We went back to Ferret's house and found the reverend waiting. Mrs. Brubaker was not feeling well enough to fix supper, so he had decided to take Ferret and TJ to dinner at Martin's Steakhouse. I was invited to go along, but I said "No, thank you, sir." I was worried about talking to Jess.

I told the reverend that I planned to go to Sunday's service for Tarzan. He told me that was a good thing for me to do and to be at his house by one-thirty if I wanted a ride. Both Ferret and TJ said they wanted to go, too.

I went home thinking about the service for Tarzan, and decided that I ought to look nice when I paid my respects. I checked my closet and found practically everything dirty, including the white shirt I'd worn to church last Sunday.

Altogether the amount of dirty clothes, between mine and Jess's, was sizable. So I did the laundry, separating the coloreds from the whites. Our washing machine was only a year old, but Mom hadn't wanted one of the newfangled hot-air dryers, preferring to hang up everything outside on the clothesline where it would get plenty of fresh air. As I pinned my jeans up, I pictured Mom standing beside me, smiling and talking, looking forward to Dad coming home from work. The image faded and I was left with nothing but wet jeans hanging heavy on the line.

Later, I fried a couple of hot dogs and took them out on the front porch to eat. I ate slowly, feeding Bopeep bits of bread from the buns, then letting her finish the last bite of each hot dog. Gratefully, she licked my fingers clean.

The sun would be setting soon, and a gentle Oklahoma breeze was cooling things off a bit. In the cloudless sky above, the blue was deepening and the air felt damp, like rain was coming. Somewhere off to the northwest, thunderstorms were probably building up.

This time of year, Mother Nature hardly allowed a week to go by without throwing some kind of violence at us. But I didn't figure the storm would hit us until much later tonight. Might even be an electrical storm.

I wondered where Jess was, and whether Sheriff Adams had talked to him yet. Would the sheriff believe me? Jess wouldn't believe me. I was just a kid.

Bopeep lay at my side, dozing comfortably, her eyes closed, letting me scratch her neck and ears. I thought about TJ, wondering whether Tarzan's getting killed was bothering her. I glanced up Ash Street, toward the Brubakers' house.

Two blocks beyond their house, a car turned off Main Street, coming from the west, from the highway. The day's brightness had faded so I couldn't see it clearly. It came south a block, then turned east again. A big car, with fins. The shape was undeniably that of a Cadillac. It was Mr. Hogan.

Why had he come back? To tell the truth? If he told the truth, then folks would believe me and not Mr. Tucker. Right now he was the best chance I had of getting Packard thrown in jail.

"Bopeep?" I said softly. "You need an outing."

She opened her eyes, then scrambled to her feet, dancing off the porch, ready for whatever adventure lay ahead. Together, we set out through the seeping twilight for Mr. Hogan's house.

Mr. Hogan's house was silent and the lights were off. The Cadillac wasn't parked there so we continued on east and then south toward the pool hall. Sensing that something was up, Bopeep trotted determinedly beside me, matching my long strides with her hurried pace.

It was a strange evening. I could feel the electricity building up in the air, flowing on the breeze around my back. The last few minutes of twilight caused the sky above to glow eerily, and hues of gold and red and yellow flickered on the cotton-woods and rooftops before me, as if a huge fire were burning in the distance, someplace behind me, far, far away.

Leaving the houses behind, we arrived at the pool hall, approaching it from the west. The lonely decrepit building stood isolated, like a miniature island surrounded by a sea of gravel. Mr. Hogan's vacant Cadillac, its left front tire perched awkwardly on a pile of garbage, was parked behind the squatty building, near the back door. Beyond the dirty, grease-laden windows, light shimmered from somewhere within, reminding me of the flickering twilight rays dazzling in the sky above.

Flickering? Near the flat tar-paper roof line, a flame burst through a thin seam, then sputtered and caught again, flaring more intensely. Smoke belched through the rapidly expanding hole, boiling upward into the evening sky. The pool hall was on fire!

I ran toward the back door. "Mr. Hogan! Mr. Hogan!"

Bopeep chased after me, barking excitedly. Smoke poured into the sky, and I knew it'd be only seconds before someone in Bob White spotted it and called the fire department.

I dodged around the Cadillac, then hesitated at the back door, wondering how bad the fire was inside. The fire hadn't gotten this far yet. But the acrid, heavy odor of burning tar paper rolled off the roof. To my right, I sensed, rather than saw, a bit of shadowy movement. Well away from the building, behind the open door of his pickup, stood Lafe Packard.

"Where's Mr. Hogan?" I hollered.

Packard pulled off his John Deere cap, scratched his head, and spat out a stream of tobacco juice. "I don't rightly know, boy," he yelled back, his voice filled with contempt. "I just got here." He chuckled, then slapped his hat on and propped his arms over the edge of the truck's door frame, as if he was enjoying the fire.

"Mr. Hogan's in there. We've got to get him out."

Packard's eyes narrowed, the merriment in them changing into hostility. "Too late, boy. Reckon that fire's pretty much already gutted the insides."

Something inside my head woke up. Packard's being here and the fire starting were no coincidence. "You son-of-a-bitch. What'd you do to Mr. Hogan?"

Packard frowned, and his voice turned ominous. "Maybe you're right, boy. Let's both go in and rescue the little turd." Packard lunged away from the pickup, and stalked quickly toward me, his right hand buried deep in the pocket of his overalls.

Menace filled the old man's face as he approached, his right arm tight against his side, his scruffy shoes crunching purposefully across the gravel. His right overalls pocket bulged, as if his hand was balled around something. It had to be his knife. He was coming for me.

Beside me, Bopeep growled. She hadn't forgotten about what happened down at the Clear Boggy River—Packard thrusting a snake at her trying to get her bitten. Already, she'd bared her teeth, her body tense, poised like hornets ready to take off.

"Got your god-damned dog, have you?" Packard kept coming, drawing his hand from his pocket. "I'll take care of that mutt, this time." Fflickkk!

My instincts told me to run, but I couldn't. I couldn't let Mr. Hogan be burned up. Warily, I backed away, trying to figure out what to do. Bopeep snarled, then darted forward, barking like she was going to take an arm off.

Packard halted, then hid the knife behind his back and leaned forward, offering his left forearm for Bopeep to bite. "C'mere, pooch."

I started to yell, then I remembered doing just that down at the trestle, distracting Bopeep, nearly getting her bitten by the moccasin. I kept my mouth shut. Bopeep could take care of herself.

Suspicious, Bopeep backed away and circled warily. Packard turned, and lunged, swiping the knife at her. Bopeep dodged it easily, barking, challenging him.

I whirled, looking for something to use as a weapon. There. In the trash next to the door. Dozens of empty beer bottles. I grabbed one by the neck and smashed its bottom half against the door frame.

At the sound, the old man jerked toward me, then pulled up short, his eyes focusing on the broken bottle in my hand.

"Packard," I yelled. I crouched slightly, and took a half-step forward, holding the jagged weapon low. I felt like James Dean in *Rebel Without a Cause*. I jabbed the bottle at nothing in particular.

From off to the side, Bopeep growled. Packard's eyes darted toward her, then back again, a sudden uncertainty clouding them.

In the distance, a siren wailed. The heavy smoke boiling upward had been spotted and help would be here within minutes.

"Fuck you, Stoddard. And fuck your fuckin' dog, too." Packard spun around and raced to his pickup, Bopeep chasing after him. He jumped in and his pickup roared across the graveled lot, a shower of rocks kicking out from under the rear wheels. "The Day of Doom, boy. The Day of Doom's . . . " The sound of his voice was lost as the truck swerved and raced away.

I didn't have time to waste. Mr. Hogan was inside. Dead or injured, I didn't know. I tossed the broken bottle aside, then touched the doorknob. It was warm, but not hot. Standing to one side, I jerked the door open. Dense, dark smoke rolled under the top of the door frame. Inside, a foot-thick layer of smoke hovered against the ceiling of the stockroom. But nothing was burning in this part of the building.

I kicked a rock against the door, blocking it open to let the smoke escape. I didn't want it to build up so I couldn't see. Ducking down low, I entered and wound my way through the stacks of boxes to the barroom door. I could hear the fire now. Crackling, hissing, whooshing, roaring like I imagined it would be inside a tornado.

The door was half open, and I could feel the heat pulsing from the fire within. I kicked the door all the way open. Fires burned practically everywhere. Flames shot up from several pool tables, more intense there than elsewhere, as if they had been set on fire first.

Burning chunks of wood littered the wooden floor, and little fires sprouted in the cracks between the floorboard. Smoke lay like a heavy blanket above, and most of the ceiling burned, flames licking downward here and there cutting through the smoke. A ten-foot two-by-four plunged from the ceiling, its entire length engulfed by flames, and crashed against a pool table, exploding sparks in every direction.

My eyes scanned the room, shadows and light alternating as the fires ebbed, then flared, bursting with renewed energy. Behind the bar, Mr. Hogan's homemade platform burned in several places. My eyes started tearing from the smoke, and the light was tricky. Then I remembered the light switch, and felt for it against the near wall. I pushed it up, and several lights glowed across the room. A split second later, two of the bulbs exploded, and all the lights went out. Bedlam surrounded me.

Hunkering down further away from the smoke, I entered the room, circling the bar carefully, my eyes searching. "Mr. Hogan!" I yelled, as loud as I could.

Then I saw the slight movement on the floor behind the bar stools, a stubby arm and a hand waving. I ran to the stocky figure. Mr. Hogan lay on his back, his eyes tightly closed, his blubbery face contorted in pain. Grabbing him by the shoulders, I shook him and his eyes flew open, a look of terror, of death. "Mr. Hogan? Are you all right?"

His lips moved. "Help me." The scared, weak voice was barely audible.

I pulled him up, slipping my arm underneath his back, supporting his head and shoulders. He groaned and his hands flew to his stomach. His shirt was matted against his belly against a mass of dark, sticky-looking red blood.

He'd been gut-stabbed. Packard!

I had to save Mr. Hogan. I pulled him forward into a sitting position, then strained against his torso. "Mr. Hogan! Get up! You've got to get on your feet. I can't lift you."

Mr. Hogan's eyes closed, and his body went limp. I didn't know if he had died or passed out.

A few feet away, another two-by-four crashed into the floor. I ducked, protectively wrapping my arms around him. A shower of sparks peppered my back and neck, stinging, burning their way through my T-shirt, random needles of pain. The ceiling would collapse any second.

Laying him back down, I seized his legs and tugged, hard. He slid across the floor, barely. I leaned backwards, pulling with all my might, inching Mr. Hogan toward the doorway, stumbling against the bar stools and against bits of charred and burning wood. My eyes ran and my lungs burned from inhaling some smoke. Behind the bar, bottles exploded like shotgun blasts. All around me, the sounds of falling wood intensified.

I leaned backward, tugging harder. Unexpectedly, Mr. Hogan slid several inches, and something underfoot rolled. I fell heavily, Mr. Hogan's legs flopping across my thighs. Above me, wood splintered and shifted. I looked up. An entire section of ceiling sagged toward me, then hung suspended, except for a flaming plank that crashed down atop Mr. Hogan. Time was running out. I scrambled out from under the stubby legs.

A hand touched my shoulder. Then Jess's face appeared,

worry weighing down his features. He lunged forward and kicked the burning plank off Mr. Hogan.

A thought flashed through my mind that Jess was here, and things would be all right. I grinned, stupidly, and I knew it was a stupid thing to do, but it felt good.

"You damn fool! I wouldn't have known you were in here if I hadn't seen Bopeep out back." He seized Mr. Hogan's upper body, and together we hoisted him between us. Looking over my shoulder, I backed toward the storeroom door. We passed through the door and then most of the barroom ceiling caved in, crashing to the floor of the room we'd just left. A wave of heat washed over me, but we were safe.

Outside, I turned away from Mr. Hogan's Cadillac, and we carried him toward Jess's Fury, parked near the edge of the gravel border, its lights flashing. In the street, the county fire truck lumbered to a brake-squealing halt, and yellow-jacketed firemen jumped off, grabbed hoses, and raced to hook them up to the hydrant on the corner.

We reached the safety of Jess's police car, out of the way of all the shouting and hectic activity. "Put him down here," Jess ordered. We lay Mr. Hogan down carefully, and Jess reached into his car and grabbed his microphone. "Lucy! You there?"

Inside the car, the radio squawked. Jess continued. "Get an ambulance here fast. Hogan's hurt bad. Abdominal injury. Looks like he's been stabbed. Hurry." Jess hung up the mike, and came back over to us, looking intently at me. "You all right?"

"Yeah." I felt okay. I was covered with soot, and my hair smelled like it had been singed, and I had a stinger on my left shoulder that I didn't know how I'd gotten, but I'd managed not to get burned.

Night had fallen, but the fifty-foot-high fiery torch fueled by Mr. Hogan's pool hall lit up the sky like midday. All around, firemen scrambled, dragging hoses into position, shooting streams of water into the blaze.

Mr. Hogan was still breathing, but shallowly, his face as red as a bad sunburn, glistening with runny sweat. A baseball-sized patch of his hair had been seared away and his stomach was a mass of blood, like Tarzan's had been. Packard was no better than Satan. He liked killing.

Jess turned to me. "What happened?"

"Packard did it," I said, nodding grimly. "He was here. Drew a knife on me, too."

"I . . . I came back." Mr. Hogan's eyes were open. He squeezed them closed and groaned, fighting the pain inside.

"Lie still," Jess said, touching Mr. Hogan's forehead, comfortingly. "Help's on the way, and you're going to be all right."

I wasn't so sure about that. Blood was pooling all over his stomach, more than when Tarzan had been killed. There might not be time. Packard had to be stopped. He was still after me . . . and after Jess. "Packard did this to you, didn't he? Tell Jess so we can get that bastard."

Mr. Hogan opened his eyes, and nodded slightly. "Yeah. Packard said he'd kill me if I didn't give him an alibi. But I came back . . . to tell the truth about that and the bootlegging. He was waiting inside . . . he cut me."

"All right," Jess said firmly. "We'll get him. We'll get him for you."

Mr. Hogan gasped, coughed, then his breath settled down. "I stopped in Tulsa . . . for gas. People laughed. Laughed at me. Like I was a stupid clown. Wanted me to do some tricks."

"It's okay now, Mr. Hogan," I said. "You're home now."

Underneath his tired face and heavy jowls, his body relaxed. "Home." he said slowly. "Yeah . . . Bob White's . . . home." The man's large head sighed, except his breath just kept coming out until there wasn't anything left.

Bopeep came over, wagging her tail, and lay down beside me, her eyes watering like she had gotten smoke in them.

44

After Sheriff Adams arrived, Jess took me and Bopeep back home. A few smudges marred his uniform, but he didn't look anything like me. He made me peel off my T-shirt and then he checked me quickly for burns. I'd been lucky. The pinpricks on my back didn't even hurt, but I accepted some salve on my shoulder. I hoped Jess would stay home, but he said he had to go out looking for Packard, and he left.

I took a bath, suddenly realizing I was dog-tired. It was all I could do to finish up, then climb into bed. Bopeep joined me, looking about as fresh as she had when we'd set out for the pool hall.

I felt good about Jess now. He was innocent. Packard had killed Hogan and Tarzan. Now, the whole state would be looking for Packard for murder. And Jess would be safe. It didn't matter when the Day of Doom was suppose to be.

I remembered Packard yelling something about that when he was driving away from the pool hall, yelling that the Day of Doom was coming. Except . . . he hadn't said that exactly. Had he said "The Day of Doom's here"? The way the pickup had spun away, I couldn't tell for sure what he'd said. Maybe I only thought he'd said it was coming. Then why was I worrying that he might have said "The Day of Doom's here"? Maybe that's what I really heard . . . mingled with the roar of the truck and crunch of the gravel. I shuddered. I tried to tell myself that it didn't matter now. Packard was as good as captured. But a cold chill ran down my spine.

The next thing I was aware of was that I was shooting up out of a deep dreamless sleep, all my senses on fire. It was dark. What had awakened me? A low growl emitted from the foot of the bed. Bopeep stood stiff-legged, staring out into the back yard.

"Packard!" my mind screamed.

"Easy, girl," I whispered, quietly slipping my legs out from under the sheet, putting the bed between me and the window, feeling the cool wooden floor under my knees. The night was lit only by starlight, and across the yard our unattached garage loomed, shadowy and mysterious.

Slowly, my eyes swept through the darkness, making out nothing recognizable. The stillness was damn right eerie. Far off to the northwest, tiny spider webs of lightning rippled through the sky. The storm was for sure going to hit later tonight.

Beside me, Bopeep trembled, breathing as little as I was. I put my hand on her back to reassure her and tried to see what her nose was pointing at. Toward the back right of the yard, something moved. Bopeep got throaty. Dark shadowy pants legs waved, suspended from the clothes line, moving gently in the breeze.

Relaxing, I said, "It's all right, girl." Bopeep remained tense, her ears pricked forward, listening as for even a randy cricket to scratch his legs. I patted her again, reassuringly. "Settle down."

She jerked her nose a few degrees to the left, where nothing had seemed to move, and growled again. Maybe Packard really was out there.

And if he was, I needed Dad's shotgun.

Quietly, I edged toward my closed bedroom door. Outside, the garage wall lit up. A car was coming down Ash Street, on its way from town, headlights piercing the night. I froze, watching the yard carefully as the darkness fled.

Shadows began to move across the garage wall, slowly at first, then accelerating toward the rear corner, leaping into the darkness, frantically announcing the car's approach. Nearing us, two sets of headlights reflected from the garage window. Two cars slowed to a halt in front of our house.

I recognized the sound of Jess's Fury. Then he killed the engine, leaving the rattle of what had to be Joyce's mom's '51 Ford. Seconds later, that engine died and the headlights went out. The sound of car doors creaking open split the silence.

Bopeep jumped off the bed and stood by the door, wagging her tail, wanting to be let out. Whatever had been bothering her was now gone. Maybe a striped skunk or a stray cat. I let her out of the bedroom, then, leaving the door ajar, slipped back into bed, listening.

The front door opened and I heard voices whispering, greeting Bopeep. Joyce first, then Jess. Soon I heard soft tiptoeing down the dark hallway. I lay still, knowing the darkness wouldn't allow them to notice I was awake.

Joyce paused at my door, then slipped into Jess's room. Jess appeared, lingering in my doorway, taking the longest time looking at me.

After a while, I couldn't stand it any longer and spoke. "Hi, Jess."

"Oh . . . hi, kid. Didn't mean to wake you."

It was strange, seeing only his shadowy outline and not being able to see his jaw moving as he talked or any part of his face. Like you'd expect if some mysterious dead person was talking. The image bothered me, so I shrugged it off and talked back to Jess. "You didn't. I was already awake. Saw your lights driving up."

It was quiet for a moment, then Jess said, "We didn't find Packard."

I knew he was going to say that. "He's about as sneaky as they come."

"Yeah, well, we'll get him. Hey?" Jess raised something in front of him that I couldn't see. "I got some cold pop here. Want the rest of it?"

"Sure." I licked my lips, still worried about Packard. Maybe he was outside waiting to kill us when we were least expecting anything.

Jess came in, shut the door, and switched on the light, blinding me temporarily. "Heard you talked to Brahma today."

I blinked and took the offered pop. "We all did. Me and Ferret and TJ." I took a big swig, feeling instant coolness circulating to all parts of my body.

Jess sat down on the bed and pushed his hat way back on his head. He was still wearing his uniform, his gun strapped to his side. "Tucker says you kids were trespassing. Stealing stuff."

"What kind of stuff were we supposed to be stealing?"

"Brahma asked him that and Tucker didn't have a good answer."

"Did he find the boxes of sugar?"

Jess shook his head. "Tucker wouldn't let him in the storeroom."

"He said he was afraid he'd go to jail."

"Not likely. But Brahma believes Tucker was selling moonshine makings to Packard. Around here most folks think that's as bad as committing adultery."

I remembered Tucker saying he'd be destroyed if people knew. With Lucy in the Sheriff's Office this afternoon, everyone in town knew by now. "So what will happen to him?"

"Probably nothing outright, but people will let him know they know. They won't forget."

So one way or another, Mr. Tucker would get what was coming to him. But now it didn't matter if he told the truth. Regardless, Packard would be going back to prison. Soon as he got caught. 'Cept he was still free. Maybe he was out there in the night right now. I thought about us here with all the lights on, the shades up. We were sitting ducks; and anyone could sneak up on us. I shuddered at the thought.

"Kid? You all right?"

Jess's eyes looked different than I'd ever seen them before. A strange worried look. I guess he was worried for me. "Sure. Why wouldn't I be?"

"Well . . . seeing two people die like they did."

I shrugged. "People try to do the right thing, then get themselves killed for it. Doesn't make any sense. But I'm all right."

I glanced at the bedroom window, seeing nothing but bugs on the screen and blackness beyond. "Packard killed Tarzan, didn't he?" It wasn't really a question.

"I think so. But what I can't figure is why he'd do that. He'd need some kind of motive. . . . " Jess paused, sorting things out in his mind.

I still didn't want Jess to know that Packard had come within an inch of killing me. I figured Tarzan's saving my life was all the reason Packard needed for the murder. "He's crazy. Isn't that reason enough for killing Tarzan?"

"Why do you keep calling him Tarzan? You told me he'd said his name was Jonathan Goldwyn."

"Yeah, just can't get 'Tarzan' out of my head."

"We don't really know the first thing about him. He say where he's from?"

"All over."

"Well, we've sent his fingerprints and picture to Washington. Maybe we'll get a match." Jess sighed, then took his hat off and scratched his head.

Fingerprints? Something about the word "fingerprints" bothered me. I remembered wiping the shotgun clean. Packard had slipped into our house, taken the shotgun, killed Tarzan, then replaced the gun. But if his fingerprints had been on the gun, I'd destroyed the evidence. It didn't matter anyway. Not now. Everyone knew Packard had killed Mr. Hogan.

I tipped the Coke up and drained the remainder. Curious, I glanced at the bottom to see where it had been made. I read the words and grinned. "Tucumcari."

"What?" Jess asked, like he hadn't heard me correctly.

I leaned over the side of the bed and set the bottle on the floor. I decided I'd keep it as a souvenir. Mr. Tucker would never see it. "Tucumcari. Bottle was made in Tucumcari, New Mexico," I explained.

"Oh, yeah, sure," Jess said, not really understanding.

I looked at Jess again, and I thought I could see the image of my father in him. Suddenly older, Jess's face was grayer than it had been a few days ago. "You look tired," I said.

Jess's brow furrowed, and he hesitated a moment before speaking. "Just keep this to yourself, now. I've been thinking about getting out of sheriffing."

Stunned, I said, "Really? Why?"

"Seems like the more of it I do . . . " Jess looked away, as if he was struggling to say what came next. " . . . the meaner I get."

I didn't say anything.

"I don't know exactly why," Jess said, a guilty look on his face, "but I've always felt like I had to be tough. Looking back now, I guess that's why I went into football. Then the MPs, and then sheriffing. Guess I had to prove I was tough."

I wasn't sure what all this meant. Jess was tough. I admired him for it, mostly. And so did everybody else in Bob White.

"I don't like being that way. Being mean. That's not really me."

I couldn't picture Jess not being a deputy sheriff. "What do you think you'll do?"

His voice got cheerier. "I might try getting on with the Oklahoma Bureau of Investigation. Maybe take some college courses."

It was quiet for a while, both of us thinking. Then I said, slowly, "This means you'll be leaving Bob White."

Jess looked away and spoke, slowly, sad-like. "Yeah, well nothing stays the same forever."

Joyce hollered from the other bedroom, "You boys going to talk all night? A gal needs her beauty rest." Even though she'd said what she'd said, her voice didn't sound complaining. She talked low and throaty, like she had the covers pulled up to her chin, like an invitation.

Sure enough, Jess looked kinda interested and one corner of his mouth turned upward. His face had lost that tired look.

"What about Joyce?" I asked.

He stood up and winked at me, then turned out the light and went into his bedroom, closing his door behind him.

I lay back down, thinking. I pictured them getting married and moving away. I'd be leaving Bob White, too. And Ferret and the Brubakers, and everything I'd known all my life.

A sudden urge told me I needed to go to the bathroom. I threw the sheet aside and got out of bed, then worried about Joyce maybe accidentally catching me in my briefs. I felt around for my jeans, then slipped them on and padded through the darkness into the bathroom.

I finished up, as quiet as I could, then left, bumping into Bopeep waiting nervously outside the bathroom door. "It's all right, girl," I whispered, bending down to scratch her ears.

Bammm!

45

The shotgun blast exploded into my bedroom, tearing into the bed right where I had been lying. Recoiling from the flash, I staggered back into the hallway. Outside, I heard a cackling sound. Packard!

I heard scrambling sounds coming from Jess's bedroom, and then his door burst open.

"Mark—" he broke off, seeing me. He had his pistol in his right hand and was dressed only in his skivvies.

"I'm all right," I whispered. "Packard's outside. I'm getting Dad's shotgun." I turned toward the closet.

Jess grabbed my shoulder, speaking low. "No, wait. I'll get him." He pushed past me down the hallway, Bopeep trailing at his heels.

I followed him. "Where's Joyce?"

"Under the bed, I hope. Damn it, Mark. Stay back." He paused at the front door, inching it open.

"Jess, be careful," I whispered. "He could be out front waiting for you."

"I'll have to chance it."

"Let me create a diversion."

"The hell with it." Jess threw open the door and charged outside, banging the screen half off its hinges. Jess leaped sideways off the porch, rolled once on the grass, then came up on his feet behind the Fury, crouching low, his pistol ready.

Bopeep flashed out the door a split second later, leaping off the porch, tearing around the house toward the back bedroom window where Packard had been. "Bopeep! Come back!" I yelled, lunging outside, hesitating on the porch. "Jess, he's still around back. Bopeep's after him."

"Get down!" Jess shouted.

I jumped to the ground and, hunkering low, ran cautiously after Bopeep. The moonless, starlit night allowed little light, but I could make out most things. I heard Jess's bare feet running after me, then, somewhere ahead, Bopeep snarled like she did when she had a rag in her mouth.

From near the garage, I heard Packard yell, "Son-of-a-bitch."

I rounded the corner and froze, seeing a shadowy figure half sitting, half lying on the ground, and a darting white blur. Bopeep snapped her teeth at the figure—Packard—who was trying to ward her off with his left arm. Suddenly, her jaws closed on his wrist.

"God-damned dog." With Bopeep hanging on tight, Packard rose to his feet, his right hand in his coveralls pocket.

An awful realization came over me. "No!" I yelled. I charged Packard, then tripped on something, sprawling flat. Horrified, I looked up, too late to stop Packard.

Packard drew his right hand out of his overalls pocket and thrust it at Bopeep's belly. Bopeep yelped and fell to the ground.

"Yeeee-hawww!" Packard screamed.

Bammm! Jess's pistol fired behind me, and I saw a chuck of wood burst from the garage wall, splintering into the darkness. Packard ducked and grabbed his shotgun all in one motion. Whirling, he fired an off-balance, wild blast in our direction, then dashed around the garage. Jess flew by, chasing him. Both vanished into the darkness down the alley.

Stunned, I rose to my feet and stumbled to Bopeep's side. She was breathing fitfully and a dark spot was growing on her stomach. "Oh, God. Oh, God, no. Please."

Dropping to my knees, I touched her gently, stroking her

head and side. Bopeep whined, her eyes darting toward her shoulder, not moving her head, not understanding, but trying to see what the terrible matter was.

I had to get her to the vet. Doc Bailey. Doc Bailey.

I slid my hands underneath her, as tenderly as I could, then turned and started for the house, hurrying but trying not to jar Bopeep. "Joyce!" I yelled.

I got to the front porch and Joyce came running to the door, mostly dressed but clutching her blouse together in front. Seeing me, she flicked on the porch light, then gasped. Blood was running down my arms. "It's Bopeep," I said, my voice hollow and empty. "Packard knifed her. I've got to get her to Doc Bailey's."

"Hold on, honey. We'll take her in my car." Joyce dashed inside, then returned seconds later clutching her keys and what looked like a towel in her arms. Rushing to the car, she flung open the door, then helped me into the passenger's seat, pressing a towel against Bopeep's stomach.

Bopeep cried, piteously. Anguish welled up in my heart, filling my insides.

"I'm sorry, Bopeep, but that'll help stop the bleeding." Joyce looked at me, her eyes anxious, but her voice firm. "Hold that tight against her, but not hard, you hear?"

I nodded, and did as she'd said. Lights had come on in the neighborhood, and I heard doors opening and questioning voices.

Jess came running up, saying, "He ran off. . . . " His eyes took in the situation. "Oh, my god." Jess reached down and stroked Bopeep's head. "I'm going to get that bastard tonight," he said, his face angry.

Joyce jumped into the driver's seat, then started the car, turning it in a half-circle back toward Main Street. Doc Bailey's place was on the westerly outskirts of Bob White, just off the highway, not far from Ash Street, so the trip would be real short, thankfully. "How's she doing?" Joyce asked, driving hard.

"She looks bad."

"Don't talk like that. She's going to be all right."

"Tarzan didn't make it. Hogan didn't make it—"

"She'll make it." The Ford rumbled off Ash Street, hitting smooth pavement, and turned west, accelerating.

Bopeep's eyes were closed and she felt heavier, like dead weight, except I could see her chest rising and falling slightly. "I've never seen her lie so still, not even when she sleeps. She's always chasing cats and mice and rabbits in her sleep."

"And she will again," Joyce said, pulling into Doc Bailey's driveway. "I promise you." She hit the horn a couple of times—the beeps loud, startling—then braked to a stop in front of the veterinarian's office, an addition he'd made to his house.

Doc Bailey's annex looked like a regular house, except smaller, with a covered porch and little flower pots decorating its edges, and curtained windows. Joyce reached across me and opened the door. I carried Bopeep toward the porch, Joyce leaping ahead of me, pounding on the door. Lights flicked on inside the annex and Doc Bailey called, "Hold your horses, I'm coming."

He opened the door, wearing striped pale blue and white pajamas, his thin white hair mussed up from sleep, spectacles set way down on his nose. "For gracious sakes," he exclaimed, staring at Bopeep, blood-covered. "Bring her in."

He stepped aside and I pushed past him. "She's been stabbed, Doc."

Doc lifted the towel from Bopeep, studying her injury. "Let's get her into the surgery." I followed him down the hallway and placed Bopeep on a gleaming metal table. Doc slipped on a white coat and yelled, "Martha? I need your help."

"She'll be all right, won't she?" I asked, anxiously hovering over Bopeep.

"We'll see," Doc answered, pushing me aside, peering closely at her through his thick glasses. "You two better wait in front. You'll just be in the way."

"But, Doc . . . "

He stood up and turned around, looking me up and down. "There's nothing you can do here anyway. There's a bathroom to the right where you can clean up."

"You've got to save her," I pleaded.

"I'll do the best I can," he said gravely, as if he'd made assurances before that hadn't worked out. "Now go on, please. Let me do my job."

Joyce took my arm and led me down the hallway. Mrs. Bailey, sleepy-eyed, wearing a flowery housecoat, her white hair sticking out at odd angles, breezed past us, smiling encouragingly, not knowing what problems were waiting for her. She closed the surgery door behind her.

I cleaned up, as best I could, knowing the blood washing down the bathroom sink was part of Bopeep's life. I sat down next to Joyce in the waiting room, neither of us saying much. I was too afraid to say anything or think anything.

Five minutes later, the surgery door opened and Doc Bailey walked down the hallway. Both Joyce and I stood up, moving closer together. "Mark," he said, gently putting a hand on my shoulder. "She's in a bad way. I'm sorry. It'd be best to let her go."

Involuntarily, I backed away from Doc, bumping into Joyce. I felt her arms go around me, holding me close, trying to give me strength.

"I'm sorry, son," Doc said. "Sometimes life is hard."

I pulled loose from Joyce, bitter hate building up, surging through my veins. I looked Doc straight in the eyes and said, "Life's not about anything, except dying."

A cold rage came over me. Packard had to die. Whirling, I dashed to the door and jerked it open. "You're not burning Bopeep up! She'll get a proper burial."

"Mark!" Joyce cried.

I lunged outside, running, bare feet scattering the rocks in the driveway. Behind me, I heard Joyce yelling at Doc Bailey. "You've got to save Bopeep!"

But it was too late. Bopeep was dying. My parents had died, Tarzan had died, Mr. Hogan had died. Life wasn't about anything, except dying.

Now Packard had to die.

My feet slapped against the still-warm blacktop highway, taking me back into Bob White. I eased into a steady run, pacing myself over the few blocks it would take me to get home. In the distance I heard a rumbling noise and caught a glimpse of a lightning flash, not so very far away.

Lights were on in several houses around the neighborhood and a cluster of people had gathered in front of my house, talking, probably speculating about what had happened. Jess's car was gone, and I knew he'd be out hunting for Packard. Seeing me coming, someone called, "Mark? What's going on?"

I must have looked a sight, wearing just jeans and barefoot besides. I didn't care. I ran up the steps, avoiding the wobbly screen door torn halfway from its hinges. Inside, I slammed the door and turned off the porch light, hoping everyone would go back home.

In my bedroom, the shotgun blast had exploded my mattress and pillow. Feathers and bed stuffings were everywhere. I dressed slowly, deliberately taking my time. In my nearly bare closet, I found a dark shirt and slipped it on. My sneakers were on the floor, covered with feathers. I shook them out and pulled them on over my bare feet.

Leaving the bedroom, I walked into the bathroom and stared at the stranger in the mirror. The reflection looking back at me was too young, too naive, too innocent. It wasn't me. Inside I was older, wiser, and I knew for sure now that I had a mean streak in me, too. I turned away from the mirror and walked down the hall to the closet.

46

Dad's shotgun rested where I'd left it. I took it and a box of shells into the kitchen, and sat down to load the gun. I put one shell in the chamber and two more in the magazine. Standing up, I grabbed a handful of shells and stuffed them in my pocket—not that I'd be needing them. Maybe I'd use just two, like Packard had done to Tarzan. Maybe I'd shoot him, then take his own knife and gut him, like he'd done to Mr. Hogan and Bopeep.

I turned the light off and slipped out the back door, carrying Dad's shotgun in my right hand. The wind had picked up, whistling around the corner of the house. Overhead the stars had disappeared and were covered by clouds high up. Lightning flashed, strobelike, making the backyard appear to be vibrating, then zigzagged overhead, not crashing to the earth.

I ran to the corner of the house and paused, listening, hearing nothing except the laundry flapping frantically on the clothesline. The neighbors must have gone back inside, worried about the storm. I broke into a trot, across the backyard, and down the alley. I knew where Packard would be hiding.

Jess had said Packard had run off. That meant he hadn't brought his truck, so it had to be hidden someplace nearby. And the only hiding place this side of the Bottomlands was the trees bordering Six Mile Creek.

I trotted west. The air was charged with the prickly smell of ozone, like needles inside my nose. A shrill, piercing, unruly wind ripped through the cottonwoods, whipping up sandpaper from the street, peppering my face. Overhead, drums rumbled and hostile clouds tossed brilliant darts across the sky to waiting shadows. Ahead, distant lightning suddenly backlit the trees bordering Six Mile Creek, and briefly illuminated the empty park where the fair had been.

I entered Will Rogers Park adjacent to the creek, still running, hanging low, heading straight for the nearest clump of trees. A crackling sound ricocheted across the sky, west to east, north to south, and all the earth around was buffeted with a living, breathing light.

I ducked into the tree line, and paused. I was at the south end of the park, and most of the trees lay to the north, up to Red Nelson's trap range, and then beyond it, all the way to the highway. It was quieter here. The wind swirled above the overhead canopy, muffled, like the sounds you hear with your hands over your ears. Packard might be able to hear me coming.

I had to stay within the interior, near the creek. Otherwise, I might miss the truck. I crept forward as quietly as I could, unable to keep from stepping on hidden twigs and leaves that somehow found their way all too often under my feet. With each snap and crunch, I froze, waiting for a shotgun blast to knock me off my feet. Each time, none came and I continued.

Several minutes passed as I moved north, keeping Six Mile Creek to my left, ignoring the trees on the far side—it seemed impossible to get a truck over there. A mile or so to the west, a monstrous lightning bolt surged to the ground, feeding its energy into the earth. Mother Nature was venting her wrath on her inhabitants. I was glad—

The explosion came from behind, lifting me off the ground and hurling me forward, dashing me against something hard. Stunned, deafened, blinded, I collapsed on the ground, my head throbbing, secondary explosions bursting inside my brain, my face embedded into a blanket of leaves and grass. I lay still.

All I could think was that Packard had got me, and I was dead or soon going to be.

Dazed, unseeing, I waited for him to come to me, to fire the second blast, to finish me off. I smelled something burning, and my whole body tingled as sensation returned slowly to it. I lay still, vaguely realizing that I was still in one piece. My back was strangely stiff and sore, but it didn't feel like I imagined being shot felt like.

Blood trickled down my forehead, but that was from the impact I'd made after the explosion. I struggled to open my eyes, to clear my head, and to raise it inches off the ground. Twenty feet away, flames licked a tree, split wide open by lightning.

About half my strength returned, and I struggled to my knees. Dad's shotgun was missing. Lightning flashed above, and I saw it lying a few feet away, looking strange in the brief flicker of light. I felt for it and picked it up. The stock had been split and the barrel was curved.

Shit! I tossed it aside and turned to get up. A massive eyeball, as big as a melon, peered into my face.

My entire body recoiled backwards, and I fell on my butt, a stab of pain searing my back. I stared at the silent buglike eye, its twin a few feet to its right, the two headlights separated by a turtle-nosed hood and scissors-like grille work. Packard's truck.

Every inch of my body ached and my shotgun was busted.

Slowly, favoring my back, I stood up and looked around. The truck was empty. Packard was out in the storm somewhere, armed with his knife and shotgun.

Cautiously, I slipped away from Packard's truck, moving to the east edge of the trees. The vague shape of Red Nelson's trap range appeared less than a hundred feet to the north. Now I remembered Red asking if I knew of any kids messing around there. It hadn't been kids. It had been Packard.

Overhead, the wind whistled and lightning flashed. The bolt skipped across the sky, echoing a rumble from cloud to cloud, illuminating the earth in a series of split-second blinks.

A single black and white car sat in the parking lot fronting the trap range. One with familiar tail fins and a domed police light mounted on the roof, still and quiet. Jess's Fury. The Fury started moving, turning this way, then veering along the trap range fence, slowly, its lights out.

Jess might not even know that Packard was here. I had to warn him. I moved quickly along the tree line.

Strangely, the night was getting lighter. I glanced upward. Stars twinkled to the northwest, the last vestiges of the storm overhead. Moonlight highlighted the clouds, painting their edges a bright silver.

I stumbled out of the tree line and headed straight for the Fury. Still jolted from the lightning that had struck earlier, my muscles worked awkwardly. Each jarring step sent a spasm of pain up my back.

I was in the open, totally exposed in the growing light. Packard could blast me at any second. But I had to warn Jess.

My back screamed like it was on fire. Ahead, the Fury crawled like a cat sneaking up on a field mouse. Why wasn't Jess using his searchlight?

The car stopped. Jess must have seen me. I covered the last few feet quickly, relieved not to feel a shotgun blasting me, and caught myself against the car frame. "Jess! Packard's here!" I said, half out of breath. "We've got to—"

At that moment, the moon peeked from behind a cloud, suddenly brightening the night. Packard's evil face leered up at me from the open window. He poked his shotgun out and rammed the barrel into my chest.

I tried to catch myself but my legs somehow weren't receiving the orders I was giving them to move. I fell backwards, like a dead tree, another jolt of pain surging through my back.

The car door opened, the dome light illuminating Packard's shape. He slammed the door shut and kicked me in the ribs. "Git up, boy. Gonna show you your brother. Today's the Day of Doom."

Jess was dead. An image of Jess, gutted like Hogan, flitted across my mind. I lay still, shocked.

Packard kicked me again, harder, the toe of his boot sending a sharp pain to my insides. I held the pain in, clenching my teeth. I wouldn't give him the satisfaction, as long as I had a breath left in me.

I rolled over and stood up, my back tingling with little shooting pains, murderous thoughts filling my mind. "Where's Jess?" I asked, not caring how much hatred colored my voice.

"You'll see." Packard shoved me toward the front of the car.

I stumbled again, but didn't fall, catching my balance with a hand on the Fury's fender.

He thrust the barrel into my back and prodded me forward, around the front of the Fury and through the gate leading into the range. I searched the area quickly, my eyes scanning from Red's storage shed across the grounds toward the low-slung trap house, and out toward Six Mile Creek. There! Facedown, lying next to Red's platform chair, was my brother. "Jess!"

I stumbled forward, falling to my knees beside him. Crazy with fear, I rolled Jess onto his back, my eyes drawn immediately to his stomach. A smudge of dirt, no blood. That was all. Thank God.

Jess was breathing normally, rhythmically, eyes closed, a bruise forming on his forehead. Jess was okay.

But we were in serious trouble.

"Jess? Jess? Wake up." I slapped Jess' face, feeling him stir slightly. An idea occurred to me, one that might work if Packard hadn't see Jess move.

Standing, I whirled around to face Packard. "What'd you do to him?" I demanded, deliberately raising my voice, clenching my fists, keeping Packard's eyes focused on me.

Packard stood a good four feet away from me, out of range if I tried to lunge for him. His eyes glowed intently in the moonlight, like I imagined the devil's might. He held his shotgun under his right armpit, cradling it with his left, his right hand folded, resting on top of the stock. He spat a stream of tobacco juice toward me, spattering my sneakers. "Nothing compared to what I plan to do."

Angrily, I stepped forward, angling to my left, pulling Packard's eyes away from Jess. "You son-of-a-bitch."

Fflickkk! Packard's knife clicked into place, and he dropped the shotgun from under his armpit, pulling it out of the way over to his left side. "Come on, you little shit. You been asking to git yourself killed. Come to old Lafe. Come see what it's like to have your guts ripped out."

I changed directions, edging sideways, further left, moving toward the trap stations, warily watching Packard, playing for time, knowing I could avoid him for a little while.

He lunged at me, his knife arcing for my chest.

I dodged, except nothing worked as fast as it used to. Packard's knife slashed against my chest. I staggered backwards and fought to regain my balance, expecting Packard to be on me any second.

Instead, he waited, grinning, cackling. He flipped his knife upward, rotating it, then caught it by the handle. "I'm just having me some fun now, boy. You ain't gittin' away this time. I cut your fuckin' dog. I'm gonna cut you and then I'm gonna cut your brother."

I felt blood oozing from my chest. My hand instinctively touched it, seeing how bad I'd been hurt, feeling a three-inch long gash in my shirt, the cut almost as long, but not deep. Jess hadn't moved yet. I needed more time. "Why're you trying to kill us? What about your son?"

Packard's eyes rolled crazily. A look of hatred crossed his face, as ugly as sin. "I saw it all. He cuffed me. Then he beat my boy senseless. Then he beat him some more."

"Your son died in prison. Jess didn't kill him."

"My boy died the day Jess beat him. He weren't never the same afterwards."

"He was killed by a convict!"

"Hell with this talk. Your time's come, boy." He stepped forward, blocking my view of Jess, looming menacingly.

I backed away, keeping my eyes on Packard, afraid to look toward Jess.

Packard's knife slashed upward, cutting across my left shoulder, inches from my neck.

Too late, I jumped back again, my reflexes not letting me avoid Packard. I raised my arms higher, defensively, protecting my throat.

Packard flicked the knife at me again, easily catching me, slicing a thin line across the muscle on my upper arm that bled immediately.

I glanced backward. Six Mile Creek trickled, the shallow water sparkling, a barrier. I thought about running, knowing I couldn't run fast with my back—it'd be like slogging through mud. I wondered how far I might get before Packard caught me, tripped me, rolled me over—belly up—and cut me.

Behind Packard, I saw a sudden movement and heard pounding feet. Jess was ten feet from us, charging. Packard's face jerked, and he whirled. Jess slammed into him, his momentum carrying them both crashing into me, all of us tumbling to the ground.

My back exploded with shearing pain and I yelled in agony, not able to keep it inside me. Fighting hard against the pain, I opened my eyes, searching for Jess.

They were halfway to Six Mile Creek, both on their feet now, locked in combat, feet shuffling, stomping, bodies straining, grunting. Jess had Packard's right wrist. Somehow Packard's thumbless left hand locked tightly around Jess's right wrist. Packard's shotgun lay on the ground near them, glinting in the moonlight.

I rolled over, struggling to my feet, forcing myself to stand up. If I could get to the shotgun . . . Clumsily, I walked toward it. I got to the shotgun, and bent down, seared by another wave of pain, fighting it, picking up the gun.

Jess and Packard staggered, straining mightily, chest thrusting against chest, pushing, waltzing like stiff-legged dancers. Jess saw me, and yelled, "Get out of here."

I raised the gun hip-high, pointing it at Packard . . . and Jess. I couldn't shoot. I'd hit Jess, too.

Packard leered over Jess. "Eat shit, Stoddard." He spat a mouthful of tobacco juice directly into Jess's eyes. Jess jerked his face sideways, squeezing his eyes shut, blinded. Packard reared back and butted his forehead into Jess's temple, knocking Jess backward. Packard wrenched his knife hand free from Jess's grasp.

"Packard! Hold it!" In desperation, I pointed the gun above their heads. Bammm!

The knife flashed backward, then forward, catching Jess in the left shoulder near his collar bone. Jess yelled, "Damn you, Packard!" He grappled blindly for Packard's wrist.

My God. Packard had stabbed Jess. I'll kill the bastard. Club him to death. I raised the gun over my head. I staggered forward, my body moving, turtlelike.

Packard pulled back on the knife, but nothing happened. He jerked harder, and his hand slid back empty, the knife stuck firm in Jess's shoulder. "Shitfire."

He closed his fist and slugged Jess hard in the face. Jess went down, falling on his back.

"Die, you bastard." I swung the gun at the John Deere hat.

Packard whirled, throwing his left hand up, catching the barrel neatly, wrapping his fingers tight around it, his strength surprising. He grinned.

I shoved the gun against him, and he sidestepped, letting me stagger forward, nearly losing my grip on the gun. I regripped, as tight as I could, something telling me that no matter what, I had to hold onto the gun. Packard's right hand closed over the stock, the back of his hand touching mine.

Locked together, we staggered and stumbled down the shallow incline into Six Mile Creek, splashing aside the cold, ankle-deep water, rocks and pebbles shifting underfoot. Packard twisted the barrel downward, angling it toward the water. My back sent millions of pinpricks racing toward my brain, and I felt the barrel sliding through my hand. I knew I couldn't hold on much longer.

Suddenly, I let go and fired my right hand into Packard's ugly face, catching him square in the mouth. He staggered backward, going down, then he twisted, ramming the barrel muzzle-first into the creek bed, catching himself. I started forward, hoping to catch him off balance, knock him into the water. He whirled, pointing the shotgun straight at me, water dripping from the barrel. "Gotcha," he snarled, triumphantly.

I hesitated. At this range, he couldn't miss. Standing here in the water, I couldn't dodge fast enough. I felt a strange peace come over me. "You go to Hell, Packard."

He spat something out of his mouth. Blood and stuff plopped into the stream and floated away. Then he laughed, his eyes wild, excited. "Yeeee-hawww!" He pointed the gun at my belly, and squeezed the trigger.

Bammm! The gun barrel exploded. Packard screamed, one hand flying to his face.

Expecting the shock of a full load of eights, all the nerves in my body jangled.

Packard dropped his shotgun and fell backwards, his body sending a shower of water splashing away from him. His John Deere cap drifted slowly down the stream.

Stunned, I hesitated, then waded forward and retrieved Packard's gun from the water. The barrel had split a few inches from the chamber, the metal bent upward and forward as the explosion had burst through the thin barrel, releasing its energy toward Packard. He must have jammed something into the barrel when he'd stuck the muzzle into the creek. Curious, I glanced at the end of the barrel. Stuck inside was a brown and white speckled agate, like one Tarzan would have used in making his jewelry.

Packard was lying partially out of the water, his shoulders and head on the far bank. His head was thrust back, his hands upraised, quivering. I couldn't see his face. I stepped forward.

His left eye was a mass of blood. A metal sliver from the gun barrel must have got him there.

Packard gasped. His face was gray and his right eye stared at the heavens. "Fuck the world. I'm dying."

I looked down. If ever a man deserved to die, it was Lafe Packard. But I didn't know how bad he was hurt. "I'll get you a doctor, Packard. But your days are nearly over. You're going to prison and you're going to die for killing Mr. Hogan and Tarzan."

Packard's face lit up and his right eye sparkled. He cackled softly.

I turned to leave. Jess needed help.

"I killed your dog," Packard said, his voice fading.

"Yeah?" I asked, hesitating, but not wanting to waste any more time.

He laughed, then choked, sucking in his breath. His voice came out hurried, straining. "I killed that stinking little turd, too. But I never killed that queer." He sighed and said softly, "Wish I had." His head pitched sideways, limp, his right eye open, unseeing.

"You're lying!" I yelled, hating the evilness in him for staying alive long enough to say that. I didn't want to hear him say that. Packard knew he was dying. He wouldn't lie.

I backed away, staring glassy-eyed at Packard, then felt dry land under my feet. If Packard hadn't killed Tarzan, then it had to be . . . I turned. Jess staggered to his feet, the knife still stuck in his shoulder. My brother, Jess. A murderer?

But Packard hadn't said Jess had killed Tarzan. He'd just said that he, Packard, hadn't. I decided that I'd never tell anyone that Packard's last words were to deny killing Tarzan.

Jess was my brother. I hurried to help him.

47

I got out of the county hospital the next afternoon, stiff and sore, a few bandages and stitches here and there, most noticeably on my forehead where I'd crashed against Packard's truck. The doctor took X rays and said my back was okay, just wrenched. I visited with Jess before I left. His collar bone had been busted and his shoulder was all bandaged up, but he was cheerful, saying we Stoddards were tough and he'd be fine in a few days.

Joyce met me at the hospital and took me to Doc Bailey's to see Bopeep. He had worked a miracle, she said. I found Bopeep lying in a big cardboard box that Joyce had brought over and stuffed with blankets. Bopeep's midsection was bandaged with gauze and hospital tape. I sat down and let her lick my face. She struggled to her feet and wagged her tail, thumping it against the box. We Stoddards were tough, all right.

The next day was Sunday, and I went to church with TJ and Ferret. Mrs. Brubaker wasn't there, still under the weather, the reverend said. During the service, he joked about the jagged stitches on my forehead, saying that now I, too, had the right to tell everyone that was where God had struck me with lightning. That put the congregation in a good mood, everyone laughing, enjoying the joke.

At the end of the service, he announced that he'd been chosen to be the pastor at the First Baptist Church in Little Rock. Beside me, TJ gasped, then looked at me with a sick expression jarring her face. She hadn't known. In the choir, Ferret looked totally surprised.

Across the congregation, there was a moment of stunned silence, then a hubbub broke out with people shouting, standing up, begging the reverend to stay. He looked embarrassed and guilty. After they had quieted down, he said he was sorry but the Brubaker family had to be moving by the end of the week.

The news hit the three of us hard, and we were feeling especially sad about our imminent separation when later we went to Tarzan's graveside service. Only TJ, Ferret, and I were there, besides Reverend Brubaker and Mr. Mulhair, the undertaker.

Just before the service began, Mrs. Brubaker arrived in her own car. She was dressed exactly as she'd been dressed at Mom and Dad's funeral. Black shoes, black stockings, black gloves, black handbag. Her black dress was a cocoon encasing her from calves to neck. Her black hat and black veil, a shield guarding her face. As black as death itself.

Tarzan got a pauper's burial, a freshly varnished pine box, at least three inches too short for him. He had to be all scrunched up inside it. Someone had sent a dozen carnations—anonymously Mr. Mulhair told us. TJ whispered that Mr. Mulhair must have stolen Tarzan's money, but there was no way to know.

The reverend's sermon was strange, talking about every man being worthy of death because of his sins. I didn't understand the point of his sermon and most of the time I paid more attention to a fly circling Reverend Brubaker's bald head.

Jess surprised us during the service, arriving late, driving up in his Fury, his left arm in a sling. Afterwards, the two of us waited until everyone else had left, and then we visited our parents' graves. I spoke to Mom and Dad, silently, telling them not to worry about me. I reckoned I'd be just fine from now on.

Jess dropped me at our house, saying he'd promised the doctor that if they released him long enough to attend the funeral with me, he'd go straight back to the hospital.

About nine-thirty that evening, I went outside and sat on the porch steps, missing Bopeep, wishing she was here with me, like she always had been.

I glanced up the dark street, toward the Brubakers' house. Someone was walking down the center of the street, just now coming out of the shadows, someone wearing familiar shorts and sneakers.

I was glad to see TJ. She wore her hair down, a blue ribbon running from under the back of her head to just above the crown of her hairline in front, and combed as smooth as black silk. I decided I liked her hair that way the best of all.

She came over to the porch and stood, not saying anything, studying me like I was a frog in science class.

"Where's Ferret?" I asked, feeling uncomfortable.

"Back yonder, I guess. Who cares?" She shrugged, trying to look indifferent, and not succeeding.

I scooted over and patted the concrete beside me.

She shook her head. "I don't feel like sitting."

"Want to go for a walk?"

"No."

I sighed and crossed my arms over my knees. Girls. You never know what they're thinking or why.

"Let's go inside."

I looked up, catching her eye, seeing something mysterious there. I felt as if that something was pulling me toward her.

Her eyes were a bright green, full of daring. She grinned. "You chicken?"

I rose to my full height plus two porch steps and looked down at her. "We'll see who's chicken."

She jumped up the steps and skipped past me, avoiding the screen door, still hanging awkwardly from its torn hinges. "Packard do that?" she asked, going on into the house.

I followed her in, closing the door. "Nope. Jess did it, chasing him."

Inside, TJ stood over by the TV set, looking at Jess's trophies. "Wow, Jess really did do all those things he said he did."

"Yeah," I said, remembering he had bragged his whole life story when he'd taken us to the Sonic for hamburgers. I wished she'd forget about all those trophies.

She picked up his two-foot-tall All State trophy, looked at it, and then fingered another. "Any of these yours?"

I thought of Jess's twenty-one trophies, and my one, sitting against the back wall in the closet. "Nope."

"Oh, don't be silly. Come look."

Silly? She'd called me silly? Irritated, I walked over, hardly looking, seeing all kinds of football trophies and junk. "None of them are mine," I snapped.

"Oh, yeah?" She picked up one about a foot high, shiny and new, and held it for me to see. It was a shotgunner, and the plate on the front read, CHAMPION, BOB WHITE, OKLAHOMA, 1957.

Jess must have come home before he showed up at the funeral, and put my trophy there. My eyes clouded up. I blinked quickly, and said, "It's no big deal."

TJ put the trophy back on top of the TV set. She turned to me and put her hands on my chest. "I think it is."

My hands found her waist. I hesitated. "What about the Brubakers?"

"I said I was tired and going to bed. Then I snuck out."

I gazed into her eyes, trying to think of something appropriate to say. "I like your hair this way."

She slid her hands upward, encircling my neck. "Thanks," she said, nodding sincerely.

I bent down and kissed her, tenderly, feeling her lips, warm and moist. Her mouth opened, and she pulled me to her. I kissed her hard, and then my hand was under her blouse, slipping her bra aside.

48

The next week went by all too quickly, with a flurry of activity over at the Brubakers' house. TJ, Ferret, and I bummed around constantly, except when Ferret had to help out, which was a lot, so TJ and I got to be alone reasonably enough. Her mom had decided it was okay for TJ to go to Little Rock, so that was settled.

Early Saturday morning, I went over to their house, taking Bopeep along. She'd been home a few days and was still bandaged up, but she'd started worrying the tape and gauze, chewing parts of it loose when she'd had nothing better to do. A little exercise would be good for her.

A big moving van was parked in front, and three men were going in and out, moving furniture and boxes. Both of the Brubakers' cars were parked in their driveway, doors open, several boxes filled with necessary traveling things sitting on the grass nearby. TJ came out the front door, carrying a medium-sized box, dressed in pink shorts, a pink ribbon in her hair. She'd been wearing it down for the last week. "Hi, Mark," she called.

"Hi," I answered, waiting for her over by the reverend's Impala wagon.

She put the box down beside the rest of the pile, and said, "Holy shit, we'll never get all this stuff in the car." Then she looked up at me, and her face got teary. "We're leaving soon."

Bopeep whined a greeting, her tail wagging hard as could be.

TJ bent down and wrapped her arms around Bopeep, gently hugging her a long time. Too long.

The shock of it all started hitting me inside. So little time left. "Let's go around back."

She nodded, and I took her hand in mine, noticing she was still wearing the bracelet that Tarzan had made. We walked around the side of the house, past flower beds of marigolds and petunias that Mrs. Brubaker had tended so carefully.

Bopeep trotted ahead, turning frequently to check on us. Out back, I saw the stack of firewood that the reverend had laid up for winter. His ax was stuck in the chopping block, keeping the edge from rusting. I wondered if he had forgotten about its being here.

Beside me, TJ started crying, sobbing softly. Stopping, she turned to me and I put my arms around her, folding her into me, her face against my shoulder, feeling her tears through my T-shirt. I took a deep breath and patted TJ on the back. My heart was filling up my chest and I felt a lump in my throat the size of a walnut.

She lifted her head up, sniffling a little, and said, "I'll write you. Will you . . . write me?"

My voice was hoarse, making it hard to talk. "Yeah."

"You promise."

"I promise, now don't cry any more."

"I just feel so sad. We've all been real sad. Aunt Josephine's been going into her room and crying a lot. I don't want to leave—" She broke off, biting her lip.

I knew how she felt, maybe better than she did. The Brubakers were leaving and I was losing another family. "People get sad, because leaving feels like people dying. Like when my folks died."

TJ nodded, her eyes downcast. "Yeah. Or like my Dad's going off. Leaving us all alone."

"When my folks died, I thought I was all alone. But I was

wrong. You'll never be alone, unless you choose to be. Love never dies, as long as it's in our hearts."

TJ wiped her eyes with her fingertips, and tried to smile. "I still love my Dad. And Mom, of course."

"And I still love my parents, even though they're gone."

She lifted her chin and spoke, her voice clear and firm. "And you've got Jess."

I thought of Jess. He'd been out of the hospital a few days, spending most of the time with Joyce. I'd hardly seen him. Not much seemed to have changed. "Yeah. Jess is family."

TJ's eyes shimmered, then she said softly, "I'll love you forever."

I touched her arms lightly, searching her eyes, wanting to tell her how much I cared for her, the words on the tip of my tongue. I grinned and said, "Yeah." I bent down and kissed her.

The screen door screeched open and I pulled back, embarrassed. Mrs. Brubaker stepped out, her gaze sweeping across the back yard, a harried, anxious look on her face. "Oh, there you are, TJ. And Mark. We're loading up. Come help us."

She led the way into their bedroom, where two cardboard cartons remained. "TJ, grab that small box and take it to my car. Mark, you take this one to Henry. It goes in the station wagon. Oh, I don't remember if I checked the closet."

TJ picked up the smaller carton, hurried past me, and winked, shyly.

The last carton was piled high, Mrs. Brubaker's mahogany jewelry box perched precariously on it. Carefully, I picked it up and started slowly toward the door.

"Oh, Mark. Leave my jewelry box. I'll carry it."

Stopping, I leaned down and the jewelry box started sliding. I dropped the carton, awkwardly grabbing for the small wooden box, but it tumbled to the floor, spilling earrings, necklaces, bracelets, and pins everywhere.

"Oh, shoot. I'm sorry, Mrs. Brubaker." I started picking up her jewelry.

She hurried across the room and pushed me aside. "That's all right. Just leave it. I'll pick it up."

I stood up, holding several silver and gold things in my hand, bracelets and necklaces. One of the necklaces had seashells and stones attached to it, and it wasn't silver or gold. It was a leather thong. I pulled it away from the other jewelry and held it up. At the bottom was a two-inch-long piece of amber.

Mrs. Brubaker sat on the floor, her eyes searching. She stopped, and looked up, apprehension in her eyes. She had been the woman in the tent, the woman making love to Tarzan.

I held out the necklace. "Tarzan gave this to you."

She took the necklace, then looked back at me. The color drained from her face. "Things aren't what they seem, Mark."

I felt weak all over, and sank slowly to my knees. "My God. The reverend killed Tarzan," I said, my voice a whisper.

Her voice was full of despair. "I . . . I knew Jonathan at LSU. We were . . . " She shook her head, and looked down at her hands, wringing them. "I hadn't seen him since, until . . . he came to the church. He . . . he tempted me. I was weak." A tear came to her eye and she wiped it away quickly, ashamed.

Her face didn't look right. She wore heavy makeup, but it was streaked now under her right eye, exposing a black mark. And there was a faint redness on her cheek, mottled, like the capillaries had been broken. The reverend had beaten her, punished her for her "sins." Like he'd punished Tarzan for his sins.

"Does . . . does Ferret know?" I asked, my voice quavering.

Her eyes darted at me, filled with pain and panic. "Oh, my God, no! Jonathan—" She froze, as if catching herself from saying something she didn't want to say.

My mind went back to the Bottomlands, seeing Tarzan lying there gut-shot. He knew who had shot him and he could have told us. The three of us—me, TJ, and Ferret. "Tarzan wouldn't tell. Why?"

Mrs. Brubaker shook her head, and bit her lower lip.

Hardly knowing what I was doing, I reached over and grabbed her by her shoulders. "Why wouldn't Tarzan . . . Jonathan tell who shot him?" I shook her, gently.

She looked down, and sobbed. "Jonathan . . . was Matthew's father."

I sank back on my heels, my mind spinning.

"Josephine?" The reverend's voice boomed from the front porch.

Mrs. Brubaker jumped, a look of fear cutting her face. She thrust her jewelry into the box and shut the lid. "You can't tell anyone. It would kill Matthew."

"Josephine!" The screen door slammed and I heard the reverend's footsteps coming through the empty house.

She scrambled to her feet. "Coming, dear." She hurried from the room. "Bring that last box, Mark," she called, struggling to make her voice sound as if nothing had happened.

Around me, time stood still. Slowly, I rose to my feet and picked up the box. Outside, Mrs. Brubaker and TJ were adjusting things in the back seat of her car, while Ferret was standing by the Impala's tailgate handing Reverend Brubaker shoe boxes. The reverend's big bald head bobbed in and out of the wagon as he stuffed them into nooks and crannies.

I walked forward, remembering how I'd always held back a little from Reverend Brubaker, feeling awed as if in a holy presence. Now, I didn't want to get close to him, except the feeling wasn't awe. It was horror, and a sense of the unholy. Reverend Brubaker had killed Tarzan, then conducted the funeral service for him. Somehow, I kept walking, straight for the reverend.

He turned, just as I arrived, and pulled the box from my hand. "Hello, Mark. Heard you were here." He shoved the box into the back and slammed the tailgate. He whirled back to me, and rose to his full height, hovering over me like he always had. Taking my hand, he pumped it vigorously. "Goodbye, son. Be a good Christian, you hear?"

My hand felt small in his, and his powerful eyes bored right through me. "Yes, sir," I answered.

Smiling, he walked around the car and got in.

Ferret shuffled over, trying to look bored, and said, "Golly damn."

I looked at Ferret, as if seeing him for the first time. With his dark features and slender build, he didn't look much like Tarzan. But then I'd always thought he didn't look at all like the reverend, either. "Yeah."

"You come see me next summer. I hear they got ticks as big as horseflies."

"Sure."

He paused, wanting to say something else. "Pals forever?" he asked, his voice uncertain.

"Pals forever."

Ferret grinned, then turned and got in the front seat beside the reverend.

TJ came flying over, clutching Andy the panda in one hand. She threw her arms around me, hugging me tight, her face buried against my neck, whispering urgently, "I love you. I love you. I love you."

"Yeah."

Backing up, she frowned and said, "And you better write, you turkey." She whirled and dashed to Mrs. Brubaker's car.

Moments later, they left, horns honking, hands waving, smiles and tears.

After they had gone, dust lingered over Ash Street as if it didn't want to settle out. My shoulders felt like they were carrying a load of bricks. Inside, I felt empty.

Things weren't always as they seemed. Reverend Brubaker represented good, but he'd committed a great sin, taking another man's life. How was he going to live with himself?

How was he going to live with his God?

Maybe he could. No one could prove Reverend Brubaker had killed Tarzan. The reverend was going to get away with murder. Unless . . . I told Jess. But Mrs. Brubaker said that if

I told, Ferret's life would be destroyed. And I'd just told Ferret that we'd be pals forever.

I realized that Bopeep had come up and sat down beside me, waiting patiently. I bent down and ruffled her fur. "Let's go home, Bopeep."

We started down Ash Street, my mind still struggling to sort things out. I thought about Reverend and Mrs. Brubaker. I'd lost them forever, and they still lived. As for Mom and Dad, I'd lost them through death, but they'd never be gone from my heart.

Different ways of living. Different ways of dying. Different kinds of losses.

Behind me I heard a car approaching. Jess slid his Fury to a stop beside me. His arm was still in a sling, but he'd pinned his deputy's badge across the fabric. He leaned across the passenger's seat and asked, "The Brubakers get off okay?"

"Yeah."

"Want a ride?"

I shrugged. "I guess so."

I opened the car door and Bopeep jumped up on the seat hardly the worse for wear for having been stabbed. I sat down beside her, the weight on my shoulders feeling twice as heavy. Jess represented the law, and I knew something the law would want to know.

Jess drove down Ash Street. I thought of Tarzan once more. He could have told us who had shot him, but he'd chosen not to. Now I understood why. Because telling would destroy Mrs. Brubaker's life. And Ferret's.

But that was Tarzan's decision—not mine. "Jess? I know who killed Tarzan."

Jess took his foot off the gas pedal and the Fury coasted to a stop. Jess's face was grim, his jaw set hard. "I know about the reverend."

I gasped. "You . . . you know?"

He turned and looked at me. "Me and Brahma have been working on it. You ready to tell us what you know?"

I met his gaze evenly. Slowly, I nodded.

Jess took a long, deep breath, then exhaled loudly. "We better go down to the courthouse." Jess made a U-turn and drove back up Ash Street toward Main, passing the van just as the movers were closing it up.

Right was right and wrong was wrong. Reverend Brubaker should pay for his crime. And Ferret should know the truth about the reverend . . . and the truth about Tarzan, his real father.

Jess turned east, cruising toward downtown, driving slowly for a change. "Mark?"

Mark? I turned and looked Jess full in the face. He'd called me Mark, instead of "kid." I couldn't remember the last time he'd called me Mark. "Yeah?"

"What say you and me go hunting when my arm gets well?"

Hunting. Suddenly, in my heart I knew there was nothing better in the whole world than going hunting with your brother. I felt a grin creep across my face.

Jess grinned back. "Well, what'd ya say, Mark?"

I put my arm around Bopeep and hugged her. "Sounds good to me . . . Jess."

My brother reached over and touched the siren. A tigerlike "rrowlll" sounded as we neared the courthouse. Bopeep whuffed.

The End